Praise for
THE LAST REFUGE

"My favorite novel in at least a decade. The writing was inherently masculine, brilliantly crafted."
—Elizabeth Blackney, *Huffington Post*

"Action, international intrigue, romance—it doesn't get any better." —*San Jose Mercury News*

"*The Last Refuge* is a winner, and it will keep readers turning the pages." —Associated Press

"Another winner from a writer who is a rising star among the ranks of the literary world's most successful authors of the international thriller." —*Nashua Telegraph*

"Fantastic . . . a terrific follow-up on [Coes's] first two suspenseful books." —Bestsellers World

"It's a thriller. It's current, and the excitement keeps going." —*Daily Oklahoman*

COUP D'ÉTAT

"High concept meets high octane in this brilliantly executed thriller. Envision Clancy, Forsyth, and le Carré all writing in their prime…then kick in the boosters. *Coup d'État* is fantastic and Ben Coes blows the competition away!"

—#1 *New York Times* bestselling author Brad Thor

"This exciting sequel to *Power Down* explores an all-too-plausible conflict . . . the plot sizzles with action, and the details have an authentic ring that put this thriller a cut above the pack." —*Publishers Weekly*

"Will keep you up at night—first with the titillation of a great read, then with dread that Ben's plot might not be all that imaginary. A sumptuous dessert for a thriller reader." —Brian Haig, author of *The Capitol Game*

POWER DOWN

"*Power Down* is terrific! With a gripping story, compelling characters, a relentless pace, and nerve-wracking suspense, *Power Down* is one of the must-read thrillers of the year. Don't miss this debut of novelist Ben Coes and the introduction of Dewey Andreas—you'll devour this one and wait anxiously for their return." —Vince Flynn, *New York Times* bestselling author of *Pursuit of Honor*

"Coes pumps new heat, blood, and flat-out action into a well-worn premise—terrorists are out to break America by attacking its energy resources—in his frighteningly plausible thriller debut." —*Publishers Weekly*

THE
LAST
REFUGE

BEN COES

St. Martin's Paperbacks

This is a work of fiction. All of the characters, organizations, and events portrayed in this novel are either products of the author's imagination or are used fictitiously.

THE LAST REFUGE

For information address St. Martin's Press, 175 Fifth Avenue, New York, NY 10010.

Library of Congress Catalog Card Number: 2012013915

ISBN: 978-1-250-02822-8

Printed in the United States of America

St. Martin's Press hardcover edition / July 2012
St. Martin's Paperbacks edition / May 2013

St. Martin's Paperbacks are published by St. Martin's Press, 175 Fifth Avenue, New York, NY 10010.

10 9 8 7 6 5 4

To Teddy
At age ten, you've given me as much
pleasure as most people do in a lifetime.

Their blood has washed out their foul footsteps' pollution. No refuge could save the hireling and slave from the terror of flight, or the gloom of the grave.

—FRANCIS SCOTT KEY, "THE STAR-SPANGLED BANNER"

1

ASPEN LODGE
CAMP DAVID
CATOCTIN MOUNTAIN PARK
NEAR THURMONT, MARYLAND

President Rob Allaire sat in a comfortable, red-and-white-upholstered club chair. His worn L.L.Bean boots were untied and propped up on a wood coffee table. Allaire wore jeans and a faded long-sleeve red Lacoste rugby shirt. His longish brown hair was slightly messed up, and there was stubble across his chin.

To his right, Allaire's yellow Lab, Ranger, lay sleeping. Another dog, an old English bulldog named Mabel, was napping by the fireplace, the sound of her snoring occasionally making Allaire look up.

To most Americans, the sight of the slightly unkempt president of the United States might have been off-putting, perhaps even a little shocking. If Allaire looked as if he hadn't taken a shower in two days and had worn the same pants an entire weekend, during which he chopped half a cord of wood, hiked ten miles, and shot skeet twice, it was because he had done just that. However, most Americans would have been pleased to see their president in his element, with his unadorned love of the outdoors, his simple joy in physical labor, his affection for his dogs. And now, at five fifteen in the afternoon on a windswept, rainy Saturday in April, his satisfaction at the sight of a bottle of beer, Budweiser to be exact, which one of Camp David's servants brought him as he sat staring into the fireplace.

"Thanks, Ricko," said Allaire.

"You're welcome, Mr. President."

In President Allaire's six years in office, he'd been to Camp David 122 times. Allaire would not, by his term's end, set any records in terms of time spent at the presidential retreat; that record would still belong to Ronald Reagan, who visited Camp David 186 times during his two terms in office. Still, Allaire loved Camp David just as much as Reagan, both Bushes, and every other president since Franklin Roosevelt had the retreat built almost a century before. Allaire loved its rustic simplicity, the quiet solitude, and he loved most the fact that Camp David allowed him to escape the backbiting, lying, sycophancy, and subterfuge of Washington. If Allaire was compared to Reagan for his constant escaping to Camp David, and for his conservative politics, that was okay by him. Allaire believed it was important to have a set of beliefs and to stick by them, through hell or high water, no matter what the polls or the prevailing wisdom said. It's why America loved Rob Allaire.

Allaire sipped his beer as he stared down at the iPad,

leaning closer to try and see, adjusting his glasses. He looked up. Seated on the far side of the room, reading a book, was John Schmidt, his communications director.

"I can't read this goddamn thing," said Allaire.

"You're the one who said you wanted one," said Schmidt. "Remember? 'It's the future' and all that?"

"Yeah, well, I changed my mind. I'm sick of pretending I like these fucking things."

Schmidt nodded.

"We'll go back to the daily notebook, sir."

"Good. In the meantime, have you read this editorial by our friends at *The New York Times*? How the hell is *The New York Times* editorial board aware of what's happening in Geneva?"

"It's coming out of the Swiss Foreign Ministry," said Schmidt. "They're taking the credit, which is not necessarily a bad thing. To the extent it adds to the public pressure on Tehran, it's helpful."

There was a knock on the door and in stepped two men: Hector Calibrisi, the director of the Central Intelligence Agency, and Tim Lindsay, the U.S. secretary of state.

Calibrisi and Lindsay, who had been out shooting at the camp's private skeet range, were both dressed in shooting attire. Calibrisi was an expert shot. He came up through the ranks of the CIA paramilitary and was deft with most weapons known to man. Lindsay, a retired former admiral in the navy, and lifelong hunter, was even better.

"Well, if it isn't Butch Cassidy and the Sundance Kid," said Allaire, a shit-eating grin on his face as he watched the two men stomp their boots on the welcome mat and remove their Filson coats. "Either of you manage to hit anything?"

"No, Mr. President," Calibrisi said politely. "We thought it would be impolite to hit more clays than you."

Allaire laughed.

"Wise guy," said Allaire as Ricko returned to the sitting area near the fireplace. "Do you two have time for a drink before you leave for D.C.?"

"Sure," said Calibrisi. "Same thing as the president, Ricko."

"Pappy Van Winkle," said Lindsay, looking at Ricko, "if there's any left. A couple rocks. Thanks, Ricko."

"Yes, sir," said the bespectacled servant, who turned and left for the kitchen.

"Seriously," continued Allaire. "Who won?"

"It's not a contest," said Calibrisi, his confident smile leaving little doubt as to who hit more clays that afternoon. He moved to one of the sofas and sat down.

"I'm sixty-four years old, for chrissakes," said Lindsay, sitting across from Calibrisi, next to Schmidt. "I'm surprised I hit anything."

"I've heard that one before," said Allaire, taking a sip from his beer and shaking his head at Lindsay. "Right before you took twenty bucks off me."

"That was a lucky day, Mr. President," said Lindsay as Ricko brought a tray with drinks on it.

The four men sat talking about skeet shooting and hunting for a long time, the president regaling the others with a story about the time when, as governor of California, he'd gone dove hunting with then vice president

Cheney just a few months after Cheney had strafed someone with an errant shot. The story, as with most of Allaire's elaborate and expertly told stories, left the other three in laughter.

Allaire stood and put more wood on the fire, played with the arrangement of the logs for a time, then returned to his chair.

"Before we take off, Mr. President," said Lindsay, "we need to discuss the proposal by the Swiss foreign minister."

"We've already discussed it," said Allaire. "I gave you my answer two days ago, Tim. I refuse to sit down with the president of Iran. It's that simple."

"Ambassador Veider believes that if we agree to a summit, with you and President Nava meeting one-on-one, that the Iranians will renounce their nuclear ambitions and might even agree to begin talks with the Israelis."

"I trust Iran about as far as I can throw them," said Allaire. "They're lying. I've seen this movie before, Tim. I don't like the ending."

Lindsay nodded at the president.

"We have to consider the larger objective," said Lindsay. "The Iranian government is reaching out to us. This meeting would be the first step toward normalizing relations between our countries."

"They're playing the Swiss and they're attempting to play us," said Allaire, nodding across the room at Ricko, indicating he wanted another beer. "President Nava has created a distraction which he's using to get us to take our eye off the ball. So while he makes the world and

The New York Times believe he's had a change of heart, Iran continues to pour tens of millions of dollars into Hezbollah and Al-Qaeda. And they continue to build a nuclear weapon."

"We don't have definitive proof the Iranians are constructing a nuclear bomb, sir," said Lindsay.

Allaire glanced at Calibrisi. "Here we go again," said Allaire, shaking his head.

"We know they are, Tim," said Calibrisi. "They have enough highly enriched uranium to assemble at least half a dozen devices. They have the uranium deuteride triggers. We know that. These are facts. They're getting close."

"Our objective, Mr. President, is to put Iran in a box," said Lindsay. "We do that by allowing the Swiss to bring our countries together, and then holding our noses and sitting down with President Nava. He publicly commits, we get inspectors in there, and the box is complete."

Allaire nodded, but said nothing.

"We have to be willing to be the adults here," continued Lindsay. "The reward is worth whatever risk we take by virtue of standing on the same stage as Nava. This is a good deal. They've agreed to on-demand inspections, access to their scientists, and details on their centrifuge supply chain."

"Tim, there are certain things that, for whatever reason, you don't seem to understand," said Allaire, leaning back. "One of those things is Iran."

"I think I understand Iran, sir," said Lindsay sharply.

"You understand Iran from a policy perspective. You

know the names of the cities, the history of the country. You've studied their leadership, their institutions, their culture. You've been there how many times? Five? Six? A dozen? I know all that. But I don't think you understand that the Iranians are, quite simply, the most dishonest group of people on this planet."

"You can't seriously mean that, Mr. President," said Lindsay.

"Yes, I can. And I do mean it. I don't trust those fuckers one bit. The Supreme Leader, Suleiman, is insane. President Nava is a menace."

"You're misunderstanding me, sir," said Lindsay. "I don't trust them either. But you'll forgive me if I take a slightly more nuanced view of Iran. It's a country ruled by a corrupt group of individuals, but a large majority of the country desires freedom. The Iranians are a good people."

Allaire paused and stared at Lindsay. He looked around the room, caucusing Calibrisi and Schmidt for their opinions.

"I think it would be a mistake," said Schmidt. "A big mistake. Nava and the president of the United States, on the same stage, tarnishes America."

"Hector?" asked the president.

Calibrisi shook his head in silence, indicating his agreement with the president's and Schmidt's negative assessment.

"For you to extend the olive branch to Iran would send a positive message to the Iranian people and to all people in the Middle East," said Lindsay.

"I understand the concept, Tim," said Allaire, "but

my decision is final." Allaire took a swig from his Bud-weiser. "I don't trust Suleiman and I don't trust Nava. They're pathological liars. I will never step foot on the same stage or shake the hand of Mahmoud Nava."

The president arose from his seat. He walked to the large picture window that looked out on the fields, trees, and forests of the Maryland countryside. The rain was coming down hard now, slapping atop green leaves that had just started sprouting in the early springtime air. He grabbed a brown coat that was draped over a bench near the door. Ranger, his Lab, awoke and moved quickly to the door, anticipating going outside.

"Come on," said Allaire. "I'll walk you guys down to the helipad."

"You don't need to do that," said Calibrisi, who stood and put his coat on. Schmidt and Lindsay followed suit. "It's pouring rain out."

"Are you kidding?" asked Allaire. "Nothing wrong with a good rainstorm. Besides, Ranger needs a walk."

"What about Mabel?" asked Schmidt, nodding to the large bulldog asleep in front of the fireplace.

"Mabel will be asleep until Christmas," said Allaire, smiling.

The four men, followed by the Lab, walked out across the terrace, then down the old road that led past the commandant's quarters, past the tennis courts. In the distance, they could hear the smooth, high-pitched drumming of the helicopter's blades slashing through the air. As they reached the edge of the tarmac, Allaire turned to the three men. All of them were soaked. Allaire smiled.

"You and your team have done remarkable work," said Allaire, staring at Lindsay, talking above the din. He placed his hand on the secretary of state's shoulder. "You, in particular, Tim, deserve a great deal of praise and credit. I will speak nothing but positively about the developments in Geneva and the potential for Iran to rejoin the civilized world. But they're going to need to do it without the involvement of the United States. They need to do it because they want to, not because I agree to sit on the stage and legitimize their past behavior."

"I understand, Mr. President," said Lindsay. "Thank you for the day of shooting."

"See you three in a couple of days," said Allaire, smiling.

Allaire shook Lindsay's, Calibrisi's, and Schmidt's hands, then watched as they climbed aboard the dark green and white chopper. A moment later, a uniformed soldier aboard the craft pulled the door up and sealed it tight. The chopper lifted slowly into the darkening, rain-crossed sky.

Allaire stared at the flashing red and white lights as it disappeared into the slate sky. He glanced around the now empty helipad, watching the rain bounce off the dark tarmac. He reached down and gave Ranger a pat on his wet head.

"Good boy," he said.

As Allaire started to walk back toward Aspen Lodge, he felt a strange warmth on the left side of his body, emanating from his armpit. He went to take a step but his foot was suddenly stuck in place, frozen still. His voice, which he tried to use to call out to the agents, now up the road more than a quarter mile, didn't work either. As the massive stroke swept down from his brain, his body convulsed in a warm, hazy, painless set of moments. He tumbled to the grass, his face striking first, the sound of the spring rain and the dog's desperate barking the last sounds President Rob Allaire would ever hear.

2

MARGARET HILL
CASTINE, MAINE

Dewey awoke with the first light. On the other side of the bed, Jessica slept quietly. Her auburn hair was spread across her face as she slept. On the table next to her were two cell phones and a specially designed, customized BlackBerry.

From the duffel bag at the end of the bed, he found a green T-shirt, running shorts, socks. He dressed quietly. He put on a pair of Adidas, then knelt to tie the laces.

He heard the sheets ruffle. He looked up. Jessica had turned and was looking from the pillow at him.

"Whatcha doing?" she asked sleepily.

"Run. You wanna come?"

"Oh, man," she said, yawning.

"You'll like it."

Jessica smiled. She reached out and put her hand gently in Dewey's hair.

"Sure," she said. "How far? This isn't going to be some sort of Delta training thing, is it?"

"I thought you played lacrosse at Princeton? You can probably run me into the ground."

"Probably," she whispered. "Princeton girls are tough. Certainly a hell of a lot tougher than Deltas."

Dewey smiled.

Jessica pulled the quilt and sheets aside and climbed out of bed. Dewey was still kneeling next to the bed, tying his shoes. She stepped in front of him, naked, less than a foot from him. She was not shy; she didn't have any reason to be. At thirty-eight, her body was the same sculpted, voluptuous object that had driven nearly every boy at Andover crazy. In silence, Dewey stared at Jessica. First at her knees, then, climbing with his eyes, her thighs, then higher and higher until his eyes met hers.

She'd watched the entire eye scan, and now a slightly scolding, slightly playful look was on her face.

"Troublemaker," she said, shaking her head. "*After* the run."

"It might help us get loosened up," said Dewey, moving his hand to the back of her thigh.

"After, dirty dog. And only if you beat me."

Softly, Dewey's hand rubbed the back of Jessica's thigh. She leaned toward him. She was silent; then she put her right hand onto his shoulder to steady herself.

"Jerk," she whispered.

He stood and their lips touched.

"I suppose we should loosen up," she whispered, opening her eyes and looking into his. She smiled and pushed him back onto the bed. She giggled as the bed-springs made a loud squeaking noise. She climbed on top of him. "I don't want any excuses after I beat you."

The idea for the trip had been Jessica's.

"I'm taking a week off," she'd said. "I want to go to Castine. Meet your parents."

"They don't talk very much. Just warning you."

"Gee, I never would've expected that," she said sarcastically.

"How can you possibly take a week off? You're the national security advisor. You're not supposed to take vacations."

"Watch and learn, Dewey."

"Who's going to be in charge?"

"Um, this guy named, wait, what's his name? Oh yeah, Rob Allaire. He's the, ah, president of the United States? You may have heard of him?"

"You know what I mean."

"Josh Brubaker," she had said, referring to her chief of staff. "I told him not to bother me unless it's a national emergency. If there's a problem, I told him to call Hector."

So far, four days in, no calls. The only visible evidence of her job was the FBI agent posted around the clock at the entrance to the farm.

Dewey and Jessica began the run down the long dirt road to the Castine Golf Club, then went right on Wadsworth Cove Road. After a mile or so, they went left on Castine Road. The small, winding road went for several miles. They ran alongside each other, with Dewey on the inside, closest to the road and the traffic, but there was hardly any. When they passed something and Jessica asked what it was, who lived there, where does that road go, Dewey would patiently answer.

At a sagging, moss-covered wood fence, they hopped over and went right. A path opened into a long, rectangular field overgrown with hay grass. The sun was out and it warmed them as they ran through the thick grass downhill toward the ocean, Dewey cutting a path, Jessica right behind him.

At the end of the field, the sea filled a rocky cove with calm blue water and the smell of salt and seaweed. A small dirt path was etched just before the rocks, and they ran along it for several more miles, trees to the right, rocky coastline left. Finally, in the distance, a church steeple, the beginning of the town proper. They came to a low, old stone wall, behind which lay row upon row of tombstones.

Dewey stopped, followed by Jessica. They were both drenched in sweat. Dewey leaned over to catch his breath.

"So," he said after several minutes. "How was that?"

Jessica breathed heavily. Her face was bright red.

"I let you win," she said.

Dewey stared at the ocean, then looked at Jessica.

"Are you hungry?"

"I like blueberry pancakes."

"I know a place," he said.

In town, Dewey and Jessica went to a small diner near Maine Maritime Academy called Froggy's. Jessica ordered blueberry pancakes and Dewey ordered eggs and bacon.

"When do you go to Boston?" Jessica asked.

"Day after tomorrow."

"Are you nervous?"

Dewey sipped from his water glass. He was interviewing for a job in Boston, an interview arranged by Jessica, running personal security for a wealthy hedge fund manager named Chip Bronkelman.

"No," said Dewey.

"Do you want the job?"

"Sure," said Dewey unenthusiastically.

"You're the one who said you didn't want to come back into government."

Dewey nodded. She was right. Calibrisi had offered him a job at Langley, and Harry Black, the secretary of defense, had done the same, asking Dewey to join his staff at the Pentagon. Black had also offered Dewey a job he came close to accepting, going back to Fort Bragg and becoming a Delta instructor. But Dewey wasn't ready to make the commitment. He'd already sacrificed years of his life for his country, had already risked his life for America more times than he could count, and he knew that if he went back in it would consume him all over again. He didn't want that.

But with that decision made, he needed a job. Bronkelman, a forty-something billionaire, was a very private man who lived in Wellesley, outside of Boston, and had homes in Manhattan, Palm Beach, Paris, Montana, and Hong Kong. Dewey would be well paid and he'd get to travel. But, in the end, he'd be little more than a glorified bodyguard to Bronkelman and his family.

"Do you want to come down to D.C. after your interview?" Jessica asked.

"I'm going to New York City," said Dewey.

"What for?"

"I'm meeting Kohl Meir," said Dewey matter-of-factly, after the waitress brought him a cup of coffee.

It had been nearly three months since the bloody night at Rafic Hariri Airport in Beirut, when Dewey nearly died following the coup in Pakistan. Dewey had been saved by a team of commandos from Shayetet 13, Israel's equivalent to the U.S. Navy SEALs. Kohl Meir was the leader of that Shayetet team who saved Dewey from near-certain death. Six of the eight-man S'13 team died that night.

Jessica took a sip from her coffee cup and slowly put it down on the Formica table.

"Why?" she asked.

"He's visiting the parents of Ezra Bohr," said Dewey, referring to one of the fallen Israeli commandos. "He asked if I'd meet him."

Dewey's face remained as blank as stone.

"Why does he want to see you?" she asked.

"I don't know, Jess," said Dewey.

"Did he say anything?"

Dewey looked across the table at Jessica.

"He said he needs my help," said Dewey.

"What for?"

"I don't know."

"Did you ask him?"

"Yeah," said Dewey.

The waitress brought over the plates of food and placed them down on the table in front of them.

"And. . . . ?"

"He said he needed to talk about it in person."

She raised her eyebrows.

"You don't find that in the least bit unusual?" asked Jessica.

Dewey smiled at Jessica, then shrugged his shoulders.

She looked back at him, raising her eyebrows, smiling, expecting him to say something. But he stayed quiet.

They finished breakfast. When Dewey asked for the check, the waitress shook her head, then nodded toward the counter. Behind the counter, a bald man with a University of Maine Black Bears baseball cap smiled, then shook his head.

"Your money's no good here, Andreas," he said.

"Thanks, Mr. Antonelli," Dewey said, smiling.

As Dewey and Jessica walked up the grass-covered dirt driveway from the golf club to the farm, a faint noise caused Dewey to turn around. Jessica's eyes followed his. Above the trees, from out over the ocean, a black object no bigger than a bird moved across the blue sky, followed, a few moments later, by the faint sound of whirring; the telltale rhythm of a chopper.

"Why do I have a sinking feeling?" asked Jessica.

3

APARTMENT OF JONATHAN AND SYLVIE BOHR
FOURTEENTH AVENUE AND FIFTY-EIGHTH STREET
BORO PARK
BROOKLYN, NEW YORK

The swaying of the white lace curtain, pushed by a soft breeze from the open window, was the only movement in the apartment.

Beneath the window was a small wooden dining table. On top of the table were two teacups, both filled, tiny clouds of steam rising up from the tea. Two plates; on top of one was a hard-boiled egg, cracked open, and a piece of rye toast, a bite missing. On the other plate lay a toasted onion bagel, cream cheese smeared on both sides, one of the pieces missing a few bites. Between the plates sat a bowl full of fresh-cut fruit—strawberries, pineapple, tangerine slices, blueberries. Two wooden chairs had been pulled out from the table.

The only sound in the kitchen came from the open window. The low background noise of Boro Park, of

Brooklyn, of New York City—car engines, an occasional distant horn, the voices of children outside playing on this warm, sunny spring day.

The empty kitchen led to an open, arched doorway.
Through the doorway was a dimly lit hallway. Across the
hall stood another door, slightly ajar, that led to a small,
plainly adorned bedroom. Above the simple wooden bed
hung a small Star of David, made out of wood. Next to it
was a framed photograph of a thin adolescent boy with a
long round nose, thick black hair in a jagged, uneven
crew cut, and a gap-toothed smile on his freckled face.

Outside the bedroom, the long hallway's walls were
covered with watercolor paintings, of various sizes,
and photographs. Photos in simple frames; of people,
family, engaged in different activities, standing in front
of recognizable landmarks such as the Eiffel Tower,
hiking on mountain passes, snow-covered peaks in the
background, or just seated at tables filled with food and
drink. Most showed the same people: a good-looking
couple with their son, a large, striking-looking boy
who always seemed to have a big, infectious smile on
his face, the same boy as in the bedroom photo. The
photos showed the progression of time, but what never
changed was the sense of family connection, of love.

Down the long, silent hallway was a living room, high
ceilings crossed with thick mahogany beams, two big
windows on the far wall partially covered in flowered
curtains. The walls were lined floor-to-ceiling in bookshelves, every inch filled, and in the corner of the room
was a simple desk, neat and orderly, a few piles of paper
stacked in the middle, and a small light on. In the center

of the room, two red sofas faced each other across a large, round glass coffee table. The living room, like the other rooms, sat in virtual silence, the only noise coming through the walls from the random clatter of the city.

At one end of the sofas sat a pair of leather club chairs, behind which hung a large, mesmerizing photograph. Slightly faded, it was an aerial photo of Tel Aviv. At the bottom of the big photograph, like paint thrown from a child, a spray of dark red liquid coated the glass; it shimmered, still wet.

In one of the leather chairs, the one on the right, a man sat, motionless. It was the man from the photos. He was, perhaps, seventy years old, his once thick hair had receded and what remained of it was mostly white. He had a thick gray and black mustache that hung down at the edges. He wore brown-framed Coke-bottle-thick eyeglasses. They were slightly askew. Behind the lenses, the man's brown eyes stared out across the room.

On the chair next to him was an older woman whose beauty was still obvious despite her years. Her long black hair was streaked in white; her simple, aquiline nose appeared as if it had been sculpted. She, too, was as still as a statue.

In the middle of the man's forehead, just above the bridge of the nose, an inch-wide bullet hole had been neatly blasted through his skull. Beneath it, a rivulet of blood oozed down the nose, then dripped in a slow but steady stream into the folds of his shirt.

The woman's skull was perforated in the identical spot.

The bullets had been fired from the same gun: a suppressed Beretta 93, clutched in the same leather-gloved hand by the same woman, who now stood, calmly, silently, as still as stone, against the far wall, near the front door.

The woman had long blond hair. It was a wig, and it covered short black locks that were slightly visible just above her ears. She was no more than twenty-five, simple-looking, a small, plain nose. The brown hue of her skin was accentuated and framed by the blond wig, and it made her look exotic. She wore a long-sleeve black Nike running shirt and matching running pants that looked as if they'd been painted on her hard, muscled body. She held the silenced .45 caliber weapon in her right hand, at her side. She stood patiently, motionless, waiting near the front door.

Next to her, on the wall, was the intercom, a black box with a pair of red buttons. Every few seconds, the young killer's eyes blinked in anticipation. It was the only movement in the room.

Outside the door, on the landing, was a brown mat with the word *welcome* in Hebrew. The landing sat empty and quiet. To the left, carpeted stairs ran up to the fourth and fifth floors of the brownstone. To the right, the stairs descended toward the ground floor.

Three floors below was a lobby. A large, antique chandelier dangled in the middle of the chamber, gold leafs wrapped around dozens of slender gold tubes with tiny lightbulbs at the ends; a gaudy, ornate, somewhat incongruous central point to the otherwise unadorned lobby. A stainless steel block of mailboxes hung on the wall across from a large glass and wood door. A tan curtain was drawn across the glass.

In the corner, behind the door, against the wall, stood a man. He was dressed in a similar outfit as the woman stationed in the apartment: black running shirt and pants, Adidas running shoes. A thin, black cotton ski mask was pulled over his head down to his neckline. Only the man's eyes were visible, two black embers smoldering, waiting. In his gloved left hand, the man held an M-26 Taser.

It was Sunday afternoon and the streets were busy. The sidewalks were filled with people. The weather was picture-perfect, a warm day, one of the first warm days of spring. Every resident of the neighborhood of brownstone apartments was out, sitting on stoops, talking with neighbors, walking young children, enjoying life.

At the corner, a yellow taxicab pulled over and a young man climbed out. He was big and athletic. His brown hair was slightly long and his face was tan. He wore khakis and a blue button-down shirt. He shut the back door then reached into the front window and handed the cabbie some cash.

He walked down the sidewalk with a slight limp. It didn't slow him down, but it was noticeable. His face had a hint of sadness to it. His brown eyes, however, told a different story. Their deep, blank pools scanned the street with trained suspicion.

But here, in Boro Park, he was among family. He was greeted by smiles from strangers, who recognized somehow his bloodline, his heritage. He returned the smiles with blank stares. He was here for a reason. A visit to the parents of one of his fallen colleagues.

Except for one, he had visited all the families of the S'13 who had died that day at Rafic Hariri Airport. He wasn't required to do so, but it was the way he chose to lead. To fly half a world away in order to sit down with a dead comrade's parents and explain to them that their son died fighting for something important, something he had believed in.

He walked up the wide steps of a pretty brownstone. He nodded to a pair of teenage girls who sat on the steps, both of whom blushed, then giggled back at him.

Next to the door was a strip of doorbells. He read the names. He reached out and pressed the button of the bottom name: BOHR.

After a few seconds, the intercom clicked.

"Yes," said a woman over the intercom.

"Hello, Mrs. Bohr, it's Kohl Meir."

At precisely the same moment, less than ten miles away, on the fifteenth floor of a nondescript office building on Second Avenue near the United Nations, a red, white, and green flag, with a strange emblem in the middle, stood near a mahogany door. Next to the door, the words were simple, engraved in a shiny gold plaque:

Permanent Mission of the Islamic
Republic of Iran to the United Nations

In a windowless, locked, highly secure room near the kitchen of the mission, two men stared at a large, flat plasma screen.

One of the men wore a black three-piece suit, a tan

shirt, a gold-and-green-striped tie. His black hair was slicked back. He had a bushy mustache, dark skin, a thin, gaunt face. The other man was stocky and had on a simple, denim button-down and khakis. The stocky man sat behind the desk, typing every few seconds into a keyboard in front of him. The man in the suit leaned over the desk, a cigarette in his hand. Both men studied the screen intently.

"It's him?" asked the suited one, Amit Bhutta, Iran's ambassador to the United Nations. "You're sure?"

"Yes, yes," said the stocky Iranian. "Crystal fucking sure."

On the screen, in fuzzy black-and-white, they watched as Kohl Meir climbed out of the cab, then walked down the sidewalk.

"And it's all ready?"

"Yes, Mr. Ambassador. It could not be any more precisely arranged."

On the plasma screen, they watched as Meir walked down the crowded sidewalk, limping slightly. Halfway down the block, he started to climb the steps of a brownstone. He moved past two girls on the steps, then put his hand out to ring a doorbell.

"Just think," said the stocky man. "The great-grandson of Golda Meir herself. We could not inflict any more damage on the Jew if we dropped a nuclear bomb on downtown Tel Aviv."

On the screen, the door to the brownstone opened, and Meir stepped through. Then he disappeared from the screen.

"Imagine," whispered Bhutta, "when we do both."

4

The chopper ride to Bangor International Airport took fifteen minutes. Jessica stepped off the Black Hawk and walked to a waiting Citation X, which flew her to Andrews Air Force Base. En route, she called Josh Brubaker, her deputy at NSC, to find out why she was being brought back early. Brubaker didn't have a clue. She called Calibrisi, the director of the Central Intelligence Agency and her closest friend in government.

"I haven't been told," said Calibrisi.

"You haven't?"

"No," he said. "Look, it's probably nothing."

"What have I missed?"

"I've read the dailies twice. ECHELON scans. Daily status call with Kratovil," Calibrisi said, referring to the director of the FBI. "Everything is quiet."

"What about Iran?" asked Jessica. "The negotiations?"

"That's all on course, Jess," said Calibrisi. "Would

the president call you back to discuss that? Isn't that a phone call?"

"I've tried calling him twice," said Jessica. "Control says he's unavailable."

"The daily briefing was canceled this morning," said Calibrisi. "Then again, it was canceled twice last week so he could play golf."

"Have you been summoned to a meeting?" she asked.

"No," said Calibrisi.

"Hector, be honest," Jessica said. "Do you think he's firing me?"

Calibrisi's laughter echoed over the phone.

"Are you kidding? You're the daughter Allaire never had. I'm guessing he's just lonely without you."

"Yeah, I don't think so."

"I don't either. My honest guess is there's something larger he's concerned with. Tell me what he says, will you?"

"Of course," she said. "I land in an hour."

They hung up and Jessica sat back in her leather seat, alone in the cabin of the jet.

Less than a minute later, her phone rang. It was Calibrisi.

"Strike that, I was just summoned," he said. "I'm meeting you at Andrews. See you in an hour."

At Andrews, Jessica stepped off the Citation and walked across the tarmac to a waiting helicopter. She climbed the stairs. Calibrisi was already seated inside.

"Welcome home, honey," he said. "How was your trip? Did you get me something?"

"Not funny," she said, taking the seat across from him.

"I just got a call from Mike Ober," said Calibrisi, referring to Vice President Dellenbaugh's chief of staff.

"What about?"

"He wanted to know what was going on."

"What did you say?" Jessica asked.

"What could I say?" said Calibrisi. "I have no idea what's going on."

"Obviously, it's something involving the vice president," said Jessica. "Why else would he call you?"

The chopper moved across the late-afternoon sky toward downtown Washington. After fifteen minutes, the chopper began to arc left and down, descending. Calibrisi glanced out the window. For the first time, he realized they weren't anywhere near the White House.

"Captain," said Calibrisi, yelling into the cockpit over the din, "where are you taking us?"

"Bethesda Naval Hospital, sir," said the pilot.

The chopper moved into a hover, dropping slowly toward the hospital helipad, noted by its large red X.

Jessica shot Calibrisi a look.

"Calm down," said Calibrisi, reaching out and patting her knee. "Maybe a heart attack. We'll see. But stay calm."

Jessica stared at Calibrisi, but her mind flashed to President Allaire. It had been more than two years now since he'd brought her from the FBI, where she'd run counterterrorism, appointing her national security advisor at an age—thirty-six—that was unprecedented. He was, far and away, the best boss she'd ever had. She pictured his block of brown hair, always neatly combed back. Allaire, at sixty years old, looked younger than his age. He was in good shape. He drank, but not too much, and he didn't smoke.

The door to the chopper swung open, the stairs fell to the helipad, and a uniformed FBI agent waved them down.

"This way, Ms. Tanzer, Mr. Calibrisi," said the agent, who held a close-quarters combat submachine gun at his side, aimed at the ground.

Jessica felt as if she was floating now. She stared blankly ahead, at the yellow letters on the back of the agent's black sweater, ignoring the noises around her, focusing on nothing save taking the next step, then the next. She had an overwhelming sense of the fact that the world, her world, was about to change. She tried to breathe.

They stepped onto a waiting elevator, which descended to the fifth floor. When the doors opened, Jessica's first sight was the grim face of Mark Hastings, chief justice of the Supreme Court. His normally ruddy face appeared gaunt, ashen; haunted.

Behind him, on his cell phone, stood Vice President J. P. Dellenbaugh, who registered the entrance of Jessica and Calibrisi, nodded at the two of them politely, then turned away.

A commotion came from down the hallway as Mary Whitcomb, the White House photographer, approached. A uniformed agent attempted to stop her, but she shouted at him, then was allowed past.

Jessica and Calibrisi were led past Hastings, Dellenbaugh, then through a doorway. Inside, a small sitting room had four chairs, all of which, save one, was empty. Cecily Vincent, the president's assistant, a woman who had worked for Allaire since the time he was governor of California, sat alone, with tears streaming down her face.

"Oh, Jess," she whispered through tears, shaking her head, her red eyes revealing utter sadness.

Jessica felt her own tears begin to roll down her cheeks. She stepped to the door and pushed her way inside.

The room was a large, modern operating room. She quickly counted four nurses and a pair of doctors. The walls were lined with plasma screens, displaying digital readouts. The steady monotone of the heart machine seemed familiar.

She felt Calibrisi's hand on her back, calming her, perhaps even holding her up lest she faint. But she didn't. Something inside her had already told her what she would see, some premonition before she left Castine that morning, whispered to her as if in a dream: *Nothing will be the same.*

In the center of the room, on a large, elevated steel table, covered in light blue blankets, was the president of the United States, Rob Allaire. His eyes were closed. An oxygen tube protruded from his mouth, running down his throat. Three separate IVs ran from his arms.

The president's physician, Lyle Cole, was standing next to Attorney General Rickards and White House Counsel Jack Fish. Cole stepped forward and met Jessica and Calibrisi.

"He had a massive stroke," said Cole. "Last night, out at Camp David."

"How bad is it?" asked Jessica. "People recover from strokes—"

"Not this one, Jess," said Cole, interrupting her. "I'm sorry. It was too big. His vitals are good, but his brain is no longer functioning. It never will."

Jessica stepped to the operating room table, to the president's side. She placed her hand on Allaire's, gripping it as tears fell down her face. The realization of what had happened struck her like a lightning bolt, hitting her with a force she couldn't tame. She held on to his hand for more than a minute, until she felt an arm on her shoulder. She turned to see Calibrisi. His eyes were red.

"Come on, Jess," he whispered.

"He had a DNR," said Fish, referring to a do-not-resuscitate order. "That said, everyone felt it was important for you two to be here."

"It was me who insisted," said Rickards, the AG. "I have no idea what the blowback will be, but I think it's extremely vital that our intelligence and national security infrastructure be prepared for this. Besides, I couldn't have lived with myself if I hadn't given you time to say goodbye, Jess."

Jessica stared blankly into Rickard's eyes. She realized, then, the very real implications of what was about to happen, and the work she needed to do immediately in terms of calming allies, and doubling down on areas of vulnerability that America's enemies might seek to exploit in the coming hours and days.

"How has it not leaked?" asked Jessica.

"We haven't permitted anyone to leave the hospital," said Fish. "We also haven't let any politicians in, except, of course, Dellenbaugh."

"When will you tell the speaker?"

"He's en route. So is the senate majority leader. But we're not going to wait. We need to get Dellenbaugh sworn in immediately."

Jessica looked one last time at the president of the United States, a man she respected, a man she loved like a father. Dazed, she turned and stepped out of the OR.

5

BETHESDA NAVAL HOSPITAL
BETHESDA, MARYLAND

Chief Justice Hastings swore in J. P. Dellenbaugh as the forty-sixth president of the United States as the sun was setting over the nation's capital. The brief ceremony was performed in the vaulted lobby of Bethesda Naval Hospital, which had been shut down to visitors.

Jessica didn't want to be there, but she knew she had to be. She stood with Calibrisi, Rickards, Fish, and a few other key figures from Allaire's administration, as well as the speaker of the house and the senate majority leader.

As Rickards had correctly guessed, the moment the politicians were summoned to Bethesda, the leaks began. By the time Dellenbaugh had placed his hand on the red leather-covered Bible that Hastings held aloft, television trucks and a line of reporters had gathered behind a secure perimeter in front of the hospital. The scene was chaos.

Dellenbaugh did the best he could to appear confident and presidential as he took the oath of office. Whereas Rob Allaire had a Kennedyesque swagger to his manner, Dellenbaugh's style was different, a more earnest, small-town charm, like Jimmy Stewart in *Mr. Smith Goes to Washington*. All politicians stay awake at night dreaming of being president. But Dellenbaugh seemed different, almost as if he could take it or leave it, but now that he was president, he would give it his best. Still, the sight of him taking the oath of office was like watching a movie for Jessica; she still couldn't process what was happening.

Dellenbaugh was a former professional hockey player from Michigan, born into a family of union card–toting GM autoworkers, who happened to be a Republican. When Rob Allaire, the conservative governor of California, had run for president, the presence of a good-looking working-class kid with a slightly crooked nose from one too many fights had been exactly what Allaire needed to beat a popular Democrat in the Rust Belt.

After Dellenbaugh shook Hastings's hand, he made a beeline for Mike Ober, his chief of staff, and Tim Sokolov, his press secretary.

"Wanna lift?" asked Calibrisi, turning to Jessica.

"Can you drop me by the White House?"

"Yes," said Calibrisi. "I assume we'll be sitting down with him at some point tonight?"

"We'll see," said Jessica. She turned to leave, then heard her name being called. It was Dellenbaugh.

Dellenbaugh walked to Jessica and Calibrisi. As he approached, he put his hand out.

"I'm very sorry, Jessica," he said.

She took his hand in hers and shook it; his hand-shake was powerful. He shook Calibrisi's hand too.

"I know how close you were to Rob Allaire," continued Dellenbaugh, looking into Jessica's eyes. "Like a daughter, everyone said. I'm just very, very sorry. I know you must be in shock. I know I am."

"Thank you for thinking of me," said Jessica.

"Please don't thank me," he said, looking at Jessica, then Calibrisi.

"If I may say something," said Jessica.

"Sure," said Dellenbaugh.

"The American government is incredibly resilient. It was designed so that the loss of one person wouldn't destroy it. My point is, Mr. President, government will function without President Allaire. It will afford you the time to take your time. I urge you to ease into your role. There are a lot of people, including myself, who will help you in the coming hours and days."

"Thank you," said Dellenbaugh. "That was probably the nicest thing anyone has said to me all day. I want us to work together. I need you. I need everyone right now. I have a lot to learn. Will you help me?"

"Of course," said Jessica. "We need to get you fully up to speed as soon as possible."

"Could you two sit down with me tomorrow?"

"Yes," said Calibrisi.

"Let's meet at the observatory," said Dellenbaugh, referring to the vice president's residence at the Naval Observatory in Washington. "I'm going to make a brief statement, then head over there. I think it makes sense

for me to reach out to foreign leaders. Let's meet tomorrow night around nine."

Back at her office in the West Wing of the White House,
Jessica and Calibrisi watched President Dellenbaugh's
statement, delivered on the front steps of Bethesda
Naval Hospital, as a wall of photographers and cam-
eramen surrounded him.

"Today, a great American has died," said Dellenbaugh. "Rob Allaire was more than just a great man. He
was more than just a president. He was, if it's at all possible, more than just a great American leader. President
Allaire was a friend. A mentor. He took strong stands
for what he believed in, and he refused to back down.
He inspired people from all political backgrounds with
his fairness, his sense of righteousness, his wonderful
humor, and his kindness. He was as tough as they come.
But even the toughest must face their maker, and tonight, God has called Rob Allaire to come home."

Jessica stared at the screen on her wall, listening to
Dellenbaugh's words. Tears collected in her eyes and
she reached up and wiped them away.

"He's pretty good," said Calibrisi, looking at Jessica.
She said nothing.

"To America's allies," continued Dellenbaugh, "I say
this to you: nothing has changed. America remains
there for you, with you, by your side. And to America's
enemies, I say this: *nothing has changed*. Do not
mistake the grief of a nation, the passing of a warrior,
for something it is not. For it is in grief, in tragedy, and
in the hard trials of our young democracy that Americans

come together, that we become stronger, that we arise in our duty to what is true, what is right, and what is sacred. Thank you, and may God bless President Rob Allaire, and may God bless the United States of America."

6

CIA HEADQUARTERS
DIRECTOR'S OFFICE
LANGLEY, VIRGINIA

Back in Calibrisi's corner office at CIA headquarters, two men sat in chairs in front of his large glass and steel desk: Josh Isler, the head of the CIA's Intelligence Directorate, and Bill Polk, director of the National Clandestine Service.

It was early afternoon. Calibrisi was quiet, sipping his Starbucks coffee, as he listened to his two top lieutenants brief him on elevated threats in the wake of Rob Allaire's death.

The phone console suddenly buzzed, and Calibrisi's assistant came on the intercom.

"Menachem Dayan is on one," said Jenna, his assistant, referring to the head of Israel Defense Forces.

"Can I call him back?"

"He says it's urgent."

"Okay," said Calibrisi. "Put him through."

He held up a finger to Isler, instructing him to stop talking.

A second later, the phone chimed. Calibrisi reached out and picked up the black handset.

"General Dayan," said Calibrisi.

"Hello, Hector," said Dayan, his deep, gravely voice booming through the handset. "And since when do you call me 'General'?"

"Sorry, Menachem. It's been a long day."

"I can imagine. I am very sorry for your loss. Rob Allaire was a true friend of Israel."

"Are you coming to the funeral?" asked Calibrisi.

"No," said Dayan. "The prime minister will be there. There's too much going on here."

"What can I do for you?"

"I apologize if I'm imposing during such a difficult time, but I need your help, Hector."

"Name it."

"We're missing a soldier," said Dayan. "He flew to New York yesterday. He hasn't been seen or heard from since he landed."

"Forgive me, Menachem, but how many Israeli soldiers visit the U.S. on any given day? This is a needle in a haystack."

"It was Kohl Meir, Hector."

Hector's mind flashed to a mental picture of Meir. It had been Dayan who ordered the Shayetet 13 team to Beirut to save Dewey's life.

"Oh," said Calibrisi, rubbing his eyes.

"He was visiting the parents of Ezra Bohr, one of the boys killed in Beirut."

"Give me a spelling on that, names too."

"B-O-H-R. Sylvie and Jonathan."

"I'll get on it," said Calibrisi. "Hopefully he met a cute girl and decided to spend a few extra days over here."

"I wish you were right," said Dayan. "But you're not. I know him. Something has happened."

"I'll report back as soon as we have something."

"Thank you, Hector."

Calibrisi hung up. He looked at Isler.

"You want me to throw a couple guys at it?"

"Yes," said Calibrisi. "Quiet. We're on domestic soil."

Within ten minutes, Josh Isler was back at Calibrisi's door. He held a piece of paper in his hand.

"I've already got something," said Isler.

"What is it?" asked Calibrisi.

"Yesterday, a couple was murdered in Boro Park, a Jewish neighborhood in Brooklyn. Slugs to the head, identical, between the eyes."

"Bohr?"

"Yes."

Calibrisi sat back, pondering.

"Did you speak with someone at NYPD?"

"Yes. And the FBI, who was unaware of it. NYPD doesn't have a clue. They assigned a detective to it last night. He hasn't even come to work yet."

"What about an autopsy?"

"I think they figured out how they died, Hector."

"That's not what I'm talking about, Josh. I'm looking for a time of death."

"Why?"

"I'm going to call Piper Redgrave at NSA," said Calibrisi, reaching for the phone, referring to the National Security Agency's Signals Intelligence Directorate. "We need Jim Bruckheimer at SID to put a couple of his hackers on this and do a little moonlighting for us. They'll need the time of death."

"Let me see what I can do," said Isler.

"*Gracias.*"

"All kidding aside, Chief, this is on domestic soil," said Isler. "It's one thing for us to do a little work on this. Involving Bruckheimer and the SID guys ups the ante. You might want to run it by counsel."

"It's Israel," said Calibrisi. "We bend the rules. As for Bruckheimer, he owes me a favor or three."

"You going to call General Dayan?" asked Isler.

"Not yet. Let's see if we can figure out who did it first."

"You know this means Meir's probably dead."

"Yes," said Calibrisi. "That had crossed my mind."

7

NATIONAL SECURITY AGENCY
SIGNALS INTELLIGENCE DIRECTORATE (SID)
FORT MEADE, MARYLAND

Hector Calibrisi's black CIA-issue Chevy Suburban exited the Baltimore-Washington Parkway, turning at a sign that read NSA EMPLOYEES ONLY. After a short drive down the private road, it went through two consecutive security gates. Beyond the gates, a cluster of black glass office buildings stood, somewhat menacingly, in a sea of parked cars. The Big Four, they're called, the glass infused with copper mesh to prevent eavesdropping. This was the headquarters of the world's foremost cryptologists, eavesdroppers, and hackers: the National Security Agency.

Josh Isler at the CIA had succeeded in getting an FBI doctor to visit the NYPD morgue in Brooklyn and do a quick and focused autopsy on the Bohrs to determine approximate time of death. Isler also had the Bohrs' phones and Internet activity run through different CIA databases to see if there were any contacts made with suspicious individuals, groups, or Web sites, but that analysis came up empty.

In addition, two witnesses emerged who had both seen a stranger on the morning of the killings, a blond woman in a dark running suit, entering the brownstone.

After getting clearance from Piper Redgrave, NSA's director, Calibrisi called Jim Bruckheimer to ask for help, describing the phone call from Menachem Dayan, and summing up the other small pieces of information. Bruckheimer had started laughing over the phone.

"That's all we got?" he asked.

"That's it."

"That and five dollars couldn't get you a coffee at Starbucks."

"Yeah, it could," said Calibrisi. "A small coffee."

"I'll get some people on it, Hector, but I'm not sure we'll find much."

"I know. But it's Israel."

"Look, if there's something findable, my Einsteins will find it. By the way, I'll handle the FISA warrant."

"Thanks, Jim."

On the third floor of the building, in a windowless conference room, Calibrisi was greeted by three individuals who sat around a large rectangular conference table: Jim Bruckheimer, director of SID, and two of Bruckheimer's SID analysts, Serena Pacheco and Jesus June.

This highly secure room was one of several command centers within the NSA's Strategic Intelligence Directorate, or SID. Etched into the center of the table was an eagle clutching a pair of keys, the NSA insignia, signifying the highly secretive agency's dual role: protecting America's secrets and stealing everyone else's.

"So you got something?" asked Calibrisi as he sat down.

"We have something," said Bruckheimer. "Serena, you good to go?"

Pacheco, a young blond woman with glasses, suddenly looked up from one of two computers in front of her on the conference table.

"Yeah," she said. "Jesus?"

"I'm good," said June, the other analyst.

"Let's see what you have," said Calibrisi.

Pacheco nodded toward a massive plasma on the front wall. The image was still. On it, there was displayed a grainy black-and-white overhead photo of a crowded city sidewalk.

"What's that?" asked Calibrisi.

"It's the street in front of the Bohrs' apartment," said Pacheco.

"This was taken about forty hours ago," said June.

"Where did you get it?" asked Calibrisi.

"We searched through everything we possibly could from any country who might have wanted to kidnap or kill Kohl Meir—Syria, Iran, Egypt, Lebanon, Saudi Arabia, Iraq, Kuwait, et cetera," Bruckheimer said.

"I tapped into every signals intelligence data cache from each country," said June. "It wasn't hard. With the exception of the Saudis, they're all sloppy."

"Who was watching him?" asked Calibrisi.

"This photo came off Iran's SIGINT," said

Bruckheimer. "It's circumstantial evidence, of course. But, it's damning."

"Let me keep going," said Pacheco.

The large, grainy black-and-white photo showed a residential street, a spring day, a sidewalk bathed in sunlight and shadows. People in short-sleeved shirts, shorts, sundresses. The sidewalks were lined with brownstones. People sat out on the stoops, families, friends, and neighbors.

"This is Brooklyn," said Pacheco. "Sunday. Boro Park. Obviously heavy Jewish population. Cue it, Jesus."

Suddenly, the video began to roll. There was no sound. The camera focused in on a man walking down the crowded residential sidewalk. The frame moved slowly down onto the individual as he walked.

"This is what they were watching approximately one to two hours after the murders, if the time of death is accurate," said June.

Calibrisi stood up and walked to the plasma, standing less than a foot away from the individual who was walking down the street.

"That's Kohl Meir," said Calibrisi, astonished.

"Yes," said June. "The limp. I understand he was shot not too long ago."

"Great work," Calibrisi said, turning to June, then Bruckheimer.

Calibrisi turned back to the grainy, black-and-white image.

The camera zoomed in on a young, athletic-looking man. He wore khakis, a striped button-down shirt. His muscles pressed against the shirt's material.

"What was he doing in Boro Park?" asked June.

"Meir is commander of an Israeli special forces unit," said Calibrisi. "He was here to visit the family of a guy in his unit who was killed; the parents of a commando named Ezra Bohr."

Everyone in the room watched, mesmerized, as the video continued to roll. Kohl Meir walked with a limp down the crowded sidewalk. The scene was simple. The camera tracked him as he maneuvered around strollers, old men out talking, a jogger.

"How the hell did they know Meir was coming?" asked Bruckheimer.

"My guess is, whoever did this knew he'd visit the Bohrs," said Calibrisi. "It was only a question of when. The Bohrs mentioned it to someone—a neighbor, someone at the synagogue. It would've been easy to elicit information from the Bohrs. An innocent question from someone concerned about their fallen son."

On the plasma, Meir continued to walk slowly down the crowded sidewalk. About three-quarters of the distance down the sidewalk, he stopped and looked up at a brownstone. He started to climb the front steps. A pair of girls, sitting on the steps, looked up at Meir as he passed. They leaned into each other. One of the young girls whispered something to the other, and they both started laughing.

"Hold it there," said Pacheco, nodding to June.

The video on the plasma suddenly stopped.

"Here's where we pick up the audio," said Pacheco. "Run it without the audio then back it up, will you, Jesus?"

The video began rolling once again on the plasma screen. The focus of the overhead camera moved in even closer to Meir, ascending the steps. He looked at the two girls, now giggling, and kept climbing.

At the top of the brownstone's steps, he studied the nameplate to the side of the door. A few moments later, Meir leaned forward and pressed one of the buttons. After a few seconds, he leaned down and spoke into the speaker. A moment or two later, the big glass door opened. Meir stepped in, then the door shut behind him. The screen remained focused on the door for a few moments longer, then cut and flashed black.

"Okay," said Pacheco. "Move it back."

The screen suddenly showed the black-and-white audio being rewound. It stopped at the point at which Meir turned and was about to climb up the steps. The angle zoomed down onto the young man's face. Meir's eyes were big, set slightly apart, a handsome man, Mediterranean-looking, with high cheekbones.

"The judge was a pain in the ass on the warrant," said Bruckheimer. "Because it's U.S. citizens talking, we have permission to listen to exactly twenty-six seconds of tape."

"Here's the audio from the point just before he enters the building. It's tough to hear. Jesus, punch it up. It'll be loud at first," said Pacheco, not looking up from her computer screen. "It smooths out, after we isolate the frequency and synthesize out the background noise."

The speakers in the conference room made a loud sonic clicking noise. A cacophony boomed through the speakers. The sound of traffic, a loud taxicab horn, blaring several times, the voice of a man, a thick New York accent; a question that quickly trailed off into unintelligibility. Then, the clamor evened out, as if someone had adjusted the volume.

In beat with Kohl Meir's footfalls up the front steps, the soft scratch of shoes striking each one as he climbed. As the video showed the man passed by the two girls, as one girl leaned into the other, the soft giggling of her voice was heard, then the words:

"Is that Mr. Monochlay's nephew?" she asked.

"No," said the other teenager, leaning in conspiratorially. *"But I bet he would kiss you if you ask him."*

The girl's comment was followed by giggling from the teenagers.

"How did you retrieve this?" the CIA director asked, incredulous.

The plasma screen suddenly froze.

Pacheco punched a few keystrokes on her laptop. On the big plasma, the view on the screen moved out. The camera angle pivoted, then zoomed in on a man standing across the street, talking on a cell phone.

"Verizon archives phone conversations for a few days. It was easy once we had the precise time he went in the building. We removed the audio of the conversation he was having with his bookie along with background echoes."

"Nice work," said Calibrisi, nodding to her.

The young analyst turned back to her computer.

"Here we go," she said, tapping her keyboard again.

The view swung back to Meir, standing on the steps. The video began to roll again, along with the audio. The sound of shoes lightly scratching concrete as Meir climbed. At the top step, Meir read the nameplate, then reached for one of the doorbells. He pressed the black button on the nameplate. The sound of a doorbell chimed.

After a few seconds, a dull click is heard; the intercom above the strip of doorbells came suddenly to life.

"Yes," said a woman through the intercom.

Meir leaned toward the intercom.

"Hello, Mrs. Bohr, it's Kohl Meir."

"Come in, Kohl."

The intercom buzzed. Then the loud click of a door latch being unbolted as, on the plasma screen, the door to the brownstone opened up. Meir stepped inside, then shut the door behind him.

"Hold for a second," said Pacheco.

As the video continued to roll, showing the door, motionless now in the moments after Meir entered the building, a strange noise suddenly interrupted the conference room speaker. It sounded like a guitar string breaking. Then, a pained grunt. The plasma went black, as the audio clip ceased.

Pacheco looked around the conference room.

"Taser," said Calibrisi.

"That's what we thought," said Bruckheimer.

"What about the voice?" asked Calibrisi. "Who is she?"

On a different plasma screen, to the right of the conference table, the empty screen suddenly displayed a green-and-black grid of an audio synthesizer. The clip of Meir climbing the steps played. Orange lines bounced in jagged bunches within the grid, like an EKG.

The woman's voice suddenly came into the tape.

"Come in, Kohl."

As it did, the black-and-green audio graph suddenly froze, then collapsed into the corner of the big plasma. It was replaced by a different application that popped up onto the screen. A square suddenly appeared, showing the darkened outline of a female silhouette. Within the silhouette, a rapidly changing series of photographs scrolled through. Then, the photos stopped, and the photograph of a woman suddenly appeared. Short black hair, small nose, a long face, dark, thin eyebrows, thin lips, tannish-looking skin, severe-looking, young, an angry look in her eyes.

After the face held the plasma for a few moments, the frame dissolved and a different application popped up, occupying the center of the plasma. The name and bio of the woman appeared on the screen.

KHANEI, ARYSSA
VEVAK OPERATIVE 2006–
ALIASES:

CASSU, ARYSSA (FR)
PAQUIN, SIRYNA
D.O.B: UNKNOWN
HOMETOWN: TABRIZ, IRAN

Calibrisi stared at the photograph of the Iranian operative.

Back at his corner office at Langley, Calibrisi phoned Jessica.

"The most important detail is the Taser," said Calibrisi. "They've taken him hostage. They're not going to kill him, at least not immediately."

"What do we tell General Dayan?" asked Jessica.

"I don't know," said Calibrisi. "Shalit will go nuts. God only knows what Israel will do to retaliate."

"You have to call him," said Jessica. "Explain that Kohl is alive. That as long as he's alive, Israel can't take action that risks getting him killed."

"We need time," said Calibrisi.

"'*We?*'" asked Jessica. "This is Israel's problem."

"So we're not going to help the people who saved Dewey's life?" asked Calibrisi. "In fact, the guy who saved him?"

"We've already helped him, Hector," said Jessica. "We found out who took him. We found out he was abducted and not killed. We should be proud of that. But we can't get involved."

"I'm going to appeal to Dellenbaugh. I want you with me."

"Of course I'll go with you. After we call Dayan."

There was a long pause on the phone.

"What is it with these fucking Iranians and their hostages?" asked Calibrisi. "It's like an industry over there. It's the only thing they're good at."

"Let's make the call," said Jessica.

"It's three in the morning in Tel Aviv."

"Let's make the call, Hector."

Calibrisi placed Jessica on hold, then had CIA Signal find General Menachem Dayan. He conferenced Jessica back in.

"Good morning, Menachem," said Calibrisi. "You've got me and Jessica Tanzer."

"Hello," said Dayan in a deep, clotted voice, the voice of a chain-smoker. "Hello, Jessica. The prettiest girl in America. How are you?"

"Thank you, General. I'm fine."

"I'm sorry to wake you up," said Calibrisi.

"Wake me up?" asked Dayan. "Is that a joke? I don't sleep."

"Menachem, the Iranians have Kohl Meir," said Calibrisi.

Dayan was silent.

Calibrisi described the evidence.

"Well, that's good investigative work," said Dayan. "Now what do we do? I will need to wake up the prime minister. He will want to bomb Tehran back to the Stone Age. I will agree with him."

"He was abducted," said Jessica, "not killed. He was Tasered and abducted, General. As long as we believe he's still alive, we need to be smart about this. Bombing Tehran back to the Stone Age won't bring him back."

There was a long pause at the other end of the phone, interrupted by the scratchy, hacking cough of the old general. Finally, he cleared his throat.

"Will you help me, Hector?" asked Dayan, a tinge of sadness, weariness even, in his voice.

Calibrisi stared at his phone. He looked through the glass walls of his office, down the empty, lifeless floor of cubicles and offices. He thought of Jessica's words, warning him not to get involved.

"Yes, Menachem," said Calibrisi. "Of course we'll help."

8

The CIA director's bulletproof, chauffeured black Chevy Suburban drove through the iron-gated entrance of the United States Naval Observatory. Outside the gates was a mob scene. The street had been shut down due to the hundreds of people who had gathered outside the gates and down Wisconsin Avenue. The mood was somber. Several held up signs: GOD BLESS AMERICA. REST IN PEACE, ROB ALLAIRE. One sign read, GOOD LUCK, J.P.

The SUV sped up the long, sloping driveway in front of the beautiful Queen Anne–style mansion that served as the official residence of the vice president of the United States. The vehicle passed more than a dozen police cars, Secret Service sedans, and assorted SUVs already parked along the driveway. The lights of the beautiful home cast a golden hue across the grounds. The driver stopped in front, and Jessica and Calibrisi climbed out.

It was the first time Jessica had been to the vice president's residence. Indeed, as she stepped toward the front door, she considered that it was a stark sign of how much President Allaire had kept J. P. Dellenbaugh out of state affairs that this would be only the third meeting she had ever had with the former vice president.

Two more soldiers stood at the front door to the house.

Inside the brightly lit entrance foyer, Jessica glanced around. It was homey, pretty, a little preppy, with Farrow & Ball wallpaper and chintz-upholstered furniture. On the ground, in the corner, she noticed a baby jogger and a soccer ball.

"Hi, Hector, Jess," said Mike Ober, Dellenbaugh's chief of staff. They shook hands with Ober. He was short, slightly obese, and young, with a mop of unruly, curly hair.

"Hi, Mike," said Jessica. "How are things going?"

"Good, I think. He's putting his daughter to bed. He'll be down in a few minutes. You want something to drink? Coffee, tea, something stronger?"

"Coffee," said Calibrisi.

"Two. Thanks."

They followed Ober into the dining room, a large room with a long table in the middle, which was covered in phones and laptops.

"Have a seat. I'll get those coffees. How do you like it? Cream and sugar?"

"Black," said Jessica. Calibrisi nodded, indicating he would take the same.

A few minutes later, Ober returned, followed by J. P. Dellenbaugh, who shut the door behind him.

"Thanks for coming, guys," said Dellenbaugh.

"How have the calls gone?" asked Jessica.

"Everyone is shell-shocked," said Dellenbaugh. "I've spoken to the Chinese premier, the Russian president, almost every European leader. Everyone is just shocked. Obviously, we'll bury President Allaire at Arlington. I want to be actively involved in the planning of that. I think we need to decide whether or not to have a parade. But we don't need to discuss that right now."

Jessica sipped her coffee as Dellenbaugh took a seat at the dining-room table.

"Before we discuss the transition, Mr. President, I'm afraid there's a situation," said Calibrisi.

"Go on."

He glanced at Ober.

"I have clearance," said Ober.

"No, in fact, you don't," said Calibrisi. "You have top secret clearance. There's a level above that."

"I wasn't aware of that. What's the process for getting that clearance?"

"It involves a comprehensive interview and reinvestigation by Langley. We can probably have you in front of the group, depending on the quality of your background materials, by midweek next week. I'll push it."

"Okay," said Ober. "I completely understand."

"Until then, I must insist that any discussion of CIA

activities or written materials be restricted to your eyes only, Mr. President."

"Of course," said Dellenbaugh.

"Do you want me to leave while you guys talk?" asked Ober.

"That might be best," said Calibrisi.

As Ober closed the door, Calibrisi turned to the president.

"It concerns Iran," said the CIA director.

"What about it?" asked Dellenbaugh.

Calibrisi glanced at Jessica.

"As you know, two months ago, the United States engineered the removal of Omar El-Khayab from the Pakistani presidency," said Calibrisi.

"I read the debrief," said Dellenbaugh.

"The American who led the coup, Dewey Andreas, was abducted in the hours after the operation was over. The military commander we initially installed as president of Pakistan, Xavier Bolin, took him and sold him to terrorists. Bolin killed Andreas's two American teammates, both soldiers, and flew Andreas to Beirut where he was to be tortured, then executed."

Dellenbaugh's eyes were wide in disbelief.

"My God . . ."

"By the time we found out, we had only a few hours to put a rescue operation together," said Calibrisi. "We had one option."

"Israel?" asked Dellenbaugh.

"Yes," said Calibrisi. "General Dayan dispatched a team of commandos to save Andreas. Israel lost six men that night saving him. One of the survivors, the man who led the Israeli special forces team, was named Kohl Meir."

Dellenbaugh nodded, sipping from his cup, rapt by Calibrisi's story.

"So how does Iran come in?"

"Iran kidnapped Meir yesterday in New York City," said Calibrisi. "He was there visiting the parents of one of his fallen teammates. Agents from their intelligence service, VEVAK, abducted him. We believe they took him back to Iran."

"The Iranians also killed two American citizens," added Jessica.

"Who?"

"The parents of that dead Israeli."

"This might sound like a stupid question, but why would Iran want Meir?"

"It's not a stupid question, Mr. President," said Calibrisi. "Meir is on an Iranian capture-or-kill list. He's a high-priority target for Tehran. In addition to being one of Israel's most highly decorated soldiers, he's the great-grandson of Golda Meir."

Dellenbaugh was silent for several moments, then glanced at Jessica.

"How does this concern us?" he asked.

"Israel has asked for our help," said Calibrisi.

"Help?"

"Finding him. Rescuing him."

"Obviously, this is complicated by what's going on in Geneva," said Dellenbaugh.

"Yes, sir," said Calibrisi.

"Can you update me on the status of those negotiations?" Dellenbaugh asked, looking at Jessica.

"The negotiations are at a delicate stage," said Jessica. "The Swiss are close to finally getting Iran to agree
to cease the development of their nuclear weapons program and allow inspectors inside the country."

"Close?"

"The deal is done," said Jessica. "Iran will receive
$150 billion in IMF loan guarantees. But they've made
another demand, one that President Allaire turned
down. We're at a stalemate."

"What was the demand?" asked Dellenbaugh.

"President Nava wants to sign the agreement on the
same stage as the American president," said Jessica.
"President Allaire wasn't willing to do it."

"Why not?" asked Dellenbaugh.

"He felt it would tarnish the reputation of the United
States," said Jessica. "He also believed the Iranians
were lying."

"I can certainly understand where President Allaire
was coming from," said Dellenbaugh, pausing. He looked
at Calibrisi, then at Jessica. "Still, do you two realize
how historic this could be?"

"I'll believe it when I see it," said Jessica.

"So you don't think Iran will go through with it?"
asked Dellenbaugh.

"They might sign it, but I'd be lying if I told you I
trust Mahmoud Nava."

"People are capable of change," said Dellenbaugh.
"This would be a major historic achievement."

"'Change,' Mr. President?" asked Calibrisi. "This is the regime that just killed two American citizens on U.S. soil."

"And whose magnetic bomb killed the scientist in Tehran last January?" asked Dellenbaugh.

"Your point, sir?" asked Calibrisi.

"My point is, they kill some of our citizens and we kill some of theirs. It's the way it works."

"Mostafa Roshan was one of their top nuclear scientists," said Calibrisi. "That's quite a bit different from killing two innocent bystanders."

"All I'm saying is, trust is not the issue," said Dellenbaugh. "It seems to me that any agreement that provides the international community with increased inspection powers inside Iran is worth the risk."

"Iran pledging to stop building nuclear weapons is just the tip of the iceberg," said Jessica. "Until we actually start to do on-demand inspections, we won't know if the agreement is being adhered to. That's at least a year from now, maybe two."

"Look, I'm as skeptical as you two," said Dellenbaugh. "But imagine if we did the signing in Tehran. At the embassy where Americans were taken hostage. It would be like Nixon going to China."

Jessica and Calibrisi were silent.

"Well, I don't expect you to jump all over it," he said. "I know it's out there."

"Iran has been trying to build a nuclear device for more than a decade," said Calibrisi.

"Well, that's up for debate, is it not?" asked Dellenbaugh. "I mean, they want nuclear power. Is that really so wrong? Who are we to dictate where they get their power from? If we go to Tehran, it might embolden the good side of Iran, the good side even of Nava, to follow through on their promises, to become part of the civilized world."

"Mr. President," said Calibrisi, "the decision as to whether or not to hold a summit with President Nava doesn't need to be made tonight. You bring up some good points. But we need to make a decision as it relates to Kohl Meir."

"I understand," Dellenbaugh said. "I apologize for changing subjects, Hector. What assets do we have inside Iran?"

"The CIA has at least a dozen operatives in or around Tehran; mostly Kurds we recruited out of northern Iraq and trained over here. In terms of informants, we have a broader set of Iranian citizens, perhaps two dozen, who provide us information on a regular basis."

"Do we know where they took Meir?"

"We believe he's in a prison on the outskirts of Tehran. Evin Prison."

"And is Evin the sort of place we could somehow penetrate? Do we have any agents or informants inside the prison capable of rescuing him?"

Calibrisi nodded, understanding the drift of Dellenbaugh's comments.

"No, sir. Evin is virtually impenetrable."

"Then what would you have the United States do, Hector?" asked Dellenbaugh. "Invade Iran? Storm a prison that you yourself just said is impenetrable? This is Israel's problem. It's not our problem. I understand

American citizens were killed, and it pisses me off. And if it makes you feel better, find out who did it and have them killed. Frankly, I don't care. But unless you can explain to me how we get Meir out, I don't see how we have a role here."

"Iran has at least fifty spies inside U.S. borders, Mr. President," said Calibrisi sharply.

"What does that have to do with anything?" retorted Dellenbaugh. "Kick 'em out. But I am not going to send in SEAL Team Six or anyone else for that matter to a situation that sounds, frankly, like a suicide mission. In addition, I disagree with Rob Allaire on this agreement signing. I want Iran to sign it. Even if you're right, that they're just deceiving us, it's worth the risk. It's a little bit of money for a lot of increased manpower on the ground over there."

"To be clear, we'll be saying no to helping rescue the man who saved Dewey Andreas's life," said Jessica.

Dellenbaugh nodded.

"What would you have us do?" asked Dellenbaugh.

"Condition our signing the agreement on Tehran releasing Meir," said Jessica.

"No," said Dellenbaugh calmly. "I'm not happy about what happened, but I am not going to risk the opportunity, the history-making opportunity, to finally get Iran to stop their nuclear weapons program. The opportunity that lies in front of America, and in front of Israel, is bigger than one man. If Iran can be brought back into the community of civilized nations, imagine the number of Israelis whose lives will be saved."

9

THE BRONKELMAN FUND
JOHN HANCOCK TOWER
BOSTON, MASSACHUSETTS

Dewey wore a navy blue suit, a white button-down shirt, and a green tie. His entire outfit had been purchased at Brooks Brothers the day before, as had a pair of cordovan wing tips, which were on his feet. Dewey's hair was short, and he was clean-shaven. He handed his license to the security guard, walked through a metal detector, then headed for the elevators. On the forty-eighth floor, he stepped off the elevator.

The floor was empty. He walked to a set of glass doors, the letters *TBF* etched in elegant cursive across the glass. Behind the doors, twenty feet away, sat an attractive brunette behind a large desk. He heard the faint click of a lock unbolting. He reached for the door and stepped inside.

"Mr. Andreas?" the woman asked. She stood up, her hand extended.

"Yes," said Dewey.

"Welcome to Bronkelman," she said. "I'm Monica George. Chip is expecting you. Please follow me."

Dewey followed her down the hall. In the distance, at the corner, a set of double doors was open. Past the doors, Dewey could see into a large office, then the windowed walls and behind them, the Boston skyline and the blue waters of Boston Harbor.

As he walked along the muted, lush brown carpet, Dewey glanced at the large paintings on the walls, an Edward Hopper oil of a diner at night, several Andrew Wyeth paintings, including one of a field running toward the distant ocean shore, which looked like a field he knew in Blue Hill, near Castine. Then a line of Picassos. The offices were quiet, nearly soundproof. He passed a line of young analysts seated in front of flat-screens, two per desk, each clotted with red and green numbers and graphs that undulated with activity.

"May I get you something?" asked Monica. "Water? Coffee? Tea?"

"No thanks."

She showed him into the corner office. The office was huge, two of its walls completely glass. An enormously large wood desk was arrayed with computer monitors, perhaps a dozen of them, and several phones. The chair behind the desk was empty, but in a seating area near the corner of the room, a large, overweight man in jeans and an untucked red button-down shirt stood up. He had a cell phone clutched to his ear, and he smiled and waved at Dewey to come to the seating area.

"Call you back," he said into the phone, then tossed

it onto the glass table and stepped toward Dewey.
"Dewey Andreas, how are you? Nice to meet you. I'm
Chip Bronkelman. Come in, sit down, make yourself at
home."

Dewey shook Bronkelman's hand.

"Nice to meet you," he said.

"Shut the door, will you, Monica?"

Dewey was at least half a foot taller than Bronkelman. The hedge fund manager was five-six or -seven,
but he weighed at least three hundred pounds. He was
bald, with glasses, and had a big, infectious smile.

Bronkelman sat back down on one of the leather
sofas. Dewey sat across from him.

"You don't look like the kind of guy who likes to
wear ties, Dewey," said Bronkelman.

"I'm not," said Dewey.

"Good. I don't let any of my people wear them. Honestly, I don't even understand what the fucking point is.
Originally ties were there to catch food before it hit
your shirt. Now God forbid you spill something on
them. Cost you two hundred bucks."

Dewey grinned, but said nothing.

"So you're from Maine, went to BC, played football
there, then served in the army, Rangers, Delta," said
Bronkelman.

"Yes," said Dewey.

"Jessica tells me you've done a bunch of other things
but that she wasn't at liberty to divulge any of it, for
national security reasons."

Dewey nodded.

"She also said you didn't talk much." Bronkelman

smiled. "That's okay. I talk enough for two people. So here's the deal. I need someone to oversee security, mainly for myself and my family. Last March, my daughter was kidnapped while we were in St. Bart's. It cost me several million dollars to get her back. I don't care about the money, but if I had lost Rebecca it would've killed me."

"Who did it?"

"We still don't know. The exchange was arranged by someone at the CIA. It's how I met Jessica. She's the one who recommended I get someone to help out."

"I understand. Do you mind if I ask what it is you do?"

"I'm an investor. Mainly currency. I'm what they call a global macro investor. I take what are hopefully educated guesses about the direction a specific country's currency is going to go in relationship to the dollar. We manage approximately thirty billion dollars. Insurance companies, endowments, wealthy individuals. Almost half of it's my own money; clients like when you put your money where your mouth is."

Dewey smiled.

"Look, Jessica told me a little bit about you. I know you view this as a lousy job, a compromise, settling. And the fact is, most of the time, you're going to be bored out of your skull. But, I don't want the kind of person who wants this job. That guy's a schmuck. I want someone who does view it as boring, as settling, because then I know I've got the right guy."

"I'm flattered you'd consider me," said Dewey. "I don't see it as settling, I'm just not sure I'm the right person."

Bronkelman leaned forward. He was an odd-looking man with a slightly nasally voice, and he spoke very rapidly; Dewey liked him.

"Here's the deal, and you think about it," said Bronkelman. "Take your time. Your base pay will be a million dollars, and I'll give you a nice bonus. You'll have access to my plane when we're not using it. I'll give you a budget so you can hire a few people so you don't have to be a constant babysitter."

"That's very generous," said Dewey.

"Something else," said Bronkelman. "We'd be spending a bunch of time together. I'll teach you how to trade. Maybe you're good at it. My best currency trader is a guy who didn't even graduate from college. He played online poker from the time he was fifteen until I hired him. I'll show you the ropes, teach you another skill. And you can teach me a thing or two, I'm sure."

Dewey grinned.

"You want some references?"

"No. Already got 'em. Jessica's the best reference I know. I can tell you're my kind of guy. I've never been wrong, at least about people. You seem like the kind of guy who's had some interesting shit happen to you. I'll take that. I always tell people, the best time to buy something is when it's undervalued. And my best traders are invariably the ones who've lost a fortune or two."

Bronkelman stood, as did Dewey. Bronkelman extended his hand and they shook hands.

"Take your time," said Bronkelman. "You know, this job would be easy for you. You'd make good money.

And I'm a good boss. My people like me because I'm fair and I'm loyal. I want you here. So let me know."

Dewey took the Delta shuttle from Logan to LaGuardia Airport outside of New York City. By the time the plane touched down, it was nearly 5:00 P.M.

Dewey was to meet Meir in the lobby of the Mark Hotel at six.

Dewey had liked Bronkelman, more than he ever would have predicted. He found him to be straightforward, kind, and not at all corporate or stuffy. Clearly, Bronkelman was also brilliant. Interestingly, what intrigued Dewey the most wasn't the money, but rather the chance to learn something new.

So, he'd take a day or two and think about it. In the meantime, he'd get together with Kohl Meir and see what he wanted. Maybe he'd head down to Washington and see Jessica. He'd call Bronkelman from there and say yes.

Dewey stepped off the plane, clutching a leather weekend bag. He walked quickly through the terminal. Outside, he made a beeline for the taxi line.

As he did, he heard a loud whistle. Turning, Dewey saw a black sedan with darkened windows idling in front of the taxi stand. The back window was halfway down. He recognized the face of Hector Calibrisi.

Dewey stepped toward the Town Car.

"Hi, Dewey," said Calibrisi. "Get in."

Dewey climbed in the front seat. A young agent was at the wheel; in back sat Calibrisi and Jessica.

He stared for several moments at her. She returned his look with a steady, blank stare.

"Hi, Dewey," said Jessica.

"Hi, Jess," said Dewey. "I'm sorry about the president."

"Thanks," she said.

Dewey glanced at the driver.

"Can you take me to the Mark Hotel?" said Dewey. "Seventy-seventh and Madison."

The CIA agent didn't move, except for his eyes, which glanced into the mirror at Calibrisi.

"He's not there," said Calibrisi from the backseat, running his hand through his mop of black hair. "Iranian agents abducted him. It happened day before yesterday."

Dewey's eyes shot from the driver to Calibrisi.

"He was coming to see you," said Calibrisi. "Do you know why?"

"I have no idea," said Dewey.

"How was it arranged?" asked Calibrisi.

"He called me. He said he needed my help on something. He wouldn't tell me what."

"Why wouldn't he tell you?"

"How the hell should I know? He called. We spoke for about a minute. He said he needed my help. He wanted to discuss it in person. That's it."

He looked back at Jessica and Calibrisi, who stared at him in silence.

"Where did they take him?" asked Dewey.

Calibrisi glanced at Jessica.

"Why are you asking?" asked Calibrisi.

"Hector, where the fuck did they take him?"

Calibrisi shook his head.

"Dewey, the president doesn't want us fucking around in Iran right now. Not with the Iranians about to stop their nuclear weapons program. Dellenbaugh doesn't want to risk it. That's why we flew up here."

"God forbid we offend the fucking Iranians," said Dewey.

"More important than the agreement is the fact that rescuing Kohl is a suicide mission," said Calibrisi. "He's in Evin Prison. No one gets out of Evin once they're inside. Not Delta, not SEAL, not Special Operations Group. Not even you."

"Is Israel going to do something?" asked Dewey.

"We assume they're going to go out and kill a bunch of Iranians," said Calibrisi. "If they haven't already."

"I meant, are they going to try and rescue him?"

"They came to us for help, if that tells you anything," said Calibrisi. "He's in Evin Prison. The only way he's coming out is in a body bag."

"What about a prisoner exchange?"

"There's no prisoner Iran would trade for Meir. He's a prize catch."

"They're going to dangle it over Israel's head," said Jessica. "Like Hamas did with Gilad Shalit, let him rot away, or else have some sort of trial and then execute him."

Dewey stared out the window, at a plane taking off in the distance.

"If you came here to talk me out of going over there, you're wasting your time."

"President Dellenbaugh wants America on the sidelines," said Calibrisi.

"I don't work for President Dellenbaugh."

"You've already done more than we ever asked of you," said Jessica. "You went into Pakistan and risked your life because your country asked you. Now your country is asking you to leave this one alone."

"Jess and I don't want you to die," added Calibrisi, leaning forward and placing his hand on Dewey's shoulder. "That's why we're here. It's a suicide mission."

Dewey's mind flashed back to the tarmac at Rafic Hariri. Pinned down by Hezbollah to the south, Lebanese Armed Forces to the north. Six dead Israelis were bleeding out on the bullet-pocked tarmac around them. The Israeli chopper, which they needed to rescue them, was nowhere to be seen. Death was imminent and both he and Meir knew it.

Dewey would never forget the look in Meir's eyes as they exhausted the last of their ammunition, as they prepared to die; a fearless look that told Dewey not to give up.

Or was it his look that told Meir to hold on?

He felt it then, a surge of warmth, bitter at first, then all-consuming, like fire.

"You think Kohl Meir and that Shayetet team thought about the risks before they went to Beirut that night to save me?" asked Dewey. He calmly turned and looked at Calibrisi, then Jessica. "Six Israelis died, men who didn't even know me. Thank you for thinking about my safety, but Kohl Meir saved my life. I know you'll understand."

Dewey reached for the car door.

"Where are you going, Dewey?" asked Jessica.

Dewey turned and looked one last time at Jessica. He opened the door and climbed out.

As he walked away, he reached into his pocket and pulled out a piece of paper. On it was a long number. He stared at it for a second, then put it back in his pocket, replaying Meir's words.

"If I'm not there, it means something happened to me. Call my father. He'll know what to do."

"What to do about what?"

"I can't tell you."

Dewey walked to the front of the taxi stand, cutting in front of a man in a suit who was talking on his cell phone.

"Hey, you're cutting," said the man, but Dewey ignored him and climbed into the cab.

"Where to?" asked the driver.

"JFK," said Dewey. "Step on it."

10

Kohl Meir opened his eyes and felt nothing but a deep sense of drift, loss, bewilderment, as if he'd been asleep for days. His eyes took several seconds to adjust to the light. *Where am I? Where the hell am I?* Meir tried to move his arm, but it was shackled. His legs were tied tight, strap restraints at the ankles and just above the knees; a belt across his torso, tightly bound so that breathing was difficult, another strap across his neck. His arms were fastened down as well, just above the elbows, and at the wrists.

The burning in his arm went from mild to severe, razor-sharp like a snakebite, and suddenly, against his will, he found himself screaming.

"There, there," came the voice.

Meir's mind was a scrambled mess, but he quickly allowed the accent to cut through the fog of his misplaced mind: Persian, some British; a cut of deep desert country. *Iran.*

His brain still worked. That was a start.

Meir looked to his left, blinking several times. He saw a short man with gray and black hair, a round face, glasses, and a big bushy mustache. He was wearing a white doctor's jacket. He stood at Meir's left arm, holding a syringe. The man pressed the plunger.

Meir screamed again as he felt whatever was in the needle invade his veins.

"It's not meant to hurt you, Mr. Meir," said the man. "It's an antidote, to wake you up. You were tranquilized. You've been out for some time. The pain will pass."

Gradually, the burning moderated. Meir stopped screaming as it went from severe to merely deep throbbing. As he calmed, Meir's mind sharpened. In front of him, blacked-out glass so he couldn't see out. He was in an ambulance. They were moving quickly. The road was rough, perhaps unpaved, or at least potholed.

The girls on the stoop.

Meir suddenly remembered his last thoughts. Walking down the sidewalk, the crowded sidewalk in Brooklyn. The warmth of the sun. The brownstone. Pressing the intercom buzzer, then waiting.

"You wonder where we are?" asked the doctor. He completed the injection, pulled the syringe out, then wiped Meir's arm with an alcohol swab.

Meir remained silent. With the pain, the consciousness, with his reawakening, he let his training begin to take hold.

Don't talk. Don't say a fucking thing.

How long had it been? Hours? Days? Weeks?

"Stop the chatter," came the order from behind his head. Another voice, this one with a deep, thick Iranian accent, telling the talkative doctor to shut up. He could hear, in the man's voice, years of cigarettes, military training, authority; a soldier, a commander of soldiers. A voice that gave orders.

He watched the doctor's eyes. Their reaction told him all he needed to know.

Meir strained to look behind him. But the restraints were too tight.

Now, his nose acclimated, he identified the smell, the cigarettes that the man's voice hinted at.

Meir shut his eyes, shut out the smell, the motion, everything.

He recalled the voice that came across the intercom. A soft, female voice.

"Yes."

"Hello, Mrs. Bohr, it's Kohl Meir."

The dull buzzer, a lock unbolting. He'd pushed the big door open and stepped into the small lobby in the brownstone. He had shut the door behind him. He had stepped toward the stairs, but he hadn't even made it to the first step. Someone had been behind him. A sharp painful electric jolt to his neck. And that was all. That was the last memory he had.

There was a low chirp from the cell phone of the man behind him. The man cleared his throat.

"Yes. One hour ago. Yes."

Meir kept his face blank. It had been a while but he could understand the words.

"It will be done." Then a click as he shut the phone.

Meir opened his eyes again.

"Evin?" asked the doctor.

The man behind him said nothing.

Evin. The word sent a small wave of dread through his body. It was the most notorious prison in Iran. They had many names for it. The "torture chamber" was the one he remembered.

Meir shut his eyes. He tried to put those thoughts out of his mind. The dark thoughts. This was how they said it started, dark, uneven, bitter thoughts, when you realized that you were a prisoner. That you would almost certainly be tortured.

Under his lids, he felt tears, which he struggled to keep away. He had to stay strong now.

"Whatever you're thinking, Commander, it's wrong," he said, coughing. "Whatever assumptions you have about where you're going, or what we are going to do to you, I can assure you you are wrong. You are about to experience hell. I know you have been trained in torture. In pharmaceuticals. I know that you know that torture always, in the end, wins out. But torture is only part of what is coming. The part that you don't yet understand is what it feels like to be the sword that slays your own people. That is what you are to become, Kohl. The symbol of Israel's defeat. How do you think your fellow Jews will feel when we parade you in front of them, shackled like a dog?"

Meir let the words wash over him then. He let the man's hatred take him over, like a sickness. He remained blank. Cold and blank as stone. For Meir knew that his strength in the coming hours would have to come from this wellspring of hatred. He would have to welcome it, draw energy from it. They could parade him in front of the world. Torture him. But if he could remain cold, unaffected, dignified, then he would win.

Meir let the thought of Israel, his country, come to him. He pictured the faces of his Shayetet unit, and the thought of the love and sacrifice of his fellow soldiers. He pictured his father, maimed permanently on the battlefield fighting in the Six Day War. He thought of all of the Israeli children who had lost their fathers, and all of the mothers who had lost their sons. He was not alone now. He let the strength of the Israeli soldiers who were still out there fighting forge like steel around him.

After what seemed like hours later, Meir felt the ambulance slow down. He heard the sound of a gate creaking open. There were voices, someone speaking with the ambulance driver, then laughter.

After the checkpoint, they drove farther on, slowly now. Then they came to a stop and the back doors of the ambulance opened.

Meir looked up. He saw no less than a dozen soldiers, standing in a loose semicircle behind the ambulance doors. Two soldiers reached for the steel frame of the gurney and pulled it out. Joined by two more men, they lifted him from the back of the van.

It was nighttime. He glanced up and could see stars.

To the right, he spied a yellow sliver of moon. The soldiers stared at him like fishermen staring at a large tuna, dangling from a hook above the dock. From the back, a short man, dressed in a suit jacket, no tie, stepped through the crowd, a maniacal smile on his face. Meir recognized him immediately. The man stepped forward, a large grin painted across his lips. Photographs did not do justice to the man; he was far uglier in person than Meir could believe.

"I had to see it for myself," said Mahmoud Nava, Iran's president. "I can't believe it. Welcome to Iran, son."

Meir remained silent.

"Would you like something?" asked Nava. "Some water? Some food. Yes, yes, they will feed you. You have had a long flight. Would that be good?"

Meir said nothing.

Nava nodded, smiled, turned to the gathered soldiers.

"Ah, yes, I see," said Nava. "Tough guy. Well, that is fine. This is not about you, Kohl. This is about your country. We will endeavor to treat you as well as can be expected, as long as you do what we say. We are not intent on hurting you. We are, however, determined to hurt your fellow countrymen. Do you see? Ah, yes, you will understand soon enough."

Nava turned, walked back through the semicircle to a black sedan that was waiting.

They unstrapped Meir from the gurney. He collapsed, his legs having been immobile so long they had become numb, but a pair of soldiers caught him before he hit the ground, lifting him by the arms, which they cuffed tightly behind his back. They left the shackles around his ankles.

"Come," said one of the soldiers, motioning toward a concrete building.

Meir walked, shackled, taking tiny steps, just inches with each step, slowly toward a door. Two soldiers, one at each side, guided him, holding his arms at the biceps behind his back.

He entered a hallway. Fluorescent lights overhead allowed him to see, for the first time, traces of blood on his shirt and khakis.

He moved down the hallway and entered a large, windowless room. A rectangular wooden table sat in the middle of the room. Two chairs, one on each side, faced each other.

The soldiers moved him to one of the chairs. They chained him tightly around his waist to the chair.

Meir sat for more than an hour in silence, alone, under the bright fluorescent lights. At some point, a young soldier brought him a bottle of water. The soldier held it to Meir's mouth and he guzzled the entire bottle down in seconds. Then the soldier left.

A short time later, the door opened again. A tall, hulking man entered. The man was bald with a thin mustache, wearing a white button-down short-sleeve shirt and dark pants. He walked around Meir, examining him as if he were an animal at the zoo, before finally taking the chair across from him.

"Hello, Mr. Meir," said the man in English with traces of a British accent. "My name is Moammar Achabar. I am your court-appointed attorney."

Meir stared at Achabar with a blank look and said nothing.

"Now, let's not have any pretense here," continued Achabar. "We both know where this is going, and frankly I will be happy the day you're found guilty. So don't consider me a friend or even your advocate. I am an actor. And this is a play. And you are the star."

Meir remained silent. Achabar removed a pack of cigarettes from his chest pocket. He lit a cigarette.

"Oh, yes," continued Achabar, "in case you are wondering, it's not a comedy. It's a tragedy. At least, for you and your country. They will keep you at Evin for a period of time. I don't know how long. You'll be charged with crimes. What I've heard is that you'll be charged with murder. You were involved with operations in the Strait of Hormuz, yes? Yes, of course you were. Well, there will be something to do with that."

Achabar took several puffs of his cigarette, held it up as he did so, watching the orange cinders burn down toward the brown filter, then stubbed it out on the table. He lit another one.

"Whatever they charge you with, they will make an example of you," said Achabar. "They'll find you guilty. Will they execute you? It depends on the mood. I think it will hurt your country much more if you are rotting in a jail somewhere. So that is what I will advocate for. It's funny, isn't it? I want you to suffer, and yet they will say I'm your friend. That I fought for you. But really all I will be doing is trying to punish you in a way I believe is worse even than to be shot by a firing squad."

Meir observed Achabar from his uncomfortable steel

chair. He remembered, then, something his great-grandmother, Golda, had written, before she died. In one of her last letters, to a man named Farger, who had written expressing his concern as to what would happen to Israel when she died, she wrote:

Do not be concerned, for it is not the end. It is not even the beginning of the end. It is merely the end of the beginning.

The stark, brutal nature of the predicament Meir was now in struck him like a slap across the face. But he didn't show it. Instead, he watched patiently, blankly, as his court-appointed attorney finished his third, then fourth cigarette.

For his part, Achabar smoked the last two cigarettes without speaking, slightly reclined, with one leg up on the wooden table, and a knowing grin on his lips.

"Would you like some food?" asked Achabar finally. He pulled his leg down from the table, stood up. "You must be hungry. Hold on."

Achabar gestured to the one-way mirror at the side of the room. Soon, the door at the back of the room opened and two soldiers entered. One held a stainless-steel tray. He walked over to the table and placed it down. On top of it sat two apples, a large piece of bread, and a small bowl of nuts, along with a bottle of water.

The other soldier went behind Meir. He unlocked the cuff around Meir's left wrist, pulled Meir's wrist around in front of him, then refastened the cuffs, tightly, so that Meir's wrists were touching in front of him. The soldiers pulled Meir's chair forward, closer to the table, then turned and left the room.

Meir stared at the food for several minutes. He did nothing.

"I'm going to leave now, Kohl," Achabar said. "Eat. You're going to be here a while."

Achabar turned and left the room. Meir stared at the tray for a few minutes. Finally, he reached out and picked up an apple. He was ravenous. He ate the apple quickly, swallowing large pieces that he had barely chewed. He then wolfed the bread down, then the nuts, then the other apple. He was surprised at how good the food tasted, even Iranian prison food, after not having eaten in such a long time.

Meir reached forward to the bottle of water. It was difficult to hold the wide bottle and unscrew the plastic cap. He struggled, then felt the bottle slipping from his shackled hands. He dropped the bottle. It bounced on the ground, then cracked. Water spilled on the ground.

After a few minutes, the door opened and two soldiers entered. One of them gathered the tray, then turned to leave the room while the other soldier reached down and picked up the dropped bottle of water. As he stood up, his head passed near Meir's waist.

Meir lurched at the young soldier. He grabbed the man's shirt at the starched collar with his manacled hands and pulled him down.

The soldier, caught off guard, screamed. He tried to push Meir away, but Meir held the shirt collar tight. The other soldier, near the door now, yelled and ran back to help.

Meir tried to move his fingers up toward the soldier's neck. The soldier pulled back with all of his strength, but the Israeli commando was too powerful. Meir held firmly, clawing at the skin above the collar, clawing upward toward the man's larynx.

Meir heard footsteps behind him, then felt a sharp blow to his left side, a boot—the other soldier kicking him with a steel-toed boot.

Meir pulled the soldier closer. His grasp was tightening. His fingers tore at the skin of the neck. The Iranian panicked as he tried desperately to pull backward and away from Meir's hands. The soldier tried to yank Meir's hands from his neck.

But Meir clawed his fingers like spider legs up the soldier's neck. His fingers, with barely room between his hands, encircled the soldier's neck in a tight grip.

More soldiers started pouring into the room, yelling and screaming at Meir to let go. The first soldier kicked relentlessly at Meir, his hard boot hitting Meir's ribs and back. Meir absorbed the blows, as he had been trained to do. Compartmentalizing the pain, he focused on what he had to do. Another soldier soon joined him and Meir suddenly felt a sharp strike to the back of his head, the butt of a rifle.

But still he held firm.

"*Stop, Meir!*" came a scream, and he recognized the voice of Achabar, his attorney. "*Stop! You'll kill him!*"

Meir was surrounded by a phalanx of men, then tackled. The steel chair cascaded over as at least four men grabbed him and wrenched him to the ground. They pulled at his head, yanked at his hands, tried to snap his fingers, which were locked around the soldier's neck like a vise.

But it was too late. As Meir toppled over, he brought the soldier tumbling down with him. They landed under the scrum of Iranian soldiers. As they hit the ground, Meir turned his powerful hands counterclockwise in a sudden, violent motion. The soldier's neck snapped, then he went limp, dead instantly on the hard, wet floor of the prison.

11

Dewey was still dressed in the navy blue Brooks Brothers suit, now wrinkled from the overnight flight from New York. The cab dropped him off in a quiet, well-to-do residential neighborhood twenty minutes east of downtown Tel Aviv. It reminded him of Beverly Hills.

Dewey glanced both ways and crossed a tree-shrouded sidewalk to a large iron gate. He pushed the gate in; behind it, a hundred feet ahead, at the end of a fieldstone sidewalk, a simple, rambling single-level home spread to the left, a large garden to the right. At the front door, a short, middle-aged woman in a green sundress was standing. Her straight gray hair was brushed neatly back. She smiled at Dewey as he entered.

"Mrs. Meir?" asked Dewey as he walked to the woman and shook her hand. "I'm Dewey Andreas."

"Please call me Vered."

Dewey towered over Kohl Meir's mother. She held his hand tightly.

"How was your flight?"

"Fine, thanks."

"Would you like something to drink? Coffee? Perhaps something to eat?"

"No, thank you," said Dewey. "I grabbed a sandwich when I landed."

"He's waiting for you," she said, nodding behind her. "The door."

Dewey walked down the hallway, through the living room. At the back of the living room, a door stood closed. He knocked.

"Come in," said a voice from inside the room.

Dewey entered a small room lined with bookshelves. Two windows looked out on a flower garden behind the house. In the middle of the room, a large man sat in a wheelchair; he was in his sixties with a thick head of black and gray hair; his features were chiseled, a sharp nose, broad forehead, tanned and ruddy. His deeply creased face looked as if it had been cut by winds over a lifetime outdoors.

"Hello, Dewey," Tobias Meir said, his voice deep and gravelly. "Please, have a seat."

"It's nice to meet you," said Dewey as he sat down in the chair next to Meir.

Meir stared at Dewey in silence.

"Did someone explain what happened to Kohl?" asked Dewey.

"Menachem Dayan called me."

"I'm sorry."

"It's the way things happen. You were a soldier, were you not? You can't think like that."

Dewey nodded.

"I need to know why he was coming to see me," said Dewey.

Meir stared for several seconds at Dewey.

"Do you believe there are good Iranians?" Meir asked. "Perhaps a guard in the prison who'll prevent Kohl from being tortured?"

"I don't know," said Dewey. "I doubt it."

"You assassinated Khomeini's brother," said Meir. "In Bali, 1988."

Slowly, Dewey nodded. "How do you know that?"

"We studied it," said Meir, "in Shin Bet. Why did you kill him?"

"It was an operation," said Dewey. "I was ordered to do it. I didn't ask why."

"Why kill Khomeini's brother?"

"He was the one charged with funding the different groups that were starting to sprout up. So, it was a message from us. A 'fuck you' to Tehran and the mullahs. A way of saying America doesn't forget. Someone else stepped into his shoes, but there was a certain amount of value in having that person's name not be Khomeini."

"It was a masterpiece," said Meir.

"No, it wasn't a masterpiece," said Dewey. "It succeeded, that's all you can say. I've seen piss-poor designs that ended up achieving the objective of the operation, and I've seen brilliant designs that go very badly, very quickly."

Tobias Meir moved his wheelchair across the library's oriental carpet to a dark mahogany rolltop desk in the corner of the room. He opened the top drawer of the desk, removing an envelope. He wheeled backward and stopped next to Dewey.

"If I tell you something, are you obligated to tell your government?" asked Meir.

"No," said Dewey.

"Not the CIA?" asked Meir.

"I don't work for them."

"So I can trust you?" he asked.

"Yes," said Dewey, "you can trust me."

"I'm going to show you why Kohl was visiting you," said Meir.

Meir clutched the white letter-sized envelope in his right hand. His hand tremored slightly as he held it. He extended the envelope to Dewey. Dewey took the envelope, but did nothing.

"Iran's president, Mahmoud Nava, has vowed to destroy Israel," said Meir.

"I know."

"They say he's trying to build a nuclear weapon."

Dewey took the envelope and lifted the flap at the side. He pulled out a photograph. The photo showed a long, roundish object in the back of a semitruck; the object was oval, long, dark silver, with a shiny steel tip. A missile. On its side, in green lettering, something was written in Persian.

"Is it—" Dewey started.

"Iran's first nuclear bomb," said Meir.

"Where did you get this?" asked Dewey.

"From an Iranian high up in Mahmoud Nava's staff. He stole the photo, then reached out to Kohl."

"Who is he?"

"He works for Mahmoud Nava himself. So you see, there are good Iranians, Dewey."

"There might be," said Dewey. "Or it was a trap. Who else have you told about this?"

"Nobody," said Meir.

"Why not?"

"According to the Iranian, they have a mole inside Mossad," said Meir. "Nava would launch the nuclear bomb immediately if he knew we had knowledge of it, before we have time to design and execute the operation to destroy it."

"*Operation?*" asked Dewey. "What operation? If Israel or the U.S. saw this photo, they would immediately blow it up."

"If they knew where it was."

"Natanz? Qum?"

"It's not at Natanz or Qum," said Meir calmly. "They've hidden it. Only Nava knows. He and a few high up in the Revolutionary Guard and VEVAK. And, of course, Suleiman, their psychotic ruler."

Dewey paused, staring at the photo.

"How did he get this to Kohl?" asked Dewey.

"A woman. A reporter for *Al Jazeera* who came to Tel Aviv and found Kohl."

"You're playing with fire," said Dewey. "You have to tell someone. Dayan. Mossad. Or let me tell the CIA."

"*No!*" shouted Tobias Meir. "No. If you tell anyone, they'll launch the bomb before we have time to react.

He specifically warned Kohl. You must promise you won't tell anyone."

"So what was your plan? What if I hadn't called you?"

Dewey looked into Tobias Meir's eyes, encircled by dark crimson, the bruises left by the aftermath of what were undoubtedly too many sleepless nights.

"That is a question I don't know the answer to," said Meir.

"What's written on the side of the bomb?" asked Dewey.

"It says, 'Goodbye, Tel Aviv,'" replied Meir.

Dewey shut his eyes for a brief moment, then swallowed hard. He reached his hand into his pocket, looking for a cigarette. On the flight to Tel Aviv, he remembered thinking that rescuing Kohl Meir from an Iranian prison was going to be next to impossible. Now it looked easy in comparison.

He felt the thin, sharp cardboard end of the cigarette pack. He pulled one out and lit it, not even asking Meir for permission.

"Do you know how to reach this man?" asked Dewey.

"His name is Qassou. I know how to get a message to him, through the woman."

Dewey held up the photo of the nuclear bomb.

"I need to meet with him," said Dewey, taking a drag on the cigarette. "Immediately."

12

At four thirty in the morning, a small plastic alarm clock made an incessant beeping noise. But the man who it was intended for, Abu Paria, was already awake. He'd arisen a handful of minutes before, as if his subconscious knew something was about to happen. Paria stared at the alarm clock for more than half a minute as the noise pealed in the air and its small light went on and off. Finally, he reached out and hit the button to turn it off.

Paria threw the sheets off and stood up, buck naked. He was a gorilla of a man, his chest, torso, and back covered in thick black hair. Paria's powerful frame looked like that of a bodybuilder's. He was a wall of muscle; big, hulking, with biceps the size of grapefruits and a barrel of a chest, legs like small trees. A lifetime's worth of weight lifting, combined with a decade as a member of Quds Force, an elite unit of Iran's

Revolutionary Guard modeled on Britain's SAS. Quds was Iran's fiercest military weapon, a commando regiment attuned to the climate and exigencies of the Middle East, designed for deep covert strike capability inside the borders of other countries. Quds Force training had been brutal—miles and miles of daily running in weighted-down gear, mountain climbing, survival training, hand-to-hand combat, and always the weights. Recruited into Quds as a twenty-year-old college student, Paria had been named unit commander by the time he was twenty-six.

Paria walked to the closet. On a hook inside the door, he removed a leather belt. He stepped into the middle of the bedroom. With the belt in his right hand, he whipped the belt across his left shoulder, so that the end of the leather smacked across his back, making a loud snapping noise. He whipped himself more than twenty times, each time the stroke became harder and more vicious. His back grew red, though after so many years, it had grown a thick, tough layer of callus. Paria repeated the exercise with his left hand, ripping the leather belt across his right shoulder until he nearly bled, all the time saying nothing, looking forward into a large floor-to-ceiling mirror, staring into his own eyes, without expression.

Everyone knew Paria was tough. Among the people within Iran's military and intelligence communities, he was widely considered the toughest man in Iran. But even those who considered him the toughest man in Iran, perhaps even the Middle East, had no idea how tough he really was.

He'd begun this sadistic daily exercise long ago, to learn how much pain he could actually endure, how he would behave and react if he was ever captured and tortured. Now he looked forward to the feeling, the utter pain of it all. It allowed Paria to begin his day with the knowledge that he could survive almost anything. It made him remember that he was just another human being; the humiliation and degradation of the lashes transported him to a level of self-awareness that was ultimately degrading, and grounded him. Paria believed it made him hungry, desperate, and brutally effective.

And these qualities were essential in the role he'd been chosen to play a decade ago: director of Iran's Ministry of National Intelligence and National Security. VEVAK, as it was known, was Iran's secret police. In theory, it was a combination of the FBI and CIA, focused both internally and externally, but rendered according to Iran's particularly evil recipe; doing anything necessary to keep Iran's ruling clergy in power. At the end of the day, it was this role more than anything that guided VEVAK.

Over the years, it was reported that VEVAK had killed more than a million of its own citizens. The truth is, even Paria didn't know how many they'd killed. He'd long ago outlawed the ministry from keeping such records.

VEVAK was everywhere. As anonymous as the wind, but as powerful and unforgiving as a hurricane. Paria had been chosen by Ali Suleiman, Iran's Supreme Leader, Ayatollah Khomeini's successor, and it was to Suleiman that Paria reported, not Nava. Once a week, Paria walked to the central Tehran mosque where

Suleiman lived and worked. There, he sat in Suleiman's office and updated him on important developments within VEVAK, both inside Iran and abroad. VEVAK was the most important weapon in the Iranian clergy's fascist-like control over the country.

Suleiman had the ear and instincts of a politician. As such, Suleiman tended to focus his questions to Paria on political developments inside Iran, especially in relation to Iran's president, Mahmoud Nava. Suleiman despised Nava, thought him volatile, ignorant, and often irrational; yet Suleiman had learned to appreciate the very considerable shield that Nava's mercurial reputation in international circles allowed him, as Supreme Leader, inside Iran.

It was Suleiman himself who had ordered the dramatic escalation in financial support for Al-Qaeda, Hezbollah, and Hamas. It was Suleiman who asked on a weekly basis how many IEDs had been trucked to the front lines in Iraq, as if keeping a mental count of the tens of thousands of bombs sent by Iran made him sleep better at night. And it was Suleiman who, early on, pushed for the development of a nuclear bomb.

But if Suleiman was the one who controlled the levers, it was Paria who was the lever itself.

After waking himself up with precisely four minutes of whipping, Paria did seventy-five push-ups and one hundred sit-ups. He dressed in shorts, a T-shirt, and running shoes. By 6:00 A.M., he was in the elevator that took him down to the lobby of his apartment building. He passed the security desk, manned with a pair of handpicked ex–Revolutionary Guards.

"Good morning, General Paria," said one of the
men.

"General," said the other, nodding.

Paria nodded at the two guards, but said nothing.

"The usual run, sir?" asked one of them.

But Paria didn't answer the soldier.

He left the building and ran to the right, down the
residential street, toward Sorkheh Hesar Park. Paria
didn't reveal information, to anyone, if he didn't have
to. As innocent as the guard's question was, there was
always the infinitesimally small chance that the guard
was working for someone, reporting to someone, and
that his question could be soon followed up by the appearance of a stranger along his running route, who,
from a few hundred yards away, would blow a hole in
the back of Paria's head.

Paria had ordered many such executions over the
years. It was a VEVAK trademark. Use informants to
learn the daily routine, then penetrate that daily routine, interrupt it, cleanly, efficiently. Kill with one
well-aimed bullet. Leave without a trace.

Even though both guards had worked in Paria's building for more than two years, and even though he knew
their backgrounds going all the way back to childhood,
Paria entered Sorkheh Hesar Park and ran in the opposite direction, taking a different route around the
large, now deserted park.

Paria ran a relaxed five miles, seeing nary a soul on
his route.

Back at his apartment, he did seventy-five more push-ups, a hundred more sit-ups, showered, then dressed in his usual attire—steel-toed black military boots, khakis, a short-sleeve button-down khaki shirt.

At 8:30 A.M., he climbed into the back of an idling black Range Rover, parked in front of his building. Waiting inside the SUV was a plainclothed man, who handed Paria a Ziploc bag. Paria took it and poured it out on the seat between them as the driver sped away from the building.

"This is everything Meir had on him?"

"Yes, General."

Inside the bag was a wad of cash, U.S. dollars and Israeli shekels, a car key with a Porsche logo emblazoned on it, a brown leather wallet, and an Israeli passport. Paria reached in and removed the wallet, inspecting it quickly, removing credit cards and examining both sides, then putting the wallet back in the bag. He opened the passport and stared for a few seconds at the photograph of Meir.

"Run the credit cards," said Paria. "See if they're dummies."

"They might set off some sort of notification."

"It doesn't matter," said Paria. "He's inside Evin. They can't do anything and they'll find out soon enough, if they don't already know. Run them. One of them might link to some sort of secret files."

"Yes, sir."

Paria held the small black Porsche key in his hand.

"They pay well in Israel, yes, General?" remarked the man.

But Paria didn't answer. Instead, he held the key and rubbed his finger across the logo, admiring it. Finally, he stuck it in his pants pocket.

As they drove down Resalat Highway, Paria opened a manila folder that was tucked into the back of the passenger seat. Inside, a sheath of papers contained Paria's daily briefing, including his schedule, press reports deemed by his chief of communications to be relevant, mostly articles about the war in Iraq, and operations briefings, which meant any activities of material nature from field operatives.

He pulled one particular piece of paper from the folder and read it twice. Attached to the sheet of paper was a five-by-seven color photograph showing a distinguished-looking man in a *bisht,* his beard and mustache trimmed neatly, a pair of round glasses on his head. The man's name was Mohammed Habib. He was a professor of mathematics at Tehran University.

Paria pressed a button on his cell phone.

"Ariz," said Paria to one of his deputies.

"Yes, General."

"Professor Habib," said Paria.

"You have the sheet."

"And you traced the transfers?"

"Yes, General Paria. The moneys were wired to an account in the professor's daughter's name in Lebanon. There can be no doubt."

"There can always be doubt," said Paria.

He hung up the phone.

* * *

A few miles east of the presidential palace, the Range Rover came to a stop in front of a beautiful red building, six stories tall, with a tan terra-cotta roof. Carved into the lintel above the doors: TEHRAN UNIVERSITY.

With one of his armed lieutenants positioned a few feet behind him, Paria walked down the fourth-floor corridor in the mathematics department of Tehran University.

They walked past legions of students, milling about in the hallway. Most were male; they stared at Paria as he strode by them. Students walking toward Paria, upon seeing the big, uniformed man, stepped out of the way immediately.

It was not that Paria was widely known; he wasn't. But a six-foot-tall, two-hundred-and-forty-pound man in a military uniform isn't something you messed with in Tehran. The fact that Paria's uniform had no markings, same with the officer trailing a few steps behind, made it clear to all that he was from VEVAK. Everyone had relatives and friends who had mysteriously disappeared over the years, and at no place was that more true than at Tehran University.

Paria came to a doorway halfway down the corridor. He opened the door. Inside, a short man in a button-down shirt, khakis, and glasses, was speaking to a classroom filled with students. The professor looked up as Paria opened the door.

"May I help you?" asked the professor nervously.

"I must speak with you, Professor Habib," said Paria. He stepped toward Habib. "Now."

"I'm in the middle of a class. Who are you?"

Paria was silent. He stared at Habib, whose eyes darted back and forth between his students and him.

Paria looked away from Habib to the classroom.

"Clear out," he said to the class. "Class dismissed."

"Wait one minute," said Habib, holding up his hand and trying to stop his students from leaving.

Paria walked to the front of the classroom, as nervous students filed quickly toward the door.

"My name is Abu Paria," said Paria quietly, so that only Habib could hear.

At the words, the professor visibly jerked backward.

"General Paria," he said, his voice trembling. "I had no idea."

Paria came closer to Habib. He turned behind him; the last of the students was hustling out of the room. Paria made eye contact with his aide, nodding at him. The aide shut the door.

Paria moved next to Habib. The professor stood no taller than Paria's neck, and was skinny and frail. Paria stood over him, staring into his eyes. Without provocation, he swung his right hand through the air, striking Habib with the back of his hand. Habib let out a high scream, then reached for his mouth, which was quickly flowing blood.

"What did I do?" he asked, holding his hand to his mouth.

"Cut the crap," said Paria. He swung again, this time hitting the other side of the professor's face with the open palm of his right hand. It caught Habib hard on the ear, and he fell to the ground. "We both know you've been selling secrets to Israel."

"No!" yelled Habib from the linoleum floor, his chin now covered in blood. "The Jews? Never!"

"Cut the crap, I said!"

Paria unleashed a boot to Habib's groin, which made him crumple to the floor, then lose his wind. He tried to crawl away from Paria, but his groans were hoarse and he couldn't draw a breath.

"We know you're an informant, Professor. We traced the funds to your daughter's account. Do you think we're idiots? Could you really have thought of nothing more creative?"

A look of pure fear washed across the professor's face.

"Answer my questions and I'll let your daughter live."

Habib struggled to breathe, looking up at Paria with a look of pathetic fear and utter surrender in his eyes. He cowered against the wall as Paria kicked him again, this time in the kneecap, connecting with it with all his fury, the steel of the boot toe ripping through Habib's pants, into the knee, shattering the kneecap, and making Habib scream as he reached for the knee. Paria descended on him, covering his mouth with his hand.

"Do you believe I'm capable of killing your daughter?" Paria asked, staring menacingly into the professor's eyes.

Habib moved his head up and down.

"Then answer me."

"Yes, okay," said Habib.

"Did you work for Mossad?"

"Yes," said Habib.

"We knew this. We've been watching you for six months now."

"I'm a mere functionary," said Habib.

"You betrayed Iran," said Paria.

"I would say it's you and your bosses who've betrayed Iran," whispered Habib weakly.

Paria shook his head. He reached down and picked Habib up by the back of his shirt. When he tried to stand, Habib almost fell over due to his shattered knee.

"Stand up," barked Paria.

"What do you want?" he said, struggling, holding his hand against the desk.

"What do they know of our nuclear program?" whispered Paria.

"How should I know this? I'm not privy to that. I simply relay insights and on-the-ground observations, once a month, that is all, General."

"I don't believe you," said Paria. "What does Shalit know?"

Habib struggled to speak as blood pooled on the ground beneath his bleeding mouth.

"Nothing, General. What is there to know?"

Paria stared down at Habib.

"There's a lot to know, Professor," said Paria, looking around at the empty classroom. "More than your big university brain can even begin to contemplate."

Paria continued to hold the professor tightly, clutching his shirt. It was like holding a rag doll. Paria's eyes drifted to the open window at the side of the room. He carried Habib toward the window by the shirt collar.

"No," said Habib, begging. "No, please. I know something."

"It's too late for that," said Paria. "An untrustworthy man will always be untrustworthy. A liar is always a liar."

Paria brought Habib to the window ledge. He leaned out and looked down at the internal courtyard, which was empty; a pair of green Dumpsters sat in the middle of the courtyard.

"It's Qassou," said Habib, blood coursing down his chin.

"Who?" asked Paria, nostrils flaring. "Minister Qassou?"

"Yes."

"What about him?"

"He's not as he appears," whispered Habib.

Paria pushed the frail man's head out over the window ledge, grasping him by the neck of his button-down shirt. Habib was now extended out over the ledge of the window; the only thing preventing him from falling was Paria, holding him by his shirt.

"What do you mean?" barked Paria. He shook Habib violently in the air. "*Speak!*"

"He's working against the Republic," Habib cried out frantically, tears streaming now down his cheeks as he stared down the empty courtyard below. "He—"

The top button of Habib's shirt suddenly popped off, then, in a matter of seconds, the rest of the buttons began popping away. Habib suddenly fell, screaming at the top of his lungs. Paria reached for him, but he was too late. He clutched at the professor's shirttail as the thin brown shirt tore away.

The squirming figure dropped quickly down the four flights, arms and legs flailing, screaming a high, horrific noise that made even the coldhearted Paria wince. His desperate screams echoed up. He landed head first in one of the empty Dumpsters.

"Fuck," said Paria.

Paria observed the Dumpster for more than a minute, scanning the interior windows of the courtyard for eyes. In his hand, he clutched the tattered shirt. He let it drop. He watched as it floated into the Dumpster, next to Habib's badly contorted corpse.

"I want all of the professor's files, computers, *everything*, on my desk within the hour," said Paria to the agent at the door as he walked quickly away from the room. "And put a tracking protocol on Minister Qassou. Immediately."

"Should I have him brought in?"

"No, not yet. But I want to know everything he does. And if he leaves the country, I want a full black team on him. We're going to find out what he's up to."

13

RESTRICTED AREA
NEAR DARBAND CAVE
MAHDISHAHR, IRAN

The mountain was anonymous-looking, just one of a series of smaller mountains at the western edge of the Alborz range. It was covered mostly in rock and dirt, with a few small trees and shrubs dotting its base and low country. This particular highland was a mile and a half inside a restricted nature preserve. Few knew the area's real purpose. A dirt road led to the base of the small mountain. A camouflaged door, large enough to allow semitractor-trailers, cranes, and other industrial equipment inside, was artfully set into the base of the mountain. In a hidden bunker next to the entrance, half a dozen armed soldiers stood guard, peering out through slats in the mortar.

Behind the disguised entrance was a cavernous, windowless, concrete and steel chamber more than fifty meters high and a hundred long. This tunnel was the only way in or out. At the end of the tunnel was a massive steel-frame sarcophagus built into the base of the mountain. Five stories high, a quarter mile in diameter, the Mahdishahr Nuclear Facility was not as big as Natanz or Qum, but it was big enough. And, it had one quality that made it, in one sense, the most important facility in Iran's extensive and growing galaxy of covert nuclear activity: Mahdishahr was unknown to Western intelligence services.

Deep inside the sarcophagus, a seventy-four-year-old man in leg braces and a light blue lab coat grasped a wooden cane and hovered alongside the object.

Dr. Kashilla ran his left hand, his only hand, along the welded seam of the object. The seam was perfect except for a small, marble-sized bump near one end. The object was dark silver-steel, shaped like a massive soda can turned on its side, tapered near the back. The object was a few inches under nine feet long. As he stared at the device for the umpteenth time, Kashilla didn't see the outside of the bomb; it had become invisible to him. Rather, he visualized the interior parts he and his team of scientists and engineers had worked so hard to design and build; the interior of the nuclear bomb he'd given the last decade of his life, his first wife, and his right arm to building.

Dr. Kashilla ran his hand over the fancy Persian script on the underside of the device. *Goodbye, Tel Aviv.* It had been his original idea to write "Goodbye Israel." Nava ordered the alteration, the edit, the specificity. As he ran his hand along the paint, that specificity sent a chill up Kashilla's spine.

The nuclear device, Iran's first, weighed exactly 9,012 pounds. Most of the nuclear bomb's weight, more than two and a half tons of it, was the high alloy steel case that held the target assembly at the front of the bomb. Inside the assembly was a target case—three feet long, two feet wide—screwed tight into the front.

Inside the target case was the target insert, eight rings stacked on top of one another like plates, their hollow centers filled with a steel rod that kept them held together within a thick alloy encasement. The stack weighed exactly one hundred pounds. A similar but slightly smaller stack of disks rested at the other end of the bomb. Combined, these disks weighed 188 pounds. This was the uranium. With an average enrichment of 87 percent, the nuclear device held a total of 164 pounds of Uranium-235, all of it enriched at Natanz, under Dr. Kashilla's direction, over a chaotic, at times danger-filled, decade.

Kashilla had seen eleven of his scientists killed over the years, assassinated by a combination of efforts by Mossad, the CIA, and MI6. He knew the risks of his profession, his mission really, because he himself had been targeted. A magnetic bomb had been attached to his car one morning six years ago by a young Kurd, a Mossad recruit from a village near the Iraq border. Kashilla had watched him do it. After the Kurd pulled his moped alongside the moving car, Kashilla heard the faint click of the bomb being stuck to the door. Kashilla had leapt from the backseat of the moving car, trying to pull his wife with him, just as the bomb had detonated. She had been killed by the blast, along with their driver. Kashilla's missing right arm was a permanent reminder of that awful day, a day that had driven him to complete the bomb, and to contribute toward the vengeance he knew would soon come.

Behind the target case at the front of the bomb, running the length of it, was a smooth-bore alloy gun tube with walls more than three inches thick, designed for a maximum pressure of 80,000 psi. It was through this gun tube that the stack of Uranium-235 at the tail of the bomb would be fired at the stack at the front, resulting in an explosion the likes of which the world hadn't seen since Nagasaki.

There were other pieces to the bomb, of course, the uranium deuteride trigger mechanism, tungsten carbide reflectors to amplify the explosive impact of the device, and even some empty space.

As Dr. Kashilla completed running his finger the length of the bomb, the serial beeping of a sideboom crane, backing up, drew closer to where he stood. The crane came to within a few feet, yet still Kashilla didn't take his eyes off the bomb. The door to the cab of the crane opened and a young man stepped down from the cab and approached Kashilla, placing his hand gently on the scientist's shoulder.

"Is it ready to be lifted, Doctor?"

"Yes, Alhaam," said Kashilla. "Take it away."

14

MARISTELLA CLUB
ODESSA, UKRAINE

In the afternoon, Dewey arrived at the Maristella Club, a modern hotel just up from Arcadia Beach.

A windswept, driving rain had delayed his connecting flight from Prague. He checked in, paid in cash, then went to the suite overlooking the Black Sea. He had less than an hour before he was to be at the restaurant, a place called Khutorok by the Sea.

Dewey glanced out the window. A large swimming pool, shaped in an unusual geometric pattern, like two ovals attached to each other, sat just below the balcony, devoid of people, steam arising into the balmy Odessa air. The ocean was just beyond it, across a small street and boardwalk, the water a black monotone to the horizon. Finally, he went into the bathroom and splashed water on his face.

A few minutes later, he stepped through the lobby and walked down a line of taxicabs. At each driver's door, he asked if the driver spoke English. At the third cab, the driver said, "Yes," and he climbed in the back.

"Pawnshop," said Dewey.

They drove through the city. A mile inland, in a neighborhood bustling with pedestrians, shops, and cafés, the cab pulled up to a small, run-down building with strange lettering on a yellow sign; behind the windows were steel bars; a photo of a Kalashnikov was the only indication of what the shop was in business for.

"Stay here," said Dewey, handing the driver a small wad of cash.

Dewey stepped inside the pawnshop. He looked at a wall of handguns, picked out a used Stechkin APS 9mm, the only handgun in the place with a suppressor. Dewey paid for the weapon and a box of slugs. He asked the clerk for a piece of twine.

Back in the taxi, he loaded the magazine and pushed it into the Stechkin. He laced the twine through the trigger guard, tied it in a loop, unbuttoned his shirt, then hung the gun from his neck. He rebuttoned his shirt and zipped up his Patagonia fleece.

At Khutorok by the Sea, Dewey took a seat at the bar. He was a few minutes early. He ordered a whiskey— even in Odessa they sold Jack Daniel's—and pounded it down, then ordered another.

He remembered the words from Tobias Meir, calling him at the hotel to tell him of the arrangements.

"Be careful; Odessa is a lawless place."

The rendezvous had been arranged by Tobias Meir and the reporter from *Al Jazeera*, a woman named Taris Darwil. Odessa was close to both Israel and Iran, and it was a popular destination for vacationers from both countries. Dewey didn't know what to expect tonight. On one level, he was here to listen to Qassou and any ideas the Iranian might have for stopping the nuclear attack on Israel. But more important than that was sizing up Qassou, determining if the Iranian was telling the truth, or whether he was a pawn in a larger plot that had already ensnared Meir.

At a quarter of nine, a tall, handsome man with longish black hair, combed back neatly, and olive skin, accompanied by a gorgeous woman with long black hair, arose from their table near the front window. The man paid the bill and, as he walked out, made eye contact with Dewey.

Two minutes later, Dewey threw cash on the bar and exited Khutorok by the Sea. Outside, Dewey stood for a moment and looked at the ocean, slapping the shore just across the street. The sound of the ocean's waves, crashing against the beach, created a steady rhythm.

Straight ahead, Dewey marked the couple, standing on the quay just up from the beach. She was pretty, dressed in a simple, sleeveless white dress. The man was dressed in khakis and a white button-down shirt with no collar. The man's arm was around the woman's back. They began to stroll away.

Qassou.

Dewey waited outside the bar for several minutes, watching Qassou and the woman walk away. The sidewalk wasn't crowded, but there were a few people out, enjoying the clear night and the sight of the ocean. He watched the couple as they receded into the distance.

"He will be with a woman. She's unaware of the purpose of the visit. Be careful. He might be followed by VEVAK."

Suddenly, to his left, in the distance, walking down the sidewalk, Dewey's eye was drawn to a short, round-ish man, smoking a cigarette, a wool beret on his head. He looked like an overweight tourist or a retiree and walked like someone who'd overeaten—shuffling, moving slowly, one hand on a thick belly.

Dewey went left, in the opposite direction of Qassou and the woman. He passed a second man, dark hair, a leather jacket. Dewey glanced at him and saw his eyes were searching, tracking, following the couple.

At the next corner, Dewey went left. He walked fast, down the block, then took another left, and kept going for three more blocks. He took one more left, slowing now. The street was thinner and darker, a service street.

After several minutes, as Dewey expected, at the far corner Qassou and the woman were crossing the street from the beach, heading up the thin service street in Dewey's direction.

Dewey walked on the opposite side of the small, dimly lit street. Halfway down the street, he tucked into a darkened alcove in front of a dry cleaner, now closed. He pressed against the glass, out of sight. Unzipping his fleece then unbuttoning the top button of his shirt, Dewey pulled the Stechkin from around his neck. He watched as Qassou and the woman passed slowly on the opposite sidewalk, chatting to each other, laughing.

Gripping the suppressed 9mm in his left hand, he lifted it into the air as the soft shuffle of footsteps came

from down the street. A shadow appeared on the cob-
blestones, a silhouette, as the lone figure stepped in
front of the alcove.

Training the Stechkin at the figure, Dewey prepared
to fire.

The silhouette turned, and in a reflection of light,
Dewey saw an old woman clutching a shopping bag. He
recoiled the weapon, and stood silently as she walked
quickly away, filled with fear, yet too old to do anything
except flee.

Dewey's paranoia had nearly caused him to kill an
innocent Ukrainian woman. *Wake up,* he thought. *How
could you come so close to making such a mistake?*

Dewey returned to the Maristella Club. He took the
elevator to the third floor, then went to his suite and
waited. After ten minutes, a knock came at the door.
Dewey stepped to the door and opened it. Qassou
stepped inside the room. Dewey shut the door behind
him.

Qassou was drenched in sweat. He looked disheveled, even slightly panicked.

"We need to hurry," he said, in near perfect English.
He was as tall as Dewey. "She's asleep, but if she wakes
up she'll wonder where I've gone. A cigarette break
lasts only so long."

"Who is she?" asked Dewey.

"Just a girl. But she's my alibi."

"Is it standard operating procedure to track government officials when they leave Iran?" asked Dewey.

"The answer is, I don't know, Mr. Andreas. Why?
Was I followed?"

"I thought so," said Dewey. "But if you were, I lost him."

Dewey walked to the seating area of the large suite and sat on a chair. Qassou followed and sat across from him on the couch.

"I have questions," said Dewey. "If I'm going to put my neck on the line, I need to be able to trust you. And right now, I don't."

Qassou stared at Dewey, nodding his head.

"I understand," said Qassou. "I can't make you trust me. What I can tell you is that I've already taken great personal risk to be here."

"What about Kohl Meir? Is he at Evin?"

"Yes," said Qassou. "He's at Evin. They are going to put him on trial. It will be a farce, but then you know that already."

"Can you do anything to get him out?"

"I have contacts inside Evin," said Qassou, lighting a cigarette, "but I don't see any way to get him out. He was a wanted man."

Qassou took a piece of paper from his pocket and unfolded it. It looked like an FBI most wanted poster from the post office, written in Persian. There were three lines of black-and-white headshots, photos of twelve different people. In the top corner, a grainy photo showed the unsmiling face of Kohl Meir.

Dewey took the sheet and studied it.

"What is this?" he asked.

"This is a VEVAK capture-or-kill list," said Qassou. "Agents are authorized to capture or kill anyone on this list."

"What's the writing?" asked Dewey.

"Various so-called crimes, real or imagined. Kohl was the number one target. As the great-grandson of Golda Meir, his capture is significant."

"How were you and Kohl going to find the weapon?"

"I don't know."

Dewey leaned forward and took a cigarette, then lit it. He shook his head, unconsciously, for the first time realizing there wasn't any sort of structure or strategy.

"Tell me about the mole."

"He works for Beijing. In turn, Beijing relays everything they know to VEVAK. It's *imperative* Mossad not know of our plan. Mahmoud Nava would detonate the device preemptively if he believes Tel Aviv or Washington knows and might attempt to destroy it."

"Let me tell Menachem Dayan," said Dewey. "They run a fucking mole hunt. They know what the hell they're doing."

"That is the precise moment when the traitor inside Mossad will call his handler," said Qassou, "and before the hour is out, the bomb will be sent on its way to Tel Aviv. I know Mahmoud Nava. This is what he will do. We only have a few days, but if he finds out someone is on to his plan, then all bets are off. Tel Aviv will be destroyed."

Qassou lit another cigarette.

"What about the CIA?" asked Dewey.

"I thought of the CIA," said Qassou. "I know the Damascus chief of station. With the CIA, it's a different problem. America will send in the cavalry. It's your arrogance. If we tell Langley, they'll want to start bombing 'in five minutes.' "

"I know people at the CIA we can trust," said Dewey.

"Mossad has people inside Langley. There is practically an open pipeline."

"So what if we *did* start bombing? Maybe that's the best solution."

Qassou blew out a mouthful of smoke, then smiled. He looked at Dewey.

"I don't know where the bomb is," said Qassou. "As you can imagine, this would make it difficult. And before the second American bomb is even dropped, Mahmoud would detonate the nuclear bomb in Tel Aviv."

Dewey reached out and took another cigarette from Qassou's pack.

"Look, I don't love Israel," continued Qassou. "But that doesn't mean I want to see half a million people die, no matter what their nationality or religion. When I found out Mahmoud's plan to use the nuclear device on Tel Aviv, I knew I had to do something. I would like to think someone in Tel Aviv would do the same if they found out someone was going to drop a bomb on Tehran."

"How did you find out about the nuclear bomb in the first place?" asked Dewey.

"Mahmoud trusts me. As much as he trusts anyone."

Qassou pulled a small letter-sized envelope from his pocket. He pulled out a short stack of photos. He placed them out on the table.

"They were taken last week. I spent more than an hour trying to guess the password to his laptop. I finally got in, and printed these. If I had been caught, he would have had me killed."

The photos showed different angles of the bomb. The final photo in the stack showed a plain-looking, new semitruck.

"Do you know the dimensions? The weight?"

"No."

"Why the photo of the truck?"

"The bomb's inside it," said Qassou. "The plan is to move it to a port, then bring it to Tel Aviv by boat."

"Who else knows about the bomb?"

"I don't know."

"Guess."

"At most a dozen people. The builder himself, Dr. Kashilla, and now, whoever is holding it. The military. Paria, of course. High-level Revolutionary Guard. And of course the Supreme Leader, Suleiman."

"You have no idea where the bomb is?" asked Dewey.

"If I knew where the bomb was," said Qassou, "I would simply have told Kohl. Israeli Air Force could get rid of it within the hour, I have no doubt. But I don't know where it is. It's the most closely guarded secret Mahmoud has. When I ask him if I may accompany him to see it, he lashes out at me."

Qassou leaned back. He removed another cigarette and lit it.

"Is the bomb launch ready?"

"What do you mean?"

"Is it on a mobile launcher? Is it in a silo? Do you know?"

"All I know is the plan that Mahmoud has bragged about. It's going to be sent by water. Hezbollah will bring it into Tel Aviv in a small fishing boat. They'll detonate it once it's in Tel Aviv."

Dewey stood up, shaking his head, his stubble-coated face lined with a look of anger, frustration, and fatigue.

"You have to find out the location. It's the only way."

"I'll find the location," said Qassou.

There was a long silence. Dewey went to the mini-bar and took out a beer.

"So you find the location," said Dewey, unscrewing the bottle of beer. "Then what?"

"That's why you're here," said Qassou, looking at him. "There will be very little notice. You'll need to be inside Iran. Then, when the bomb is being moved, you'll have to intercept it."

"Oh, that should be easy," said Dewey sarcastically. "I'll just go up and knock on the door. Maybe they'll even help me load it into the back of my car. What do you think?"

Qassou was silent for several moments. Then a grin spread across his face. He laughed.

Dewey took another sip and laughed with him.

"I do know that it's within a two-hour drive of the presidential palace," said Qassou.

"That narrows it down," said Dewey. "You're talking about a massive area."

"By my math, approximately a thousand square miles," said Qassou.

Dewey stood at the minibar and slugged the rest of

the beer down. He opened the minibar again, pulled out a small bottle of Jack Daniel's, twisted the cap off, and downed it in one gulp. Then, he grabbed one more beer, another bottle of Jack Daniel's. He sat down again, unscrewed the cap of the whiskey bottle, and took a sip.

Qassou stared at him in disbelief.

"What?" Dewey asked.

"You like to drink, don't you?" asked Qassou, laughing.

"When I'm planning my own funeral, yes," said Dewey.

Dewey stared at Qassou. He couldn't imagine how he'd hijack a nuclear device; he would have to involve the CIA. He thought of Calibrisi, Polk, and the rest of the team that had helped execute the coup in Pakistan. He thought of Jessica. He would need their help.

But then, he realized, if he were to tell any of them, no matter how much they promised, they would have to elevate it. Especially Jessica.

"How much time do we have?" asked Dewey.

"Days," said Qassou. "Taris will e-mail you. I'll try to figure out how to free Kohl before they execute him. But you have to know something. I probably won't succeed."

"Why are you doing this?" asked Dewey.

"Why?"

"You heard me."

"Not every Iranian hates Israel. You wouldn't know that, would you? The day Iran destroys Tel Aviv will be celebrated by a very small, very vocal minority of Iranians. Most of us will be deeply embarrassed, ashamed, and angry. I would not have been able to live with my-self if I didn't try to stop this. When I die, I want to be proud of what I did while I was alive."

With those words, Qassou stood, walked to the door, and disappeared into the night.

Dewey sat on the sofa for several minutes, closing his eyes, trying to think. Finally, he stood up and went to the minibar. He took the final bottle of whiskey from it. He stepped to the window. Lights dangled from lampposts along Arcadia Beach every hundred feet, il-luminating the sand in small, eerie tan circles. He un-screwed the bottle and, as he put it to his lips, suddenly saw Qassou walking beneath the lights of the the board-walk back to his hotel. Dewey slugged the whiskey as he continued to watch Qassou trail away.

Dewey was exhausted, both mentally and physi-cally. He'd barely slept the night before, staying at a run-down motel near the airport in Tel Aviv. His flight tomorrow was at 11:00 A.M. He would sleep in. There was so much to think about now, the complexity of a mission whose parameters had just changed, a mission he could tell no one about. His mind was too frazzled to think about any of it.

"Tomorrow," he whispered aloud.

He would figure it out tomorrow. He watched as Qas-sou's dark frame receded down the boardwalk to the left. He put the small bottle to his lips and drained it.

And then he saw it.

Out of the corner of his eye, to the right, along the beach. Almost imperceptible. A shadow passing be-neath a lamppost. Then, whatever it was disappeared as it moved to the left, to the south, tracking Qassou at a distance.

It was at the opposite end of the beach from where he'd just seen Qassou, at least two hundred yards away.

Maybe it's nothing. A shadow. A whore. Nothing.

But he knew it wasn't nothing.

Then, at the next lamppost, the dark figure appeared from behind the shadows, stalking. He was large, a tall man, dressed in black. He moved calmly.

Was Qassou followed? Was *I* followed? Was it the man from earlier?

The man below, whoever he was, now was aware of Qassou's meeting with Dewey.

Dewey picked up the Stechkin off the bed and ran to the door. He stepped into the hallway, then ran toward the elevators.

As he rounded the corner to the elevators, he came upon an agent in a leather jacket, bearded, young, olive skin, carrying a weapon Dewey recognized immediately, a H&K VP70M. Instinctively, Dewey stopped in his tracks, ducking as bullets tore from the muzzle. He pulled himself back, behind the corner, as bullets struck sheetrock next to his shoulder.

Shielded by the wall, Dewey moved backward, toward the fire stairs, as fast as he could, pressing his back against the wall, his right arm raised, pointing the Stechkin back at where he knew the gunman would emerge. His head swiveled between the corner of the wall, near the elevator, where he knew the killer would be coming, and the door to the stairs.

Then, with a suddenness that caused Dewey to jump

back against the wall, the glass in the fire stair door shattered as shots were fired from the stairwell. There was a second killer.

Dewey flattened his back against the corridor wall and fired, causing whoever was in the stairwell to duck. Dewey's eyes shot in the opposite direction, back to the elevator, as a black cylinder emerged from behind the corner of the wall. Bullets sailed blindly down the hall in his direction.

In front of Dewey was a hotel room door. As a hail of silenced slugs encroached now from both directions he raised his right foot and kicked the door violently in.

A woman inside the room screamed, her voice pitched with terror. Dewey lurched forward into the hotel room, sprinting. He fired one last round toward the stairwell, striking the Iranian in the forehead, dropping him. The woman screamed as Dewey crossed the carpet, running toward the deck. He fired toward the glass as he ran for his life, taking out the terrace door with a slug. The sound of shattering glass mingled with the young woman's hysterical screams.

The other killer entered the room, weapon out, cocked to fire. He pulled the trigger. The girl's screams were abruptly silenced as a slug ripped into her head, slamming her hard against the headboard, killing her instantly.

Dewey sprinted through the terrace door, onto shattered glass, then jumped, right foot first, to the railing, then out into the open air. As he leapt, he turned, rotating, and looked back up at the terrace. His legs flailed wildly as he fell. When the dark-haired killer stepped onto the terrace, Dewey fired a slug that ripped into his head, kicking the Iranian backward. A moment later, Dewey crashed into the swimming pool, back first, striking the water with a painful splash.

From three stories up, hitting the water was not like it was with a casual dive, but more like falling onto a piece of plywood. Dewey slammed down into the hard water of the pool; the wind was knocked out of him immediately. But he expected it, anticipated it, and in the moments after landing he let his body relax. He absorbed the trauma, swallowing the pain, then kicked his way slowly back to the surface. He left his gun at the bottom of the pool, swam to the shallow end of the pool, and stood for more than a minute, catching his breath.

He climbed from the pool, slowly now, leaning over and coughing. He tasted whiskey, cigarettes, and chlorine. He walked down the deck of the pool. His wet shoes made a sloshing noise. He took a set of stairs down to the beach. It was desolate, the only sound the soft, lazy patter of surf slapping atop the sand at water's edge.

In the shadows beneath the boardwalk, he stopped and removed his shoes, socks, pants, and shirt. He was now dressed only in a pair of soaking-wet navy blue underwear. He ran down to the water, in the darkness, then sprinted along the surf line toward the south, running parallel to the path Qassou had taken back to his hotel.

Dewey felt his lungs burn as he ran. Looking up, the lampposts along the beach and street cast diffuse yellow light. After several minutes of hard running, Dewey spotted the red ember of a cigarette in the shadows along the dark buildings across the street. He slowed to a jog, moving along behind the ember. It was Qassou.

He scanned the sidewalk. The dark figure appeared again, a quarter mile or so behind Qassou, who was oblivious to the man tracking him. He was big and tall, and walked with the bowlegged gait of an athlete or soldier.

Dewey moved to the edge of the concrete boardwalk, aiming toward a midpoint between two lampposts, a place that was in total darkness. He hunched over next to the overhang, waiting for the man to pass, watching him. When the man was a hundred feet farther along, Dewey reached up and pulled himself onto the boardwalk. He stepped silently across the cobblestone street. He began a slow run along the edge of the dark buildings, beneath canopies, hidden by shadows. He came to within five feet of the dark figure; close enough to smell cologne; close enough to hear him breathing.

Dewey took the final barefoot steps in silence, timing it so that he reached the man beneath a restaurant canopy. In one swift motion, he wrapped his right forearm around the front of the man's neck and his left forearm across the back of his neck, locking his left hand to his own armpit, rendering the man's neck in a vise-like grip that was unbreakable.

The killer was solid, resilient, and he struggled, flailing his arms wildly, fighting to pull Dewey's arms away from his neck, but it was futile. He kicked backward, then attempted to pull Dewey over, but Dewey was simply too strong. Dewey yanked back with his right forearm, snapping the man's neck like a tree branch.

Setting the body down, he searched his jacket and clothing, finding nothing except some money, a fixed-blade combat knife, and a black Glock G22C. He took the gun and the knife. Making sure no one had seen him, Dewey ran back across the street and jumped down to the cold sand. He threw the knife and gun as far as he could out into the surf.

He ran back to the hotel, barefoot, in his underwear, along the water's edge. Near the hotel, he retrieved his wet clothing and shoes. Looking down, he saw that his feet were bleeding from rocks and shells along the beach that he hadn't even felt.

He needed to get out of Ukraine before the proverbial shit hit the fan. But beyond that, he needed help. He was in over his head, far over his head, and he knew it.

15

The dais is prepared. Whenever you're ready, sir."

"Good. How many reporters are there?"

"The usual pool."

"Are any of the U.S. networks there?"

"Yes. Fox has a camera. The others will pull off the pool. The correspondent from NBC, Richard Engel, has requested an interview afterward."

"Tell Mr. Engel I will be happy to do it, after *Al Jazeera* gets their turn. Who is the correspondent?"

"El-Bakhatr."

"That's good. That's very good."

"Please, Mr. President, remember my advice. Do not smile. Do not gloat. This is about *justice*. This is about holding a *criminal* accountable. You must stick to the message."

President Mahmoud Nava adjusted his glasses as he

studied the paper in front of him. He lowered the glasses on the bridge of his nose, then looked across the mahogany desk at his minister of information, Lon Qassou.

"But how can we not gloat today, Lon?" asked Nava, smiling.

"Please, sir," said Qassou. "As it is, the announcement will be a lightning bolt across the sky. A majority of world opinion will be deeply critical."

"We're used to that."

"Yes, but if you gloat you'll only build sympathy for Israel. Even from our natural allies. You cannot express personal satisfaction. This is about *justice*."

Nava stood up.

"I understand. Do you think we would be better off if the adjutant justice made the announcement instead of me?"

Qassou shook his head, closing his eyes, his frustration impossible to hide. "Yes, you know I think Rafsanjani should make the announcement. I practically begged you. You are once again needlessly politicizing this. But that is your style. It will be your downfall. And now it is too late. Rafsanjani is not even in Tehran and there are fifty hungry reporters out there."

Nava watched with a big smile on his face as Qassou railed at him.

"You know me too well, Lonnie." Nava laughed. "No one could deprive me of this announcement. This will be the greatest day of my presidency. This will strike like the plague on all of Israel. There will be only one thing better, the day we drop—"

"Stop," interrupted Qassou, anger in his voice. "It's all a joke to you."

Nava stepped to the door, opened it slightly. The sound of the crowded communiqué room, filled with reporters, burst inside the office. He stared out through the crack, into the room.

Nava, still facing the door, searched the crowd of reporters through the crack, then looked back at Qassou. A maniacal smile crept like a small garter snake across his lips.

"Justice will be when we have wiped Israel from the face of the earth."

A thousand miles to the west, near the center of Jerusalem, in a heavily guarded six-story building made of tan-colored Jerusalem stone, Israeli Prime Minister Benjamin Shalit rubbed his eyes.

The cabinet room, a spacious room down the hallway from the prime minister's office, was crowded. Jerusalem was enjoying an unusual heat wave and the air-conditioning in the cabinet room wasn't working. The members of Shalit's cabinet sat around the square wooden conference table, cigarette smoke cantilevered in hazy lines across the sunlit air, sweating.

A door to Shalit's left burst open.

"Mr. Prime Minister, excuse me, sir," said the young man nervously. He looked about the room. "Come quickly."

Shalit, followed by his cabinet ministers, walked quickly down the hallway. In the cramped press office, a large television was turned on.

"Hurry," said Eli Ziegler, Shalit's press secretary. "He's about to come on."

"Who is about to come on, Eli?" demanded Shalit.

"Nava," answered Ziegler, ashen.

On the screen, a long, empty conference table with a cluster of microphones at the center. Behind the table, on the wall, to the left, the red and green flag of Iran. Next to the flag, three photos: Iran's president, Mahmoud Nava; Iran's supreme religious leader, Ali Suleiman; and the ubiquitous photo of Ayatollah Khomeini.

Beneath the screen, which was empty, the ticker scrolled: LIVE PRESS CONFERENCE WITH PRESIDENT NAVA.

Shalit, tired and angry, stepped to the television and stood directly in front of it.

From the side of the screen, Iran's president, Mahmoud Nava, entered and took a seat behind the microphones.

"Just over three years ago, a group of Israeli soldiers killed four Iranians. This was not a battle. These Iranians were ambushed on a boat in the Strait of Hormuz by Israeli special forces. One of those men was positively identified. His name is Kohl Meir. Mr. Meir was indicted by the highest court in Iran for his role in the deaths of the four Iranian citizens.

"Recently, Iranian police captured Kohl Meir. I am not at liberty to describe how or where. What I can tell you is that the capture of Kohl Meir is about justice. Under Islamic and Iranian law, he will be given a fair and proper trial. He will experience the benefit of

Iranian justice as we look with equilibrium and propriety on his transgressions."

Shalit reached out and pressed a button on the television set, pausing Nava's speech. Steadying himself, he looked back at his ministers, all of whom were equally speechless. His bloodshot eyes found Dayan, his military chief.

"What are we to do then, Menachem?" Shalit whispered. "Our boy is now beyond the gates. He cannot be saved."

Dayan stared at the image of Nava on the television screen, then turned to Shalit, saying nothing.

"This is now beyond the scope of Mossad or the Central Intelligence Agency to deal with," continued Shalit. "He's gone public. They will have a public trial followed by a public execution. Nava is going to torture an entire country."

Dayan, looking back at Shalit, showed no emotion, only calm. He pulled his cell phone from his pocket and dialed a number, then held the phone to his ear.

"Unleash the dogs," said Dayan calmly.

16

At just before seven in the morning, Ariq el-Sadd knelt down on the kitchen floor to tie his running shoes. Behind the counter stood his wife, Ara, glasses on, reading the newspaper.

"Do you want to go to the beach today?" he asked.

She ignored him.

"Ara?" he asked.

She continued reading.

He stepped forward, ripping the paper away from her.

"Why do you not answer me?" he asked, a hint of anger in his voice.

His wife looked up, pulled her glasses calmly from her face. She looked angry.

"What?" she asked quietly.

"Can we go one day without this fight?" he asked. "One day."

El-Sadd looked at his wife. She remained silent.

"I have no friends in Lisbon," she said, shaking her head. "I want to go home."

"Ara—"

"You said that after a year in Lisbon you would ask to go home. It has been four years. I have no friends."

El-Sadd, Iran's ambassador to Portugal, smiled at his wife.

"So go home," said el-Sadd. "Take a trip. Go see your sister. Or better yet, make some friends. Why do I have friends and yet you cannot find it in your heart to like anyone in the entire city?"

El-Sadd turned and walked to the door at the side of the kitchen, which led to the outside. He turned at the doorway.

"I grow tired of your anger at me, Ara," he said. "You are starting to distract me. I love you but I need your support. The complaining is getting very old."

El-Sadd stepped outside.

The Iranian ambassador's house was situated on a hillside, down a tree-lined street from Parque Eduardo VIII and its modern, geometric gardens. Its views, to the south and west, were stunning; the bold ocean, beneath the cliffs that ran along Lisbon's coast.

El-Sadd stood in the driveway. He closed his eyes, trying to put the conversation with his wife out of his mind. He stepped slowly down the large granite steps at the side of his house. The early morning sun had begun to warm the air. It was el-Sadd's favorite part of the day. He placed his left foot on the granite step to the right, leaned down to stretch. As he did so, he looked left. The black ocean shimmered in a million silver cuts that dotted the surface as far as he could see, to the horizon. A white sedan moved into the street. It slowed as it came to the end of his driveway. He finished stretching as the sedan passed the end of the driveway. The back window of the car slid down. Before he could even process what was about to occur, he had a vague premonition. He saw the black circular abyss of a weapon's tip. He felt his feet start to move, ordered by a part of his brain he didn't know even existed, telling him to run.

Inside the sedan, Ziefert, a thirty-four-year-old Mossad operative, held a suppressed Ruger 10/22 rifle with subsonic ammo. Ziefert locked the Zeiss optic scope on the man's skull. The man stood motionless for several moments as Ziefert moved the rifle into position. Then the man started to move back up the steps. Ziefert fired, just once, as the car continued to drive slowly down the quiet residential street. The suppressed bullet ripped into the Iranian's head just above his left eye. Blood sprayed across the stucco wall of the house behind him. The Iranian diplomat, Ariq el-Sadd, was pummeled backward as the bullet tore part of his skull off. He crumpled to the ground.

"Let's go," said Ziefert.

17

IQASS AVENUE
TEHRAN

The shiny black Range Rover stopped in front of the imposing, sterile, square concrete headquarters of the Ministry of Intelligence and Security. Abu Paria climbed out and walked quickly up the front steps of the building.

When he arrived at his suite of offices on the third floor, Paria swept past his three assistants. Inside his office, two men were seated.

"What the *fuck* is going on?" asked Paria as he crossed the room.

"What do you think is going on, General?" replied one of the men, a short, fat bald man with a mustache and glasses, who sat at the conference table. It was Paria's number two, Qasim Atta. "Israel is taking its revenge."

"Where was the ambassador killed?" asked Paria. He reached out, took Atta's cigarette from his deputy's mouth, and stubbed it out in the half-filled coffee cup in front of Atta.

"I was still drinking that."

"Where was el-Sadd killed?" repeated Paria, moving behind his desk, ignoring Atta's complaints about the destruction of both his cigarette and cup of coffee.

"Outside the residence in Lisbon," said Sasan Shahin, the other man seated at the table.

"Did President Nava really need to go on national television and rub Israel's nose in it?" asked Paria rhetorically, shaking his head in anger as he stared down at photos of the blood-covered corpse of the Iranian ambassador to Portugal. "Send out a black flag immediately to all embassies and consulates. Mossad will be looking for revenge, everywhere."

"Yes, sir," said Shahin.

Paria threw the photos down onto his desk.

"What's the report on Qassou?" asked Paria.

There was a long moment of silence as Atta and Shahin exchanged glances across the conference table.

"We've been unable to reach any of the agents we sent to track him," said Atta.

"What do you mean, 'unable to reach them'? Pick up the fucking phone."

"We've tried."

"Who did you send?" demanded Paria angrily. "A bunch of girls? I told you to track him full black; a kill team."

"We dispatched an S7 and two QUDS commanders," said Atta, barking back at Paria. "Three highly trained operatives."

"So where are they?" yelled Paria.

Again, Atta and Shahin exchanged nervous glances across the conference table.

"I spoke to Odessa police," said Shahin quietly. "Three men were killed. They match the descriptions of our men."

Paria stared at Shahin, incredulous.

"Two were shot. The S7 had his neck broken."

Paria was silent. He looked surprised, shocked even.

Paria knew Qassou. Everyone knew Nava's young minister of information; his propaganda chief. It was said Qassou alone had the president's ear. Paria knew that with Qassou, he needed to tread carefully. Of course, Paria knew that if Qassou had Nava's ear, it was he, Paria, who had the president's balls. So he didn't worry about Qassou. At least not until now.

"Qassou is a small man. He went to Oxford. I would be frankly surprised if he knew how to shoot a pistol."

"Mossad?" asked Shahin.

Paria shrugged. "Perhaps. Who the fuck knows. Who was the S7?" asked Paria, looking at Atta.

"Azur. Kiev chief of station."

"Did he send reports?"

"Yes," said Atta.

He leaned forward and pulled photos out of an envelope. He stood and placed them on Paria's desk. Paria picked them up.

"He tracked Qassou from the moment he landed. Qassou and the woman had been out at dinner. That was the last we heard from him."

Paria flipped through the photos, which showed the couple in various settings, taken from a distance. He took one photo and tossed it down onto the desk. It showed the pretty face of an Iranian woman, long black hair, dark sunglasses.

"Who is she?"

"Sara Massood," said Salim. "Just a woman. She works for a member of Parliament."

"Bring her in," said Paria. "This afternoon. I will handle the interrogation myself."

"She's already here," said Shahin. "She's waiting downstairs."

"Should we bring Qassou in?" asked Atta.

Paria paused, thinking for a moment. He reached for his pocket and removed the Porsche key that he'd taken from the Ziploc bag, the key belonging to Meir. He palmed it absentmindedly. Then, he started to shake his head.

"No," Paria said, calmly. "No, not Qassou. But I want to see a complete dossier on him. Get access to his spending habits. Phone logs. Internet. *Everything*. Make sure the men tailing him are good. Our best."

"Yes, sir," said Shahin.

"And get the black flag out, immediately."

Paria walked out of the office, walked down the corridor, then took an elevator to a floor two levels beneath the ground floor.

He stepped out of the elevator and moved past a pair of guards. He saw Salim, VEVAK's chief of staff, standing next to a steel door.

"Did she come easily?" asked Paria.

"Yes, General," said Salim. "She was in her apartment, preparing to leave for work."

"Who is the member of parliament she works for?"

"Khosla."

Paria entered the room.

Inside, a pair of bright halogen lights shone down, making the room feel like a sauna.

Seated in a wooden chair was the woman from the photos, now wearing a stylish red hijab that covered her hair. She wore a long yellow dress.

Paria had long ago given up the pretense of treating certain individuals with deference. He knew, as he entered the hot interrogation room, that the polite thing to do would have been to arrange for a meeting so that Massood wasn't embarrassed by the sudden intrusion. He also knew he should have conducted the questioning in his office or at least in a place that wasn't so unpleasant.

But he quickly brushed the thought from his mind. After all, Paria didn't care. It wasn't that he was within his rights; it was the fact that rights no longer mattered. The law was irrelevant; he *was* the law. She would undoubtedly walk out of the ministry a changed creature, every step filled with a sense of fear for the rest of her life.

He shut the door. Stepping to the table, he flipped a switch on an electronic panel that had been on, turning off a device that automatically recorded the audio of the interrogations.

"Miss Massood," said Paria. "I am Abu Paria."

The woman was expressionless. Her face and forehead had a sheen of perspiration on them. Paria noticed that her upper lip quivered slightly.

"You have nothing to worry about, if you tell me the truth," continued Paria. "I have a few questions for you. If you lie to me, on the other hand, I cannot protect you."

Slowly, Massood nodded her head in acknowledgment.

Paria remained standing.

"Where were you this past weekend?" asked Paria.

"Odessa," said the woman.

"With who?"

"You know with who," she said, barely above a whisper. "Lon Qassou."

"What were you doing in Odessa?"

"Visiting," said Massood. "A long weekend. We've been there before. We went to the beach. Restaurants. Shopping."

"How many nights were you there?"

"Two."

"Tell me, how long have you been dating Qassou?"

"Why do you ask?"

Paria paused, then leaned over. A maniacal smile crossed his face.

"I will do the asking here," he whispered, then slapped his hand hard on the table. Instinctively, she lurched back.

"A year," she said. "Maybe a little longer."

"Will you marry him?"

"I have no idea. I don't know if he wants to get married."

"Why not? Why do you think this? Tell me!"

"I just don't know if Lon is the type who wants to get married. He likes his freedom. I'm not . . . I'm not the only one he dates."

"A woman as beautiful as you?" Paria asked, smiling. "Come now. He would be crazy to let you go."

The woman frowned, and a look of fear came into her eyes.

"We've done nothing wrong," she said.

"I'll be the judge of that," said Paria.

"When I tell Representative Khosla—" she said.

"He will tell you to keep your mouth shut," said Paria, who moved now around the table and placed his thick fingers around her small neck. Paria squeezed his hand around her neck, choking off air. "Nor should you tell Qassou, do you understand?"

She struggled, nodding her head, but Paria maintained his steely grip.

"Were you ever apart?" asked Paria, taking a step back, but still gripping her neck with his meaty paws.

She shook her head back and forth, indicating no.

She reached her hands up, trying to pry Paria's fingers from her neck.

"Not even once?" he whispered.

She struggled to breathe. Tears streamed down her cheeks.

"Saturday," she coughed.

"What about Saturday?" Paria asked, menace in his voice. "He went out?"

"Yes."

"Where?"

"I don't know," she pleaded. "He left the hotel room. He thought I was asleep."

Paria let go of her neck. He stood back. Her eyes were bloodshot. Then, he swung his right hand through the air, slapping her hard across the cheek. She screamed.

"You lied to me," he said. "How long was he out?"

"Two hours," she cried. "Maybe longer."

"Did you see him when he returned?"

"Yes, of course."

"Was he bleeding?"

"No," she said, shaking her head.

Paria stared down at Massood. Her cheek was bright red. Her hijab had fallen off and was on the ground, and her long black hair was now a mess.

Finally, the woman looked up at Paria.

"There was a man," she whispered. "At the restaurant. A large man."

"What about him?" asked Paria. "Did they speak?"

"No," said Massood. "But they exchanged a look. A knowing look. I swear by it."

"What did he look like?" asked Paria.

"I don't remember exactly," she said. "Just that he was mean-looking, and American."

Turning, Paria signaled to the one-way mirror, waving. A moment later, the door opened and Salim poked his head in.

"Get the sketch artist in here," he commanded Salim, "*immediately!*"

18

On the thirty-third floor of a high-rise in downtown Tehran, a man named Ahmet Garwal wrapped a soft, navy blue bathrobe around his shoulders. Garwal, Iran's minister of housing, looked down at the huge king-sized bed of his twenty-eight-year-old mistress, Paisa. Slightly overweight with a cute face and short black hair, she lay sprawled across the bed, naked.

"Champagne, Ahmet," she said.

"Your wish is my command, my dear."

Garwal leaned down and picked up the two empty champagne glasses. He walked from the bedroom through the big, open living room to the kitchen. He took the open bottle of Veuve Clicquot from the refrigerator and filled the glasses.

In a half-constructed office building across the street from Garwal's building, a space on the thirty-fourth floor sat empty. It consisted of steel beams, concrete floors, piping, and clusters of wires dangling from the ceiling and walls, stacks of sheetrock, all cloaked within the darkness of a Tehran evening.

A lone man lay on his stomach on the concrete floor, near the edge of the building. Positioned on the floor in front of him was a long-barreled weapon with a wooden stock and a distinctive square muzzle brake: a PGM Hecate II heavy sniper rifle. The front of the weapon was supported by a small bipod, the back by a small monopod, steadying the high-powered weapon. The man lay still and quiet. His right eye was pressed against a SCROME LTE 10x telescope, customized with thermal-imaging technology. His right index finger lightly touched the trigger.

Through the telescope, he watched as Garwal put the bottle back inside the refrigerator.

Across the dark Tehran evening and the wide city block that separated the half-built office building from Garwal's luxury apartment building, the air was humid and blisteringly hot, nearly a hundred degrees. The humidity would affect the flight of the slug as it coursed across the sky. But the Israeli gunman had already made the precise countercalibration to accommodate for what would be a slightly altered, a slightly lower, trajectory.

As Garwal shut the refrigerator door and then reached for the champagne glasses atop the counter, the gunman pulled the trigger. A low boom like a bass drum sounded, but no one except the gunman heard it. A split second later, there was the sound of shattering glass.

Garwal was kicked violently backward through the kitchen and slammed hard into the stove, glasses dropping to the floor, the walls beyond him suddenly ruined in a miasma of red. The gunman removed his finger from the trigger as he watched Garwal fall in a contorted heap to the ground.

19

A pair of Iranian soldiers dragged Meir down the hallway, pulling him along like a slab of beef by the shackles at his feet. His head scraped against the concrete floor.

The guards spoke Persian, which Meir understood, but the dialect was rough. They were angry; he had killed one of their friends.

"Cell block one," said one of the men, dragging him down the corridor.

"Yes, sir."

"Where is Achabar?" the first one asked.

"He left."

"Get him back here, now."

"Yes, Colonel."

A latch on a door ahead unbolted. They stopped. Upside down, he turned his head and saw a small cell, empty except for a steel bed frame jutting from the right-hand wall and a toilet. A bright light hung from the ceiling.

"Get the machine," ordered one of them. "When Achabar gets back, keep him in the waiting area. Until I'm done."

"Yes, Colonel."

The soldiers lifted Meir, each grabbing him at the shoulder and along his pants leg. The guards threw him face-first into the cell. Instinctively, he tried to shield the coming crash with his hands, but then felt his shackles at his wrists behind his back; reflexively he tried to kick, but his feet were bound tight by the flex-cuffs. As his head was about to strike the concrete floor, he wrenched himself sideways, avoiding the direct hit to the head, his shoulder striking the ground first, a hard, painful crash into the concrete.

"Fucking Jew," barked the colonel.

Meir felt sharp pain in his shoulder. He looked right and watched as the cell door slammed shut.

Meir closed his eyes and didn't move. He had to gather his thoughts now. It was likely the last time for some time he would be able to find the calm place inside where he could steel himself.

He pictured his father, Tobias. It was always the same image: his father arriving at the playground at the elementary school in Savyon. Meir was five, in kindergarten. His father had on his military uniform. A broad smile was on his face. All of the other children looked over at him: Meir had been playing with a yellow toy dump truck on the pile of dirt. He pictured his father as he suddenly spotted him, their eyes meeting across the playground. His father's mouth moved; what had he said? He stood up and ran from the mound of sandy dirt. He ran across the lot to his father, kneeling, arms out. He'd run into his father's arms, who had lifted him up, then swung him around through the air.

It was always the same memory. It brought warmth to him. The images ran through his mind like a movie. At his hardest times, it was this clip that brought him back to the core of who he was.

Son of a soldier.

Meir knew why he held the memory so close. It was the day before it all changed. The day before someone from Hamas ended it all—a homemade IED put his papa in a wheelchair forever. That was okay. He had survived. He didn't understand it yet, not at that point. But at age five, Kohl Meir had suddenly felt the responsibility being moved from his father's to his shoulders. Like all Israeli sons, his time had come. That memory, of his father walking across the playground, was his last day as a boy.

The latch on the cell door creaked. The loud scraping of steel against steel as someone unbolted it. Then there was a noise of wheels turning, squeaking.

"They say I'm not to kill you." Again, the voice of the colonel. It was a deep voice, chilling. "I'll do my best. But I never was very good at following orders."

The door slammed shut.

Meir didn't move his head. He remained still, on his back, staring up at the bottom of the filthy steel toilet. He felt the wet of blood dribbling down from his forehead. The colonel's hand suddenly grabbed the shackles at his ankles. He pulled him into the middle of the cell.

Meir was on his side now. He opened his eyes. Blood had pooled in his eyes and he blinked to see.

The colonel was a short, obese man. His black hair was shaved close to his head and he had a beard and mustache. He wore glasses. He knelt down so that he was next to Meir. He pulled a knife from a sheath at his waist belt. He took the blade and moved it slowly across the air, toward Meir's face. He rubbed the side of it on the tip of his nose, pressed it against the flesh just not quite hard enough to break the skin, but close. Then he moved the blade down to his neck. He put it inside the neckline of the shirt, then quickly sliced the blade down toward Meir's waist, ripping the shirt wide open.

The colonel stood. He turned. Meir watched as he stepped toward a trolley, atop which stood a machine which Meir recognized; a red and black box with dials, and electronic cables crisscrossed at the back. The colonel took a pair of the cables and moved back toward him. On the ends of the red wire cables, Meir recognized small clips. The colonel bent down. He attached one of the cables to Meir's left nipple. The other clip the Iranian attached to Meir's right ear.

Meir concentrated, as he'd been trained to do. He forced his mind to compartmentalize what was coming, to mark off a mental border around the coming seconds and minutes. To seal it off and trick the mind into thinking that somehow it was happening to someone else. The barrier, he knew, was only in his mind, and it didn't make it hurt any less, but it would let him absorb the pain until he was unconscious.

The colonel stood. He stepped to the trolley. He turned a dial and a low hum could be heard. Then, the first bolt of electricity shot like fire into Meir's nipple, his ear, wrenching him sideways, his head jerking up, then slamming against the hard concrete. The pain shot through him for five seconds, and he felt himself urinating as his body lost control. After too long, the electricity suddenly stopped.

"I would ask you how that felt, but I already know," said the colonel. "Hussein tortured me during the war. The worst part is still coming."

The charge surged yet again, this time searing through his nipple like lightning. His ear took the electricity and it made an inhuman screaming noise in his ear, which, after a few seconds, he recognized was his own voice screaming.

"The worst part is when your body remembers the pain," said the colonel. "It will be at odd times. You're lying in bed. Maybe you're driving or at a restaurant. Your mind will suddenly replay the pain. You'll jump. Or turn suddenly, like a madman. Everyone will wonder why. That's the worst part."

Meir heard the torturer's words, vague, far-off sounds, like the tinkling of glass breaking in a distant room somewhere.

"Of course, you'll never know any of those situations again," said the colonel, laughing. "I have a feeling you won't be eating at too many restaurants."

In the pause before the next pulse of electricity, Meir smelled his own flesh, burning.

"Would I have done this had you not killed my man?" asked the colonel. "The answer is no. So don't blame me."

Then the pain began yet again, and his body, now resigned after only a few turns of the torture, shut down and he slipped into unconsciousness.

20

EMBASSY OF THE ISLAMIC REPUBLIC OF IRAN
BEIJING
PEOPLE'S REPUBLIC OF CHINA

In downtown Beijing, the sun was setting.

Inside the Iranian embassy, Tariq Ghassani, Iran's ambassador to China, loosened his tie. Inside his office, he stared down from the second floor of the embassy through a large, floor-to-ceiling bulletproof window. Outside, the streets were crowded with people. In his hand was a glass half filled with vodka and lime juice.

After two years in Beijing, Ghassani and his wife, Sacha, were starting to like the city. Ghassani spent time here when he was younger, as a spy, working for SAVAMA, VEVAK's predecessor. It was in China that Ghassani had brokered the deal to purchase several pounds of medium-enriched uranium from a rogue within the Chinese Ministry of Defense. Now Ghassani was too old for the work and sacrifices necessary

for VEVAK. Paria had offered Ghassani a posting anywhere and he'd chosen China.

The phone on his desk buzzed.

Drinking the last of his gimlet, he walked across the
large room and pressed a small white button on the
phone console.

"Yes," said Ghassani.

"Mrs. Ghassani called, Mr. Ambassador," said his
secretary. "She'll meet you at the theater."

"Fine, fine," said Ghassani. "Is she on the phone?"

"No, she said she had to get ready. Seven thirty."

Ghassani pressed the console button and stepped
around to the front of his desk. He grabbed a stack of
papers and placed them in his leather briefcase. The
top sheet was the day's press clippings, which showed a
photograph of Nava, sitting in front of the Iranian flag,
announcing the capture of Kohl Meir. Ghassani shut
the briefcase, buckled the two locks on the side, then
left his office.

Ghassani stepped through the massive front door of
the embassy and down the steps to the street. Reflexively, he glanced around, paranoid.

In front of the embassy, a long, black Mercedes had
its red parking lights on. He opened the back door and
climbed inside.

"Good evening, Ling," said Ghassani, shutting the
door behind him.

"Good evening, Mr. Ambassador," said Ling from
the front driver's seat. A low thud echoed in the luxuri-
ous car as Ling locked the doors with a button on the
car's console.

* * *

As he greeted his boss, Ambassador Ghassani, then locked the doors, Ling felt the sweat drips on his forehead, wetting the inside of his black cap. He glanced to his right. Crouched on the floor, out of sight to anyone but him, was a man. The man wore black jeans, a black shirt, and a thin ski mask pulled down over his face. He had a handgun with a long black suppressor screwed into its muzzle, aimed at Ling's skull.

The man nodded, flicking the muzzle of the weapon forward, silently ordering Ling to drive.

The Iranian ambassador's driver pushed the gas pedal and moved the Mercedes forward, lurching into traffic. He drove for several blocks, taking a left at Xin Dong Lu, and then rushing through central Beijing.

"Penghao Theater," said Ghassani from the back. "I forgot to tell you."

"Yes, of course, sir," said Ling nervously, watching the gunman out of the corner of his eye.

Ling had been at the light, several blocks away, after refueling the limousine. The blond woman had approached him. She looked like a student; young, jeans, backpack, carrying a fold-out map of the city.

"Do you speak English?" she had asked as he lowered the window. When he lowered the window, she reached out, placing the map in front of Ling. "I'm trying to find the Marriott Hotel."

"That is easy," he had said, flipping on the switch for the hazard lights, taking the map, orienting himself. He found the location on the map, then looked up. When he did, the young woman had the suppressor of a handgun an inch from his left eyeball, cloaking the view by covering the window with her frame.

"I have very little money—"

"Unlock the doors and you won't die," she whispered in perfect Mandarin. "Now. Use your right hand. Keep your left hand on the steering wheel. If the car moves even an inch, I will blow your head off. Understand, Mr. Ling?"

"Yes," Ling responded.

Ling had reached down with his right hand, crossing it over his left arm, finding the unlock button, pushing it, raising the locks.

A moment later, the passenger door had opened.

"Keep your eyes on me," the young woman had said. She thrust the black steel hard into his left eye.

Ling heard the sound of a man climbing into the passenger seat, to his right, then the door shutting. Then, he felt the hard steel of a gun against the back of his neck. He looked one more time into the blue eyes of the girl. Suddenly, she pulled the weapon from his eye, tucked it into her jacket, then abruptly turned, disappearing into the crowded sidewalk along Cho.

"Face the front," said the man in the passenger seat. His Mandarin was not nearly as good as the girl's, but it was proficient. It was good enough. "No sudden moves, Ling. Hand me your cell."

Ling had turned to face the front. He reached into his pocket, grabbed his cell phone, handed it to the man. Ling dared not look in the direction of the passenger seat.

"We're not after you," the man said. "Do exactly as I

say and you will be home to see Tammy and your two children tonight."

Those final words. . . . Ling had not, to that point, harbored thoughts of trying to do something, to be a hero, or even notify someone. Those words guaranteed what would be, over the next few minutes, his absolute fealty to the stranger in the passenger seat.

Ambassador Tariq Ghassani, in the backseat, was reading some papers by the lamplight. Ling thought briefly about trying to do something. After all, Mr. Ghassani had been so kind to him. The only thing he could think of would be to drive the right-hand side of the Mercedes into something hard, to try and crush the intruder.

He glanced down at the gunman. As if the intruder somehow knew what Ling was thinking, he slowly moved his head from left to right, then back. The message was clear: whatever you are thinking, Ling, stop thinking it.

Ling saw the red light ahead. He came into the traffic lane behind a red delivery truck. Less than a block away was the Penghao.

The intruder moved. He crawled forward, knees atop the leather of the seat, weapon out. He thrust the muzzle of the handgun forward, over the top of the seat. Ling saw, in the rearview mirror, the ambassador's eyes as he suddenly became aware of the gunman. There was a brief moment of silence, then Ghassani lurched for the door handle.

The commando fired. A dull thud, then an arc of blood sprayed across the black glass behind Ghassani.

Ghassani reached for his throat, where the bullet had entered. Then, as he held his throat, the assassin said, in Persian: "This was for Kohl Meir."

The gunman fired again. This bullet ripped into Ghassani's forehead, blowing the back of the ambassador's skull across the back bulletproof glass of the limousine, killing him instantly.

The killer turned, aiming his weapon at Ling.

"Railway station," he said calmly.

Ling's hands, shaking like leaves, gripped the wood veneer of the Mercedes's steering wheel as he drove toward the massive Beijing central train station.

At Beijing Railway Station, the man opened the door, climbed calmly out, then stepped away from the Mercedes. He disappeared into the busy crowd.

21

Dewey walked out of the Pierre Hotel, crossed Fifth Avenue, then took his time meandering through Central Park, which, at 8:00 P.M. on a Thursday night, was filled with people.

Reaching the west side of the park, Dewey exited at Sixty-first Street, crossed Central Park West, then walked north. He looked at his watch: 8:45 P.M. He still had time to kill. At Eighty-first Street, just past the Museum of Natural History, he took a left. At Columbus Avenue, he went left again, doubling back downtown. He walked down Broadway until he saw the fountains of Lincoln Center.

He walked around the big, softly lit fountain in front of the white granite opera house. A crowd of people was gathered around, mostly couples, a few smoking, all dressed in formal evening wear, long dresses on women and tuxedoes on men. It was intermission, and he'd timed his arrival perfectly.

Dewey was dressed in a blue blazer on top of an orange T-shirt, khakis, Frye boots. His brown hair was short, cut somewhat unevenly, as if he'd done it by himself. He was starting to get a layer of stubble. As he walked around the fountain, a few of the women standing outside watched him. He was handsome, tan, big, muscular; but it was something more that drew their eyes to him.

As usual, Dewey didn't notice the women, or pretended not to anyway, as he walked around the perimeter. Standing on the far side of the fountain was a large, slightly overweight man with black hair combed neatly back. It was because of how neat his hair was combed back that Dewey at first didn't recognize him.

They made eye contact. The man turned and started walking away from the fountains. Dewey stayed behind him, at a safe distance. The man walked briskly to Columbus. At Seventieth Street, he went right. It was a quiet residential block of pretty town houses. A third of the way down the block, the man climbed a set of stairs and disappeared inside.

Dewey registered the width, the location, the look of the town house as he passed by. He walked for ten minutes up Columbus, turned around, then walked back down. He went left on Seventieth and entered the town house.

On the third floor, Dewey knocked twice on the door. A moment later, the man in the tuxedo opened the door.

"Hi, Dewey," said Calibrisi. "That's the first time I've ever been followed by you. It's not a very pleasant feeling."

"If I ever come for you, you won't know it, Hector."

Calibrisi laughed. "That makes me feel better."

"What happened to your hair?" asked Dewey.

"What do you mean?"

"I didn't recognize you. You look like Liberace."

"It's my cover," said Calibrisi.

"Why the logistics?"

"Because I'm disobeying a direct order from the president of the United States, that's why," said Calibrisi, exasperation in his voice.

Dewey followed Calibrisi down a hallway, into a living room. They sat down across from each other.

"You wanted to see me," said Calibrisi.

"I need to tell you something and trust that you won't tell anyone. I need your word."

Calibrisi reclined, then folded his fingers together across his belly.

"What is it?" he asked finally.

"Do I have your word?" asked Dewey. "You can't tell the president. You can't tell Harry Black. You can't tell Jessica. You can't even tell your dog."

Calibrisi grinned.

"Yeah, you have my word."

"Iran has a nuke," said Dewey.

He removed a small stack of photos from his jacket and handed it to Calibrisi. Calibrisi pored through the photos.

"Kohl was working with an informant inside the Iranian government," said Dewey. "High up. A top aide to Nava. They were working on an operation."

"An operation? Why? What is Iran planning to do with the bomb?"

"Bring it into Tel Aviv, by water."

"Why didn't Kohl go to Menachem Dayan?"

"The Chinese have a mole inside Mossad. They're relaying any information they get back to Tehran. By the way, Mossad, as you probably already know, has spies inside Langley."

"That's debatable," said Calibrisi.

"Well, the point is, Hector, if Iran knew that Mossad or the U.S. had knowledge of the bomb, they'd move on Israel preemptively. It's why Kohl couldn't tell Dayan or anyone inside IDF or Mossad. It's why you can't share it with anyone."

Calibrisi nodded.

"I met with the Iranian in Odessa," said Dewey.

"Do you trust him?"

"I don't trust anyone. But I'm not playing with a full deck here. I don't have a lot of options. Do I believe him? I have to believe him. Kohl believed him. I'm not sure I can exfiltrate Kohl, but if he was working on preventing the Iranians from detonating a bomb in Tel Aviv, then I feel it's my duty to complete that mission."

"I don't agree," said Calibrisi, "but I get it."

"The Iranian is a guy named Qassou," said Dewey. "He was being tracked by Iranian intelligence."

"How do you know that?"

"Because I killed three of them. There could've been more. I didn't have a choice; they marked our meeting."

"Jesus Christ," said Calibrisi. "They already suspect him?"

"Yes," said Dewey.

"Let me take it to Dellenbaugh," said Calibrisi. "To Shalit and Dayan. We should invade the fucking place."

"You and I both know that's not an option. Besides, the point is, the moment Tehran gets an inkling we or Israel know about the bomb, they'll move to detonate it."

Calibrisi shut his eyes. He reached his hand up and rubbed the bridge of his nose.

"You trusted me to lead the coup in Pakistan," said Dewey. "If you'd found this out on your own, would you have come to me, Hector?"

"No," said Calibrisi.

"Why not?"

"Because Iran is different. Pakistan was mismanaged. Disorganized. Chaotic. I knew you'd be able to weave your way into that chaos. Iran is a different place altogether. It's structured, disciplined, and highly competent, especially VEVAK. I have a bad feeling about this, Dewey."

"What would you have me do?"

"I would say to you, let me tell Menachem Dayan. *Let Israel deal with it*. They're the ones facing the threat. They're not encumbered by bed wetters and second-guessers in Congress or a new and inexperienced president. And their military isn't spread thin."

Dewey was silent. He knew Calibrisi was right. But he also knew it didn't matter.

"I need help," said Dewey. "That's why I called. Non agency. The best you have."

"You have a design?"

Dewey was silent. He looked at Calibrisi, staring into Calibrisi's eyes.

"No."

Finally, Calibrisi smiled. He wrote down a phone number on a piece of paper.

"These guys left National Clandestine Service a couple years ago," said Calibrisi. "Set up their own shop. You'll get a recording saying you've reached a senior citizens' home. When it comes on, hit the number eleven. Then leave a voice mail saying Red Rover told you to call and leave a number for them to get a hold of you."

"What part of NCS were they?"

"Special Operations Group. One of them, Tacoma, is a former SEAL. The girl, Katie, came to Langley right out of the University of Texas."

"You know their work?"

"Yes. They're very good."

"Are they good with computers?"

"They have a couple beefed-out analysts and an absolutely top-notch hacker they brought out of NSA. Let's just say they may have been peripherally involved with Stuxnet."

Dewey reached into his pocket. He removed a pack of cigarettes.

"So they know Iran?"

"Yes."

"Do you mind?" he asked, lighting a cigarette.

"No," said Calibrisi. "What else? I have to get back."

"I need a weapons expert."

"What kind of weapons?"

"The kind that go boom, Hector. A nuke expert. I have an idea and I'll need some help."

"Go on."

"I want to build something that looks like that one. A fake bomb."

"A fake?"

"If we could steal the Iranian device and replace it with a fake, I could buy myself time to get it out of the country."

Calibrisi sat back, deep in thought.

"Has anyone ever told you you're nuts?" asked Calibrisi. "Even if some agency could do this—the Pentagon, Energy, Langley—it would ring huge alarm bells. If you go outside of those groups, you'd still need someone who knows what the hell they're doing. That's not a big group of people and every nuclear weapons expert, intermediary, midlevel yellowcake runner, are being watched, by us, by MI6, by Russia, by China. Plus, that thing probably weighs several tons. I don't see how you could do this anonymously."

"What's your point?"

"You need a rogue. You need an arms dealer. A powerful arms dealer."

Dewey stared at Calibrisi as the CIA director stood up. He walked to the window and looked out on the street. Calibrisi was deep in thought, and Dewey left him in silence.

"There is one," said Calibrisi. "A real beast. A German. His name is Borchardt. We try to avoid him, but it's hard to; he's at the center of a lot of weapons activity, particularly advanced satellite systems and centrifuges. He's very powerful. And very dangerous."

"Where is he?"

"London. I'll get you his address. There's something you should know, though."

"What?" asked Dewey.

"You have a history with Borchardt. He's the one who sold photos of you to Aswan Fortuna, the photos they used to find you in Australia. He almost got you killed."

Dewey was stone-faced, remaining silent, then a slight, almost imperceptible grin flashed across his lips.

Calibrisi opened his briefcase and removed a pad of paper, then jotted down some notes.

"What else?"

"What I asked you for over the phone," said Dewey.

Calibrisi reached into the briefcase and took out a manila folder.

"You need to burn these after you memorize them."

There were four sheets of paper inside, each with a photograph in the corner, and a biography.

"These are the top assets Iran has in the United States," said Calibrisi. "Either current or ex-VEVAK."

Dewey quickly scanned the bios. Two of the Iranian operatives worked in the private sector: one as an accountant for a meat-processing plant in Georgia; the other as a staff attorney at NBC.

The other two VEVAK operatives were on the staff of the Iranian Mission to the United Nations.

"Why don't you guys kick these guys out of the country?" asked Dewey. "Or kill them?"

"We can't touch the UN guys unless they commit a crime on U.S. soil," said Calibrisi. "The other two are a pipeline. We know everything they're doing, we listen to every conversation, read every e-mail. They're a source of information, even though they don't know it."

Dewey laid all four sheets out across the table.

"This isn't going to work," said Dewey.

"What do you mean?"

"I need someone high up," said Dewey. "Someone with the clout to make a phone call at the right moment."

Calibrisi leaned back, folded his hands across his chest, then smiled.

"There is somebody else," said Calibrisi.

"Oh yeah?"

"He's got clout. He might even have some knowledge of their nuclear program. He would be missed."

"I'm listening."

Calibrisi reached into the steel briefcase. He pulled out a piece of paper. He pushed it across the coffee table to Dewey.

"I'm handing you a piece of C4," said Calibrisi. "And I don't want you to get mad when it blows your hand off."

Dewey unfolded the piece of paper. It was a photocopy of a *Wall Street Journal* article entitled THE MOST UNPOPULAR AMBASSADOR AT THE UN. It was a profile of Iran's ambassador to the United Nations, Amit Bhutta.

"Oh, this is perfect," said Dewey. "You weren't kidding, were you?"

"About what?"

"About the C4," said Dewey. "I'm guessing there's

some sort of rule against killing these guys when they're on U.S. soil?"

Calibrisi stared at Dewey and laughed while shaking his head.

"How well guarded is he?" asked Dewey.

"Are you kidding?" said Calibrisi. "Like a fucking rock star. You got a better chance of kidnapping Queen Elizabeth."

"I'll need to borrow *Double Jeopardy*," said Dewey.

Calibrisi paused, his mouth dropping open. He stared at Dewey.

"How do you know about *Double Jeopardy*?" Calibrisi asked.

Dewey returned Calibrisi's stare with a wide smile.

"It doesn't matter how I know," said Dewey. "The point is, I'm gonna need it."

22

The crane operator maneuvered the steel jib at the top of the crane over the bomb, then slowly released the thick wire rope. A large steel hook came down just above the bomb.

Four workers, two on each side of the bomb, lifted the sides of the steel hammock beneath the bomb, wrapping the heavy sides of the hammock up and around the top of the bomb. At the top of the steel hammock was a pair of large steel rings. The crane operator inched the hook down and the workers pulled the rings over the end of the big hook. The crane operator moved the cable slowly up, until the wire rope was taut.

Dr. Kashilla watched from a chair at the side of the room as the crane operator lifted the four-and-a-half-ton nuclear device into the air. When the bomb was a few feet off the steel platform, the cab of the crane wheeled around, then moved forward, toward the back of a semitruck. The top of the truck trailer was open, and the operator moved the bomb inside the trailer as the workers guided it to a specially designed steel container inside the trailer. The semitrailer sagged noticeably under the weight as the bomb was lowered. The workers unhitched the steel rings from the wire rope and the operator raised it back up, then moved away from the truck. They shut the top of the steel container.

Kashilla stood and walked across the concrete floor to the truck. He watched as the workers, using ladders at each side of the trailer, closed and sealed the roof hatch.

It was a silver trailer, anonymous-looking even down to the license plates, which gave no indication as to its contents. Kashilla looked up at the shiny container holding the bomb, then reached his arm out and touched the side of it, wanting one last moment of connection to that which he'd spent so long creating.

"Can you believe it?" one of the workers said to him.

But Kashilla ignored the worker. He looked at his watch. It was late afternoon. They would come for the bomb at midnight.

"Do you need a ride home, Doctor?" asked one of Kashilla's assistants.

"No, thank you. I will wait until it's gone."

23

In the foothills of the Carpathian Mountains, a pair of shiny silver Audi S8s moved quickly along a winding mountain road. To the north, the white tops of the Carpathian Mountains were visible in the distance.

The meeting had gone well, Yuri thought, relaxing in the backseat of the lead car. Now they would all go to dinner at the Star, drink the best wines in Mukacheve, then retire for the night. Normally, Yuri would have asked Victor, his assistant, to procure a few of Mukacheve's best *poviya*. Perhaps having them waiting in his guest's hotel rooms to seal the deal with some of the Ukraine's legendary female companionship.

But not this night.

The Iranians were different. They were Muslims. There were plenty of Muslims in Ukraine, but when it came to how devout and what sort of particular practices each sect and country had, Yuri thought it best to avoid introducing elements that could strain what was a business relationship. He didn't like religion, didn't understand it, and found it was better to just leave it all alone. So no whores tonight; at least not for the Iranians.

They would have a hearty meal at Star, go to sleep, get up, and sign the letter of intent. And by this time two months hence, if due diligence went smoothly, he would be worth more than a billion dollars.

"I'll be a billionaire," said Yuri from the backseat. "A fucking billionaire."

"Yes, yes," said Victor, who was seated next to him. "I know."

"You say that as if you're disappointed," said Yuri. "What's with the attitude, Vic?"

"Nothing," said Victor. "The end of an era, that's all. I don't like the Iranians."

"Like them or not, it doesn't matter. They like my copper. And that's *all* that matters."

"Yes, yes. They like your copper. And you and Olga can go live in Paris. But I'm from here and this is all I know."

"I'm sure you can still work for them if you want," said Yuri. "They will need someone to run the operation. You heard them."

"I don't want to work for the Iranians," muttered Victor, running his hand back through his longish brown hair. "They smell."

"They smell?"

"The cologne. My God."

Yuri started laughing and looked at his assistant, who had grown into his closest friend. Victor tried to show no emotion, but Yuri poked his elbow once, then twice, and Victor grinned.

The Audi moved quietly along the curvy road that laced the hills near the mine operations. It was still light out, barely. The road was remote, cutting around a series of mountains at their tree-rung bases. A sign for the M06 appeared. Soon they would see the lights at the outskirts of Mukacheve's quiet, quaint downtown.

"Are they still behind us?" Yuri asked, looking in the rearview mirror at the driver.

"Yes, sir, Mr. Anton," said the driver. "That's them, the lights just behind."

Yuri nodded, saying nothing. His grandfather, after whom he was named, had bought the land from the Ukrainian government, using political connections to win the bid for the valuable state-mining operations near Mukacheve, paying little and being allowed to re-pay the government with a cut of the profits. *What a deal,* thought Yuri, shaking his head. It wasn't Ukraine's biggest mining operation, nor its most profitable. Just a little mine, enough to make one family very rich, and that is all.

Now, at age forty-four, Yuri would turn that simple transaction into more than one billion dollars.

Inside the tail Audi, a stone-faced Russian driver stared straight ahead as two men in the backseat spoke to each other in a high-pitched, rapid dialect that the driver couldn't understand. The third Iranian, who sat in the passenger seat in the front of the expensive vehicle, re-mained quiet.

The men were the three top executives at the National Iranian Copper Industries Company, or NICICO, one of Iran's largest mining conglomerates.

"You read the engineering report," said Esh, one of the men in the backseat, speaking in Persian. "They have barely scratched the surface of territories fourteen and fifteen."

"I know, I know," said the other man in the backseat, Harui, NICICO's vice president for development. A tall man, younger, with a thin mustache, he was giddy with excitement. "If they were smart, they would expand the operations, then sell. We're lucky they're not charging us five times the price."

"Yes, but there is the cost to get it to market," argued Esh. "This detracts from the beauty of this deal."

"How much does it detract?" said Harui. "Really, come on. We are stealing this mine from the stupid Russian."

"He's Ukrainian," said Esh.

"Ukrainian, Russian, who cares."

The man in the front seat suddenly whipped his head around, a cold stare of anger on his face.

"Shut up," barked the man, looking at Harui, then Esh, nodding ever so slightly at the driver. "Your wild tongues will see this deal ruined. Or worse, the price doubled. Keep your mouths shut."

The man, Marsak, was NICICO's chairman and chief executive officer.

Marsak stared for several more seconds at his underlings, scolding them with his eyes, then turned back to the front of the sedan. Glancing at the driver, he saw that the big man had had no reaction. Still, he hated the lack of discipline from his vice president. He made a mental note to fire him after the deal closed. Fire him, that is, if he could. After all, Harui was the son of Nava's brother. Perhaps he could just demote him instead.

Marsak leaned back and stared out the window. He loved traveling, especially to places that had colder climates than Tehran. That would be one of the biggest benefits to the deal, he thought. He would visit Mukacheve once a quarter, bringing his wife, Kessola. It was getting darker outside by the minute.

The Audi came to a sudden stop. The red brake lights of the forward car were bright, the car having come to an abrupt halt on the winding, remote mountain road.

"Buck," said the driver in rough English, so that they could understand. He pointed toward the front of the car. "Buck. In road. Deer. Big deer."

Slowly, the driver maneuvered the vehicle next to the other Audi, then stopped. Lying across the road was a massive deer, a fourteen-point buck by the driver's quick count. On the buck's chest, next to its leg, was a large bullet hole. From the front legs down, blood covered the big animal's brindle coat.

Next to the animal, backs turned, stood two men, inspecting the buck. Hunters. As the vehicles came to a stop, the men remained standing over the dead buck, still as statues, not turning.

"What is it?" asked Harui from the backseat.

"A deer," said Marsak, smiling. "Let's go see." He reached for the door handle.

The Ukrainian driver, a former officer in the Kiev Police Directorate, reached for Marsak's arm.

"No," the driver said, "I will look."

The driver opened the glove compartment and removed a handgun.

"What's wrong?" asked Marsak.

"Perhaps nothing," said the driver. He opened the door to the car.

As if choreographed, the two hunters turned. Each clutched not a hunting rifle, but submachine guns: HK MP5s, sleek, tight to the torso, long black suppressors screwed to the muzzles.

Yuri's driver stepped on the gas pedal, sending the first Audi lurching toward the gunman on the right. At the same time, the driver of the second Audi started shouting.

"Down!" he screamed as he tried to get behind the now open door.

The first Audi aimed at the hunter to the right; he stepped nimbly aside and started firing his SMG. The Audi slammed into the 1,500-pound buck as the gunman pelted the car with slugs. The windshield shattered, then bullets struck the driver. The gunman moved the weapon methodically along the driver's side of the car, stepping toward the vehicle as he did so. He mowed down Yuri and Victor in the backseat.

The hunter on the left opened fire, sending bullets beneath the second driver's door, into the driver's legs, who screamed for a brief moment until, through the Audi's aluminum, a tungsten-tipped bullet cut through the door and killed him instantly, his large frame falling to the road next to the car.

The gunman stopped firing and stepped to the side of the Audi. He looked inside the car, counting three men.

"Mr. Najar?" he asked politely in perfect Persian, stepping over the dead Ukrainian driver, aiming the weapon and looking inside the car at Marsak in the passenger seat.

Car lights suddenly danced in the distance, coming toward the scene.

Marsak's fear-filled eyes flew from the gunman, hopefully, to the oncoming vehicle.

"It's our car," said the gunman. "Sorry."

He aimed the tip of the silencer at Marsak.

"Whatever you want," said Marsak, pleading.

He fired the MP5, riddling Marsak's chest with a short spray of bullets.

"Who is Harui?" the gunman asked, again in Persian, looking onto the backseat.

"I am," said Harui with surprising confidence despite his predicament, perhaps believing he was to be saved.

The gunman aimed, then fired, ripping a quick slug through the Iranian's head.

The gunman stepped back, aimed the weapon at the car's tires, then fired. He punctured all four tires. He leaned into the driver's seat and looked at the last remaining person alive, Esh.

"Today's your lucky day, Mr. Zamia," said the gunman to Esh.

The gunman opened the door. Esh, whose cheek was now covered in blood spray from Harui's skull, stepped from the back of the automobile.

The gunman grabbed Esh by the collar of his jacket and directed him around the dead driver.

The headlights of the approaching Mossad recon team moved in behind the dead animal.

The gunman pushed Esh to the buck.

The other gunman waiting there took a pair of flex-cuffs and put one on the base of the buck's antlers, then looped the other end around Esh's wrist. He yanked tight.

"I will freeze to death out here," said Esh.

"No, you won't. Someone will come along. If not, here, take this."

The gunman reached into his pocket. He pulled out a folding combat knife. He handed it to the Iranian.

"If no one comes, gut the animal and climb inside. It will keep you warm. It's better than dying, yes?"

Esh looked down in horror at the blood-soaked animal, just in front of his black Gucci loafers.

"Who are you?" Esh asked as the two men stepped around the animal and walked to the waiting Range Rover.

The gunmen ignored the question. The first gunman climbed into the backseat of the SUV. As the second gunman, a Mossad operative, opened the passenger door, he turned to Esh.

"Go back to Tehran," he said. "Tell them everything that has happened. Tell the midget we will find you anywhere you walk. Tell Nava no Iranian is safe, not until Kohl Meir is returned."

24

WANG BAO HE
SHANGHAI

Wang Bao He was, as usual, crowded. At half-past eight on a Friday evening, the large waiting area of bamboo chaises and window seats was filled with those people who didn't have reservations. Out the door, a neat line stretched halfway down the block, beneath the restaurant's garish, mammoth red signs that hung overhead.

Past the lobby, a central dining area held a dozen tables, all filled with patrons. A din of laughter and chatter, in Mandarin, inhabited the space as waiters moved quickly between tables and the kitchen in back, porting bottles of Shaoxing wine from the small bar and food—the hairy crab was the house specialty—to the tables. The restaurant was filled with wealthy patrons from Shanghai, mostly Asians but a few Aussies, Americans, and Europeans. Wang Bao He seemed to always be crowded, but rare was the customer who walked out afterward thinking it hadn't been worth the wait—and the cost.

Most diners, however, were not in the public dining area. A pair of corridors stretched out and around the perimeter of the establishment. Down each dimly lit hallway were private dining rooms; intimate, windowless rooms set off from public view, with a large round dining table in the center and a beautiful crystal chandelier hanging overhead. If the central space held walk-ins, last-minute reservations, or tables set up by a concierge from a Shanghai hotel, these private dining rooms were the provenance of Shanghai's elite. On any given night, one of China's newly minted millionaires was entertaining colleagues in one of the private rooms.

In the last one down a corridor, a neatly attired waiter slid the bamboo and paper door aside, then stepped in. He was carrying a tray with two large plates piled high with Xiao Long Bao, the restaurant's famous crab roe dumplings. Though the table seated eight, it was occupied by only two people, a pair of gentlemen dressed in suits, one Chinese, the other with darker skin, short-cropped black hair, slightly overweight, with a sinister, almost sneering look on his wide face. They halted their conversation as the waiter placed the plates down on the table.

"Another bottle," said the Iranian, his Mandarin flawless, holding up his wineglass. "Colder this time."

The waiter nodded without saying a word, without even making eye contact with either man. He took the empty bottle of Shaoxing from the table, and left, sliding the door quietly closed behind him.

"Your fears are an illusion," said the Iranian, leaning in toward the other man. "There is no way anyone knows."

The speaker, Hasim Aziz, was an operative with VEVAK. He was, in fact, head of VEVAK in China. The man he was seated with was his main point of contact within the Chinese Ministry of Intelligence, Liu Ban Ho.

"It's not my fears," said Ho, reaching for his plate and picking up a dumpling. "It's the fears of my superiors. What do you do with our secrets? We're concerned about what happens when we tell you something. It is imperative that the Iranian government not react immediately upon receipt of information."

Ho stuffed the dumpling in his mouth.

"You're referring to the abduction of Meir?" asked Aziz.

"Yes, of course," he said with his mouth full. He swallowed, then washed it down with a gulp of wine. "Minister Bhang is very concerned. He himself spent more than a decade cultivating the relationship with our friend inside Mossad. He is among our most valuable assets. Not only is he privy to what is happening inside Israel, he is always on the receiving end of information out of Langley. We cannot see him put at risk."

Aziz leaned back in his chair. He took a sip from his glass.

"And what would you do if somehow General Dayan discovers this mole?" asked Aziz. "You jump to the conclusion that somehow it is Tehran who has erred."

"We would never jump to a conclusion, Hasim. We

would investigate. And if it was discovered that somehow Tehran had outed our man and got him killed, suffice it to say, Beijing would be very upset."

"And if Tehran were falsely accused of committing some form of error that led to the exposure of China's agent, we would be upset too," said Aziz. He squinted his eyes, then let a maniacal smile come to his lips. "In fact, I believe the oil ministry would be more upset than perhaps any other part of the republic. And I don't need to tell you what that means."

"Right," said Ho, laughing. "The only thing more powerful in Iran than hatred of the Jew is greed. You would sell oil to Satan if he had cash in his wallet."

Aziz grinned.

"Perhaps," said Aziz. "Though it is unfortunate your Sinopec holes are always so dry. China has many wonderful things." He reached out, picked up a dumpling, nodding to it. "Oil is not one of them."

Aziz tossed the dumpling into his mouth.

"Your threats are meaningless to me, Hasim. I am a deliverer of a message. The point is, be careful with our asset."

Aziz finished chewing and swallowed, then washed it down with the last sip of his wine. He reached his hand out and patted Ho on the shoulder.

"We value your asset perhaps even more than you do, Liu," said Aziz. "For China, it's a game. For Iran, we are talking about life or death. Israel is our mortal enemy. We would never do anything to compromise what Bhang and the ministry have created inside Israel. Never."

Ho smiled.

"I know that," he said. "I just need to remind you from time to time."

"No, you don't," said Aziz.

"Yes, I do," said Ho. "For I have a particularly juicy and delectable present for you tonight, my friend."

Aziz's eyes widened.

"I'm all ears, Liu," he said, leaning closer to the Chinese agent.

The door abruptly opened and the waiter from before stepped inside the room. He quickly slid the door shut, then turned, arm raised, in his hand a dark object; the green bottle of Shaoxing. Ho and Aziz remained silent, waiting for him to finish his business. He refilled the glasses, then placed the bottle in the middle of the table. He turned and left, sliding the door shut behind him.

"What is it?" asked Aziz. He took his wineglass and gulped nearly half of it down.

"An accidental discovery," said Ho. "Uncovered by Mossad. A juicy little morsel that will make Abu Paria get an erection."

"For God's sake, tell me," the Iranian whispered, urgency in his rasp.

Ho reached to his left. He lifted a thin silver briefcase from the ground and placed it on his lap. He adjusted the six-digit lock out of sight of Aziz, then popped open the case. He removed a manila envelope, then handed it to Aziz.

"Happy birthday, Hasim," said Ho, closing the briefcase and placing it back on the ground. He reached for another dumpling, tossed it in his mouth, then picked up his wineglass.

Aziz ripped open the envelope. He pulled out a small stack of photos. All were black-and-white, grainy.

The first photo showed a tall, handsome man walking with a gorgeous dark-haired beauty; both were Middle Eastern.

"Do you recognize him?" asked Ho.

"Yes," said the Iranian. "Lon Qassou. A cabinet member. Of course I recognize him."

"These photos were taken less than an hour apart, at Odessa Airport."

"Odessa?"

"Yes."

"Our Kiev chief of station was killed in Odessa last weekend," said Aziz, flipping to the second photo. "Two Quds soldiers too."

"Do you know what date?"

"Yes. September tenth."

Ho reached out and yanked the top photo from Aziz. It showed a digital time stamp:

10-09-12

Aziz placed the second photo on top, at first his head seemed to jerk backward ever so slightly at the subject. The photo was the clearest of the three. It showed an American with short hair, unkempt. He wore a suit coat with a button-down shirt. He was good-looking. But the camera also caught something else in his demeanor;

his dark eyes had an angry edge. A silent wave of electricity, composed partly of fear, moved through Aziz. He reached for his wineglass, then drank down the remaining wine as he continued to stare at the photo of the man.

"Who is he?" asked Aziz.

"His name is Dewey Andreas," said Ho. "Have you heard of him?"

"No," said Aziz. "Should I have?"

Suddenly the door opened again. Aziz swung around just as the waiter was entering, a tray full of food on his shoulder.

"Out!" barked Aziz, his voice trembling with anger. "Now!"

The waiter almost dropped the tray, but managed to hold on. He slipped quickly out, then slid the door closed.

"He's American," said Ho calmly. "He's the man who led the coup in Pakistan."

"Special Operations Group?"

"No," said Ho. "He doesn't work for the government."

"What do you mean he doesn't work for the government?"

"You heard me correctly. He's a free agent, a former Delta. He's a mean son of a bitch."

"Mean?"

"Very. He's the one who stuck a knife into Khomeini's brother more than a decade ago."

"Bali?"

"Yes."

Aziz flipped back through the six photos. He swallowed hard.

"What's going on?" asked Aziz.

"I have no idea," said Ho. "And frankly, I'm not sure China cares. You, however, would seem to have a situation on your hands."

"It could mean anything," said Aziz.

"Or nothing."

"You don't believe that."

"No, I don't. Perhaps Abu should grab a cup of coffee with Mr. Qassou."

Aziz stood up. He quickly put the photos back in the envelope. Aziz stepped quickly toward the door.

"You're welcome," said Ho. "By the way, Minister Bhang has a simple favor to ask. Not urgent, but if you happen to think of it . . . If the situation presents itself."

"What?" asked Aziz.

"Kill Andreas, if you have the opportunity. For all our sakes, Hasim. It's not good to have an American running around with such—how shall I put it—*skills*."

25

Mahmoud Nava walked down the hallway next to his office to a private elevator that led to the basement garage. Instead of pressing the button that would take him to the garage and one of his waiting limousines, Nava pressed the button for basement two, one floor below. When the doors opened, he stepped out into a dimly lit hall.

He walked quickly to the right, to a door at the end of the hall. He looked back over his shoulder; he thought he had heard something, but he saw no one. He took a silver key from his pocket and unlocked the steel door. A black Range Rover sat just outside the door, idling, windows completely dark in black tint. Nava stepped over to the SUV, opened the front door on the passenger side, climbed in.

Seated in the driver's seat was a man in a khaki military uniform, sunglasses, a beard and mustache, long-ish black hair.

"Colonel Hek," said Nava, climbing in.

"Mr. President."

An hour later, the shiny Range Rover moved quickly through the half-paved, half-dirt streets of downtown Mahdishahr. Dust churned into the afternoon air behind the black SUV as it sped through the crowded streets, as many pedestrians on the streets themselves as on the sidewalks. The vehicle attracted stares but for the most part it blended into the general chaos of the small city, sixty miles east of Tehran.

They turned off the A83 Highway south of Mahdi-shahr. At a traffic light at the end of the exit ramp, they went left. Trees dotted the sidewalks, bushy cypress that provided little relief from the scorching sun that had the city, at 2:45 P.M., cooking at 101 degrees. They drove into an area of warehouses and lots piled high with industrial equipment. At one of the warehouses, a light yellow unit with nothing particularly distinguish-ing about it, the Range Rover slowed and entered the parking lot. Hek pushed the vehicle quickly across the parking lot, then around back. He sounded the horn once and a door at the back of the warehouse began to slide open.

They drove inside and the door quickly slid shut be-hind them.

Bright lights shone down on a clean concrete floor, the building empty except for one item. In the middle of the floor, a big semitruck; eighteen-wheeler, blue truck cab, a long silver trailer hitched to it. A dozen soldiers stood with weapons pointed at the SUV. Colonel Hek was the first to climb out, followed by Nava.

Nava followed Hek across the concrete floor. At the back of the truck, Hek stepped up a small set of steps. Nava followed him, his eyes growing wide as he climbed.

Resting inside the trailer was a long object that resembled a steel can, except that it was much, much bigger. The underside was emblazoned with Persian lettering. The object was squat—no more than ten feet long—and bulky. The front was shoulder-height to Nava.

Nava was speechless. His trembling hand arose from his side. He touched, gingerly, the steel tip of the missile. He ran his finger down the cone, then along the smooth side of the missile, his eyes like a child's on Christmas morning. Nava traced the lettering on the side, shaking his head.

"It is magnificent," Nava said, barely above a whisper.

"Yes, Mr. President," said Hek. "That is the perfect word for it."

An hour later, as Nava walked into the entrance foyer to his office, his assistant held up a piece of pink paper.

"Your brother called, Mr. President. He said it was urgent."

Nava kept walking, shutting the door to his office, and went to his desk. He dialed his brother.

"What is it?" he said into the phone. "They said it was urgent. Is it Father?"

"No," said Nava's younger brother, Davood. He spoke softly, as if he was crying. "It's Harui."

"Harui?"

"He's dead," moaned Davood. "He was on a business trip to Ukraine. Israel murdered him."

"How do you know this?"

"They let a man live. The Israelis said they will keep killing until Meir is returned."

For several seconds, Nava stared at the phone, as if dazed.

"I'm sorry, Brother," he said, anger in his voice. "But if it means anything, Harui did not die in vain."

26

Nava climbed out of the back of a black Mercedes limousine. He walked up the steps of the Beit Rahbari, House of the Leader, a former palace, through a set of heavily guarded steel gates. He went by a small coterie of worshipers and imams. Inside, he was met by one of Suleiman's assistants, who nodded to Nava.

"Mahmoud," he whispered.

"Imam," said Nava.

"The Supreme Leader is expecting you."

They went down a long, dark corridor, illuminated by candles. They came to a large wooden door, the top of which was arched like a half-moon. Suleiman's assistant knocked on the door.

"Imam," he said. "The president is here."

The door handle turned, then the door opened. Ali Suleiman, a short man like Nava, stood behind the door. He waved his hand quickly.

"Come in, Mahmoud," he said.

Inside, six other men, all dressed in the attire of imams, sat in chairs along the walls. The office was small and had a single window that looked out on the mosque and behind that, in the distance, mountains covered in snow. It was a simple office, with a table beneath the window, and no artwork. It always amazed Nava that the Supreme Leader of the country, who could have availed himself of any material comfort he so desired, would choose to exist so simply.

Nava bowed, holding his head in fealty for several seconds, then stood again.

Suleiman shut the door behind him.

"Please, Mahmoud," said one of the clerics. "Sit down. Take a load off, as they say."

"Thank you, Imam," said Nava.

Nava sat in a wooden chair at the end of the line of clerics.

"You have asked for this meeting of the Supreme Council, Mahmoud."

"Indeed," said Nava. "Members of the Assembly of Experts, thank you. I will get to the point. Today, I believe, has the potential to be an important day in the history of the Islamic Republic, one of *the* most important, perhaps the biggest day since February first, 1979."

Nava looked around the room, meeting the eyes of the bearded clerics one at a time. He ended with Suleiman.

"Our Iranian scientists have made all citizens of Iran proud," continued Nava. "I am pleased to report that the first nuclear device has been completed. Today, I seek the official sanction of the Supreme Leader for the use of the device."

"The use of the device?" asked one of the clerics. He looked at Suleiman. "Were you aware of the completion of the nuclear device, Imam?"

"Yes," said Suleiman, nodding.

"And you didn't inform the assembly?"

"Since when do I have to inform the assembly of anything? If you don't like it, appoint someone else in my place. I grow tired of your complaining, Mashiri. Besides, are you not here today? Am I imagining this meeting? Please, someone pinch me; Mashiri seems to think today's meeting isn't in fact taking place."

Several of the other clerics started to laugh as Suleiman shook his head back and forth, a wide smile on his face beneath brown, bespectacled eyes.

"The assembly has been fully aware of the process for the development of the nuclear device," Suleiman continued. "It was completed less than two weeks ago. We have not had a meeting of the assembly in this time. Besides, Mashiri, I have no need to tell you or anyone else. I am aware of many things. Until there is a call for some sort of action, I have no obligation to blather to you or anyone else about developments."

"Iran has completed its first bomb!" said the cleric.

"That's right," retorted another cleric. "Under the leader's guidance! Stop your complaining!"

Suleiman stared at Mashiri, then raised his hand and, in a casual flicking motion, dismissed his comments.

"Continue," he said, staring down the cleric.

"Yes, Imam," said Nava. "Today, with the blessing of Allah, I seek the sanction of the Supreme Leader for the use of the bomb. It is time for Iran to begin the process of wiping the Zionist from the face of the earth. I believe we must detonate the device in Tel Aviv."

The room was silent. For several moments, the clerics, to a man, stared at the ground in contemplation. Then another cleric, a short, rotund man to Suleiman's right, cleared his throat.

"Why?" he asked.

"Because we are the chosen ones who will stab the blade of Allah into the Zionist," said Nava. "First, with the capture and, soon, the execution, of Kohl Meir. Then, when the dust has settled, and the Israelis believe they can take no more punishment, we shall ignite Tel Aviv with the majesty of Iranian technology."

The room was silent. One of the clerics looked up from the ground.

"What will happen after we drop the bomb?" he asked. "How many weapons does Israel possess of its own?"

"Yes," said another cleric. "So we drop one bomb, our first bomb, and Israel drops ten bombs. Soon, how much of Iran is destroyed?"

"But therein lies the genius of our plan," said Nava, smiling. "We will move the bomb by water into Tel Aviv. A small fishing boat is all that is needed. Israel won't even know it's Iran that has done it."

"Who will do this?"

"Hezbollah," said Nava. "Colonel Hek will oversee

it. The bomb is in hiding. It will be transported to the port at Bushehr. A martyr from Al-Muqawama will then spirit it into the belly of the beast, Tel Aviv."

"What about Washington?" asked another cleric. "Surely, they would come to the defense of Tel Aviv?"

"How?" asked Nava. "They won't have a clue. None of them will. And when they want revenge, which they will, who will they blame? They will have to blame the entire Middle East. Look at how weakened the Americans are. They were badly scarred by their failed experiments in Iraq and Afghanistan. They're impoverished by their debt to the Chinese. Their economy is in ruins. Perhaps most important, Israel's main ally, Rob Allaire, is dead now. President Dellenbaugh is a weak, naïve man. Will he come to the rescue of Israel?"

"I agree," said another man, seated next to Nava. "Please don't any of you take this the wrong way, but Iran is not entrapped by the logic and moral quandaries of the West. America will not respond because America is shackled down by its own rules, laws, congresses, treaties, but most of all by its own Western morals."

"Well put," said Nava.

"It's not the United States I'm worried about," said one of the clerics. "It's Israel. They *will* counterattack. They know one rule, and it's self-defense. If necessary, Israel would drop a bomb on every city on the Middle East in order to survive."

"So what are you saying?" asked Suleiman.

"I'm against it," said the cleric. "We have a bomb. *Iran has the bomb!* Let us celebrate that. Kill the Jew

Meir. But must we kill a bunch of Israelis? Let us not forget that many of these Israelis will be children."

"I must tell you something else," said Nava. "In the past twenty-four hours, no less than half a dozen Iranians have been murdered by what we believe to be Israeli Mossad agents. This includes the Iranian ambassadors to China and Portugal. Two officials at NICICO were killed, including my own nephew. Imam, I implore you: let me take this next step."

Suleiman looked at Abdollahi, the cleric who was against the strike.

"Your concerns are sincere, Abdollahi," said Suleiman. "And well considered. But the blood of the child is part of the tide that will wash away Israel forever."

Suleiman stood. He stepped to the window.

"Kill the Zionists," said Suleiman.

27

The sun was rising, bright orange on the horizon, as Dewey drove slowly along Washington Street, through downtown Middleburg.

Middleburg was a picturesque rural town in Virginia horse country; neat brick and clapboard homes, shops, inns, and municipal buildings located a little more than an hour outside of Washington, surrounded by horse farms and fields, streams and forest. The town itself was a simple grid of streets lined with antique shops, restaurants, gourmet food stores, and other establishments catering to Middleburg's equestrian set. There was even a place to arrange a private jet out of nearby Dulles Airport, about a half hour away. In the town center, the shops, restaurants, and inns transitioned quickly into small homes, then the land opened up and spread out, becoming rolling country of large estates with fields of verdant blue and green, stone walls, big, sweeping, tree-filled vistas leading to the Blue Ridge and Bull Run mountains in the distance.

The estates were owned, for the most part, by old-line Virginia gentry and their descendants, along with the new wealthy; businesspeople working along the tech corridor near Dulles. Every year, the area was the site of well-known equestrian events, including the oldest horse show in the United States, the Upperville Colt and Horse Show, and the Gold Cup, a day of steeplechase racing attended by most of Washington's elite, sponsored by Tiffany's, BMW, Range Rover, and other luxury brands.

After passing through town, Dewey went left on Zulla Road, driving his rented Chevy Tahoe for precisely three and a quarter miles, along a thin winding road. Dewey had flown into Dulles the night before from New York City, staying at a Marriott near the airport. He'd risen at 4:30 A.M., showered, then checked out, grabbing a coffee at a gas station in Chantilly.

The meeting had been hastily arranged the night before. Dewey was to meet two ex–CIA agents, Katherine Foxx and Rob Tacoma, at the farm that served as the headquarters for their firm, Riscon. Legally, Riscon LLC was a consulting firm that specialized in risk management. Its only official listing was in the tax rolls of the town of Middleburg and the Internal Revenue Service. Riscon had no phone number, Web site, or other means of identification.

Dewey knew there were many entities such as Riscon sprinkled throughout the Virginia and Maryland countryside. As with any government agency, the CIA had plenty of people who ultimately tired of the relatively low pay of being an agent, just as other executives in other branches went into the private sector.

Other than speaking briefly with Foxx on the phone, Dewey had done no research or background checking on Riscon, Foxx, or Tacoma; he was relying solely on the recommendation of Calibrisi. He had no idea what to expect. But then again, this world was somewhat foreign to Dewey. His interactions with the CIA when he was in the military were limited.

When he was in Delta, he was used to receiving detailed operational plans. The design of the operations themselves was always done by someone else, someone who knew more than Dewey about the various aspects of an operation necessary for success. Travel arrangements, funds flow, armaments, local political situations, everything was done, for the most part, by someone else.

In the Pakistan coup, the key to Dewey's success had been based on three factors. First, research conducted by the CIA, in conjunction with a team of UAV pilots and analysts out of the Pentagon. It had been the CIA's National Clandestine Service and its Political Action Group who knew the political lay of the land well enough to select the right military leader to replace Omar El-Khayab. The second key was Special Operations Group, the other arm of the National Clandestine Service, who planned out the on-the-ground tactical support Dewey needed to take out El-Khayab, including the weapons planning and intra-Pakistan travel, from automobiles to the chopper that took

Dewey and his small team from Islamabad to the Kashmir war front in order to find Bolin, El-Khayab's replacement. The third factor, of course, was Dewey and his team and their in-theater decision making and actions.

But in Iran, it would all be different. Dewey didn't have the CIA to help him this time. With Calibrisi sidelined, Dewey couldn't count on any support whatsoever, whether it was the basic logistics of travel inside Iran, or weapons. Even manpower.

Dewey had never been much of a planner; he was the one who executed the plans of others, no matter how chaotic, fluid, or dangerous the environment. He was also good at improvisation. But now, he knew, he needed a plan. And he needed to design it in such a way that he kept certain end goals hidden.

As he rounded a corner on Zulla Road, edged with a low stone wall and a faded yellow ribbon tied loosely around the trunk of a tree, he checked his watch: 5:38 A.M.

He slowed, then went right onto a pebble driveway that meandered between white horse fence, thick pine trees every hundred feet or so, then, beyond the trees and fence, green fields that were neatly cut. Dewey drove for half a mile and came to a set of steel gates. The gates opened as his SUV came closer. The pebble drive continued for another quarter mile, opening up into a large circle, behind which was a simple, pretty two-story house, with white shingles, green shutters and dormers.

Standing in the middle of the circular parking area was a man dressed in an orange T-shirt, running shorts, and flip-flops. He was tall, with a mess of brown hair that looked like it hadn't been brushed in several weeks. He also had a mustache, which looked slightly out of place. He was young, athletic, with thin arms. He leaned back against a mud-covered white pickup, a cup of coffee in his hand.

Dewey pulled up alongside the pickup and climbed out. The man walked toward him.

"Hi, Dewey," he said, extending his hand. "I'm Rob Tacoma."

"Hi, Rob," said Dewey, shaking his hand.

"How was your flight?"

"Fine. I got in last night."

"Well, shit, you should've told us that. We could've put you up here."

"Thanks. Next time, maybe. You guys live here?"

"No," said Tacoma. "I live in London. Katie lives in Paris. We stay here when we're in the States."

"Is Katie here?"

"Yeah, she went for a run."

Dewey followed Tacoma to the front door. The entry foyer was empty except for a long table, on top of which were several firearms, most of which Dewey recognized: SMGs, a few sniper rifles, handguns. On the walls, there was no art, just faded sun-marks outlining where frames had once been. The kitchen was off the foyer, and was also sparsely furnished, except for a round table and chairs. The countertops had boxes of cereal, a coffee maker, stacks of books, and newspapers. On the countertop nearest the stove, at least two dozen combat knives were laid out.

Dewey couldn't help staring, trying to take it all in. It looked like a fraternity house for assassins.

"I know what you're thinking," said Tacoma. "It's a fucking mess, right?"

Dewey grinned. "No, I wasn't thinking that."

"The truth is, it's a pain in the ass hiring a cleaning woman," said Tacoma. "Sure we can vet them, that's not the problem. The problem is, we have to hide everything before they get here. It's just a logistical nightmare."

"So what do you do to clean up?"

"We sort of take turns," said Tacoma. "Emphasis on the sort of. We also try and do everything electronically, so there's less paper we have to worry about burning or disposing of. Once in a while, when we need it, we ask Bill Polk at NCS to send out a cleaning crew."

"When did you start the firm?"

"Three years ago," said Tacoma. "Katie was number two in Special Ops. I worked for her. By the way, you want some coffee?"

"Yeah," said Dewey.

Tacoma crossed the kitchen and opened a cabinet, pulling out a coffee mug with a Boston Bruins logo on it.

"Bruins fan?" asked Dewey.

"Fuck no," said Tacoma. "I'm from Philly. Flyers."

"So what's your deal?" asked Dewey. "I know you probably, by this point, know a little about me, but tell me about your background."

"Yeah, I studied you," said Tacoma. He smiled. "You've seen some shit."

Dewey remained silent.

"So me," continued Tacoma. "I went to UVA, then worked on Wall Street. After a couple of years, I got sick of it. I tried out for the SEALs, made it through Hell Week, then did that for six years, mostly Iraq, a little Afghanistan. Katie recruited me into Special Operations Group. All in all, not too dissimilar from a lot of other guys inside. Especially since nine-eleven, a lot of jocks working out in the real world, realizing they could be over in Afghanistan killing jihadists and risking their lives. I had to have some of that, know what I mean?"

"Yeah, I know what you mean."

"Come on, let's go out back," said Tacoma. "Katie should be here soon."

Dewey trailed Tacoma through a living room, decorated with a few chairs and couches, a flat screen on the wall. From every window, Dewey could see empty, overgrown sun-covered green fields, running away toward the horizon. They walked through a set of French doors to a brick patio. They sat down in wooden Adirondack chairs.

"What about security?"

"Yeah, that's pretty covered. Two motion layers and a thermal scrape, all state of the art. We know when someone arrives, anywhere on the property. The small stuff gets weeded out. But, truthfully, if someone tried to penetrate, somehow got through the layers, then most of the time we're not even here. The computers are in the basement and you can't get inside the room without passing the biometric scanner. If we are here, and we don't know you, you're not going to last long."

Dewey scanned the grounds behind the house. A neatly trimmed lawn ran from the edge of the patio for a few hundred yards to a field, covered in knee-high, olive-colored grass. The field spread out beyond, in an undulating pattern of wild green, pushed by a gentle morning wind. It rolled gently for what seemed like at least a mile, away from the house, far into the distance.

A small black dot appeared at the end of the field. It was a person.

"How many acres?"

"A few hundred."

Tacoma pointed to the black dot, now moving toward them.

"Now take that individual, for example," said Tacoma, sipping his coffee. "I knew when they crossed the first and second perimeters. I received a signal here."

Tacoma took out a small device that looked like a credit card. He handed it to Dewey. It had a small screen with some letters on it, indecipherable to Dewey.

"Thermal scanner tells me he or she weighs about one hundred and twenty-five pounds. Now if I didn't know who it was, I would start getting slightly more serious about things in a minute or two. Grab one of the sights or even the sniper rifle. I'd arm it with a tranquilizer, of course."

The black dot started to take shape. It was a woman, running quickly across the field; Dewey estimated a six-minute pace.

"Then again, if I shot Katie with a tranquilizer, I don't think she'd be very happy."

The runner moved swiftly through the field. Her

blond hair was in a ponytail, which bounced as she moved toward the patio. Dewey sipped his coffee and watched her as she came closer. It took several minutes for her to cross the field. At the edge of the lawn, she slowed down, leaning over to catch her breath. She walked slowly across the lawn toward the house.

The running pants and shirt were tight, and clung to her body. Her face was bright red from the exertion, covered in perspiration. Her nose was sharp, longish, and tan. She looked like she was in her late twenties. She smiled. She was cute, like the girl down the street, or a little sister; more Mary Ann than Ginger. Except for her eyes. As she walked closer and Dewey's eyes met hers, he saw the cold look of a trained operative.

"Dewey," she said, huffing as she stepped onto the patio, extending her hand. "I'm Katie."

Dewey stood up, shaking her hand.

"Hi," he said.

"I hope I didn't keep you waiting long."

"Not at all."

"Let me grab a water. Be right back. You want a re-fill?"

"Sure," said Dewey, handing her his empty Bruins cup.

When Foxx returned, she handed Dewey the coffee cup, then sat down on a wicker couch across from Dewey and Tacoma.

"Hector called me yesterday afternoon," said Foxx. "Other than telling me your name, and giving us some access to your background, he wouldn't tell me anything. Except to say everything had to be done outside Langley."

"It involves Iran," said Dewey.

"Okay. That explains a lot. They've shut down offensive operations inside the country until this agreement is signed."

"Look, we know Iran," said Tacoma. "We know the players. What do you need?"

"Before we get to that, how do you guys work?" asked Dewey.

"What do you mean?" asked Foxx, smiling, curious.

"How much do you cost? Who designs the actual operations? Do you go into the field?"

"If you were the head of security for a Fortune 500 company, we would probably design the OP. Looking at your background, I would say we could go either way. You're obviously capable of designing it. Who goes into the field from our end depends on the OP design. Sometimes we'll use subcontractors. As for the cost. . . . Hector didn't tell you?"

"No," said Dewey.

"We work on retainer. We get half a million a week with a minimum six-month retainer. Plus expenses. We'll need the first million today."

Dewey took another sip from his coffee cup, then calmly set it down on the arm of the Adirondack chair.

"I don't have that kind of money."

Foxx looked at Dewey with a mischievous smile.

"I'm just fucking with you," she said. "Hector said he would cover it. You have a fan at Langley."

"What's your deal?" asked Dewey. "How did you get into this line of work?"

"When I was a senior in high school, my mother was

killed on United Ninety-three in Pennsylvania," said Foxx. "I went to the University of Texas. I was so miserable for four years all I could do was study. I was valedictorian. After graduation I joined the CIA. At some point, I realized that the only thing that would ever make me happy would be killing terrorists. And I was right. That's about it."

"Why did you guys leave?"

"Same job, more money," said Foxx. She leaned forward and reached her hand up for her ponytail, removing the rubber band. "I used to be the person who hired firms like ours, then managed them. I realized I could easily do what any of them was doing. So I did."

"So what do you want to know?"

"What's the OP?"

"It involves Israel," said Dewey.

"Kohl Meir. I read about it. Do you know where he is?"

"Evin Prison."

"So what do you want from us?"

"I need a clean insertion into Iran. And I need to talk to someone, someone who is very well protected."

"Who?"

"Amit Bhutta, Iran's ambassador to the UN."

"Are you crazy?" said Foxx.

"He has information. I need that information. I also need his participation."

"So what do you want to do?"

"First, I need a biograph on him," said Dewey. "His background, family, that sort of thing. I want to know if he has any weak spots. Any vulnerabilities."

"Why?"

"It'll make the interrogation go quicker," said Dewey. "I want to talk with him in a controlled environment."

"Interrogation?" asked Foxx. "He's ambassador to the United Nations. What are you planning?"

"What *we're* going to do," said Dewey, "is take him hostage. In New York City. And we have to move *now*."

"You realize we're private contractors?" asked Foxx.

"If any of us gets caught, it's ADX for twenty years," said Tacoma. "What information does he have that's so valuable?"

"I can't tell you that," said Dewey.

Foxx stared at Dewey, then her eyes moved to Tacoma, a look of annoyance on her face.

"That's a deal breaker," she said.

"I gave someone my word."

"That's not good enough," said Foxx.

"The information Bhutta has is necessary for me to exfiltrate Kohl Meir. That's all you need to know. If you can't live with that, I'll find someone else to help me. I'd rather have you, though."

Foxx leaned forward, wiping her still sweaty brow with her arm. She stared into Dewey's blue eyes, at his big chin, at his mouth.

"Is the idea that we're going to free Kohl Meir from an Iranian prison?" asked Tacoma.

"Yes," said Dewey.

"Evin is a fortress," said Tacoma. "That's even assuming you can get into the country. Iran's borders are without question the tightest borders in the Middle

East—outside of Israel, of course. There are no leaky holes."

"I know," said Dewey.

"Let's just say you're in-country," continued Tacoma. "You're talking about a place that's covered with secret police. VEVAK is everywhere. A big American guy with blue eyes, maybe carrying around an SMG, might set off a few alarm bells."

Dewey grinned, but said nothing.

"VEVAK catches you, and you can say goodbye, Dewey," added Foxx.

"But say we figure that all out," said Tacoma. "We alter your appearance a little, dye your hair, that sort of thing. We get you inside Iran. Then you have to get him out of a prison that ranks among the tightest security prisons in the world. What are you going to do? It's a triple-gate complex. You can't even get close to the front door."

"I need Bhutta," said Dewey. "And I need a clean insertion into the country. If I get caught in Iran, then it's none of your concern."

Foxx looked at the ground. She stood up, then leaned over to stretch. Try as he might, Dewey couldn't help checking her out; her long legs, outlined in the stretch nylon material that clung to every inch of her legs and thighs. She leaned over, stretching out her hamstrings. When she was done, she walked inside.

After more than a minute of silence, Dewey looked at Tacoma.

"Are you two dating?" he asked.

"No." Tacoma laughed. "Katie's like my older sister. She doesn't date much. All work."

Dewey sipped his coffee. He wanted to confide in them. If they were cleared by Hector, and recommended by him, they were obviously trustworthy. What Dewey had in mind was complicated. He hadn't run it by anyone. Getting feedback—and help—from two veteran NCS operatives would be incredibly valuable.

But another voice told him not to. *Keep your cards close to your vest.* If he informed them that Tehran had a bomb, there existed the very real possibility they would tell someone else at CIA. Then, all bets would be off. The operation would be outside his control. And Dewey didn't trust the CIA to do what was necessary to succeed. Not to mention whatever CIA channels to Mossad existed, permitted or otherwise. If Lon Qassou was right, and a mole inhabited the upper echelon of Israel's spy agency, he couldn't run the risk of tipping his hand.

Keep your cards close to your vest, he repeated to himself.

Finally, Foxx returned from the house. She was eating an apple.

"I'm afraid we can't help you," said Foxx. "I'm sorry."

"Is it because you think taking Bhutta will be too difficult?" asked Dewey. "Because if it is—"

"I don't like being kept in the dark," interrupted Foxx. "If you don't trust me, that's fine, but I'm not working for you. Besides, if I don't know the full details of the operation, I'm relying completely on your skills and judgment. And from what I saw of the coup in Pakistan, you guys made a bunch of mistakes that cost lives."

"What the fuck are you talking about?" asked Dewey, slightly irritated.

"Don't take it personally."

"We had less than thirty-six hours to remove Omar El-Khayab from power. We're talking about the president of the sixth-largest democracy in the world. If you ask me, it was a pretty good goddamn operation."

"Dewey, yes, you're a talented in-theater commander. Hector certainly thinks you are. But you lost two very valuable men. Accident or not doesn't matter. Alex Millar and Rob Iverheart died. Not to mention the fact that you came within a hair of dying too. You also caused the death of six Israelis."

"The mission was, remove El-Khayab from power," said Dewey defensively. "Avoid a military confrontation with China. We succeeded."

"Yes, on the larger objective, you did," said Foxx. "But it was a sloppy operation with unnecessary casualties. That's my only point. And on this thing, we're the equivalent of Millar and Iverheart. Unless we know the details, you can find someone else to carry your fucking water."

Dewey was silent. He stared at the young, innocent-looking face of Katie Foxx. She looked like she would have been more at home in a college dorm than planning black-on-black operations for the CIA and other well-heeled clients. She was blunt, arrogant, and smart. And she was right.

"I know what you're thinking," she said, smiling. " 'Who the hell is this girl? She thinks she knows everything.' Right? Well, I don't. On the Pakistani coup, I'm an armchair quarterback, assessing the facts after the events have taken place. That's easy. All I'm saying is, I don't want to die or anyone else to die on the next one, including you."

Dewey smiled. He nodded.

"I get it. So what do you want to know?"

"What's the OP?" she asked. "What are you hiding from us?"

"Iran has a nuclear bomb," said Dewey. "Kohl Meir was working on an operation to destroy it with an informant high up in the Iranian government. Hezbollah or Quds Force is going to bring the bomb by water to Tel Aviv, then detonate it. It's going to happen in days, not weeks."

"So why not tell the Israeli government? Our government?"

"The informant doesn't know where the bomb is located, so we can't just take it out. More important, there's a mole inside Mossad. Kohl knew if he told anyone in the Israeli military or intelligence hierarchy, Iran would find out, then move preemptively to detonate the bomb."

Tacoma whistled aloud, shaking his head in disbelief. Foxx was silent.

"Kohl Meir saved my life," said Dewey. "That's it. I

owe him. I owe the Israelis who lost their lives that night in Beirut."

"You also see it as a challenge, right?"

"What is that supposed to mean?"

"I read your psychographic, Dewey," said Foxx.

"Oh, did you now?"

"Yes, I did."

Dewey was silent.

"Loner," said Foxx. "Heavy drinker. Not afraid to kill first and ask questions later. The loss of your wife and son over a decade ago only exacerbated your tendency toward self-reliance and your drinking. Tell me this, did you drink during the Pakistani coup?"

Dewey stared ahead, into the distance, at the empty field.

A phone in the house started ringing. Tacoma stood up and walked inside.

"Your file goes on to say that you blamed yourself for the loss of your wife," said Foxx. "I don't mean to bring that up, but is it true? Was it your fault?"

Dewey stared at Foxx. He said nothing.

"If you want my help, I need to understand you," continued Foxx. "I'm not going to risk my life, or Rob's, because I didn't understand a piece of your character that might endanger us inside the theater of operation."

"It was my fault," he said, still staring out at the field. "I should have been there for Holly. I should've quit Delta. But I didn't."

"One of the conclusions of the psychographic is that blaming yourself for your wife's suicide enables you to take a higher level of risk than most people," said Foxx.

"In other words, you hate yourself, so you're willing to expose yourself to higher risks."

Dewey smiled.

"Of course, the implication of this, for us, is that being involved with you on a mission is also going to be higher risk," continued Foxx. "The problem is, unlike you, I don't want to die. I'm only thirty years old. I have a long life in front of me. Kids. Marriage. You name it. So what I need to ask myself is, do I want to ride shotgun with a kamikaze pilot, so to speak."

Dewey stared into Foxx's pretty blue eyes. Her blond hair was tucked back behind her ears. The perspiration had dried on her tanned, freckled face. He let his eyes move down to her arms, then to her legs. Dewey appreciated beauty in women; he appreciated Foxx and he wasn't shy about it. She knew it, and let him look at her, without apology or shyness.

"I don't care what your fucking report says," said Dewey. "I don't have a death wish. I take risks to save lives, including my own. It's why I agreed to the coup. I take risks for my friends. I take risks for the United States of America."

"Killing Aswan Fortuna?" Foxx asked. "Vic Buck? Who was that risk for? You didn't need to do that."

"The only person at risk in those operations was me," said Dewey. "And, of course, them."

Foxx smiled at Dewey, staring for a long, pregnant moment into his eyes.

"As for *your* file, Katie," said Dewey, "have you ever read it?"

"Well, no, not exactly."

"I have. Hector gave it to me. You say you're thirty and you don't want to take risks because you want to someday get married? The CIA brain trust, just so you know, believes you'll never get married. Your rise at NCS was in some measure predicated on a belief by your superiors that great value existed in the fact that you are unwilling to make personal attachments to people, especially romantic ones. According to your partner here, you rarely even go on dates, at least not that he's aware of."

Foxx stayed silent, glancing at Tacoma through the French doors with a perturbed look.

"Despite the fact that you're smart, accomplished, and, at least to my eyes, pretty good-looking," Dewey added, looking directly at her.

"Flattery won't get me involved in something that's going to get me killed," she said, adding, "and I'm more than 'pretty good-looking.' "

"Not all CIA reports are accurate. I don't have a death wish. I would never put you or anyone else into an environment they weren't trained and prepared for. And I have no doubt that you will soon be dating someone and on the road toward marriage and a white picket fence."

Foxx laughed, shaking her head.

"Jerk."

"I need your help."

Foxx ran her hand back through her hair.

"We won't be able to exfiltrate him from Evin," she said. "You know that, don't you?"

"I know. We're not going to."

"How are we going to get him out?"

"The barter system."

"And what in the world would cause the mullahs in Tehran to give up their prized prisoner?" asked Foxx.

"A nuclear bomb."

"For Kohl?"

"Yes."

"And where are we going to get a nuclear bomb?"

"We're going to steal it from them."

Dewey's lips formed into a devilish grin. Foxx stared at him for several moments.

"You're crazy," she said, then started to laugh. He joined her and for a few moments they laughed with each other.

Tacoma returned from inside the house.

"What's so funny?" he asked.

Down a flight of stairs, they came to a steel door. Tacoma stepped in front of a key fob next to the door and stared into a glass ocular. A bolt clicked. Tacoma reached for the door and swung it open.

Inside, the windowless room was brightly illuminated by overhead lights. The room was large, perhaps forty-by-forty. The floor was concrete. A series of half a dozen plasma screens hung on the far wall. In the center of the room, a massive square glass and steel table held computers. Beneath the table was a neat stack of servers.

Tacoma walked to a computer keyboard and keyed in his password. One of the plasmas came to life. A light blue screen suddenly appeared, followed soon thereafter by the letters, in black block letters, RISCON.

Tacoma typed into his keyboard. A series of photographs burst onto the screen. All of them displayed the same man; a tile of photos populated the plasma. He had thick black hair, a bushy mustache, dark skin, and was handsome. The words, BHUTTA, AMIT G, appeared at the top of the screen.

"Let's get to work," said Tacoma.

28

Hasim Aziz walked quickly out of the main entrance of Khomeini International Airport. His eyes darted furiously about; he found the black Mercedes S500, with blackened, bulletproof windows, idling at a curb a hundred feet away, guarded in front and back by police cruisers, lights flashing. He walked to the Mercedes and climbed in the backseat.

Abu Paria said nothing, a blank, unsmiling, severe look on his face.

Aziz sat down and placed the steel briefcase on his lap. He adjusted the four-digit lock on the side of the briefcase and popped it open. He pulled a small stack of photographs out of the briefcase and handed them to Paria.

There were six photos in all; all were black-and-white. The first three displayed Lon Qassou, taken by security camera as he walked through Odessa Airport.

Next to him—in two of the three photos—was Sara Massood, the woman he'd just interrogated.

The next three photos showed Dewey. In all three, he wore a dark blazer with a white button-down. His frame towered at the center of each photo. The last photo showed Dewey's face from the closest point of view. His look was menacing. Paria stared at this photo for nearly a minute. Behind the photo was another small stack of papers; a report, written in Chinese.

"Who is he?" asked Paria.

"His name is Andreas," said Aziz. "He's American, ex–special forces, a former Delta. Dewey Andreas. He has a long and rather interesting history, General."

"Talk," said Paria, holding the report, which he couldn't read.

"He led the coup in Pakistan. He's also the one who killed Alexander and Aswan Fortuna."

Paria again studied the photos of Dewey, his nostrils flaring with contempt. From his pocket, he removed the sketch done by the artist, based on Sara Massood's description. There was an unmistakable similarity between the sketch and the photos, though it wasn't definitive.

"There is new information in the report, General," said Aziz, pausing, looking at Paria. "Andreas is the one who killed Rumallah Khomeini."

"How did you get these?"

"From Bhang," said Aziz, referring to the head of the Chinese Ministry of Intelligence. "They're from the Israeli."

"What I want to know, why would Mossad be interested in Andreas?" asked Paria.

"I don't know, sir," said Aziz. "Technically, there's nothing connecting Andreas to Qassou, other than the coincidence of their both being in Odessa."

"Two Quds commanders and an S7 were terminated the night these photos were taken," said Paria.

"And you believe it was this American?" asked Aziz.

"Think about it," said Paria. "It had to be Andreas. They were sent to Odessa to track Qassou. Andreas must have been tracking Qassou to see if he was being followed."

"It's still circumstantial, General," said Aziz.

"The woman saw something," said Paria.

Paria flipped his phone open and pressed a button.

"General—"

"Don't let the woman leave."

"It's too late," said Paria's chief of staff. "She's already gone."

"What?" demanded Paria. "*Why?*"

"She had to be taken to a hospital, sir."

"Find her!"

"The speaker of the parliament called. He's called three times looking for you. Miss Massood has lodged a formal complaint."

"*Find her!*" barked Paria. "*Now!*"

29

Meir awoke to the smell of cigarette smoke.

He looked up. He was still in the cell, but not on the ground any longer. They had moved him to the steel bed sticking out from the wall.

His entire body was sore. He trembled uncontrollably, like a leaf dangling from the branch of a tree. Soreness emanated from his nipple, a raw feeling that burned.

His eyes adjusted. He saw legs in front of him; gray slacks. His eyes drifted up. Sitting in a chair in front of him, less than two feet away, was Achabar, his so-called lawyer.

"You've been unconscious for nearly twenty-four hours," Achabar said. He blew out a cloud of smoke that traveled toward Meir's face. "The warden saved your life. Colonel Atta got into some trouble. Of course, if it were up to me, I would have let him kill you. Why is your life more important than the sergeant's you killed?

But what do I know. I do what I'm told. They have plans for you, obviously. A trial. Then you will be found guilty. Then the firing squad."

Meir focused his mind, then catalogued his pain. He saw a puddle in the middle of the cell. He smelled, and then recognized the stench of his urine. Somehow the fact that it was his own urine made it slightly better than if it had been someone else's, but not by much.

"So you know, I am having you moved, cleaned up," said Achabar. "Frankly it's for my benefit, not yours. I can't be expected to work with the smell of your waste in the air. It's inhuman. But don't think it's because I feel sorry for you. I hate you more than even the soldiers hate you."

Achabar caught Meir's eye, smiled at him.

"As I said before, I am your lawyer. There will be the tribunal. It will begin tomorrow or the next day. It will be filmed and they will release parts of it to *Al Jazeera*. They will cut it to make it look like the trial is a fair one. I will play the part of the fierce, fair-minded advocate."

Achabar reached into the pocket of his blazer, grabbed his pack of cigarettes, lit another one, pulled a long drag on the end, then exhaled.

"But it won't be fair," continued Achabar. "It's rigged. Perhaps, before they shoot you, you can write a letter to the newspaper complaining? What do you call it in America, a 'letter to the editor,' yes?"

Achabar laughed. Meir remained silent. He stared blankly ahead at Achabar.

"I will ask this, however," said Achabar, leaning

forward. He put his face up close to Meir's. "In theory, how do you expect me to represent you if you will not even say a word?"

Achabar puffed the cigarette, then exhaled, blowing the smoke into Meir's eyes. Meir blinked as the smoke burned his eyes.

"Tough guy, huh," whispered Achabar, shaking his head. "Shayetet thirteen."

Meir's mouth was dry. He was thirsty. He felt sick to his stomach. He tasted the remnants of blood in his mouth, now sour.

Achabar took another puff, then exhaled again, blowing the smoke at Meir's eyes yet again. Again, he blinked as the smoke burned his eyes.

Achabar began humming a tune, then smiled.

"Smoke gets in your eyes," he sang in a low, playful voice.

Achabar puffed one more time, then leaned forward to exhale.

Meir pulled his head slightly back, then thrust forward. He sent a bloody wad of saliva flying into Achabar's face. It struck him in the right eye.

Achabar lurched backward, the chair tilted, he lost his balance, the cigarette dropped from his mouth, then the steel chair with Achabar on it fell backward. Achabar landed on the ground, at the edge of the wet ring of urine in the center of the cell. He paused, horrified, then stood up. His face was as angry as any Meir had ever seen. He stood, his mouth ajar, breathing rapidly, glaring at Meir.

"You asked for it," said Meir, his first words since arriving at Evin.

* * *

Several hours later, three soldiers came into Meir's cell. One of the men unshackled his feet and made him stand up. His legs were like two sticks of butter on a hot day. He could barely hold himself up. He was shirtless and one of the guards pushed Meir's pants down to his ankles with the muzzle of a Kalashnikov rifle.

Looking down, his left nipple was crisscrossed with red and black burn marks.

"Come," said one of the guards, then Meir felt his hands, shackled tightly behind his back, being forced forward. He followed the soldier down a long hallway.

He looked up. It was a different section of the prison and for the first time he saw the eyes of men behind bars, small slats no more than six inches by six inches, staring out at him as he shuffled slowly down the hallway. Meir knew Persian, but a few muttered words in a dialect he couldn't understand.

"Run while you can," he heard in broken English from one of the cells. Then there were a few hoots and curses. Finally it spread out in a low din.

Finally, one of the guards had had enough. "Shut the fuck up!" barked one of the soldiers behind him. "No water today if I hear another word!"

They took a right, and continued down another long hallway, more eyes behind small openings and silence.

Meir entered a large, windowless room that was tiled, the floor wet. The soldier pushed him against a wall. One of the soldiers turned a faucet on and he saw a long black hose being stretched across the floor. The soldier aimed the hose in his direction. Cold water sprayed from the end of the hose. For several minutes they shot cold water against his body, cleaning him off.

The water helped awaken Meir. He felt gauzy, in a stupor, a natural reaction; he had been in shock from the torture. He probably should have received some sort of medical attention. But the body was an amazing thing, especially that of a healthy twenty-five-year-old. The electricity yesterday would have killed most men.

They led him back to another cell, shut the door. It was a different cell from before; cleaner, with a small window. Meir could see the buildings of Tehran in the distance.

After several minutes, the door opened again and Achabar stepped in. He removed his cigarettes and lit one. Then, he removed a black rectangular object, which he held in his other hand.

"This is a Taser, Kohl," said Achabar. "Set to the highest level. Spit at me again and I will take great pleasure in frying you until you scream."

"Then don't blow smoke in my face, asshole."

Achabar smiled, but his nostrils flared, revealing anger.

"Your trial docket has been set," said Achabar. "It will begin this evening, in front of the judge. It will be a military tribunal. It will last at most two days."

"And what are the charges?" asked Meir.

"The specific charges relate to an operation you were part of three years ago," said Achabar. "Off the coast of Bandar-e-Abbas, in the Strait of Hormuz."

"What about Bandar-e-Abbas?" asked Meir.

"A group of Israeli frogmen boarded an Iranian

Navy cruiser," said Achabar. "Four Iranians died that night."

"How do you know it was Israel?" asked Meir.

"I don't," said Achabar. "And the truth is, I would have argued, not very forcefully, mind you, but I would have argued that point exactly. How do we know it was Israel? It's just circumstantial evidence, as they say. And more to the point, how do we know that you were even on the team? I had my arguments all worked out. Not that it would have mattered. They will find you guilty no matter what I say or do."

Meir stared out the small window, ignoring Achabar.

"Yes, yes," said Achabar. "Whatever. It doesn't matter now because the killing of the prison guard is now the main charge. It's a rather open-and-shut case. It would have been a much longer trial and I would have presented various evidence. But you have saved me a great deal of time and effort, so I should thank you."

"Then what?"

"After you're found guilty, you'll be sentenced to death. There is a question right now as to whether it will be a public execution or not. There is an argument for doing it in private, then releasing the photos."

Meir felt a tremor move through his body. He clenched his teeth and pushed the fear from his mind. He closed his eyes. He forced himself to think not about his own life, or Achabar, or Evin; but rather about Israel. He imagined Talia.

Sometimes, at night, she would stand on the deck, overlooking the Mediterranean, with nothing on except one of his T-shirts. Would he ever see Talia again? His beautiful fiancée, Talia. The thought of her dark skin, her voluptuous body, her silly, infectious laugh; all of it tortured him. But it helped him escape, if only for a few moments. And it helped remind him that he had much to live for.

"I would like to be alone," he whispered to Achabar.

At a little before seven that evening, Meir awoke from a deep sleep to the sound of iron keys turning the latch on his cell door.

He moved down the windowless corridor, inch by inch, as the chains that bound his feet only allowed him baby steps. They passed other cell doors, each with yellow writing, though in this section the cell doors were windowless, so prisoners couldn't look into the corridor. Still, his chains made a loud clanking noise on the concrete, and an occasional, distant scream could be heard. Meir's hands were out in front of him. A soldier stood to each side. In front of him, Achabar walked, smoking a cigarette.

They entered the elevator and descended one flight. Meir was led down another corridor, through two sets of steel doors, out into the humid night air. In a courtyard, he was led to the back of a dark blue van. The soldiers lifted him up. A pair of soldiers was already inside the van. One of them grabbed his cuffs and locked them to a steel bar that ran down from the ceiling to the floor, then did the same with his ankle cuffs.

"I'll be in another car," said Achabar, standing in the open door and looking into the van.

Meir said nothing, not even looking at his Iranian lawyer.

The doors shut and the van started to move.

A corrugated steel fence separated the back of the van from the front, but still, Meir could see out the front. The van left the prison grounds and moved onto a busy street, fell anonymously into traffic, just another set of headlights in a long line of cars.

They drove for twenty minutes, then entered an underground parking garage. Meir looked up at one of the guards.

"Where are we?" he asked in Persian.

"Ministry of Justice," mumbled the guard.

The courtroom was on the sixth floor. The corridor was empty except for soldiers, all armed with SMGs, wearing the uniforms of the Revolutionary Guard. Near the door, Meir glimpsed Achabar standing near a tall, stocky man with a bushy mustache, dressed in a short-sleeve blue button-down, arms crossed on his chest as he listened to Achabar.

Meir immediately recognized Abu Paria.

Paria was studying Meir as he inched along the linoleum floor, toward a door with the number "seven" on a sign above it.

Meir knew about Paria. Over the years, through his generosity to Hezbollah, Paria had single-handedly killed more Israelis than any man alive. When the PLO needed bombs, grenades, and firearms, it had been Paria who funded and organized the efforts to keep the fatah alive and flourishing. It was Paria who pushed Hezbollah to infiltrate, grow, and take over Lebanon, then provided the weapons and even some troops for various skirmishes against Israel over the years. It was Paria who directed, from afar, the war between Israel and Lebanon. Paria's support of Hamas was no less generous. Over the years, Tel Aviv estimated that VEVAK, under Paria's direction, had funneled more than half a billion dollars' worth of missiles, firearms, and cash to Hamas, enabling the rogue terrorist group to build a fortress on the Gaza Strip.

In Iraq, Paria was the strategist who, upon seeing Al-Qaeda's early success with roadside bombs, struck upon the idea of dramatically expanding the IED program, turning whole factories in eastern Iran into IED-manufacturing facilities, with regularly scheduled semitrucks that would take loads of the highly lethal bombs into Iraq, to then be dispersed among different groups fighting the Americans.

At the same time, he created the industry of suicide bombers. It was said that VEVAK offered families fifty million rials, about five thousand dollars, for every son or daughter willing to travel to Israel or Iraq to sacrifice themselves. That was a Paria touch; Paria had long ago recognized that beneath all of the veneer of religiosity, within all jihadists lurked the rank greed they claimed to so adamantly abhor in the West.

This was the first time Meir, or any Israeli for that matter, had seen Paria in person. Even photographs of Paria were hard to come by. As Meir came closer, he felt the urge to grab Paria by the neck, to kill the man who had caused so much misery. But he couldn't, not as long as he was shackled. Even unshackled, as he glimpsed Paria's big frame, the steel darkness in his eyes, Meir knew that Paria would represent a tough battle. But he would have given anything for just one shot.

"I know what you're thinking," said Paria as Meir passed, his voice deep and gravely. Paria had a look on his face that could only be described as vicious.

"Fuck you," said Meir.

Achabar laughed derisively, but Paria did not. Instead he took a step toward Meir.

"What did you say to me?"

"I said fuck you, Paria. Go fuck yourself."

Paria moved closer, his face now just inches from Meir.

"The great-grandson of Golda Meir with such a foul mouth," said Paria. "Do you think she would be proud of you now, Kohl?"

"Don't ever say her name again."

Paria stared for a moment, then stepped back.

"You'll soon see her," said Paria.

Meir, pulled along by the two soldiers, stepped past Paria and through a set of steel doors, into the courtroom where the tribunal would take place.

The courtroom was large, windowless, and smelled stale, like a classroom. The gallery contained at least fifty chairs and was empty except for a pair of men in khaki military uniforms who sat near the back. Meir inched down the center aisle. Through a wooden balustrade that separated the gallery from the front of the courtroom, Meir stepped forward. Behind a massive table near the front of the room sat a uniformed man, who was reading a file folder, not looking up. This was the judge. To his left, on a raised platform, stood a chair, surrounded by bars. It looked like a cage.

After several minutes, the man looked up.

"I am Adjutant Judge General Rumallah Khasni," he said, looking at Meir. "I will be presiding over your case. Is defense council here?"

"Yes, Your Honor," said Achabar, who'd moved to a table at the left.

"Good evening, Moammar," said the judge. "And for the Islamic Republic?"

"The government stands prepared to present its evidence, Your Honor, sir."

Meir looked to the right. The two men who'd been sitting at the back of the gallery were now at a table across from Achabar.

"Very well, Mr. Qazr," said the judge. He scanned Meir with his eyes. "I understand you speak Persian, Mr. Meir."

Meir said nothing.

The judge glanced at Achabar.

"Please explain to your charge why I ask this question," said Khasni.

"He knows," said Achabar. "He speaks Persian."

"I will be happy to have an interpreter brought in, Mr. Meir. Would you like me to do that? This is why I ask."

"That's not necessary," said Meir in Persian. "What does it matter anyway?"

"It matters because I want you to understand the charges being made against you, as well as the evidence being presented. In my opinion, justice is not served if the accused doesn't understand what is happening. If you are innocent, you don't know what you are innocent of because you haven't heard the charges, and you therefore can't make rational arguments on your own behalf. If you are guilty, there is no chance for redemption."

"I speak the language," said Meir. "So let's get on with this puppet show."

Khasni stared at Meir, his look blank and severe.

"Do not speak that way in my courtroom," said Khasni slowly, his voice rising slightly. "I'm not the one who captured you or who is charging you. I am a purveyor of justice, that is all. And I will not tolerate disrespect of my courtroom or the law. Do you understand?"

"This is a farce," said Meir. "Do whatever you want with me, I don't care. If it helps to have your little show before you pronounce me guilty, then do so. Or you can save us all a lot of time and just send me to the firing squad right now."

Judge Khasni nodded and paused. He leaned forward in his chair.

"Clearly someone has polluted your head about the fairness of the Iranian justice system," said the judge. "Or perhaps you bring with you bias borne of your own system, Mr. Meir. In either case, your opinion is irrelevant. So is the opinion of your counselor or that of the prosecutors. There is only one opinion in this room that matters, and that is mine, and right now, I have no opinion. Do you understand?"

Meir stared at Khasni.

"When was the last time this man ate?" the judge asked, looking at Meir, then glancing to Achabar.

Achabar stood up.

"I-I-I don't know, Your Honor," stammered Achabar.

"Mr. Meir, when did you last eat a meal?"

"It doesn't matter," said Meir. "I'm not hungry. The electricity from the torture session ruined my appetite."

Khasni ignored the comment.

"Bring him something to eat," Khasni barked to a soldier standing near the entrance to the courtroom. "Now."

The soldier left the room.

"I will have the shackles at your ankles removed," said Khasni. "But if you do anything, such as try to run, or try to harm anybody in this room, the soldiers at the back of the room have permission to stop you by all means necessary, including shooting you. Do you understand?"

Meir said nothing.

Khasni nodded to one of the guards, who came forward and removed the steel chain and cuffs at Meir's ankles. He was led to a set of stairs which he climbed. He took a seat in the cage. There was a small table in front of him with a pencil and a pad of paper.

A soldier entered at the back of the courtroom carrying a small steel plate upon which was a stack of bread. He rushed down the center aisle, waited for Khasni to nod permission to enter, then walked it up the stairs to Meir, placing it on the table.

Judge Khasni stood up.

"With the permission of Allah, the case of the Republic of Iran versus Kohl Meir now begins," said Khasni, reading from a sheath of papers. "Docket seventeen hundred forty-seven. Mr. Meir, you are charged with crimes against citizens of the Islamic Republic of Iran. All five of these crimes involve the capital murder of citizens of Iran. Four of the five men were members of the Iranian Navy. One was an employee of the prison system who was also a reservist in the Revolutionary Guard. These are each serious charges. The penalty for each of these crimes, if you are found guilty, is death."

Khasni took his seat.

"Colonel Qazr, are you prepared to present your evidence?"

One of the prosecutors stood up. He stepped in front of the table.

"Yes, Your Honor," said one of the men at the table across from Achabar. "The government is prepared to make its case."

"Very well, continue."

"Your Honor, on the night of August twelve, 2009, a vessel of the Iranian Navy, the *Adeli,* was in patrol in Iranian waters in the Strait of Hormuz, near the port of Bandar-e-Abbas. On board were four men, Iranians all, members of the Iranian Naval Defense Forces. They were Siamak Azizi, age twenty-nine, of Chabahar; Payman Kadivar, age thirty-nine, of Bukan; Massoud Norouz, age twenty, of Kermanshah; and Akbar Tabatabaei, age thirty-three, of Ilam.

"Fourteen miles to the south of Bandar-e-Abbas, near the coastline, a team of Israeli commandos, part of a group of special forces commandos called Shay-etet Thirteen, of which the accused was and remains a member, attacked the *Adeli* by masquerading as an Iranian fishing vessel with engine problems. As the *Adeli* came to the side of the fishing boat, the Israelis murderously, and with malevolent intent, attacked the unsuspecting vessel, killing all four Iranians. This was a tragic evening for Azizi, Kadivar, Norouz, and Tabatabaei, all four men patriots who had faithfully served our great republic.

"As to the second charge," said Qazr, the prosecutor. "Two days ago, in a conference room on the first floor of Evin Prison, Mr. Meir did brutally and in an unprovoked manner assault and murder Akbar Javadi, age twenty-five, of Tehran, by strangling the man as he was attempting to merely pick up a water bottle that was on the ground. As more than half a dozen witnesses watched, Mr. Meir attacked Javadi and broke his neck."

Khasni, leaning back in his chair, nodded his head as he listened to Qazr. When Qazr finished his summary of the charges, Khasni turned to Achabar.

"Mr. Achabar?"

Achabar stood and moved into the open area in front of the judge's table.

"Your Honor," said Achabar. "My charge, Mr. Kohl Meir, pleads not guilty to the charges contained in this docket. While the death of any Iranian, especially a young man in the prime of life, serving faithfully to defend our republic, or serve in our penal system, is a tragedy, my charge, for reasons to be detailed and explained, is not guilty.

"As to the first allegations, involving the *Adeli*, there is no evidence that my client, or indeed, that Israel itself, was even involved in the actions of August twelve, 2009. It is no secret that Iran has many enemies, including Israel, but also including America and other countries. It is our contention that Mr. Meir represents merely a convenient figurehead upon which to place the blame for this horrid and unresolved crime. As to the second charge, the murder of Akbar Javadi, my client was in a state of extreme duress, having been taken against his will and incarcerated. This state of duress produced an action that, while certainly regrettable, does not warrant the penalty of death that the prosecutors have argued for."

Meir listened to the words of the lawyers, reaching to his mouth with his cuffed hands, eating the bread from the plate on his lap. He glanced to the back of the courtroom, where Abu Paria stood against the wall, watching everything. Above his head, the clock read 10:00 P.M.

"Mr. Meir," said the judge, "it is at this point that the prosecutors are entitled to ask you some questions. Are you prepared to answer some questions?"

Meir chewed the bread, but remained silent. Khasni waited for several seconds for him to acknowledge the question.

"Very well, let the record show that you refuse to answer the question. Should you refuse to answer any questions posed by the prosecutor, it is my duty to inform you that, in the opinion of the court, your lack of cooperation and response will be seen as a desire to avoid what would otherwise have been admissions of guilt or acceptance of facts as set forth by the prosecution."

"Ask your fucking questions," said Meir, pushing the steel plate from the table, which made a loud clanging noise as it struck the steel ground and rolled down the stairs.

"I would ask you to refrain from such language in my courtroom," said Khasni sternly.

"Fuck off, Judge," said Meir. "What will you do? Lock me up?"

Khasni shook his head in exasperation, then nodded to the prosecution table, signaling to Qazr, the prosecutor, to proceed.

Qazr stood up.

"Mr. Meir, where and when were you born?"

"Tel Aviv," said Meir. "1987."

"Were you in fact a member of Shayetet Thirteen?"

"Yes."

"How long have you been a member of Shayetet Thirteen?"

"Four years."

"And what is the role of Shayetet Thirteen, in your opinion?"

"It's not opinion, it's fact. The role of Shayetet and the role of all Israel Defense Forces is to defend the citizens of Israel from attacks by our enemies."

"So if the role is, as you state, defensive in nature, would members of Shayetet Thirteen ever have need to go outside Israel's borders?"

"Yes, of course," said Meir. "To kill terrorists. Because Iran and Syria fund so many terror-related activities intended to kill innocent Israelis, it is necessary to try and stop these terrorists before they harm Israel."

"Let the record show," said Qazr, looking at Judge Khasni, "that the government, by continuing to ask the accused questions, does not agree or acknowledge the slander that Mr. Meir just spoke, namely that Iran sponsors terrorism."

"So noted," said Khasni.

"If you don't believe me," said Meir, "ask Abu Paria. He's standing at the back of the courtroom."

Meir raised his cuffed hands and pointed at the back of the room at Paria.

"He's the one who funds the terrorists," continued Meir, his voice rising. "Hezbollah, Hamas. Al-Qaeda. He's the one who slaughters innocent children. If you don't believe me, ask him."

Paria stared back at Meir without expression, saying nothing.

"Mr. Paria is not the one on trial," said Qazr.

"He should be!" yelled Meir.

"Where were you on the night of August twelve?" asked Qazr, stepping toward the cage where Meir sat.

"What year?" asked Meir. "Can you be more specific?"

Qazr shook his head, glancing at the judge.

"You know what year," said Qazr. "2009. Where were you on the night of the alleged crimes against the men on the *Adeli*?"

"I was in a fishing boat," said Meir. "In the Strait of Hormuz."

Qazr stopped, looked back at the other prosecutor, then regained his composure.

Achabar suddenly stood up.

"Judge," said Achabar. "May I have a short consultation with my charge?"

"I don't want to talk to you," said Meir. "Sit down and shut the fuck up."

Achabar raised his hands in mock resignation, then sat down.

"You were where?" asked Qazr again.

"You heard me," said Meir.

"What were you doing in the Strait of Hormuz?"

"I was sent there to kill."

Qazr paused, again momentarily taken aback.

"To kill? By who? Who sent you?"

"None of your fucking business, that's who."

"Who were you sent to kill?"

"Terrorists," said Meir. "The men you listed, Azizi, Kadivar, Tabatabaei, were all Hezbollah. Kadivar himself was a commander in Al-Muqawama, the military arm of Hezbollah. You can call them Iranian Navy or Revolutionary Guard or Quds or fishermen or whatever you want, but the fact is, they were all Hezbollah. My mission was to kill Kadivar. The other two were an added bonus. The other man, the skipper of the vessel, was collateral damage."

"So you are admitting to killing all four men?"

"Yes. In point of fact, I killed three of them. Another member of my team killed the fourth. Frankly, it was an easy operation. We expected more of a fight.

But then, perhaps we overestimated the intelligence of the Iranians, yes?"

"Which man was killed by the other frogman?" asked Qazr.

"What does it matter?"

"Well, perhaps you've been falsely accused of killing a man?" Qazr said, smiling.

"You're a jackass," said Meir. "None of your fucking business, that's who."

"Do you remember which man you did not kill?"

"Yes, I keep a picture of him in my wallet," said Meir.

"Mr. Meir, which man did you not kill?" asked Khasni from the bench.

"I don't know," said Meir, exasperated. "What does it matter? I just know that I killed Kadivar. A bullet through his head. If you want me to take credit for all four, fine with me. Would that make the paperwork easier, Judge?"

Meir looked at Khasni, then Achabar, then to the back of the room.

"Kadivar was a classmate at the University of Tehran, yes?" said Meir, staring at Paria in the back. "Was he a friend too, Abu? Did you talk as students about how much fun it would be to kill Israeli children?"

"Silence," interrupted Judge Khasni. "You will not do the asking of questions, Mr. Meir. You're accused of crimes that could result in the imposition of the death sentence. You're not helping your cause by—"

"Fuck off, Judge," said Meir. "Who's fooling who? This is a kangaroo court and we both know it."

Khasni leaned forward in anger, then stood up, pointing at Meir.

"You will not disrespect this courtroom," he barked.

"I will never respect this courtroom," shot back Meir. "Send me to the firing squad now, will you, you fatuous ass!"

Khasni stared at Meir in anger. He paused, flummoxed, his face red. He breathed deeply for several seconds, trying to calm down, then sat back down.

"We will complete the trial, Mr. Meir," Khasni said quietly. "It might be short, and you might plead guilty to every charge, but we will impose justice, which means a complete trial, with all charges and defenses, as appropriate. Mr. Qazr, continue."

Qazr looked at Meir.

"What evidence did you have that Kadivar was Hezbollah?"

"None of your fucking business," said Meir.

"How long had you been planning the mission?"

"Again, none of your business."

"Can you tell me how long you were in the Strait of Hormuz before the incident?"

"No, I can't tell you that either," said Meir.

"Why can't you tell me?"

"Do you think I'm going to give Paria insights as to Shayetet's internal workings?" asked Meir. "Are you a fucking idiot?"

"You're the one who's in jail, Mr. Meir," said Qazr.

"Yes, after you kidnapped me on U.S. soil. Has Israel begun its reprisals, Abu?" Meir looked toward the back of the courtroom.

"Have you killed other Iranians?" interrupted Qazr. Achabar stood.

"Objection," said Achabar. "This is a question that forces Mr. Meir to present new evidence against himself."

"I am attempting to establish a pattern of behavior," said Qazr. "So that we can determine if Meir's mission was premeditated. Since he won't tell the court how long he was in the Strait of Hormuz, I need to attempt to learn more about the background of the accused."

"Your objection is sustained," said Khasni. "Mr. Meir does not have to answer this question."

"I'll answer," said Meir. "I've killed many Iranians. How many? Even I don't know that number. And if I were to get out of here, I will kill more. But I have never intentionally killed an Iranian woman, child, or man I knew to be uninvolved in Iran's war of terror against Israel. I kill terrorists. That's what I've been trained to do. As long as Iran sends terrorists to Israel, my brothers back home will kill Iranians. That is the simple fact. After you shoot me my place will be taken by another man, just as strong, just as willing to die in order to protect our homeland. Leave us in peace and Israel will leave you in peace."

The prosecutors, Achabar, even the judge, sat rapt, motionless.

"Abu Paria," said Meir, again pointing with cuffed hands from the cage. "He is the father of the terrorists. He funds them. The suicide bombers. The missiles that rain down from Gaza and Lebanon into the schools in Haifa, Jerusalem, Tel Aviv, Jericho. In Nazareth."

"Mr. Meir," yelled Khasni, striking the gavel on the table. "Stop these outbursts at once!"

"If you need more evidence of my murderous ways, unshackle me right now," said Meir, standing up and pointing with cuffed hands at Paria. "I will kill another Iranian in front of your very own eyes. Would you like to watch me, Judge?"

"Be quiet!" yelled Khasni to little effect.

"Of course, Abu will have his henchmen stop me," said Meir, his voice calm, almost quiet, yet somehow cutting through the racket of Khasni's gavel and shouting. "He could never fight me himself. Paria could never actually get his hands dirty himself, could you, Abu? We both know who would win if they gave me a chance to fight you."

"I order you—"

As Khasni hammered a gavel on the table in front of him, trying to get Meir to be quiet, Paria, whose arms had been crossed, let his hands fall to the side. He said nothing. His anger was obvious. He stared at Meir across the largely empty courtroom. Then, he walked out of the courtroom, slamming the door behind him as he departed.

Meir smiled, then looked down at Achabar. His defense attorney was leaning back, reclined in his chair, in quiet resignation.

"Do you want to go to your boss?" asked Meir, looking at Achabar.

All the while, Khasni's hammering of the gavel had become a steady monotone, which Meir ignored.

Finally, Meir sat down, a gentle smile on his face. He looked around the courtroom and then at Judge Khasni.

Khasni stopped hammering the gavel, but remained standing. He leaned over the table, looking at the ground, shaking his head in disgust.

"In my twenty-four years as a judge, I have never seen such behavior," said Khasni. "It is as if you want me to impose the gravest possible sentence. Or perhaps by your abhorrent behavior, you wish to dare me. Is that it? To dare me into being lenient?"

"Yes, that's it, Your Honor," said Meir sarcastically. "I would much prefer to spend the next fifty years of my life in an Iranian gulag than die. That sounds like it would be a lot of fun. Especially the torture with the car battery. And the cuisine. The bread was superb."

"Your Honor," said Achabar weakly. "My client is under extreme emotional duress. He is out of his mind, as they say."

Meir glanced at the clock above the door. It was now eleven.

"We will take a recess until tomorrow evening," said Khasni. "At which time, Moammar, you will have the opportunity to present the defense of Mr. Meir."

Khasni hammered the gavel once, then turned and stormed out of the courtroom.

30

KARBU
TIME WARNER BUILDING
NEW YORK CITY

There were only six tables at Karbu, despite the fact that the restaurant could have routinely filled five times that number any night of the week; this lack of seating only served to heighten the allure of the exclusive, incredibly expensive establishment. Considered the best sushi restaurant in the city, it was practically impossible to get a reservation at Karbu. Entrees at the tiny restaurant on the forty-fifth floor of the Time Warner Building started at $375 per plate, individual chef tastings, single pieces of sushi made by Karbuyoshi Takayta himself, ranged from a simple piece of fresh tuna, flown in that morning from Iceland, for $175, to a more complicated and rare strip of Blue Marrow Osso Bucco, a soufflé of raw bone marrow and roe taken from the vertebrae of a female blue whale off the coast of Japan. Its price was a cool $4,000 per piece.

On a typical evening, Karbu played host to people for whom dropping thirty or forty grand on a meal was no big deal. Russians, usually oligarchs, their wives, girlfriends, or mistresses. Middle Eastern oilmen, Saudis mainly, some Saudi royalty, the occasional banker or real estate developer from Dubai. Some Europeans, fourth-generation royalty or telecom billionaires. Increasingly, Chinese entrepreneurs, some of whom were already billionaires despite living in a country that billed itself as a communist people's republic. From the United States, it was hedge fund managers who came, private equity guys, some investment bankers, the occasional celebrity. Though not often. While the food was outstanding, Karbu had started to earn a reputation as a place for foreigners, impossible to get into, crowded with Arabs, usually with some sort of thuggish guard contingency just outside the restaurant's doors. Takayta had to install a small waiting area for just this purpose, to keep some of these security types from loitering outside the restaurant's entrance, a tight square of comfortable orange Barcelona chaises to the side of the entrance. On some nights, the chairs were filled with odd combinations; ex–KGB agents, now private security, guarding Russian mobsters, seated across the glass table from ex–British MI6 guarding Chinese Internet billionaires.

Katie Foxx was dressed in a simple red and black dress. She looked down at her plate. She did not like sushi. Where she grew up, in Canton, Connecticut, the thought of eating raw fish would have made her and her three older brothers laugh in disgust. But here she was.

She smiled at Tacoma. She watched as the tall, brown-haired Nebraska farmboy wolfed down his fourth piece of raw flounder.

"Hey, slow down, Robbie," said Foxx. "That's two hundred bucks a pop."

"Yeah, but it's so fucking good, Katie," said Tacoma, smiling. He reached up to wipe his mouth. As he did, Foxx caught a glimpse of Tacoma's weapon, tucked in his shoulder holster, .357 magnum SIG P226, suppressed. It was standard-issue SEAL armament, where Tacoma had come from before joining Foxx's paramilitary team within CIA National Clandestine Service.

Over Tacoma's shoulder, she watched Iran's ambassador to the United Nations, Amit Bhutta. He was seated with two other Iranians, both unquestionably security guards.

"He'll be finished soon," Foxx whispered.

Foxx reached down. She picked up the piece of reddish fish, threw it in her mouth. After all, if he was going to pound down hunks of raw flounder at two hundred bucks a pop, she was damn well going to join him. She started chewing. It tasted like raw fish. It felt, in her mouth, like raw fish. She looked agonizingly across the table at Tacoma. He had a big, mischievous, gloating grin on his face.

"That bad, huh?" he asked.

"Disgusting," she said, swallowing.

At Bhutta's table one of the big, dark-haired Iranian security guards stood, whispered something into a wrist comm.

"They're moving," said Foxx.

Tacoma picked up the cue and nodded at the waitress for the bill. A minute later, it arrived.

Bhutta, Iran's ambassador to the United Nations, stood. He stepped toward the marble counter, behind which was a short Japanese man with a bright red chef's hat. Takayta smiled as Bhutta approached.

"Here he goes," Foxx whispered.

Foxx stood up as the bill came. Tacoma paid with cash.

They moved to the restaurant entrance. Foxx reached for Tacoma's hand, looked up into his eyes as they walked past one of the three Iranian security detail.

"I love you," said Foxx as Tacoma held the door, playing to the Iranians, who watched the swooning couple pass in front of them to the door.

"Thank you," said Tacoma to one of the men as he held the door.

"Congratulations," the man said in a thick Middle Eastern accent, smiling.

At the elevator door, they stood. Tacoma leaned forward, holding Foxx's face gently between his hands. He leaned forward and kissed her. They embraced and kissed for more than a minute.

"You taste like fish," she said, pulling back for a breath before locking lips again and closing her eyes.

Behind them, the sound of Bhutta's entourage. The two security guards from the restaurant were joined by three others. Five Iranians in all, along with the Iranian ambassador.

One of the Iranian guards came to the elevator. He pressed the button.

Tacoma, sensing the approaching group, pulled his lips back from Foxx. He acted slightly embarrassed.

"Sorry," Tacoma said bashfully to the Iranian who pressed the elevator button behind his back.

"It's no worries," said the Iranian in a thick accent.

"Were you engaged this evening?" asked another man, behind Foxx, in near-perfect English. *Bhutta*.

"Yes, sir," said Tacoma, smiling. "Tonight. Thank you for asking."

"It's always nice to see," said Bhutta. "It reminds us that there are other things that matter in this world. Sometimes we forget, don't we?"

The elevator door opened.

"Please," said Tacoma, glancing down at Foxx. "We'll take the next elevator."

"Are you sure, then?" asked Bhutta. "All right."

The Iranians moved past Tacoma and Foxx, stepped into the open elevator.

"We don't mind," said Bhutta from inside the elevator. "There is plenty of room."

"Are you sure?" asked Tacoma, glancing in at the tall, distinguished-looking Iranian.

"I insist," said Bhutta, reaching forward, pressing the door open button.

Tacoma and Foxx stepped into the elegant, mahogany-walled elevator. The doors closed behind them. Foxx quickly scanned the group of Iranians. In addition to Ambassador Bhutta, there were five men guarding him. Foxx noted the small gumdrop camera in the upper-right corner of the elevator.

The elevator began to descend.

"Did you enjoy your meal?" asked Foxx, smiling at Bhutta.

"Yes," said Bhutta. "It was wonderful. My favorite restaurant in New York."

"That was our first time," said Foxx, wide-eyed. She looked up at Tacoma. "It was amazing."

The elevator dropped silently. Foxx watched the green digital on the wall as the numbers descended: 35 . . . 34 . . . 33.

"And where are you from?" asked Bhutta, directing his question to Foxx.

She smiled, glimpsed the digital: 24 . . . 23 . . . 22.

"Canada," she said. "I moved to the U.S. ten years ago."

Foxx moved her right hand behind her as she smiled up at Bhutta, smoothly, unnoticeably. She quickly felt for the folds in her overcoat behind her, then, like riding a bike, moved her fingers to the small custom-made sew-in along the back of the wool coat. She glanced up at the elevator digital: 15 . . . 14 . . . 13.

She felt the butt of her Glock 18, already set to full auto.

"Canada," said Bhutta, nodding. "I love Montreal."

Tacoma's eye caught the digital. He got the signal, the number "ten" used by Foxx, a double meaning. He reached his right hand inside his blazer, gripped the butt of one of the SIGs. He moved his left hand behind him, against the elevator wall, then to the small of his back, gripping the other suppressed SIG P-226, which had been tucked uncomfortably behind him the entire meal.

12 . . . 11. . . .

Foxx swung the weapon from behind her back in the same instant Tacoma ripped the pair of SIGs out, crossing his arms, left aimed right, right left.

Bhutta's mouth opened in shock and surprise. The Iranian security guards reached for their weapons.

Foxx swung the Colt sideways, firing. Slugs tore from the muzzle as she moved the gun left to right, hitting the mahogany of the elevator wall, tearing up chips of wood, then striking the first guard chest high, knocking him backward. A second guard, to Bhutta's right, was struck by a bullet to the forehead.

At the same instant, Tacoma pumped the triggers on his guns, blasting a guard to Bhutta's left through the eye socket, then, to that guard's left, another thug, a slug through the forehead.

It all took less than three seconds.

Bhutta lurched at Foxx amid the tornado of wood dust and blood that quickly fogged the small elevator in chaos.

The last Iranian, immediately to Tacoma's right, found his handgun in his shoulder holster, pulled it.

Bhutta dived toward Foxx, but she greeted his lurching frame with a quick, brutal martial kick to the neck, which sent him flying backward and down, landing awkwardly on top of one of his dead security guards. Bhutta watched from the ground, helpless, clutching his throat as Tacoma finished off his last surviving security guard with a bullet through his neck, dropping him before he could get a shot off.

Tacoma turned, pulled the red emergency door

alarm. The elevator came to an immediate, rough stop. The floor counter read two.

Tacoma removed a small silver key from his pants pocket. He stuck it in the console above the alarm. Turning it, the elevator moved again.

"Who are you?" asked Bhutta as Foxx moved above him, Colt trained at his skull.

The elevator bypassed the first floor. It continued down into the building's basement.

"Stand up, Mr. Ambassador," said Foxx calmly, staring hard into the black eyes of the Iranian ambassador.

The elevator came to a stop at B4, a service floor in the building's basement. The doors opened. Waiting outside the doors was Dewey; dressed in jeans and a blue button-down shirt, his arms crossed on his chest in front of him. His bright blue eyes were as blank, as expressionless, as stone. Behind him were two men, machine guns trained on the elevator door. Behind them, a black Chevy Suburban.

"We need a cleanup crew," said Foxx to one of the men behind Dewey.

Dewey stared at Bhutta, still down inside the elevator.

The Iranian looked thoroughly confused and disheveled, and he struggled to stand. He looked around him as he made it to his feet. Along the back wall of the elevator, five corpses lay in a growing pool of crimson, which moved quickly across the tan carpet.

"This is against the law," said Bhutta, regathering himself, anger and outrage in his voice, sticking his finger out toward Dewey. *"It's against international law!"*

"Shut the fuck up," interrupted Dewey, grabbing Bhutta's outstretched hand, quickly flipping his wrist backward, then yanking his arm behind his back and thrusting him toward the back door of the Suburban. "You're the last son of a bitch I want to hear talk about international law."

31

The sea, this far north in the Atlantic Ocean, lay cold and empty. A horizon of black. Brutal, shearing winds cut like a knife through salty, rain-soaked air. Jagged, foam-crossed peaks of massive waves stretched in steady lines for literally hundreds of miles, followed by stunning, deep black canyons that dropped like cliffs into the chasm.

Here, in the waters above the Mid-Atlantic Ridge, sunset had come quickly. To anyone unlucky enough to actually be here on this night, the passage from dark gray to black was practically a nonevent. It was a place uninhabited by anyone or anything; endless, black, bitterly cold, infinitely turbulent.

The waves out here, more than a thousand miles from either North America or Europe, moved like walls of granite, their force more powerful by far than any tidal wave to ever strike land. The fact that the waves moved in steady succession for weeks on end only served to make the point that what the ocean finally does send ashore is but a dim shadow of the epic forces at work in the deep ocean.

Above the sea's disorder, six miles directly overhead, the sky was black and clear, covered in stars and an orange half-moon. An unmarked, unlit jet moved at more than 700 miles per hour toward London. Except for a small panel of one-way glass at the front of the fuselage, the gray-black plane was windowless. External lights were extinguished, replaced by infrared beacons that were usually kept in the off position. The effect was that of a dark mantis, the proverbial black cat, moving surreptitiously, invisibly through a barren sky.

Six round communications disks, each the size of a car tire, lay at regular intervals across the top of the fuselage. Strapped to the underwings of the dark plane were twelve missiles; a combination of AGM-114 Hellfire air-to-surface missiles and AIM-120 advanced medium-range air-to-air missiles. All of the plane's missiles could, if necessary, be targeted using passive infrared and low-light-level television sensor systems. It wasn't normal for a P-8A to have missiles, but then, this wasn't a normal P-8A. The entire surface of the strange angular-looking jet was coated in dielectric composites, designed to appear transparent to radar, then covered in matte paint. Multistatic radar acted to disperse incoming radar signals. The leading edges of the plane's wings and the tail surfaces were set at the same angle, as were the air-intake bypass doors and the air-refueling aperture; the effect of this so-called plan-form alignment was to return a radar signal in a very specific direction away from the radar emitter rather than returning a diffuse signal detectable at many angles.

Even if someone was in a plane flying within a few hundred feet of the mysterious object, they would not have been able to see the plane, unless a cut of light from the moon illuminated the silhouette of the dark, fast-moving object. But then, the plane's antiaircraft defenses would have long since torched any would-be witness long before they had gotten within viewing distance of the $1.6 billion technological marvel known by its owners, the Central Intelligence Agency, as *Double Jeopardy*. So called because, among other covert activities, it was aboard this plane that questions were asked; it was here that interrogations of high-value terror prisoners took place, away from the rules and regulations associated with specific geographies. Technically, at times like tonight, the 1,400 square feet of territory now encased within the plane's hard steel frame occupied a time and a place that in legal terms did not exist. *Double Jeopardy* was a lawless country.

Dewey and Tacoma exited the conference room. Tacoma carried a large IBM laptop. They walked down the plane's windowless corridor. After passing three of the interrogation rooms, all empty, they came to the fourth. The ceiling lights in the room were lit. Light poured through the one-way glass. They came to the glass and stopped, looking inside.

Bhutta, seated beneath bright LED strips, was sweating profusely. His black hair, flecked with gray, was drenched atop his head, as if he'd just returned from a long run. He was shirtless. His body was wrinkled and soft, years of easy diplomatic work, late-night meals, and no exercise revealed themselves through his pasty, light brown skin. He wore black slacks. His bare feet were shackled to the steel chair. His torso also. Bhutta's hands were cuffed out in front of him. His right leg bounced nervously up and down. He glanced about the empty room, nervously.

At the door, Dewey reached his hand out, then paused. "Your guy's in place?"

"Danny's all set," said Tacoma. "I'll pipe him in."

Dewey unbolted the door and they entered, Tacoma first, Dewey shutting the door behind him.

Bhutta looked up, momentarily surprised. He blinked his eyes, trying to focus.

"Water," Bhutta said. "Please."

"When we're done," answered Dewey. "As much water as you can drink."

"Where am I?" asked Bhutta. His eyes moved from Dewey to Tacoma then back to Dewey.

Tacoma stepped to the steel conference table, setting the laptop on top of the shining steel, in front of Bhutta. Dewey stood behind Bhutta.

"Where am I?" Bhutta repeated, pleading.

Tacoma typed into the computer, not responding.

"Please," said Bhutta.

"In a plane," said Dewey. "A big plane. Pilots,

engines, wings, that sort of thing. You've been on a plane before, yes, Mr. Ambassador?"

"Where are we going?" asked Bhutta. "*Where?*" he asked again, anger in his voice. "*Tell me!*"

Tacoma's eyes looked up briefly, calmly, from the laptop at the inflection in Bhutta's voice. His eyes met Dewey's. Then he looked back without saying anything.

"Israel?" asked Bhutta. "Is that it? Where are we going, Mossad?"

"Where are *we* going?" answered Dewey pleasantly. "I can tell you where *we* are going. *We* are going to find Kohl Meir, who you kidnapped from a sidewalk in New York. *We,* however, does not include *you,* Mr. Ambassador. You are going to a different place. You are going to a small, windowless room in a nondescript building on the outskirts of London where you will remain and where you will help us until Kohl Meir is returned. What happens next is not up to me to say. What I do know is you're going to help us, Mr. Ambassador."

"Who is Kohl Meir?" Bhutta asked. "I know nothing—"

"Stop the bullshit," interrupted Dewey, crossing his arms.

He moved around Bhutta, in front of the table, and glared at the Iranian.

"We know that you had knowledge of Meir's abduction. Don't waste my time. Do you think we don't have the capability to listen to what your VEVAK goons plan out of the consulate?"

"I knew nothing."

"Okay, okay, whatever," answered Dewey, shaking his head. "I don't care about that anyway. It doesn't matter. Kohl is gone. He's taken. We know you knew, Bhutta, you little fuckhead. But even if you didn't know, it doesn't change a thing. We're not here to establish your guilt or innocence. Frankly, I don't care."

"So you think you can kidnap a sitting ambassador to the United Nations in direct violation of international law?" asked Bhutta. "Do you understand the implications? This is an act of war."

"Kidnap?" asked Dewey, a smile spreading across his lips. "You weren't kidnapped. At least, if you were, we can't seem to find any witnesses."

"There will be such an outcry."

"From who?" asked Dewey, looking inquisitively at Bhutta, then grinning and shaking his head. "Do you actually think anyone in the world gives a damn about you? You're the world's pariah. Nava? I mean, come on, give me a fucking break. Besides, your government will have much more to deal with in the coming hours than simply the loss of its ambassador to the UN."

Bhutta stared at Dewey for several moments, then shut his eyes. He sat quietly as Tacoma leaned down and typed into the laptop.

"You can wear your Hermès and go to nice restaurants, but we all know your past. You'll help us. You designed this hit, we know you did. You'll help us get Kohl back."

"I won't," said Bhutta angrily. "Fuck you."

"Oh, I think you will," answered Dewey. "I just have

a feeling. I have a feeling I can convince you. I can appeal to that human side of you we all know is in there somewhere."

Tacoma turned to Dewey and smiled. He typed a few more strokes, then stood up.

"We're good to go," Tacoma said.

Dewey leaned down, placing his right hand on the table.

"We need your help," said Dewey. "We know you're one of the top officers in the Ministry of Intelligence. We know you've been one of the principal architects of the Iranian covert war on American troops inside Iraq. We know you're connected. You have the capability to help us now."

"I know torture," said Bhutta. "I'm willing to die for my country."

"Is Mira?" Dewey asked.

Bhutta looked at Dewey, curious, speechless, a rising tide of shock and anger on his face. His eyes shot to the computer screen. He studied the screen, blinking, leaning in closer, trying to lurch at the screen, his torso restrained to the steel chair, which was bolted to the ground.

"Mira," Bhutta whispered, his eyes bulging, transfixed.

"Ah, yes, that's the question now, Mr. Ambassador," said Dewey, looking down at the computer screen. "Have *they* been trained to endure torture? You would know better than me."

On the computer screen was a live video, the picture decent if slightly grainy, of a hotel suite. Inside, a young woman with long black hair sat on the edge of a massive bed. To her side, three children sat. They were watching something on the television in front of them.

"Dora," said Dewey. "Can you hear it? They're watching *Dora the Explorer*."

Dewey leaned down and hit a key. Suddenly the sound of the cartoon grew louder.

"*Mira!*" screamed Bhutta at the computer, his face turning red. "Mira! Run, dear!"

"She can't hear you," said Dewey.

"You . . ." Bhutta tried to speak, but struggled to catch his breath.

"You don't like that feeling? Watching someone you love who's been kidnapped? Funny how it feels, isn't it?"

Bhutta paused and tried to collect himself. He shot Dewey a look.

"A lie," he said. "This is old film."

Dewey shook his head. He nodded at Tacoma, who pulled a cell phone from his pocket.

"Danny," Tacoma said. "Flick the lights in the room." He glanced at Bhutta. "How many times, Mr. Ambassador?"

Bhutta said nothing.

"Flick them three times," said Tacoma.

On the screen, the hotel room suddenly went dark for a split second, then lit up as the lights were back and on. Bhutta's daughter looked around the room, wondering what was going on. She stared in the direction of the camera. For the first time, the look of fear and stress could be seen on her young face. The lights were turned off and on two more times.

"If I want," said Dewey, a stony look on his face, "I could have someone come in and cuff your daughter a few times, just to prove it to you."

"Savages!" Bhutta screamed. "You would torture a little child."

"We will do anything to retrieve Kohl Meir," said Dewey, anger in his voice rising like mercury. He paused. "Anything to stop Iran from detonating a nuclear bomb in Tel Aviv."

Bhutta looked up, unable to hide his surprise.

"Yes, I know about it," said Dewey. "And the sooner you understand I mean business, the sooner we can begin, and the sooner your daughter and her children, your grandchildren, can leave that room and walk back to their lives."

"You would torture—"

"*No!*" screamed Dewey, anger and fury exploding in his voice. He lurched suddenly out across the table and slapped Bhutta ferociously across the face. Blood shot from the Iranian's mouth from the vicious slap. "*You* would torture them! *You alone!* It's in *your* hands and your hands alone!"

"*Leave them alone!*" begged Bhutta, wiping his face of the blood. "They're innocent!"

"It will start with the youngest first," barked Dewey. "Do you hear me? Your daughter will watch. The youngest will be taken. She'll be flown to the United States. She'll be placed in a foster home. Your daughter will never see her again. You'll watch your daughter's reaction as we remove her children in this way, one by one. And then, when her children are gone, we'll beat your daughter until either you talk or she dies. Do you understand? Before she dies, she'll be told that you, Amit, you alone sanctioned the removal of her daughters and caused her death. You might be prepared to die for your country, for your hatred, but did Mira, did this innocent creature make the same promise? Is she prepared to lay down her life, to lose her children, just to hurt Israel?"

Tears suddenly began to course from Bhutta's eyes. His head tilted back, sobbing. Blood dripped from his mouth, down his chin, onto his chest.

"Iran began this cycle of violence," said Dewey. "Thirty years ago. Time to pay the piper."

"How did you find them?" Bhutta asked.

"Another stupid question. So many things you Iranians don't know. It's almost comical. You're like cavemen."

Bhutta leaned his chin forward, sobbing. For several moments, he cried uncontrollably. He would get control over his emotions for a few moments, look up to see the screen, then begin again.

Dewey hit him again, swinging his right hand through the air and striking Bhutta across the cheek.

"Stop crying," said Dewey. "You're like a little girl. Are you ready to help us now?"

Finally, Bhutta steeled himself. He looked up at Dewey.

"Yes, I'll help."

Dewey removed a photograph from his pocket. It was a photo of the nuclear bomb.

"How long is it?" asked Dewey. "And what is the weight?"

Bhutta studied the photo.

"Eight feet, eight inches," said Bhutta. "Weight is approximately nine thousand pounds."

"Good start," said Dewey. He took the photo and put it back in his pocket. "I'll get you some water now."

32

Petros Towers arose from the sand in black refraction. The red, Middle Eastern sun smacking off the mirrored glass had the effect, at certain angles, of making the building look like it was on fire.

The floor-to-ceiling glass took up every inch of the outer-facing walls of the skyscraper, Dubai's third-tallest building. Oval-shaped, designed by Frank Gehry, the building seemed simple enough until you stood at its base and stared up at it. There, looking straight up, the building swayed noticeably in the prevailing wind off the Persian Gulf. The skyscraper also tapered as it ascended; the top floor of Petros Towers was less than a quarter the diameter of the bottom floor. The effect was magical and strange, as the architect had intended, like a spindled black caterpillar spiraling up into the endless blue sky.

On the sixtieth floor of Petros Towers, a visitor could be temporarily stunned by the view. The outer-facing walls were all glass, so too were the inner office walls. From every angle and point of view, except of course for the restrooms, the feeling was as if one was trapped inside a sun-blasted prism, with sunlight being cut and recut a hundred times by different angles of glass, and where shards of multicolored light seemed to always be noticeable in rainbowlike chutes. At the same time, the feeling was like flying. To the east, the Persian Gulf in a bold half-circle; oil tankers, container ships, transocean liners, and pleasure boats dotted the blue waters. In the other direction, westward, the city of Dubai, skyscrapers, apartments buildings, then suburbs, and then, starting at midview, the endless, light orange sands of the Arabian desert.

At a quarter after three in the afternoon, a tall man with curly, dirty blond hair and a neatly trimmed beard stepped out of the elevator. Tim Bond, the director of French oil conglomerate Totalfina Elf's Eurasian Operations, swiped a gray plastic card at an infrared reader next to a set of doors that had a geometric triangle logo and the word TOTAL etched in its glass. The lock on the doors clicked and Bond pushed into the lobby.

"Hi, Tim," said the receptionist, who was middle-aged with a short, perfect Dorothy Hamill bob to her blond hair. "How was Africa?"

"The same as always," said Bond in a British accent,

smiling. "Hot, smelly and, in its own way, amazing. Did I miss much?"

"No." She smiled. "They're waiting for you in two."

"Okay," he said. "What's this?" He nodded at the folder.

"Your manifest for Riyadh."

"Thank you."

"Also, you have a visitor," the receptionist said, subtly leaning her head to the left and back.

Bond glanced in the direction of where she was indicating. In the large waiting area, a woman stood, back turned, staring out the glass at the Persian Gulf. Her long blond hair was braided neatly down in back. She wore a stylish white leather jacket. As if sensing Bond staring at her, the woman turned. She had a serious expression on her face.

"I'll be damned," whispered Bond.

He walked from the desk to the entrance foyer and pushed the door open.

"Katie," he said.

"Hi, Tim," said Foxx.

"How long have you been standing there?" Bond asked, staring at her.

"Half an hour," said Foxx. "Nice view."

"How'd you know how to find me?"

Foxx looked at him blankly.

"Stupid question," said Bond. "Give me a few minutes, will you?"

"Sure."

* * *

Ten minutes later, Bond returned.

"I'm sorry you had to wait, Katie," said Bond.

"It's okay. I didn't have an appointment."

"You're lucky I'm here," he said.

"It wasn't luck," she said, smiling.

"Troublemaker."

Foxx followed Bond down the long, glass-walled hallway. They turned right at the end of the hallway. He led her to the corner office. Foxx stepped inside the large office. Its walls were entirely glass, the Persian Gulf's dark blue waters everywhere like wallpaper.

Bond shut the door. Foxx walked to a modern white leather couch and sat down. Bond sat down in a red leather chair across from her.

Bond stared at Foxx for several moments. She had on knee-high black Prada leather boots, a navy blue skirt that only came halfway down her thighs, showing off her legs, and a jacket, which she removed and placed on the couch, revealing a red sleeveless blouse and sculpted, honey-colored arms. Bond scanned her up and down several times, trying without much luck to hide his obvious admiration.

"You got more beautiful," said Bond.

Foxx was silent. She stared at him, saying nothing.

"Are you not going to say anything?" he said.

"Like what?"

"Like, 'gee, Tim, thanks for the compliment.'"

"Thanks for the compliment."

"Are you still mad?" asked Bond.

"No," she said. "Why would I be mad?"

Bond chuckled and shook his head.

"Well, that's good," he said.

"We'd be divorced by now anyway," Foxx said.

"I don't know about that," said Bond. "But you'd probably be dead. All I asked was that you give it up."

"I know what you asked. I was there, remember? The one with the big smile, the engagement ring, the Vera Wang dress. The broken heart."

Bond smiled.

"I didn't want to see you die, Katie."

"It's what I do for a living, Tim," Foxx said. "What if I had asked you to give up what you do?"

"What I do won't get me killed," said Bond. "What I do won't leave children without a parent."

"It doesn't matter anyway," said Foxx, waving her hand in the air. "It's over. You did me a favor. I'm not cut out for marriage."

"I heard you left Langley."

"Yes," said Foxx. "A couple years ago."

"You need some work?" asked Bond.

"No," said Foxx. "But I do need something."

"I figured that," said Bond. "What?"

"A clean insertion into Iran," said Foxx. "Through Turkey. Doğubayazit. I need a deep cover that will back-check at the border and withstand a database pull; VEVAK, China, Interpol. That's it."

Bond nodded.

"A little vacation?"

"Funny guy."

"Who's it for?"

"Male, age thirty-nine."

"American?"

"Yes. The cover needs to be someplace else, obviously."

"If he looks non-Arab or has a stamp that's not from the area, he'll get interrogated."

"We'll dress him up. Language will be a problem."

"Let me think about that," said Bond. "We can make him Iraqi or Turk, but born somewhere else, London or Montreal."

"Okay."

"Why not let the CIA drop you in at the Iraq border? Isn't that the obvious access point?"

"It's a private operation. Also, I need to do it in broad daylight. It's the working permit that's most important. He needs to be some sort of truck driver."

"Truck driver?"

"Yes," said Foxx. "He'll be driving something that looks like this."

Foxx reached to her Hermès Birkin bag and removed a photo of a semitruck; blue cab, silver trailer. It was the photo provided by Qassou of the truck holding the bomb, though that wasn't visible.

Bond inspected the photo.

"What's going to be inside said truck?" asked Bond.

Foxx stared at him, her expression as blank as a wall.

"If you're going into Iran to cause trouble, if it's going to trace back to Totalfina, that would be a problem," said Bond. "Total is not a branch of the British government or the U.S. government. I work here. We're dancing a delicate dance over here, as you can imagine."

"I won't make promises I can't keep," said Foxx.

"There could be trouble. There's no reason it should result in Total taking any blame."

"What do you mean by trouble, Kate?" asked Bond. "If this has something to do with Natanz—"

"I can't get into details," said Foxx. "You know that."

"You're about as easy to read as a brick wall," said Bond, staring at Foxx. "So I'm not going to try and guess what you're doing. But I know your background. If you're going in to take out Nava or, God forbid, Suleiman, as much as I personally wouldn't give a shit, the fact is, they would come after any and all Total employees inside the country. I can't allow that."

"It's not an assassination," said Foxx. "Your precious oil fields will be fine."

"Fuck you. I don't need attitude from someone asking for a major fucking favor, a favor that could get me fired and probably killed."

Foxx smiled and shook her head.

"If you don't want to help me, fine," she said. She reached for her coat.

"I'll help you," he said. "But you have to protect me. The only reason I'm doing it is because I still love you."

Foxx stood up, leaving the photo with Bond. She put her leather jacket on, then picked up her bag. She took a step and stood next to Bond, who was still seated, just inches from her. He reached his hand out and softly touched the bare skin just above her left knee, just above the dark leather of the Prada boot. Foxx looked into Bond's eyes as he did it, expressionless. After half a dozen seconds, she stepped away and walked to the door.

"I'll e-mail you the details," Foxx said from the door, not turning, not looking at Bond. "I'll let myself out."

33

Golestan Street was dark and empty. Omid steered the truck along the potholed, dusty two-lane road, past small homes with sleeping families, past a strip of shops, then a closed gas station. Omid was alone. He wore civilian clothing, despite the fact that he was a commander in Quds Force, the special forces division of Iran's Revolutionary Guards. Normally, Omid operated in Yemen. He'd been flown back to Tehran the day before for the sole purpose of making the delivery.

It had seemed irrational to him as he departed from the cavelike nuclear weapons lab outside of town to travel unaccompanied by patrol vehicles. *Why would we travel alone with the republic's first nuclear bomb?* It was insanity, he thought to himself. Now, as he moved along the dark street, he comprehended the logic to the orders. He was just a truck driver, any man, moving in the night.

Then he remembered: the Americans. If they knew who he was and what he was doing, they would light him up with a missile from one of the dreaded UAVs. Omid knew that they were out there. The drones were the one thing that sent a shiver up the spine of any Quds soldier with half a brain. They could strike you whenever, wherever, and you wouldn't know it until the moment just before you were hit, as the high-pitched whistle of the incoming missile screamed in the air. For a few moments, he listened for it, then reached and turned the radio on. *If they're going to kill me, I'd rather not know*, he thought.

But his fears were baseless. His drive went without incident. At a plain-looking warehouse off Golestan, he took a right into a parking lot. He chugged across the tar, behind the building. As he came closer, a pair of large steel doors slid open. Bright lights shone abruptly out through the door. He drove through the doors and watched, in his side mirror, as they quickly slid shut. He came to a stop, then shut off the truck.

In front of him, his commanding officer, General Soleimani, stood, arms crossed. Next to him was a man he recognized, but had never met. Omid climbed down from the cab and stepped toward the two men.

"You're late, Omid," said Soleimani.

"Rush hour," said Omid.

Soleimani smiled.

"Omid," said Soleimani, "General Paria."

"It's an honor, sir," said Omid.

Paria nodded at Omid, but said nothing. He stepped past him and walked briskly toward the back of the truck, whose doors one of the soldiers had already opened. Omid followed him. At the back of the truck, Paria looked up at the bomb. He turned to Omid.

"Good work," said Paria, reaching out and patting Omid on the shoulder. "You can tell your grandchildren you were part of history."

34

President Dellenbaugh sat behind the desk in the Oval Office, running his right hand absentmindedly along the burnished edge of the old, majestic block of wood as he stared into the half-filled coffee cup in his hand.

On the desk in front of him was the morning's *Washington Post*. A photo of Amit Bhutta, Iran's ambassador to the United Nations, was displayed in the lower right-hand corner of the paper, next to an article entitled THE MYSTERY OF IRAN'S MISSING AMBASSADOR.

There was a knock on the door to the Oval Office. The door opened; Jessica and Calibrisi stepped inside.

"Good morning," said Dellenbaugh.

"Good morning, Mr. President," said Jessica.

"Morning, Mr. President," said Calibrisi.

Jessica and Calibrisi moved to the two chesterfield sofas in the middle of the room and sat down.

"I want to start by clarifying something," said

Dellenbaugh, standing up and walking around the desk. He took a seat in one of two navy blue wing chairs in the center of the room. In his hand was the newspaper he'd been reading. "I've been on the job for less than a week. I think it would be an understatement to say I'm still getting my feet wet. It's been a confusing and, to be honest, difficult week. I liked President Allaire. I didn't agree with him on everything, but I liked the man. Now I'm forced to figure out a way to both honor his legacy and those policies he espoused, and which citizens voted for, and my own set of beliefs, which as you know are different from his; not on everything, mind you, but on certain subjects."

Jessica and Calibrisi were silent.

"You two have been enormously helpful," continued Dellenbaugh. "And I appreciate it. But what I need to know is whether or not you are with me going forward. I'd like you to be. For my sake and for America's. Not only are you both widely respected, you're good at your jobs. I also think continuity at this hour in our national security infrastructure, both at home and abroad, is important."

Dellenbaugh paused. His nostrils flared slightly.

"If you're on board, though, I need you to be willing to work for, to fight for, to adhere to my policies, even those that are different from President Allaire's. Do you understand?"

Calibrisi glanced at Jessica, then looked at Dellenbaugh. In his hand, the president held *The Washington Post*.

"You're referring to this morning's story in the *Post,* Mr. President?" remarked Calibrisi.

Dellenbaugh tossed the paper down onto the glass coffee table.

"Yes," said Dellenbaugh. "I'd like to know what's going on."

Calibrisi glanced at Jessica.

"*The Washington Post* has been known to make mistakes, sir," said Calibrisi.

"Did they make a mistake?" asked Dellenbaugh.

"I don't know," said Calibrisi.

"I think you do, Hector," said Dellenbaugh. "What happened to Amit Bhutta?"

"My guess is he's not missing," said Calibrisi. "If the article is correct, however, then it's probably Mossad."

"So this wasn't Langley?" asked Dellenbaugh.

"No, sir," said Calibrisi.

"I would think we could find out who did it."

"Maybe," said Calibrisi. "But Mossad keeps their own counsel, sir."

"I just read the line-by-line of the negotiation session yesterday between Iran and the Swiss ambassador," said Dellenbaugh. "The Swiss have succeeded in getting Iran to agree to halt their nuclear program. We're talking about stopping it. A completely transparent inspection framework; monitors on the ground feeding real-time data into IAEA; unlimited, unannounced on-demand inspections, access to their centrifuge supply chain; everything we wanted."

"Mr. President," said Jessica, "the Iranians are the

most dishonest group of people on this planet. They're playing the Swiss. They're playing you."

"You can't honestly say that and mean it, Jess," said Dellenbaugh.

"Yes, I can. And I do mean it. I don't trust Nava and Suleiman one bit."

"I don't trust them either," said Dellenbaugh. "But not everyone over there is evil. There are good Iranians."

Dellenbaugh sipped from his coffee cup.

"That might be true, but we're negotiating with the bad ones."

"I've decided to accept President Nava's invitation," said Dellenbaugh, staring down Jessica and Calibrisi. "I'm going to meet Nava and sit with him onstage. I'm willing to take the risk in order to get the possible reward. If there's even a ten percent chance Iran will rejoin the civilized world, isn't it worth the risk?"

Jessica was silent, as was Calibrisi.

"Does what happened to Kohl Meir not alter your thinking, President Dellenbaugh?" asked Jessica. "Meir was abducted on U.S. soil by the Iranian government. They killed two U.S. citizens in the process and now they're going to execute him."

"One life, even Meir's, is irrelevant in the larger course of human events," said Dellenbaugh. "We have the opportunity to bring peace and stability to the Middle East. Not to be blunt, but isn't that worth the sacrifice of Kohl Meir's life?"

Dellenbaugh paused. He stood up.

"The time and place have been set," said Dellenbaugh.

"Tehran?" asked Calibrisi.

"No," said the president. "The Swiss thought we should do it on neutral ground. It'll take place in Buenos Aires. Jessica, I want you there. In the meantime, I want to reiterate what I said about leaving Iran the hell alone. Once they sign the agreement, we're going to be all over them. For now, we need to steer clear."

Jessica seethed, saying nothing.

"Yes, Mr. President," said Calibrisi.

Jessica let Calibrisi enter her West Wing office, then slammed the door behind her. Calibrisi's head turned, jolted by the noise.

"Thanks for supporting me," said Jessica. "What the hell was that?"

She walked around to her chair and sat down. Calibrisi remained standing.

"We're stepping right into Nava's clever little trap," continued Jessica. "And we're abandoning Kohl Meir. Frankly, we're abandoning Israel. I'm resigning over this."

Calibrisi stared at her.

"Say something, Hector."

"What is there to say?"

"You know something, don't you?" she asked.

Calibrisi remained silent.

"*Was* that you? My God, Hector. That was on U.S. soil. Do you realize what would happen—"

"It wasn't me," said Calibrisi.

For several seconds, Jessica studied his face. He remained calm, placid even.

"What are you not telling me?" she asked suspiciously. "It's Dewey, isn't it?"

Calibrisi's face remained blank.

"You're lying to the president of the United States."

"No, I'm not. Dewey doesn't work for me."

"You just told Dellenbaugh you thought it was Mossad who took Bhutta."

"Maybe it was," said Calibrisi. He turned to leave.

"Where are you going?" asked Jessica. "We're in the middle of a conversation. I want to know what the hell is going on."

"I just told you."

"No, you bloody well didn't."

"Yes, I did."

Jessica stood up. She leaned forward, looking angrily at Calibrisi.

"I want to know what the hell is going on, Hector."

Calibrisi met her angry stare with a look of placid frostiness.

"No, you don't," said Calibrisi.

Jessica's face flushed red. She marched around the desk and moved in front of Calibrisi. She was shorter than Calibrisi, and much thinner, but her Irish temper was blazing and she looked as if she might reach out and slap Calibrisi. She raised her right hand and jabbed her finger into his chest.

"You tell me what the fuck is going on," she said. "Right now."

"You want to know what's going on?" countered Calibrisi, leaning closer to Jessica. "Then you better be ready to put aside your little goddamn rule book, Jessica Tanzer, national security advisor. This is the real fucking world now."

Jessica stared into Calibrisi's brown eyes.

"I'm ready," she said, calmer now. She paused. "I want to know. I want to help."

"Then get your shit. We have a flight to catch."

35

The restaurant in the Azadi Grand Hotel in downtown Tehran was packed with people. Jean-Luc was Tehran's most exclusive restaurant, run by a Frenchman named Jonas Le Chene, whose father, Jean, had started the restaurant in 1966. Somehow, the Le Chenes, devout Catholics, had managed to stay in business through the massive, violent, radical Islam–fueled upheavals of the late seventies up to the present, remaining agnostic to it all, allowing the stunning gourmet food, the timeless, intimate atmosphere of the restaurant, to transport its customers away from the chaos.

A favorite of Westerners, journalists, businessmen, along with European and Russian diplomats, Jean-Luc was always crowded. Its deep wood walls, abstract French oil paintings, thick carpet, its blocked-off, smallish interior rooms, all helped to muffle the noise of so many patrons, to foster intimacy, to hush the outside world.

But on some nights, even Jean-Luc couldn't get away from it all. Tonight was one of those nights. The capture of Kohl Meir and the announcement by Mahmoud Nava had the entire city of Tehran on edge. Would the Israelis invade? Would they launch missiles?

The mood at Jean-Luc was electric; a combination of celebration, excitement, even pride. But with that victorious feeling, there was also a sense of foreboding, sadness, anger, and even embarrassment.

The announcement of Meir's capture the week before, like every other political development in Iran, impacted people in sharply different ways. Some Iranians, a growing number, it seemed, were happy about it. These were the people who hated Israel, of course. But more than that, they hated America. These were the supporters of Mahmoud Nava. And Suleiman Islamic jihadists. It used to be that this coarse group was confined to the countryside. Increasingly, they were willing to make their presence known even in Tehran, the country's political and cultural epicenter.

Just as strong, however, was a feeling of remorse among the moderates within Iran. This was by far the larger number. The Iranian government's dirty little secret: most Iranians were kindhearted and fair. They craved democracy and peace. They were religious, but they hated extremism. Seventh- and eighth-generation Iranians, descendants of a time when Iranians—Persians—were known throughout the world for their stunning artistic achievements, writing, philosophy, and even more so for their kindness.

It was a dangerous time, ever since the days when

Ayatollah Khomeini had come to Iran from Paris and established the Islamist Republic. Some Iranians had fled the country. But many didn't, couldn't afford to, or didn't want to, believing it would all soon pass, this temporary insanity, and Iran would get its country back. But the temporary insanity had grown into permanent schizophrenia. The moderates now didn't dare make too many waves, didn't dare fight too hard. Everyone knew what would happen if they did. Everyone had a family member or a friend who had disappeared at the hands of the Revolutionary Guard or VEVAK. For this group, the quiet ones, the kidnapping of the Israeli soldier was yet another embarrassment in a long list of embarrassments. It was the beginning of yet another dark chapter brought on by the malevolent, cancerous tide that was slowly but inexorably destroying their beloved country.

At the restaurant's long, crowded, and elegant mahogany bar, a series of flat-screen televisions behind the bar were turned on, volume down. They usually showed a football match. But tonight, all the television channels in Iran had been preempted by coverage of the trial of the Israeli soldier.

Every channel on the screen now showed, for the umpteenth time, a replay of Nava's press conference that day. The clip of the press conference would soon be followed, also for the umpteenth time, by a biased report by an *Al Jazeera* correspondent named Samir el-Bakahtr discussing all of the crimes the Israeli soldier, Kohl Meir, had supposedly committed, as well as still photos of Meir from the trial.

Iran's Minister of Information, Lon Qassou, the man who had given the order to state TV to preempt all other coverage, the man who had hand-fed the bogus charges to the *Al Jazeera* reporter, sat at the end of the bar, a stone expression on his face.

He watched his handiwork, the clip of his boss, President Mahmoud Nava, impassively. He sipped a glass of bourbon. It was his third of the night. Like every night, he would stop after four, after he was numb enough to go to sleep. Only he and Karin, the beautiful bartender, knew that he drank bourbon. Nothing illegal about that, but it wasn't something he wanted people to know, that he drank the most uniquely American of whiskeys.

Qassou looked around the bar. The bar was packed two deep, mostly male, a few women. He didn't see many Westerners. Not a journalist in sight, but there were a few Europeans. On nights like this, after a big, hateful, anti-American speech by Nava, or an announcement by Nava about the nuclear program, it seemed like the Americans and Brits in Tehran remained inside their apartments and hotels, holed up, fearful of the cutting edge that always lurked in Tehran. For 1979 would never leave the city, it would always be there forever, an indelible mark, to some a defining event, to others a permanent scar.

Qassou had removed his Prada glasses, tousled his long, black hair. He did this every night. He was one of the most recognizable faces in Iran. But by altering his appearance slightly in this way, he was able to enjoy relative anonymity on Tehran's streets, and especially in the slightly darkened atmosphere of Jean-Luc. Had

Qassou not altered his appearance in this way, he would not have been able to unplug from it all. Had he not messed up his hair and put in his contacts, he would not have been able to listen, as he did now, to the true, unvarnished opinions of Iranians.

To his left, two Iranian businessmen sat at the bar, one drinking a beer, the other a glass of red wine. Without looking, pretending to ignore the pair, Qassou stared at the TV screen.

"It sounds like Meir committed crimes."

"Bullshit, Mohammed. Bullshit by the midget. Are you that gullible?"

"He ordered a missile strike on a hospital."

"Right. And I discovered oil in my front yard this morning. They abducted him on American soil. Have we lost our minds?"

"Do you think America will invade?"

"No, of course not. They might bomb us, though."

"I think Israel will bomb us. That's what I think. And we deserve it. This time we deserve it."

"Listen to your talk. VEVAK would drag you away if they heard you."

At the end of the bar, Qassou noticed a woman staring at him. She had long brown hair, her hijab pulled down to her neck to show her face and pretty smile. She looked out of place, academic, a little older than a college student.

Qassou moved down to the seat next to her. He ordered another whiskey.

"Hello, Taris," said Qassou, speaking to Taris Darwil, a reporter for *Al Jazeera*.

"What does it mean?" Darwil asked, barely above a whisper, a hint of urgency in her voice. "With Meir gone?"

Qassou pulled a bill from his wallet. He placed it down on the bar. It was an innocuous gesture; still, someone inspecting the bill closely would have noticed the handwriting, written in pencil, in the corner of the bill.

"Everything remains the same," said Qassou. "There is somebody new. When I find out the location, I will call you. Send the location to this address. That is all."

"But Meir—"

"Shush!" hissed Qassou, under his breath, glancing about nervously.

"But what about him? Were you aware of this abduction?"

"No, of course not," snapped Qassou under his breath.

"Are you any closer to finding out the location?"

Qassou nodded. He glanced at her.

"He's taking me tomorrow."

"What if the American never contacts me?"

"Do you think I'm not trying?" he asked.

"Perhaps you can talk Nava out of it," said Darwil.

Qassou stared at Darwil, expressionless.

"I'm worried," said Darwil.

"You should be," said Qassou.

He stood up, turned, and walked out of the bar.

* * *

In a low, plain-looking six-story apartment building in the Norlina neighborhood of east Tehran, Paria sat in a wooden rocking chair, staring at a television set. The news was on, volume down.

The apartment belonged to the parents of Sara Massood. Paria's VEVAK agents had thus far been unable to track her down. Paria had men at her building as well as at the Parliament building. A simple tap on the parents' phone had enabled VEVAK to learn that Massood would be staying at her parents' small apartment that night—fearing for her safety after the interrogation.

Massood's parents, both in their sixties, sat petrified on a small, shabby sofa across from Paria, whose large frame spilled over the arms of the rocking chair. They had muttered nary a word since Paria and the two large VEVAK agents, both carrying machine guns, had knocked on the door then, when they'd cracked it to see who it was, pushed it in.

At a few minutes after 11:00 P.M., the sound of a key being inserted into the door lock caused Paria to look up from his catatonic stare at the silent TV. He nodded at one of the gunmen, then stood.

"Please don't hurt her," whispered Massood's mother.

Paria ignored her.

The gunman ripped the door open.

Massood stood in the door frame, momentarily shocked, her mouth dropping open at the sight of the gunman, and behind him Paria.

Her mother let out a small yelp as she looked at her daughter's face, her eyes solid red from the burst blood vessels and a bandage around her neck. Massood suddenly lurched backward to run away but a third gun-man, who'd followed her up from the parking lot, was standing behind her, weapon aimed at her skull.

"I'm not going to hurt you," said Paria.

Massood stepped inside as tears suddenly burst and started to flow down her cheeks.

Paria stepped forward, pulling the folded-up photo of Dewey from his chest pocket.

"What do you want from me?" she pleaded in a hoarse whisper.

He held out the photo of Dewey in front of Massood.

"Is this the man you saw in Odessa?" asked Paria.

She reached out and took the photo from him.

"Yes," said Massood, nodding up and down as she stared at the photo of Dewey. "I would stake my life on it."

36

UPPER PHILLIMORE GARDENS
KENSINGTON
LONDON, ENGLAND

At just after five o'clock in the morning, a dark green, old-model Saab moved slowly down Upper Phillimore Gardens, a quiet residential street in Kensington lined with brick mansions. The driver of the Saab, a nineteen-year-old Somali immigrant, stared at each of the houses as he drove slowly past. He stopped at each house for a brief moment, then tossed a *Times* newspaper from the passenger seat, trying to land each paper as high up on the wide granite steps as he could.

At number seven Upper Phillimore, a short, wiry man in a black bathrobe watched unnoticed from behind a first-story window as the Saab passed by. He noted the trajectory of the plastic-bagged newspaper as it lofted toward the top of the steps. A short burst of electronic beeps suddenly chimed faintly in the room; a sensor, indicating that something or someone had come into the airspace of the mansion, in this case, the newspaper. The beeping stopped as the motion of the paper stopped. The man sipped his coffee and watched as the Saab disappeared into the dark morning mist.

Rolf Borchardt was five feet four inches tall. His thinning brown hair was combed unnaturally, from the back to the front of his head, over his pasty skull, which was noticeable to everyone it seemed but Borchardt. Those who knew Borchardt found it hard to understand. Why not just admit that you are bald? they thought. Someone even joked that he couldn't understand why a man with Borchardt's vast wealth, who obviously cared enough about not wanting to appear bald to go through the effort of such an elaborate combover wouldn't simply buy a toupee.

Those people didn't understand Borchardt. The ones who did stayed away from him. If Borchardt appeared scrawny, short, weak, and clueless, professorial, clerkish, and distant, in fact he was precisely the opposite. Like everything else in his life, Borchardt's hair was designed to effect; subterfuge, disharmony, the breaking of visual equilibrium, the desire to trigger, on a very primordial level, avoidance by strangers and underestimation by adversaries.

This man is Borchardt? The weapons dealer? You've got to be kidding me.

Borchardt stepped from his massive, crimson-walled library to the ornate front entrance atrium of his mansion. After Buckingham Palace, the eighty-foot-wide brick building was the largest home in Kensington. It was six stories high, and spread into the back twice as deep as any other home on Upper Phillimore. According to public records, in 2006 Borchardt paid exactly one hundred and twelve million dollars for the place, but that didn't tell the true story. In fact, the building was worth far more than that amount. It wasn't supposed to be for sale. The Saudi government had owned it; it had, in fact, served for more than fifty years as the Saudi embassy. But when the Saudis needed Borchardt for something, he happened to be looking for a home. So the Saudis got exactly six pounds of U-235, highly enriched weapons-grade uranium, and Borchardt got his 53,599-square-foot mansion on Upper Phillimore. It was no secret that the Saudis feared Iran's nuclear program almost as much as Israel did. The uranium was purchased as insurance.

Borchardt was regarded by intelligence agencies and governments around the world as one of the top weapons dealers in the world. In point of fact, he was, by revenue, number of transactions, and by the hard-to-calculate metric of weapons quality and rarity, by far the most powerful weapons dealer in the world.

Borchardt was a man without morals or allies. He dealt with the United States, Britain, Germany, Israel, and just about every other democratic government. He was involved in a very high percentage of deals involving Russia and China. Borchardt also, just as easily, dealt with rogues such as Iran, Somalia, North Korea, and Cuba. He even sold weapons to terrorist organizations such as Hamas, Hezbollah, and even Al-Qaeda, though he refused to sell them anything more powerful than guns. His logic was selfish rather than moral.

The last thing Borchardt wanted to see, as his Gulf-stream 200 took off from Heathrow, was the sight of a Stinger surface-to-air missile smoking through the air toward his plane.

The reason legitimate governments dealt with Borchardt, despite the fact that he sold weapons to rogues and terrorists, was because they had to. And if Borchardt were to somehow cease to exist, everyone in the complex framework of shady deals knew the ramifications would be severe. For more than two decades, to every London station chief from the CIA, Mossad, KGB, and others, Borchardt had made it crystal clear: I will retire someday and when I do, so will my records. But if I die before then, the front page of every newspaper in the world will tell the story of our dealings for many, many years to come.

Borchardt opened the twelve-foot-tall glass and iron door at the front of the mansion, stepped to the front stoop, reached down to pick up that morning's copy of the *Times*. He stepped back inside, shut the door, walked through the front atrium to the large kitchen. He placed his empty coffee cup down on the marble counter of the kitchen's square center island. He reached into the plastic to pull the paper out. As he did so, he heard a momentary click, then, as his mind raced to process the sound, felt a sudden, sharp, painful stinging sensation. He ripped his hand out of the paper. Dangling from the end of his index and middle fingers, a mousetrap clutched his fingers.

"Fuck!" he screamed, frantically shaking his hand to release the trap. *"Fuck! Fuck! Goddamn it! Fuck!"*

But the trap would not release. He saw that blood now coursed from the tops of the two fingers, and his shaking the trap only made the steel bar dig deeper. He reached down with his free hand, pulled the bar up, released his fingers, then hurled the trap against the white marble floor.

"Goddamn it!" he yelled again.

Borchardt stepped around the blood, walked to the sink, turned on the water. He rinsed the cuts on his fingers, examining them; the small steel bar had cut his fingers straight down, almost to the bone. His mind raced. *Who the fuck would do this?* Anger boiled up like mercury.

"Control yourself," he said aloud to no one.

He wrapped a dish towel around his right hand. He stepped back to the mousetrap, reached down and picked it up. The metal bar at the trap's front had been sharpened. Lifting it from the side, he saw the wet blood, covering the glinting steel that was as thin, as sharp, as a razor.

Dropping the mousetrap, he pulled the newspaper gingerly from the plastic bag with his left hand, placed it down on the marble island. Nothing. No note, or other object. He flipped through the paper, page by page. He went quickly through the front section, then the business section. In the sports section, he suddenly saw handwriting. Scrawled across a woman's leg in a beer advertisement, black handwriting:

Queen's Gate near park entrance, one hour, or next time it will be your head

Borchardt wrapped bandages around each finger. Later, he would need stitches, but right now he didn't have the time.

He scurried upstairs. In his bedroom, he picked up the phone and dialed a number.

"Yes," came the voice, groggy.

"Wake up," said Borchardt.

"Yes, what is it?"

"I'm meeting someone at Kensington Gardens in an hour. I need you to be there."

"What happened?"

Borchardt explained the incident with the mousetrap, then read his bodyguard, an ex–KGB agent named Vlad Kellner, the note from the woman's leg.

"Why are you going?" asked Kellner after hearing the note. "We can construct a safety protocol within the hour. You stay at Phillimore and we can have this thing locked down by the time you finish putting your hair in place."

"Fuck you," said Borchardt.

"A little morning humor."

"You know how I feel," said Borchardt. "I'm more afraid of living my life surrounded by guards and fences than I am of being shot in the head."

"So you want to meet this person, who just almost cut your fingers off?"

"No, you stupid son of a bitch, I have no intention of meeting him," said Borchardt impatiently. "I want you to kill him."

"Forty-five minutes to assemble a kill team?" asked Kellner, incredulous.

"Yes!" barked Borchardt.

"It's clearly an individual," said Kellner. "A rogue. Not someone you've dealt with. You'd already be dead."

"Can you bring Anna?"

"Yes, fine. Where will you enter the park?"

"Queen's Gate."

Borchardt hung up the phone. He didn't bother showering. He dressed quickly, a dark blue suit, no tie.

Borchardt took the elevator to the basement. The lights in the darkened garage went on when he entered. He looked at the line of cars, chose the Bentley, started it up, then drove up the ramp, waiting for the automatic garage door to rise. He pulled out of the garage onto Upper Phillimore Gardens and sped toward Kensington Gardens.

He didn't notice the man seated in the backseat of the parked Mercedes across the street.

Borchardt drove quickly to Queen's Gate and parked on Kensington Road. He waited, picked up his cell, called Kellner.

"Are you there?"

"No, not yet. Five minutes out."

Borchardt flipped his phone shut. He waited in the Bentley. Ten minutes later, he dialed again.

"We're here," said Kellner. "Anna is reading a book left north of the gates. I'll be walking a vector."

"Okay. I'm parked at the gates."

"Look, I've been thinking about this," said Kellner. "Obviously, this knucklehead selected Queen's Gate because it's visible. Getting a clean shot off, leaving a body in the middle of the park. It's, well—"

"What are you saying?"

"I'm saying what I just said," said Kellner. "Getting a clean shot off will not be easy. Look around you."

From the front seat of the Bentley, Borchardt turned and ogled the gates surrounding Kensington Gardens. The sidewalks outside the park were beginning to get crowded; people walking to catch a bus or the tube to work; dog walkers, joggers, mothers and fathers pushing baby strollers.

"Do the best you can."

"This is not an ideal environment," persisted Kellner. "I don't particularly feel like spending the rest of my life in prison. We should take the time to design something correctly."

"So should I ask him to reschedule?" asked Borchardt sarcastically. "What are you, a fucking imbecile? What is it about you Russians? You manage to be both lazy and stupid at the same time. It's actually quite an accomplishment."

"We simply don't show up," said Kellner. "If it's so fucking urgent, they will get back in touch with you."

In the rearview mirror, Borchardt spied the entrance gates in the distance.

"Stop complaining. Unless you kill the queen, I should be able to get you sprung from a British prison. That's if they catch you, which, of course, they won't."

"That's reassuring. Anna has the Nikon. If she can get a clean shot, she will take it. Me too. But if she can't, she'll take some photos."

Borchardt flipped the phone shut. He shook his head. He wasn't good at this part of it. His world, his professional world, existed largely on the computer. The most important part of his job, the critical, objective assessments of weapons and weapons systems, was conducted by a field team of more than two hundred men and women who worked, secretly, for Borchardt. He had spent his life building this network of covert freelancers and highly compensated experts, and he dealt with them for the most part virtually. He didn't like people. He didn't like what occurred when he was forced to coexist with people nearby and visible.

Borchardt's fingers throbbed in pain. He didn't like pain, not at all. The bandage on the middle finger had a small dot of red where the blood was seeping through. As soon as possible, he would need sutures to fix the deep gashes.

He went to look at his watch, then realized he'd forgotten to put it on. He glanced down at the clock on the dashboard of the Bentley. It was five minutes before he was due to meet the son of a bitch who had sliced his fingers open. He climbed from the car, walking casually toward Queen's Gate. He consciously tried to keep his head calm and still. His eyes, however, darted about, wild with curiosity and paranoia. At Queen's Gate, he stepped left and went into the park, which was crowded with people. Christ, he thought. Kellner was right.

Okay, so he would meet the man. Or was it a woman? Whatever, he would meet the person who'd nearly sliced his fingers clean off, find out what the hell they wanted. Anna could snap a few photos. Kellner would get one of his contacts in Kiev to run the photo. Kellner could organize a proper hit, do it right. He would get extra protection for a week or two, until it was done.

Borchardt walked to a kiosk inside Kensington Gardens and purchased a small cup of green tea. He glanced left. Benches lined the edge of the grass meadow for as far as the eye could see. They were crowded with people, sitting and reading. On the fourth bench, he saw Anna—tall, gangly Anna, like a librarian on steroids. She sat, reading a book, one of three people on the bench.

Borchardt stood near the entrance and sipped his tea. He finished the cup. At least half an hour passed. He paced from one side of the park's large entrance to the other. He felt perspiration beginning to wet his underarms. He removed his suit coat. He went and sat on a bench near the entrance. What had happened? On the woman's leg, he'd written one hour, but perhaps he thought Borchardt wouldn't retrieve the paper so early. In fact, now that he considered it, what did "one hour" actually mean? One hour from *when* exactly? Would he be forced to wait at Kensington Gardens all day? Fuck that.

An hour turned into two, then three. Finally, at nine o'clock, Borchardt stood. He glanced at Anna, then exited the park. He walked to the Bentley. A bright orange slip of paper was tucked into the right windshield wiper; a ticket.

"Fuckhead," he muttered as he removed it, and threw it to the pavement, then climbed in the large sedan. He put the keys in the ignition, then started the Bentley.

"Hi, Rolf," came the voice from the backseat.

Borchardt practically jumped from his seat. He lurched his head violently around, his comb-over came flying off his head as he did so.

"Christ, you scared me," yelled Borchardt at Kellner seated in the backseat.

"Sorry," said Kellner. "At least I didn't wait until you were driving."

Borchardt shook his head, then leaned against the steering wheel.

"I practically had a heart attack. How the hell did you get inside the car?"

"You left it unlocked," said Kellner. He lit a cigarette, then opened the window.

After a few minutes, a tall, severe-looking woman with a broad forehead and long, brown hair climbed into the front seat of the car. Anna, Kellner's assistant. She said nothing.

Borchardt pushed the car out into traffic.

"Let's go back and look at the note," said Kellner, a hint of exasperation in his voice. "The mousetrap. Maybe it was a prank, yes? Some kid from down the block."

"Yeah, sure," said Borchardt. "Some little teenage prankster who almost severed my fingers off, Vlad."

Borchardt paused.

"Am I inconveniencing you, Vlad?" Borchardt asked, looking into the rearview mirror.

"No, Rolf. Come on. What's that for?"

"How much did I pay you last year? Three million euros? Four? To do what? You let me know if I should just drop you off right here. You miserable Ukrainian—"

"Estonian."

"Estonian, Ukrainian, who the fuck cares, you're all the same. You miserable *Estonian* fuckface douche bag. I mean, ex-agents, looking to bodyguard billionaires, are so hard to find. I'll have a rat's nest full of them by lunchtime."

"Whatever you want to do, Rolf," said Kellner, calmly puffing his Dunhill in the backseat.

Borchardt drove in silence for several minutes. Finally, he spoke.

"So what happened?" asked Borchardt.

"He didn't show up," said Kellner.

"Gee, you think?" Borchardt shook his head. "Or he did show up, mark me, and is now following us. Or he saw you or Anna and got scared."

"He already knows where you live, so he wouldn't need to follow. I doubt he marked Anna or me. But maybe you're right. Who knows. We'll go back and look at it. Maybe we ask Trudeau to look at it."

"Maybe," said Borchardt, beginning to calm.

He pulled onto Upper Phillimore Gardens. At his mansion, he turned into the brick driveway that sloped down beneath the enormous building. He pressed the door opener and the door moved quickly up. Borchardt moved down the driveway into the garage, then parked as the garage door slid back down behind them.

They climbed into the building's elevator. Anna pressed the button for the first floor. The elevator climbed, then came to a smooth stop on the first floor. Borchardt exited the elevator first, followed by Kellner and Anna.

They walked from the elevator, off the main entrance foyer, down the hallway toward the kitchen. From the hallway, Borchardt could see the plume of blood, now dried, spread in the middle of the kitchen, next to the island, the size of a large pancake. The mousetrap sat in the middle of the puddle, on its side. Borchardt entered the large kitchen, followed by Kellner and Anna. Kellner and Anna entered the large, sunlit room. The three crossed the kitchen, eyeing the bloody scene on the floor. Kellner looked somewhat uninterested as he stood above the bloody scene. He reached for his box of Dunhills.

"Welcome home," came a voice from behind them, to the right, in the corner of the kitchen.

The three heads rotated, in shock.

He held a handgun in each hand, suppressors jutting out from the barrels, aimed calmly at them. The weapons were held by a man in a red Puma T-shirt, face brown from the sun, short hair, handsome, stubble, eyes as blue as the ocean.

Anna, ex–French intelligence, wheeled her torso, and grabbed her Para-Ordnance P12 .45 caliber from a leather holster beneath her left armpit, swinging the weapon around. Before her arm could complete its arc, he fired the weapon in his right hand. The bullet struck her forehead and kicked her backward. She tumbled onto the white marble floor, which was now littered in skull, brains, and blood.

Before Kellner could do anything, the man pulsed the trigger from the other weapon. This slug hit Kellner in the middle of his forehead and sent the large Estonian lurching back. Borchardt's bodyguard landed in a contorted heap on his side.

Borchardt stood motionless, looking at the stranger in his kitchen.

The man held Borchardt within the frame of both weapons now. For several seconds, Borchardt just stared at him. He looked calm, even serene. His blue eyes were icy, as serious as any he'd ever seen.

Borchardt glanced down to his right side, then his left, at the two corpses on his kitchen floor, blood rioted across the room, then back to the man. The accent: American.

"What do you want?" asked Borchardt.

"Payment."

"For what?"

"The debt you owe me."

The man nodded at the marble counter behind Borchardt.

Borchardt turned. Next to the newspaper was a manila folder. Borchardt looked back at the man, who stared blankly back. Borchardt stepped over Kellner's body to the marble island. He glanced behind him at the gunman, who still hadn't moved. He kept the weapons trained on him. Borchardt reached down. He opened the manila folder.

Inside the folder was a black-and-white photograph. It was a surveillance photo, taken from a distance with a telescopic lens. It showed the head and shoulders of a soldier: good-looking, young. A small American flag patch on the chest placed the soldier's nationality. He wore a military uniform. In his right hand, he held an M60, pointed up at the sky. Thick stripes of eye black ran beneath the soldier's eyes. He had short-cropped hair, a sharp nose. The soldier stared straight ahead, laserlike, past the camera, a look that even the surveillance photo was able to capture in its raw aspect: danger.

It came back to him now. Was it two years ago? Such a small deal. He shook his head.

"Ring any bells?" asked the stranger.

"Yes," said Borchardt quietly. "Aswan Fortuna wanted to know who killed his son. I remember."

"That photo cost a lot of lives," said the man. "Including Fortuna's."

Borchardt nodded.

"So I heard," he whispered.

"The way I see it, you owe me."

Borchardt put the photo down. He turned around, faced the stranger.

"Yes, I do," said Borchardt. He nodded, managing to look the gunman in the eyes. "I owe you more than a favor."

The man stood, motionless, not moving. He studied Borchardt for more than a minute.

"I never got your name," said Borchardt. "Fortuna would have paid double for it. My contact wouldn't give it to me."

"Andreas," said the man, his arms still crossed, his weapons still pointed menacingly at Borchardt's head. "Dewey Andreas."

"So now you get your revenge, yes?" asked Borchardt.

"I'm not looking for revenge," said Dewey. "Frankly, I don't care whether you live or die. If you help me, you'll live. It's that simple."

"I understand."

"Look under the photo," said Dewey.

Borchardt turned back to the folder and flipped the photo to the side. Beneath it, another photo, this one of the Iranian nuclear bomb.

Borchardt stared at the photograph for several seconds.

"Whose is it?" he asked.

"Iran's," said Dewey.

"What do you want?" he asked quietly.

"A replica. Exactly the same."

"I need to know precisely how big it is."

"Eight feet, eight inches," said Dewey. "It weighs four and a half tons."

"How soon?"

"Yesterday."

Borchardt lifted the photo and looked at it closely.

"Do you see the writing on the side of the bomb?" Dewey asked.

"Persian," Borchardt noted. "Goodbye Tel Aviv."

"I want something a little different," said Dewey. "Can you do that?"

"Yes, of course," said Borchardt, "whatever you like, Mr. Andreas."

A dull mechanical thud interrupted Borchardt as Dewey fired the Colt in his left hand. Borchardt lurched back, but felt nothing, then realized he hadn't been hit. His eyes moved down and he saw specks of material from his coat floating in the air, toward the ground. He looked behind him and picked up the neat hole in the wood of the island, where the bullet had settled after passing through the linen of his blazer, near his waist.

"Why did you do that?"

"Because I want you to understand something, Rolf. If you fuck with me again, you'll get a bullet in the head."

"I'll do it," said Borchardt. "And not because of your threats. I'll do it because I owe you one. But afterward, we're even."

Dewey stared at Borchardt.

"It will be down and dirty," said Borchardt. "Where do you want it delivered?"

"I'll call you," said Dewey.

Dewey holstered one of his weapons beneath his left armpit as Tacoma entered the kitchen.

"You done?" asked Dewey.

Tacoma nodded.

"One more thing," said Dewey, turning to Borchardt. "There's a bomb in your house, remote detonator. I'll tell you where it is when we're done."

37

Paria walked into the conference room. Inside, half a dozen senior staffers from the Ministry of Intelligence were waiting.

Paria's adrenaline was coursing through him, keeping him in a state of near fury. The facts were presenting themselves only gradually, in bits and pieces and fragments. It had started with the mention of Qassou by the professor at Tehran University. Then came the deaths of the VEVAK S7 and the Quds commanders in Odessa.

Now the plot was beginning to take shape, its vague outlines were becoming more sharp and defined. Qassou was working on something with an American. And not just any American.

In the center of the table was a glass pitcher with water in it. He walked to the table and grabbed the pitcher and a glass from the tray. He was only able to fill half the glass before the pitcher was empty.

"Would you like me to refill the pitcher?" asked one of his men.

Paria ignored the question. He stared for a brief, anger-filled moment at the empty water pitcher, then hurled it at the wall, where it shattered. He gulped down the half glass of water, then hurled that at the identical spot on the wall, shattering it as well.

The men at the table were silent.

"Have the Israelis killed any more people?" Paria barked.

"No, sir," said one of his men. "We've increased protection at embassies across the globe."

"What about Bhutta? Where is he?"

"We don't know."

"What of Qassou's computer?" yelled Paria. "His expense reports. E-mail. Speak!"

"Nothing so far, sir," said one of the men at the table. "Not a thing. He travels quite a bit. He spends money. But there's nothing that connects him to the American. He has correspondence with Western journalists, of course, but nothing even remotely mysterious."

Paria scanned the room, barely controlling his anger and frustration.

"What about the American?" asked Paria. "What more do we know?"

"Andreas is thirty-nine or forty years old, General," said one of his aides. "He was a member of Delta. We don't know anything more than that. We've been unable to corroborate that he was involved in the Khomeini assassination or the coup in Pakistan; Beijing is the source for this intelligence and we've asked for backup."

Paria stared at him.

"Backup? Why the fuck do you need backup? Why would the Chinese lie?"

"I don't know, sir."

"You're a fucking idiot," said Paria contemptuously.

"The American is coming to Iran," said one of the men. "That's my guess. He's probably coming to try and rescue Kohl Meir. Meir saved him in Beirut."

"I want his photo sent out to every border crossing, every news outlet, every police station, every hotel or motel, every military outpost in the country. *Immediately!*"

"Should we move Meir?" asked another agent.

Paria thought for a moment, then shook his head.

"No," said Paria. "There's no need. He's in Evin. Let Andreas come for him. Triple the guards at Meir's cell. Shut off all traffic within a square block."

"Yes, sir."

"But why Qassou?" asked Paria. "Why meet Qassou in Odessa?"

"We still don't know that he did meet him in Odessa," said one of the agents.

Paria stared around the table. He was silent. Then, he put his fist down on the table.

"It's time," said Paria. "I want Qassou brought in. Make it invisible. No one can know we have him. *No one!* I want it to look like a ghost stole him. That way, if we have to dispose of him, Nava will not know it was me. Go. Get the traitor and bring him in."

38

It rained in Tehran for the first time in more than a month. Beginning at daybreak, sheets of water came down like wet nails on the dust-quilted city, washing down its buildings, streets, cars, filling drainpipes with brown-red water until, after more than an hour of downpour, the water began to run clear, if only for a little while. After the initial wave of thunderstorms, which lasted nearly two hours, the weather in Iran's capital city settled into a steady, light rain.

In his apartment on the fourteenth floor of the Aqusah Luxury Complex in the northern part of the city, Qassou was awakened by the first clap of thunder. He rubbed his eyes and looked at the clock next to his bed: 6:00 A.M. He closed his eyes for several minutes, then opened them again. Eventually, he threw the sheets off himself and stepped to the large window. In the distance, he watched as, within the ominous shroud of black storm clouds, a crooked white line of lightning abruptly shot down toward the highest peak in the Alborz Mountains, Mount Damavand. It was followed, just a few seconds later, by a loud thunderclap.

"Thank God for that," Qassou said aloud to no one.

The heat and humidity had lingered over the city for weeks now; Qassou knew the rain would bring cooler temperatures, at least for a few hours. He opened the window, stuck his hand outside, and felt the water.

He made coffee, rubbing his eyes and watching as it brewed. He was hungover. He drank too much as it was, but the past weeks had exacerbated the stress. His head hurt, but at least the alcohol had enabled him to escape for a few hours.

When the coffee was finished, he poured himself a cup, walked to the laptop on the kitchen table, then checked his e-mail.

There was an e-mail from Taris.

Still no contact

That was all.

Qassou sipped his coffee, staring at her words. Even if he were to find out the location of the bomb, the fact is, without Andreas contacting Taris, there was nothing. He could pinpoint the precise location of the bomb and if Andreas hadn't made it safely over the border, if he'd encountered problems, if he'd just plain given up, it wouldn't matter.

Qassou clicked the icon for the *Tehran Times*:

ISRAELI KOHL MEIR FOUND GUILTY OF MURDER

Seeing the words, a sour, tight feeling came to Qassou's stomach. Meir had been found guilty. The clock was now officially ticking. The day when the bomb would be used was coming.

Qassou couldn't escape one awful thought. Could he have inadvertently gotten Meir killed, while at the same time *not* stopping the destruction of Tel Aviv?

If the plan ended up not working, he would have a hard time going on. Life would simply be too unbearable. It had to work. The American had to make it into the country. And today, Mahmoud Nava had to take him to the location.

He shook his head, lit a cigarette, leaned back in the wooden chair, and put his bare feet up on the kitchen table. As he did every morning, he would finish his smoke, then get ready for work.

In an apartment two blocks away, a large, thin man with a sliver of a mustache and no hair was lying on his stomach, propped up on his elbows, staring into a high-powered telescope. He watched every move of the man in the high-rise apartment building, Lon Qassou. He watched through the driving rain as Qassou lit his cigarette. It made him want one as well. Without removing his eye from the end of the telescope, Pavil reached for the cigarettes next to him, put one in his mouth, then lit it.

Pavil and another VEVAK agent, Marwan, had been watching Qassou all night. The two operatives had flown back yesterday, by chopper, from Baghdad, under orders of Abu Paria himself.

When Qassou took his feet down from the table and leaned forward to stub his cigarette out, Pavil cleared his throat.

"We've got activity," Pavil said. Hearing no response, he repeated himself. "Marwan," he whispered, this time with impatience in his tone. "He's moving."

The other agent suddenly sat up. He was reclined in the apartment's only piece of furniture, a brown leather chair.

He stood up and moved quickly to Pavil, stretching as he walked, then yawning.

"Let me see," he said.

Marwan got down on his stomach next to Pavil and looked through the end of the telescope.

"What's he doing?" he asked as he watched Qassou place a coffee cup in the sink and walk out of the kitchen.

"He's climbing into the shower," said Marwan. "Should I send him?"

"Yes."

Marwan pulled a small mic that was clipped to his neck and pressed it.

"You can move now," said Marwan, into the mic.

"Yes, sir," said the voice over Marwan's earbud.

"Come in through the kitchen window," said Marwan. "He opened it. And be careful; it'll be slippery."

"Got it."

"Don't kill him. Remember, we need information."

"Yes, yes, I know."

"Good luck."

* * *

A minute later, through the telescope, Marwan stared as a black figure emerged, like a large insect, from a window one story above Qassou's apartment on the fourteenth floor.

The rain was pouring down. It made the image of the man look blurry and slightly misshapen. Like a snail, the figure moved slowly. He climbed out of a window near the corner of the building. Gripping the stonework next to the window, he placed both feet on a small ledge. The man inched slowly down the face of the concrete toward the fourteenth floor and the window to Qassou's kitchen. Marwan watched as his foot seemed to tap against the window. Was it not open after all?

"I thought the window was open," said Marwan.

"It was. He opened it. Why?"

"He's having trouble."

"Let me see."

A lightning strike hit in the sightline just above Qassou's apartment building, which rattled the sky. A moment later came a low growl of thunder.

Pavil pulled the end of the telescope to his eye.

"He's at the wrong window," said Pavil. "The one next to it. The room next to it."

Pavil watched as the dark figure struggled to open the window. Through the telescope, he watched as the figure punched at the window. He looked as if he could lose his grip. Finally, his arm went through the window, shattering the glass. A moment later, he opened the window and climbed in through the opening.

"He's in," said Pavil.

"I can see that," said Marwan. "How did he get in?"

"He punched in the glass," said Pavil.

"Well, let's hope he didn't hear."

"What's Qassou going to do?" asked Pavil, looking at Marwan and smiling. "Beat him up with his typewriter?"

"Good point," said Marwan. He got on his knees, then stood. "Let's move. We need to deliver him to the general."

Pavil got to his knees, reached for the telescope to put it back in the long case lying next to it.

Qassou was rinsing shampoo from his hair when he heard the noise. It was faint, and because of the storm and the sound of the shower, he couldn't be sure if it was anything, but it did make him stand still for a brief moment. It was the high pitch of the noise that made him stop moving. And then he realized what it was: the sound of glass breaking.

Why should that alarm him? He was, after all, on the fourteenth floor of a highly secure building.

Nevertheless, he felt a sudden wave of coldness; a feeling of fear.

He started to turn the shower off, then decided against it. He climbed out, then stood on the shower mat, dripping wet. He looked at the white door, which was slightly ajar. He stared into the dimly lit apartment through the crack, dripping wet, naked. He stared down the carpeted hallway for more than a minute, unsure of what he was looking for, but seeing nothing except the daylight coming in from his bedroom.

And then he saw the light coming in from the

bedroom suddenly darken, then lighten again, as if something or someone had crossed in front of the bedroom window. It was just a shadow, but Qassou realized someone was in the apartment.

Qassou looked around the small bathroom for something to defend himself with. There were various items—soap, deodorant, toothpaste—but nothing he was looking for. Nothing sharp. He saw a toothbrush, a hairbrush, his electric razor. He picked up the razor. Then, he put it back down.

He reached for his toothbrush, picking it up from the side of the sink. Then he stepped back, behind the door, as the water continued to pour down in the shower.

The bathroom became thick with steam.

For several minutes, Qassou waited behind the door, until he was no longer wet.

He could feel his heart racing as he stared at the door. A minute became two minutes, then five. He clutched the toothbrush in his right hand, raised next to his head.

The black forehead of a figure slowly moved past the edge of the door, emerging just in front of where Qassou stood. He had a ski mask on. Lower, Qassou saw something that was colored red; metallic. Was it a gun?

He lurched at the figure's head, swinging the end of the toothbrush as hard as he could toward the intruder's skull. He struck the man's skull, and where he expected it to bounce off hard bone, he felt instead some give, and an instant later heard the man scream out as blood suddenly spurted forward. The man fell to the ground, screaming and clutching his eye.

Yanking the door open, Qassou fell atop the man and started stabbing wildly with the toothbrush, aiming at the man's other eye as blood coursed onto the white bath mat. The man kicked out and sent Qassou flying through the air, striking against the shower curtain and falling into the shower.

Qassou clawed his way up. He climbed out of the shower as the man moaned and clutched at his eyes, trying to remove the ski mask.

On the floor, beneath the intruder's leg, he saw the red weapon. He leapt for the red object, which looked like a gun, and grabbed it before the man could find it; he was clutching his eye and moaning.

Qassou picked up the weapon and aimed it, then fired. A small dart shot out and punctured his neck just to the left of the nape. He went limp.

Qassou reached down and pulled away the man's ski mask. Beneath, his face was covered in blood. His right eye was gone. The socket was a pool of dark red. Long tendrils of veins hung to the side, down his cheek.

Qassou turned off the shower. He rinsed his hands and face in the sink.

What just happened? he asked himself as his hands shook like leaves and he threw water onto his face, which was now covered in perspiration.

He ran to the bedroom and quickly got dressed. He went back to the unconscious intruder. Kneeling, he removed the dart from his neck. He inspected it, even smelling the small object, but it was no use. He felt the man's neck for a pulse—he was still alive, the dart was some sort of tranquilizer.

Qassou tried to organize his thoughts, but they were frazzled.

Someone knew something. Someone suspected something. It was Abu Paria. It had to be. He knew enough to stage an abduction, but not enough to kill him or arrest him. Which meant that Paria was working without Nava's knowledge. If Nava was in on it, the VEVAK agents would simply have walked in and taken him into custody. No, this was to be a VEVAK special. Abduction, a long drive to a house in the suburbs, a dirty basement, torture, then his body would be deposited in a landfill somewhere.

But he wasn't dead yet. Which meant Paria suspected him and now needed information. Paria was searching for answers; he didn't have them yet.

He searched the intruder, looking for identification, but found nothing.

Qassou picked up the dart gun and fired another one into the man's neck.

He went to his bedroom and packed his leather weekend bag; a change of clothing, money, his passport, a photograph of him and his brother, a leather-bound Koran. Glancing about the apartment, he realized it was the last time he would ever step foot in the place.

Qassou picked up the tranquilizer gun, then walked to the door of his apartment. He looked through the peephole into the hallway, seeing nothing. He opened the door. He walked past the elevators, to the fire stairs, and began his descent.

39

Jessica stood in the galley kitchen in the midsection of the plane, watching as the Keurig coffeemaker pushed out black liquid into a Styrofoam cup beneath.

The idling supersonic jet hummed low in the background. Through the galley window, black tarmac stretched for a mile or so, then the main terminal buildings.

Jessica glanced at the silver Cartier watch on her wrist. It read 7:00 P.M., but she was in Spain now, so technically it was one in the morning. It felt like one in the morning. The hours were beginning to meld into a haze.

She picked up the cup of coffee and walked to the front of the heavily customized CIA-owned and -operated Gulfstream G150. She flopped into one of the big leather seats in the middle of the cabin. She rubbed her eyes, then looked across the aisle at Hector Calibrisi. The

CIA director was reading something on his thin silver laptop, running his right hand back through his thick, unruly hair.

On the flight over, Calibrisi had briefed Jessica on everything; the nuclear bomb, Qassou, the mole inside Mossad, Bhutta, everything. To say she was shocked was an understatement. But at some point, she realized that she had no choice other than to help Calibrisi help Dewey. Even if it meant losing her job and being hauled in front of Congress.

"How long, Hector?" Jessica asked wearily.

"He should be here in a few minutes," said Calibrisi, not looking up from his laptop.

"What are you looking at?" asked Jessica.

"I'm reading about the killing spree Mossad has been on," said Calibrisi. "They've killed three officials inside Iran, as well as the ambassadors to Portugal and China."

"They asked for it," said Jessica.

"True."

Outside, the high pitch of a jet landing echoed across the empty tarmac, making the Gulfstream rock slightly. After several minutes, Jessica saw movement outside her window. She leaned across the seat and peered outside. The lights of a Citation 655, painted in a muted camouflage print of tan and green, pulled slowly alongside the Gulfstream. It came to a stop. Hebrew lettering was visible along the tail. Suddenly, the jet's front hatch cracked, then opened. A stairwell fell down. A few moments later, a tall man, his face dark and tan, a block of gray hair atop his head, emerged. He wore a tan military uniform, a thick belt around the waist, ribbons decorating both the left and right chest, epaulets atop the shoulders. He was in his fifties. He climbed down the steps of the jet, alone.

Calibrisi stood up, walked to the front of the cabin, and pressed a button. The Gulfstream's stairwell fell ajar, then lowered.

"Good evening, General Dayan," Calibrisi barked down the stairwell.

"Hello, Hector," said Dayan from the tarmac.

Jessica watched as General Menachem Dayan ducked his head and entered the cabin. He reached his hand out and shook Calibrisi's hand. He shot a look down the aisle to Jessica, who stood.

"Jessica," he said, a serious expression on his face. "I didn't know you would be coming."

"General Dayan," she said. She stepped forward as he moved back to her. They shook hands. Dayan smiled at her.

"You look as beautiful as always, Jessica," said Dayan.

"I don't feel beautiful, General Dayan," she said. "I feel tired. But thank you."

"You called this meeting," said Dayan. "What can I do for you?"

"It concerns Iran," said Calibrisi, motioning for Dayan and Jessica to sit down. "Kohl Meir. But before we start, I need your assurance that this is off-the-record. Dead-man talk."

"Of course."

"Not Shalit," said Calibrisi. "Not anyone. Are we clear?"

"Yes."

"Our hands are tied," said Calibrisi. "We're under strict orders by President Dellenbaugh. We're not supposed to have anything to do with Iran right now."

"I figured as much," said Dayan.

"President Dellenbaugh believes we're within days of getting Iran to agree to stop the development of its nuclear program," said Jessica.

"And you believe them?" asked Dayan.

Jessica stared into Dayan's eyes, then looked at Calibrisi.

"Iran has completed its first nuclear device," said Calibrisi. "We're estimating it at fifteen to twenty kilotons."

Dayan was silent for several moments.

"How do you know this?"

"An informant within Nava's administration."

Calibrisi pulled the photo that Dewey gave him out of a folder and handed it to Dayan, who stared at it for more than a minute.

"My Persian is rusty," said Dayan, staring at the photo. "Does that say what I think it does?"

"Yes," said Calibrisi. " 'Goodbye, Tel Aviv'. The informant believes it will be brought in by water."

"When?"

"We don't know."

Dayan closed his eyes and rubbed them for a moment.

"Do we have any idea where it is?" asked Dayan.

"No. There's something else. The reason Kohl was in the United States, in addition to visiting Ezra Bohr's parents, was to ask Dewey Andreas to help him design an operation to destroy the bomb."

Dayan's face flushed red.

"And he didn't come to me?" asked Dayan, anger in his voice.

"Before you get mad, you need to know something: Mossad has a mole. Someone high up. Someone feeding intelligence to the Chinese, who are then handing it over to VEVAK."

Dayan was silent.

"We've been looking for more than two years," said Dayan.

"So you know?"

"Yes."

"The Iranian informant understood the danger this double agent represents. If Nava or Suleiman or whoever is running this thing from Tehran's perspective gets wind that Israel or the U.S. has knowledge of the bomb, they'll launch it preemptively. We can't confide in anyone. *You* can't confide in anyone, General."

"What am I supposed to do?" asked Dayan, gesticulating with his arms. "Let them sail into Tel Aviv and destroy the city?"

"No," said Calibrisi. "That's why I asked you here. We're doing something. It's being run outside Langley. Andreas is running it. But I need your help."

"What?"

"You have a kill team inside Tehran?"

"How do you know?"

"Someone's killing politicians."

"Yes. We have some men there from Sayeret Matkal."

"How is Iran not spotting them?"

"The same way the CIA does it; they're all recruits from Kurdistan."

"Dewey's going to need help. I can't put CIA paramilitary on the ground in time or without risking the president finding out."

"How many men are we talking?"

"Three or four. Position them in Tehran on my go."

"What if Andreas doesn't succeed?"

"You need to watch your ports, General. Amp up your naval perimeters immediately."

Dayan held the photo out toward Calibrisi.

"Look at this fucking thing," said Dayan. "You could fit it on a fishing boat. Do you realize how many small little chickenshit fishing boats come into Tel Aviv each day? Not to mention sailboats and cigarette boats?"

Calibrisi met Dayan's gaze.

"I don't know what to tell you," said Calibrisi. "Get Geigers into the hands of your patrol vessels. Restrict entry. Get planes in the sky."

"Hector, we don't have the boats necessary to enforce a blockade of smaller vessels," said Dayan, rubbing his forehead. "Even if we wanted to. Not to mention the fact that Tehran would know immediately if we did move to tie-off the ports. Then they could simply fly the fucking thing in in a private plane. Or bring it into Haifa."

"Dewey knows what he's doing," said Jessica.

"What *is* he doing?" asked Dayan.

Calibrisi paused.

"We don't know exactly," said Calibrisi.

Dayan was silent. He looked worn-out. A sheen of perspiration covered his balding forehead.

"You have to understand something," said Dayan, his voice hoarse with emotion and anger. "If Iran detonates a nuclear device in Tel Aviv, or anywhere in Israel, we will eradicate them from the face of the earth."

40

ERZURUM, TURKEY

From London, Dewey and Tacoma flew with Borchardt on one of Borchardt's private jets—a buffed-out, used Boeing 757. He'd spent more than $10 million retrofitting the plane, turning the interior into a luxurious fortress, with four staterooms, a large dining room and kitchen, a game room including a pool table, and a media room with several flat-screen TVs. The plane was designed to allow Borchardt to travel anywhere in the world in comfort.

Before leaving England, from a pharmacy near Borchardt's house, Dewey had purchased black hair dye. From an Islamic men's clothing store, he'd purchased a hijab to cover his head, a few shirts and pants.

Once they were airborne, Dewey went to one of the stateroom bathrooms and dyed his hair, beard, and mustache. He put on a pair of the pants, a tan button-down work shirt, then wrapped the hijab about his head.

From his traveling case, he took out a small plastic

contact lens case. He hated contacts, but he put the brown-hued lenses into his eyes.

He stepped out of the bathroom and stood in front of the mirror in the bedroom. At first, he didn't even recognize himself. He looked like a working-class Arab, except for his size.

"Praise Allah," he said into the mirror. "Give me three falafels and a grenade, please."

When Dewey stepped out of the stateroom and into the media room, Borchardt almost fell out of his seat.

"Not bad, Mr. Andreas," said Borchardt.

They landed in the small, remote Turkish city of Erzurum as night was approaching. From the airport, a sedan took Dewey, Tacoma, and Borchardt into the low hills east of the city, toward a farming village called Maksut Efendi.

Borchardt smoked the entire ride out in the car, sitting in the front seat.

"Who are we going to see?" asked Dewey.

"His name is Tuncay Güney," said Borchardt. "An old friend."

"Who is he?"

"Have you heard of Ergenekon?" asked Borchardt.

"No," said Dewey.

"I have," said Tacoma. "Ultranationalists."

"Yes, that's right," said Borchardt. "It is a deep state."

"What is a deep state?" asked Dewey.

"Within Turkey, there is a shadow government that is trying to form," said Borchardt. "Ergenekon. They say upward of a third of the Turkish military hierarchy has loyalties to Ergenekon."

"Who is Tuncay Güney?" asked Dewey.

"Their strategist. Very smart. I have . . . helped them out on occasion. That said, I also have very close ties to the elected government. I keep my options open."

The road was pitch-black, and rutted with holes and bumps. Peasants every few hundred yards could be seen walking along the road.

The driver, a young Turk with shaggy black hair and a mustache, who had remained silent until that point, looked at Borchardt. He said something in a language Dewey couldn't understand, his voice deep; there was a hint of anger in his words.

Borchardt responded by nodding, then barking out a few equally unintelligible words in Turkish.

"What did he say?" asked Dewey.

"He told me that to speak to you about Ergenekon was bad. He told me to shut my mouth."

"And what did you say?"

Borchardt craned his thin neck around, his eyes meeting Dewey's.

"I told him if he said one more word I would have General Güney execute him."

Fifteen minutes later, they pulled off the main road onto a dirt driveway. After several hundred yards, they stopped at a small rectangular, one-story structure made of brick. Several old pieces of equipment, including a few bulldozers, and a sideboom crane, stood next to the building. Standing outside, smoking a pipe, was a tall man with brown hair, dark-skinned, clean-shaven.

Borchardt climbed out of the sedan, joined by Dewey and Tacoma.

"General," said Borchardt, "good to see you again."

Güney nodded matter-of-factly, extending his hand to shake Borchardt's. As he did so, he scanned Dewey and Tacoma, an unfriendly look on his face.

"These are the Americans?" asked Güney, his accent thick.

"Yes," said Borchardt. "Have you finished the bomb?"

"We did as good a job as we could," said Güney.

They followed Güney through a door. Inside the building, the floor was concrete. A large, long steel workbench ran along the side of the room. Bright halogen lights, like an operating room, shone onto the center of the floor, where, on a steel platform, stood a bomb.

Two other men were sitting in the room, on the workbench, both smoking cigarettes. Each man wore a dark green soldering smock.

Dewey and Tacoma stepped to the bomb. It was like a large, elongated football with flat ends.

"Eight feet, eight inches," said Güney as he watched the two men inspect the device. "The weight is within a few pounds."

"What did you weigh it down with?" asked Dewey.

"Lead and concrete," said Güney. "It wasn't easy figuring out the math. But we did it."

"What about the Geiger? Will it set it off?"

"A handheld one, yes."

From a drawer in a red, metal tool cabinet near the door, Güney removed a small yellow Geiger counter. He flipped it on. It made a crackling, high-pitched noise. He moved it toward the bomb and the beeping became faster, more intense.

"How?" asked Tacoma.

"X-ray waste," said Güney. "From the hospital. If they use a sophisticated detection device, it will be exposed for what it is. If a simple handheld Geiger is used, it should fool them."

Dewey walked to the workbench. Taped to the wall was the photo of the bomb that Tobias Meir had given to Dewey, and which Dewey, in turn, had provided Borchardt. Dewey pulled the photo from the wall. He stepped back to the bomb and, holding the photo next to it, compared the two.

The seaming on the fake bomb looked rougher. The patina of the steel was smoother. The nosepiece didn't look exactly right; it was somehow flimsier-looking.

Still, to a casual observer, or one who had never seen the real thing before, the resemblance was striking.

Dewey pointed to the Persian script on the side of the bomb.

"It says what you asked for," said Güney.

"Will it work?" asked one of the Turks seated on the bench.

"It'll work," said Dewey. "Let's get it loaded."

Dewey stepped toward the door, where Borchardt was standing.

"Now will you tell me where the bomb in my house is?" asked Borchardt.

Dewey grinned.

"Not yet, Rolf. When I'm safely out of Iran, that's when I'll tell you where the bombs are."

"*'Bombs'?*" asked Borchardt. "That sounded like you just said bombs, plural?"

"Did I forget to tell you there's more than one?" asked Dewey, patting Borchardt on the back. "My bad."

41

They came and got Kohl Meir as the distant lights of downtown Tehran were beginning to twinkle, like stars, in the darkening sky, visible through a small window in his new cell.

The cell itself was clean. Unlike his previous cell on the first floor, this one contained a chair, a small sink, and a bed with an actual mattress, albeit one that was barely one inch thick.

They brought Meir two meals. As if they knew he would soon be found guilty and sentenced to death, whoever made such decisions—Evin's commandant, Achabar, perhaps Paria himself—had decreed that Meir receive not only a cell that was comfortable, but some food that would make his last hours decent. By feeding him they no doubt imagined the gesture would somehow cleanse the guilt of their actions.

He'd awoken to a tray that had fruit on it—two bananas and a handful of figs—as well as a glass of milk and a bowl of muesli. At lunch, half a loaf of bread had arrived along with several pieces of cheese, slices of some sort of meat that he couldn't identify, and a soda, which was very sweet and had the faint aftertaste of formaldehyde.

Because they had barely fed him since his abduction, Meir ate ravenously, then got sick afterward, both in the morning and in the afternoon. Still, when he heard the steel key turning again in the early evening, he anticipated another round of food.

Instead, the door opened and Achabar, his attorney, was standing in the doorway with two armed guards.

"Do you like your new accommodations, Kohl?" asked Achabar, a cigarette in his hand, which he brought to his mouth. "It looks like a room at the Hilton. I understand they even brought you food from the staff cafeteria."

"Come to Tel Aviv sometime and I will return the favor," said Meir, lying down on the cot.

Achabar laughed.

"Tel Aviv," said Achabar. "I hear it's beautiful. A pearl, as someone once told me. The problem is, Jews make me break out in hives."

"That's the difference between us," said Meir. "I don't hate you just because you're Iranian; I hate you because you're trying to destroy us. You hate me simply for being Israeli."

"Actually, that's quite well put," said Achabar. "I couldn't have said it better myself."

"The problem you will have is that you are in the minority, even in your own country," said Meir.

"What do you mean?" asked Achabar.

He stepped into Meir's cell. As he did so, he tossed his cigarette on the ground, then stepped on it with his shoe. He took a seat in the steel chair that was bolted near the bed.

"You know exactly what I mean, Achabar. You're outnumbered. Iranians want freedom. Your mullahs are growing old. The only thing that keeps them in power is thugs like Paria and VEVAK, and, of course, vermin like you."

Achabar grinned, but a flash of anger creased his lips.

"Ah, there you're wrong," said Achabar. "There is always more clergy. Meanwhile, the numbers of citizens who desire a caliphate, who want strict Islamic rule, those numbers grow every day. It is an inevitable tide. The time to have beaten us was in the nineties. Perhaps even a little earlier. But we're too entrenched now. You missed your window."

"We'll beat you. Unlike Iran, unlike every country in the Middle East, Israel is united with its people. Its people *are* the country. Here, you kill your own citizens simply for something they say. No, you can't survive as long as your rule is based upon the enslavement, the murder, the abuse of your own citizens, which it is."

Achabar leaned back.

"Well, let's agree to disagree then, yes," said Achabar. "Unfortunately, you will not be around to win this debate, I'm afraid. Judge Khasni has made his decision. That is why I'm here."

Meir stared at Achabar's brown, snakelike eyes.

"I assume I'll be able to appeal?" asked Meir as he sat up.

Achabar laughed.

"You have a strange sense of humor," he said.

At the Supreme Judicial Court, Meir was led to the cage at the front of Khasni's courtroom.

The room was mostly empty. Paria, Meir noted as he sat in the chair inside the cage, was absent. Behind the prosecution table, a photographer was seated, holding a large camera and snapping photos of the whole proceeding.

Judge Khasni was writing on a pad of paper, and he continued to do so for several minutes.

Meir glanced at the clock: 8:10 P.M.

Finally, Khasni stood up. He picked up a gavel and hammered it gently down on the table.

"Good evening, everyone," said Khasni. "It's my duty to reconvene the matter of the Islamic Republic of Iran versus Kohl Meir. Before I begin, I must ask Mr. Achabar, do you have any further exculpatory evidence to present on behalf of your client?"

"No, I do not," said Achabar, who looked at Meir and grinned.

"Very well," said Khasni. "Let us begin. With the permission of Allah, I am here this evening to render justice on behalf of the Islamic Republic of Iran and five of its hardworking citizens, all of whom lost their lives due to the actions of the defendant, Kohl Meir. While one could argue, as the defense has, that the four

Iranians killed aboard the *Adeli* lost their lives in battle, in an undeclared war, so to speak, between Iran and Israel, and that the defendant was merely following orders and acting in self-defense of his nation, I found this line of reasoning to be a fallacy. This was an offensive operation conducted in Iranian waters—"

"No, it wasn't," said Meir.

"Please, let me finish," barked Khasni, looking at Meir. "I will not have you once again turn this courtroom into a circus."

"But you're wrong," said Meir calmly. "It was in international waters. At least get your facts straight, dickhead."

Khasni scrambled for his gavel, found it, then hammered it down on the table several times.

"I told you to be quiet or else—"

"Or else what?" said Meir. "What will you do? Take away my conjugal visit privileges with your wife?"

"*Silence!*"

"Everyone in this courtroom knows what your verdict is," said Meir. "Even that silly pimp of a photographer knows what the verdict is. Don't you?"

Meir nodded toward the photographer, a pimply faced young man with greasy hair who glanced nervously around the courtroom, but said nothing.

"*Fine!*" yelled Khasni, leaning down and scribbling onto a piece of paper. "In *international* waters! Is that better?"

"Much," said Meir. "I'll sleep better now."

Khasni breathed in deeply, regaining his composure.

"As I was saying, this was an offensive operation conducted by Israel in international waters. The court acknowledges that the defendant himself believes the men to be members of the political party known as Hezbollah, but that, in this judge's opinion, is an obfuscation designed to cloak the facts of his own murders in the shadowy, rumor-filled world of such affairs. The defendant has failed to demonstrate the victims' purported membership in this group, and, more to the point, even if there was in fact proof they were members, it still would not change the fact that Kohl Meir murdered these men."

"Brilliant," said Meir. "You'll win a Nobel for this, Khasni."

Khasni's nostrils flared and his face began again to redden in anger, but he breathed in deeply and said nothing for several seconds.

The photographer continued to take photographs of Meir.

"In addition, there is the matter of the dead prison guard," continued Khasni. "If a case could be any more clear-cut, I have not yet seen it in my twenty-two years as a jurist. Without provocation, and by his own admission, as seen by several witnesses, Mr. Meir did cruelly and with malicious intent strangle and kill an innocent prison guard who, according to witnesses, was simply picking up a plastic water bottle from the ground."

"I broke his neck," interrupted Meir. "I didn't strangle him."

"Thus, it is my duty to render the following verdict," continued Khasni, ignoring Meir. "In the matter of docket seventeen hundred forty-seven, I find the defendant, Mr. Kohl Meir, guilty in the murders of Siamak Azizi, of Chabahar; Payman Kadivar, of Bukan; Massoud Nouruz, of Kermanshah; and Akbar Tabatabaei, age thirty-three, of Ilam. In addition, I find the defendant guilty for the murder of Akbar Javadi, of Tehran."

The photographer stood now and moved closer to Meir, continuing to take pictures.

"The penalty for each individual murder is left to the discretion of the judge, but we must follow the rules as set down by Iranian law and judicial precedent," said Khasni. "After much reflection and contemplation, I do hereby sentence the defendant to death by firing squad. For each murder, this is the sentence. Obviously, due to the nature of the sentences, it would be impossible to administer these penalties consecutively. In other words, there is no way to shoot the defendant five times in a row."

A small cough emanated from Achabar.

"If you don't get a raise after this I'm going to kill myself," said Meir.

Khasni shook his head, but ignored Meir's remark.

"The date of the firing squad is tomorrow," said the judge. "As to the location, due to security ramifications, that decision is confidential. The execution of Kohl Meir will take place in a secret location. Thank you all for your hard work and participation."

"You're welcome," said Meir from the cage. "Let's do it again sometime."

42

DOĞUBAYAZIT, TURKEY

Doğubayazit was a small, ramshackle town with unpaved roads in the far eastern reaches of Turkey. It was the closest town to the Iranian border, mostly inhabited by Kurds; a rural town in the dusty, often cold high plains, surrounded by hills dotted with small farms and mud huts.

Some people came to Doğubayazit in order to see Mount Ararat, about ten miles to the north. For most, the town was a convenient pit stop; travelers on their way to Iran, and truckers needing to get a meal, a night's sleep at one of the seedy motels. The central town had more than a dozen Internet cafés.

It took Dewey six hours to drive the semi from Erzurum to Doğubayazit. He exited the paved Turkey–Iran highway and headed into the town.

Dewey passed through Doğubayazit's central square just after two in the morning, driving slowly and avoiding the few pedestrians still out, even a few dogs and chickens, wandering around the town's dirt roads oblivious to the cars and trucks driving through on their way to the Iranian border. The few people still up were dressed in traditional Kurdish attire. The town itself looked like something out of the Old West with a smattering of austere, plain-looking concrete buildings.

A few miles from the center of town, Dewey pulled into a dilapidated series of trailers and a lit sign reading ISFAHAN HOTEL. Another sign read INTERNET. He parked the truck next to a gasoline tanker; then went inside the small concrete building that looked like the entrance.

The lobby was empty except for an elderly man with gray hair and a neatly trimmed mustache. He said hello to Dewey in Turkish.

"Internet?" Dewey asked.

"Internet." He pointed across the lobby to a table with a keyboard and a large, older computer on it.

"Thank you," said Dewey.

The computer was an old Sony. Dewey went to his e-mail and signed in.

There was one message, from Tacoma. The message had been sent the day before.

Meir guilty

Nothing from Taris, the reporter. He was about to enter Iran, a country bigger than the state of California, with a fake nuclear bomb and absolutely no clue where to go with it.

"Fuck me," Dewey whispered.

He stood up and went to the bathroom at the back of the lobby, closing the door behind him. The bathroom was squalid. He went to the bathroom, washed his hands, then looked in the mirror. He smiled as he looked at the brown-eyed, dark-skinned man in the hijab staring back at him from the mirror. He didn't even recognize himself.

He went to the front desk, paid, then went back to the truck.

He walked in front of the semi's grille, heading for the passenger door. As he rounded the front of the truck, Dewey was surprised to see two men. They were standing in front of the door. Both had black hair, cut short. They wore jeans and T-shirts. Both men were small. There was nothing unusual about them, except that one clenched a long fixed-blade knife in his right hand.

The man without the knife stepped forward, a grin on his face. He said something in Kurdish, which Dewey didn't understand. Dewey stood still.

"What do you want?" he asked.

"Money," he said in broken English. "Your truck too."

Dewey nodded. He couldn't help smiling. Curiosity got the better of him.

"Why do you want the truck?" asked Dewey.

"Gasoline," the man said.

"Why do you need gasoline?"

"We sell it," said the Kurd with the knife, smiling conspiratorially.

They were young and small, each about five-five, and thin as beanpoles. He assessed the blade; he held it reasonably well. Part of Dewey wanted to simply walk past the two and go about his business. But sometimes, Dewey knew, desperation created unpredictable and irrational behavior.

"When it rains, it pours," said Dewey.

"What?" asked one of them.

"Nothing."

If they were surprised by Dewey's six-four height and his wide berth, they didn't show it.

Without taking his eyes off the thief with the knife, Dewey took a step back, then squared off against the pair.

"Walk away," said Dewey, pointing at the field next to the truck.

The one with the knife smiled and giggled, almost like a cackle.

"Walk away," he repeated a bit louder.

The other one reached behind his back. He pulled a small handgun out.

Dewey remained still.

"Money and keys," the Kurd said, a hint of anger now on his dark, stubble-covered face.

"I'll give you some money," said Dewey, raising his hands. "I can't give you the truck."

"Keys!" the short thug screamed.

And then he fired the weapon. The crack of the bullet sounded like a firecracker. It was a warning shot; the bullet sailed past Dewey's head.

"Really simple," said the one with the knife. "Money and keys."

Dewey's eyes moved back and forth between the two thugs.

"Okay," Dewey said. He reached into his pocket and removed the keys to the truck. Holding them in his right hand, he took a step forward.

The knife-wielding Kurd was to his left, the gunman to his right.

He stepped toward the one with the knife. He held his left hand out toward Dewey. Dewey let the keys drop to the ground. In the moment after they hit the dirt, with both Kurds watching them fall, Dewey grabbed the small man by the left wrist. The thief swung the blade at Dewey. As his arm slashed through the air, Dewey grabbed him at the wrist, ripped his arm hard, then threw him like a rag doll at the gunman, who, in his panic, fired, sending a bullet into the leg of his knife-wielding friend, who screamed. In the same moment, before the gunman could fire again, Dewey reached over and struck the Kurd, lurching at the gunman, thrusting with his fist; all his strength behind the blow, which he aimed at the man's neck. It was a ferocious blow and Dewey knew immediately that he'd broken the young man's trachea.

As the first man screamed in pain from the bullet in his leg, Dewey pulled the gun from the other, who now lay on the ground next to his blood-covered friend. He held his neck with both hands and stared, bug-eyed, up at Dewey, fighting for air. He would live, in fact, both men would live, but they wouldn't be hijacking trucks for a while.

"You two might want to consider a different profession," said Dewey.

43

Marwan and Pavil sat in the front of the brown Samand sedan, across the street from Qassou's apartment building.

The rain had again picked up, and both men strained to watch the front entrance, waiting for their man, Vesid, to bring out Qassou. It was likely that Qassou would be walking, but groggy from the tranquilizer.

After fifteen minutes of waiting, both VEVAK operatives began to get antsy.

"Where the hell is he?" asked Pavil.

"I'm sure he's coming. We know Qassou wouldn't have put up a fight. He's probably heavily sedated and Vesid doesn't want to carry him out."

After waiting another ten minutes, Pavil reached for the door handle.

"I'm going up."

The possibility that Qassou had subdued Vesid didn't occur to either man. Qassou had come to the front entrance, looked out through the window, and spotted the two men sitting in the sedan. Upon seeing the two agents, Qassou turned and walked quickly through the service entrance, out the back alley, then hurried several blocks to a taxi stand in front of the Grand Tehran Hotel.

Qassou entered the presidential palace at half past seven. He was drenched and his skin looked ashen. As he approached the security desk, he realized it was only a matter of time before the VEVAK operatives put two and two together and discovered he'd escaped. Whether it was Paria himself or someone lower on the totem pole, they would quickly seek to arrest him. Still, the fact that they had tried to take him surreptitiously meant that Paria was suspicious but not certain. Paria had likely not told Nava.

You have time.

He walked up to the uniformed soldier and handed him his laminated government identification. The soldier inspected it, then passed it beneath the scanner.

"Good morning, Minister Qassou," he said. "You're here awfully early."

"What is it to you when I arrive?" asked Qassou.

"It's nothing," said the soldier. "I was just making conversation."

"Sorry," said Qassou, attempting a smile. "I have a busy day in front of me, that's all."

"Good luck," said the soldier.

He walked to his office and shut the door. From his leather case, he removed his change of clothing and quickly got out of his wet clothes. He went to his computer. Nava had yet to respond.

"Fuck," he yelled.

He went to his private bathroom, closed the door, then looked in the mirror above the marble sink. His eyes were badly bloodshot, and the skin around them looked purplish. His skin had a sheen of sweat on it, which he tamped with a hand towel. He was pale, ashen even.

He went back into his office, sat behind his desk, and kept a close eye on his e-mail.

At a little after eight, his door opened and he jumped up from his seat. It was his assistant, Firouz.

"What?" he barked.

"Morning to you too, boss," said Firouz.

"What do you want?"

"Nothing," said Firouz. "They said you were already here and I had to see it for myself."

"You're funny," said Qassou. "Your tongue will land you in the unemployment line."

"Would you like an espresso?"

"Yes. Now close the door."

Qassou picked up the phone. He dialed the number he knew by heart.

"*Al Jazeera*," said the voice.

"Taris Darwil," said Qassou.

"May I tell her who's calling?"

"The Minister of Information."

"Yes, Minister Qassou, I apologize. Right away."

He waited on the line for several seconds.

"Lon," came the soft voice of Taris. "Where have you been?"

"I can't talk. Listen to me: I will call your cell and

leave the name of a place. If I don't, it means Paria has found me. If they do, I fear they will find you. Leave Tehran."

"Lon—"

"Don't argue."

"What will happen with Meir?"

"It's over," said Qassou. "The only possibility is to stop the bomb. Meir has been sentenced to die."

"Should I call the Americans?"

"I can't think anymore. Call whoever you want."

Qassou hung up the phone just as his door opened. It was Firouz with his espresso.

"Here you are," said Firouz, handing him the small cup.

"Thank you."

"You're welcome."

"Now get out."

Firouz's smile turned into a frown. He turned and walked toward the door.

"By the way," Firouz said, turning at the door. "The president just called a minute ago."

"Why didn't you put him through?" asked Qassou angrily.

"You were on the phone."

"If, God willing, I'm here tomorrow, I will fire you."

Qassou went to his desk.

"Now shut the door," he commanded. "Now!"

He dialed Nava's office as Firouz stepped out. Nava's assistant put him through.

"Hello, Lonny," said Nava. "An important call, yes?"

"Yes," said Qassou. "Though that bonehead should've interrupted me."

"We'll have him beheaded," said Nava, laughing. "How about that?"

"You kid, but the thought did cross my mind," said Qassou.

"What's wrong, Lonny? You're finally getting your big wish. Shouldn't you be happy?"

Qassou winced.

"Can you go earlier?"

"I can leave right now," said Nava.

Pavil stepped off the elevator on the fourteenth floor. The floor was empty. He went until he found a door with the number four on it. Looking around one last time, he saw no one. He removed a handgun from his shoulder holster, took two steps back, raised his right foot and kicked the door just above the doorknob. The door ripped open, a chunk of wood falling to the ground from the sash. Pavil stepped inside and shut the door.

He moved, weapon out, down the hallway. In the kitchen, he smelled burning coffee. He moved from the kitchen to the bedroom. Several drawers on a desk were open, as was the top drawer of the dresser.

He ran down the hallway to the bathroom, where he found the VEVAK operative, Vesid, unconscious. Beneath his head was a pool of blood that had spread out like a red pancake around his head.

He saw the grotesque pool of black liquid in Vesid's eye. Kneeling, he felt for a pulse on the wrist. He was alive.

"I think we have a problem," he said into his cell phone, speaking to Marwan, waiting in the car below.

"What is it?"

"Qassou isn't here. Vesid is unconscious, tranquilized by his own gun. Someone stabbed him in the eye. You better call General Paria."

"Right now? He's going to be pissed. Should we at least give ourselves a few hours to look for him?"

"Don't be a fucking retard," said Pavil. "Make the call. Then get an ambulance over here."

They moved east from Tehran in a dark green Range Rover customized with bulletproof glass and steel and with every inch of its glass tinted black. Nava was paranoid about the possibility of being followed, something that the presidential motorcade would have practically guaranteed. A watch car with soldiers trailed a quarter mile back.

Nava and Qassou sat in the backseat; in the front were two Revolutionary Guards, both armed, the soldier in the passenger seat holding an UZI SMG across his lap.

Tehran spread out in the vale of the Alborz Mountains. Iran's largest city was in some ways similar to another mountain-ringed metropolis half a world away, Los Angeles—both chaotic, traffic-filled cities that were confusing to all except those who lived there. After pushing through a mess of traffic near the government center, the Range Rover climbed onto the highway and went east.

Nava slouched back in the seat and smiled, relaxing. He reached out and put his small arm around Qassou's neck affectionately.

"You're sweating like a pig, Lonny," said Nava.

"It's ninety-five degrees out."

"You know, it is very hard to trust people when you are the leader," said Nava, looking out the window. "So many people want things. I realized yesterday that you have never wanted anything, Lon. Not once have you asked. That is why I am showing you."

Qassou nodded to the front seat, referring to the two soldiers.

"Are they . . . ?" asked Qassou, his voice trailing off.

"Trustworthy?" answered Nava, whispering back. "Let me see. Tarik, Anwar: Can you two be trusted?" His voice was louder as he posed the question, then he started laughing.

The two soldiers did not look back, instead they glanced at each other, their faces remaining stone-cold.

"Yes, Lon, they can be trusted," said Nava. "They'll be driving it to the port."

Paria was in a meeting when the call from Marwan came in. His assistant knocked on the office door, then peeked his head in.

"Excuse me, General. Marwan is on the phone. He says it's urgent."

Paria picked up the phone on his desk.

"What?" he demanded.

"He's not here," said Marwan.

"What do you mean he's not there? You had him under your surveillance an hour ago. Am I correct?"

"Yes, you're correct, General Paria. But he escaped.

When Vesid came in through a window, Qassou stabbed him in the eye with a toothbrush. He's on his way to the hospital."

"I don't care about Vesid. Find Qassou!"

"What do you want us to do?"

Paria was silent. He held the phone against his ear, thinking.

"Nothing. You two fucked this up. So go fuck yourselves back to Baghdad."

Paria hung up the phone. He looked at the two men seated in front of his desk.

"What is it, Abu?" asked one of the men, his top lieutenant.

"There's something going on," said Paria quietly, his eyes searching the room as he appeared lost in thought.

"What happened?"

"He escaped," said Paria.

Paria looked down at his desk. Other than his telephone console, the desk was bare—except for two photos of Qassou and Andreas, the American.

"This is no longer a discreet project," said Paria, opening his desk drawer and removing his shoulder holster. He wrapped it around his left shoulder, then tightened it. From the same drawer, he pulled out a handgun. "I want an All Points Warrant for the immediate arrest of Qassou put out. Get it out through VE-VAK, then disseminate out to Tehran central police as well as the Guard. Lon Qassou is working against the Republic. I'd bet my life on it."

"Yes, sir."

"Dead or alive. He is to be considered armed and

dangerous. An enemy of the state. I don't care if he's in a meeting with the president himself: shoot this son of a bitch before he does something to harm us all."

The green Range Rover exited the A83 Highway near Mahdishahr. At the end of the exit ramp, they went left. They drove through the town of Mahdishahr, through the small city's crowded main street, then into an industrial area of warehouses, scrap yards, a long line of large gasoline tanks, then more warehouses.

Qassou registered the name: *Golestan Street*.

At one of the warehouses, a light yellow unit with rust along the building's roof eave, the Range Rover slowed and entered the parking lot. The driver pushed the vehicle quickly across the parking lot, aiming for the corner of the building without slowing down, punching into a thin alley that ran around back. They sped along the edge of the warehouse into another parking lot out behind the building. The driver stopped in the parking lot, the front of the SUV aimed at the middle of the warehouse. They waited for nearly a minute, then a large door at the back of the warehouse began to slide slowly open.

They drove inside and the door quickly slid shut behind them.

Inside, a dozen or so soldiers stood; their weapons trained on the Range Rover. Nava was the first to climb out, then Qassou. One of the soldiers inspected the inside of the vehicle, the trunk and engine, then the undercarriage; when he held his left hand up, signaling that it was clean, the others moved their weapons down to their sides.

"Good morning, Mr. President," said the soldier who had just conducted the inspection, a middle-aged man with graying hair and a mustache. "We weren't expecting you until after lunch."

"A change of plans, Colonel," said Nava.

Qassou stepped around the SUV.

"Follow me," said Nava.

There were several military vehicles parked inside the warehouse, including a pair of tanks, which Nava pointed at.

"An old army storage facility," said Nava. "Rather than build something new and raise suspicions."

They walked through the empty warehouse, past piles of parts, tools, a Dumpster. They came to a shining silver chain-link fence, which looked brand-new. The fence was built in a square box, twenty feet wide, ten feet high, twenty feet deep. Behind the fence, a silver semitrailer was parked.

Qassou looked down and saw that his hands were shaking. He put them in his pockets. He felt, all at once, a sense of sickness and triumph, anger and jubilation. His plan had worked; he was within a stone's throw. It was the nuclear device Iran had denied trying to make for the past decade, a bomb that, had its existence been known, would likely have led to an invasion of the country. He felt triumph at his having made it here, to the center of it all.

But, in the same moment, he felt incredible regret

and shame. The brilliance of the scientists who had created this object was now to be used to destroy countless innocent people whose only sin was to have been born Jewish. How could a country, a people with such skill be capable of such an atrocity? he asked himself as Colonel Hek unlocked the chain-link fence and stepped inside the protected enclosure.

Qassou followed Nava. A set of stairs was set against the back steps of the truck. Nava stepped first into the open bay. Qassou followed him inside.

A pair of halogen lights, set on temporary orange parapets, shone down on a shining steel table. On top of the table, tied down with steel wire rope, was the bomb. It was dark silver, with a patina of scratches and small dents. Qassou was surprised at the shape of it; like an elongated soup can. At one end, the bomb was tapered and pointed. At the other, a rectangular attachment, the size and shape of a shoe box, made of a different shade of steel, jutted out.

"It's larger than I imagined it would be," said Qassou, stepping forward.

He moved alongside the device, then ran his hand along the steel, from one end to the other.

"Be careful," said Nava, grinning. "Don't set it off by accident, Lonny."

"What is this?" asked Qassou, nodding to a boxlike object that jutted from the tail.

"A stabilizer, useful if we were to drop it from a plane. But we don't need it."

Qassou looked at Nava. Nava's smile looked manic as he waited for Qassou's approval somehow. Qassou examined the Persian writing, scrolled along the side of the nuclear device in red paint.

Goodbye, Tel Aviv.

Qassou read the words, felt his heart beating, then looked at Nava. He kept his tongue silent. He knew he could show Nava no trace of doubt, no hint of betrayal. He knew the name of the city, the street, the location. In his pocket, he felt the slight lump of his cell phone, pressed against his chest. He was so close.

For the first time in weeks, Qassou smiled. Nava thought it was because his aide shared his twisted vision, his excitement at the coming annihilation of Tel Aviv. Only Qassou knew that it was precisely the opposite.

44

TEHRAN

Paria stormed into the presidential palace. The guards at the entrance stepped back, for while protocol dictated that all visitors be carded and their identification checked, all six Revolutionary Guard soldiers knew who Paria was. They saw the anger in his gait, the hatred in his eyes, and, perhaps most important, they all noted the handgun now grasped firmly in his right hand, cocked to fire.

As the head of VEVAK pushed through the short line, knocking a man down as he did so, then leapt past the line of soldiers, and began a full sprint down the hall, the guards to a man thought the same thought: Paria might be going to kill Nava himself. They all knew Paria answered only to the Supreme Leader, Suleiman, and as long as that was so, the combustible, rabid wolverine of a man could do whatever the hell he wanted to, including put a bullet in the head of the president of Iran.

Paria took the stairwell three steps at a time, running, sweat dripping down from his forehead, his khaki shirt half drenched. Two flights up, he went left and began a full-out sprint. He barreled into Nava's office at full speed, moved past the president's three assistants in the antechamber.

One of the three assistants stood, saying, "He's not in, General Paria."

But Paria continued on, grabbing the brass doorknob and lurching inside Nava's office.

"Where is he?" screamed Paria, turning from the empty office and looking at the assistant.

The assistant was speechless, trembling in fear.

Paria raised his handgun. His eyes widened as he aimed the muzzle of the weapon at the man's head.

"Where is he?" repeated Paria, slower this time, without yelling. Yet the words seemed to hold even more anger than when he'd yelled.

"He left with Minister Qassou," said one of the other assistants, an older man with thick glasses, seated near the doorway. "Exactly one and a half hours ago. He did not say where he was going, General."

Paria bolted through the door, then down the hallway.

He approached the door to the Ministry of Information. Despite the fact that it was unlocked, he kicked the door just above the doorknob with every ounce of strength. The kick sent the door flying in, and tore the top hinge from the frame.

Paria entered Qassou's antechamber. Firouz stood up. Paria rushed past him, without even acknowledging

Qassou's assistant. He did the same thing to the door to Qassou's office, kicking it just above the knob. This time, the entire door went flying off the hinges, landing with a crash inside Qassou's large office, crushing a tall glass lamp on its way to the ground.

Inside, Paria walked to Qassou's desk and began opening drawers, pulling documents out from the drawers as he did so, looking through them.

Firouz followed Paria into the office. He knew who Paria was, but his loyalty to Qassou got the better of him.

"General Paria," said Firouz. "Does Minister Qassou know that you're in his office?"

Paria looked up from his desk.

"Where did he go?" Paria asked, raw rage in his voice.

"I . . . I don't know," Firouz coughed out.

Paria flipped open Qassou's laptop. A security page appeared.

"What's Qassou's password?"

"I have no idea."

"Where is he?" screamed Paria, stepping around the desk, the muzzle of the weapon shaking slightly as he trained it on Firouz's head.

"He didn't say . . ."

He lifted the weapon and aimed it at Firouz.

"The fucking password. What is it?"

Firouz stood in silence, a look of resignation and fear causing his brow to furrow and then tears to begin streaming down his cheeks. He raised his hands.

Paria fired the handgun. The crack of gunfire was

followed, a moment later, by the thud of Firouz falling to the ground, a single slug between his eyes.

The Range Rover left the warehouse, with Qassou staring out the window as they passed the last of the soldiers, standing inside the building. All Qassou could think about, as the SUV passed through the doors and the soldiers inside slid them closed, was Taris. He had to call her.

A low ringing noise came from a cell phone. It was Nava's phone.

"Yes," he said.

Qassou tried to listen. He looked away from Nava, out the window. They were moving at least thirty miles per hour back toward the city.

"Really," said Nava into his phone.

Had they found the man in his apartment?

But what if it hadn't even been a VEVAK thug, Qassou considered. What if it was simply a thief? A common criminal, there to steal his television?

But Qassou knew the truth.

Qassou felt the adrenaline rush through his head. His nerves, which had made it hard to even walk across the floor of the warehouse, washed away in a wave of confidence.

This is why you were put here.

Qassou placed his right hand on the door latch, while in his left hand he clutched his cell phone. The Range Rover continued to move, faster now. The way Nava looked at him, his black eyes scanning his face suspiciously, sent a burst of fear through him. All he had to do was tell the soldiers in front, and the whole thing would be gone. Taris would never receive the call. Andreas would never be told the location. The bomb would leave the port at Bushehr on a small fishing boat, bound for Tel Aviv.

Nava hung up the phone. He was silent for several moments. He stared forward. Then he turned to Qassou.

"Meir is to be executed this afternoon," said Nava. He was strangely quiet as he relayed the information.

"How?" asked Qassou.

"Firing squad. They haven't determined where. I would like it to be in public. The fear is that Israel, once apprised of the location, will send their jets in. After all of the Iranians Mossad has murdered in the past week, I feel why not shoot him in public? Let the world see."

"We should allow the court to make the announcement," said Qassou.

"Why? Why not us?" asked Nava.

"It will look like we're gloating. Unpresidential. It will look like we're killing him for political reasons, not for justice."

"So smart, as always," said Nava. He looked into Qassou's eyes. "It's really going to happen, Lonny."

The SUV came into the crowded main street of Semnān. There was a small traffic jam.

Qassou kept his fingers gripped on the door handle.

As they approached a red light on a busy Semnān street, filled with shops and vendors, Nava's cell rang again.

"Yes," he said.

Qassou froze. He held on to the door latch. His heart started to beat wildly.

"Yes, he's right here."

As the light changed, the soldier stepped on the gas pedal, and the Range Rover began to move. Qassou waited a moment, then yanked the door latch.

He leapt from the back of the accelerating SUV as he heard the words, barked loudly, from Nava.

"Stop him!"

Qassou's right foot hit the ground first and before his left could touch the tar he went tumbling to the ground, landing on his right arm, which he felt snap at the elbow. He screamed as he rolled, his head striking the ground next. He heard brakes as the rusted grille of a Paykan sedan in the other traffic lane nearly slammed into him.

The Range Rover's brakes screeched. Qassou reached up with his other arm and touched his forehead; the palm of his hand ran red with blood.

He looked up from the ground and saw Nava through the open door of the Range Rover, which was now stopped. Nava was pointing at him and trying to climb out, but the driver held him by the shirt. The passenger door opened next, and from the ground Qassou saw the shining black boot of the other soldier, leaping from the car to give chase.

The pain in his elbow was acute. Sharp pain shot up from the elbow to his shoulder and down to his hand. He couldn't move his fingers. His arm was twisted sideways, like a pretzel, unnaturally, enough to make him nauseated. But Qassou knew he had to run.

"Get him!" came the words, screamed this time, in the familiar voice of Mahmoud Nava. *"Traitor!"*

Qassou grabbed the cell phone with his left hand, stood up, and through the torpor of dizziness that the fall had caused, began a furious dash for the sidewalk, his right arm now lame, dangling awkwardly at his side.

He ran between two cars and jumped to the sidewalk.

As he ran, he pulled the cell phone from his pocket. He looked behind him and saw one of the soldiers following; clutching a black submachine gun in his right hand, waving it like a baton as he sprinted between the cars. Qassou kept running, feeling his lungs burning. Then he heard the staccato bullets of the machine gun. A burka-clad woman in front of him, strolling along the sidewalk, was suddenly hit with a spray of bullets and pummeled to the ground. Qassou weaved to the right just as bullets from the SMG struck a parked car, piercing through steel.

Then the gunfire abruptly stopped. The staccato was interrupted by the screech of car brakes, then a loud slam; Qassou jerked his head around to see a white taxicab slam into the soldier and send him tumbling to the tar.

As screaming and chaos enveloped the street and sidewalk where the woman had just been gunned down, Qassou sprinted as fast as he could. A block away, he saw a men's clothing store called Semnān Eka. He slowed as he approached the store, went inside, then looked back out the window.

Coming down the sidewalk was the other soldier, SMG in hand. Nava was right behind him, and behind them was a swarm of soldiers. Nava was yelling and pointing at the store.

The pain in Qassou's broken arm was debilitating. Turning, he glimpsed his reflection in the mirror; the arm dangled down and bent sideways, unnaturally.

The store was empty except for a man looking at shirts. The owner of the store came rushing from the back.

"What do you want?" he asked. "Can I help you?"

Qassou grabbed a pair of pants from a shelf.

"A changing room," Qassou said, panting and trying to catch his breath. "I'm in a rush."

"This way."

He led Qassou to the back of the shop. Qassou went inside, then shut the door. He slid a lock to the side.

Qassou pulled his cell phone from his pocket. He dialed Taris's number.

He looked at his watch: 9:15 A.M.

"You've reached the voice mail of Taris Darwil . . ."

The first shots came through the wood of the door and were low. They struck Qassou's legs and sent him falling to the ground onto the dirty carpet of the changing room, writhing in pain.

"I'm not available to take your call. Please leave a message after the tone . . ."

The next bullets tore through the thin door, but were higher. They flew over Qassou's head. Then a bullet hit him in the chest, kicking him sideways, and he felt blood come to his nose and mouth.

"Mahdishahr," he whispered in a clotted voice. "Golestan Street. A yellow warehouse . . ."

The door suddenly was kicked in and the soldier stood looking at Qassou. He paused for a split second, then swiveled the weapon at Qassou's head. The next bullets ripped through his skull and killed him instantly.

45

TURKEY–IRAN BORDER
BAZARGAN, IRAN

Dewey had reached the border at four thirty in the morning.

The line of trucks at the border numbered in the hundreds, by Dewey's estimate, and stretched for miles. The trucks all seemed to perform the same ritual. The drivers would turn their engines off, then wait for the truck in front of them to move down the line some distance, far enough to make it worth the fuel it would take to turn the engine back on. Dewey was behind a rusty green flatbed. He would wait until the truck was fifty yards in the distance before he would turn the engine of the Mack back on and slowly crawl forward and catch up.

Through the early morning, cars and motorcycles moved in a steady parade to the left of the truck line. Even a few people on bicycles passed by. The sheer volume of traffic gave Dewey a sense of confidence, knowing that in order to process this many visitors, the soldiers and customs officials at the border needed to move quickly. A sparse line of traffic would have been much more worrisome. That said, by ten, having barely moved since 8:00 A.M., he began to worry about running out of time.

Dewey pulled the empty fuel truck beneath the first set of lamplights that encircled the border patrol.

A sign overhead read GÜRBULAK SINIR KAPISI.

The facility comprised two long sets of ramshackle concrete buildings, one on the Turkish side of the border, the other, separated by about a hundred feet of space, the Iranian port of entry.

Dewey moved his truck to the head of the line, where two Turkish customs agents stood. Both looked tired. Dewey handed his passport and visa to the first agent.

The agent looked at his papers briefly while the other Turk walked to the front of the truck, then around the entire tanker.

"Which refinery?" he asked without looking at Dewey.

"Tabriz," said Dewey.

He stamped Dewey's passport, handed it back, then waved Dewey through the imposing iron gates.

After the Turkish gates, the road went straight in a single line toward the Iranian side of the border. The ground was littered with bottles, cans, and other trash, as if no one was responsible for cleaning up this no-man's-land, seemingly outside the border of either country.

Dewey's eyes looked to the Iranian side of the border. The round building was cleaner, with spotlights in a line on lampposts, six in a row. The Iranian customs building looked like a UFO that had landed in the middle of nowhere. The line of trucks fanned out into five different lines. Standing at the front of each line were at least three agents, along with a pair of Revolutionary Guard soldiers, SMGs strapped across their chests. Dewey did a quick count. He counted twenty soldiers in his line of sight alone. There were no doubt others in the regular car traffic lanes farther left, inside the rambling corrugated steel and concrete building, and on the other side of the gates.

He glanced in the mirror. Despite the fact that he was looking into his own eyes, he saw a different man. The sight of the dark beard and mustache, the tan skin, the brown eyes shaded by contacts, gave him a renewed sense of ease.

In Delta, they were trained in all aspects of border infiltration. It was a core competency, an absolute necessity both at the start of an offensive mission, but also in emergencies, when you found yourself in enemy land and had to escape.

There were the basics of passport control and paperwork; airport and rail penetration; memorizing the variegated, often differing regimes required by different countries; which airports were behind when it came to technology and weapons detection. They learned how to cross borders illegally, whether on foot or later on by vehicle, learning about the porous nature of most borders in the world, and how easy it was if you really wanted to cross illegally into a country. At first, they

used U.S. borders as test labs. Dewey spent weeks crossing the border between Canada and the United States,
and Mexico and the United States.

But by far the most important part of his training,
Dewey knew, was in the sessions on mock interrogation and deception techniques, in which they were
trained to lie. In two separate weeklong sessions during Delta training, Dewey spent time studying lying
techniques, then practicing and honing the craft. The
first sessions took place at CIA headquarters in Langley, where Dewey and a dozen other Deltas were stuck
in a classroom, learning from veteran agents the funda-
mentals of deception, gleaned over decades of practice
and analysis. You learned that the liar always had his
biggest advantage at the beginning of an interrogation,
before the interrogator knows you. A trained interrogator quickly picked up on nonverbal cues, such as shifting in your seat, blinking too much, or changing your
stance, to clue into the fact that you were lying. They
learned how to beat lie detectors; this had to do with
breathing and heart rate control. As with human inter-
rogators, a liar's best method for beating the lie detector
was to believe your lie before you stepped foot in the
room.

The second session, the final exam, took place, at
least for Dewey, at Dulles Airport. Dewey and fourteen
other Deltas were sent to London and given a week to
assemble the parts for an explosive device powerful
enough to destroy an airplane. They were also instructed
to procure fake papers that would enable them to get
into the United States. A week after getting to London,

they were all put aboard the same British Airways flight in London, bound for the United States, each Delta carrying a fake passport, and each man carrying components of a bomb, which, if put together with parts from the other Deltas, could be assembled to form a bomb. When asked what would happen if they were caught, Dewey's commander had responded: "Don't get caught."

The exercise was multifaceted. It was about teamwork in homegrown munitions, and the need, in this case, to make do with off-the-shelf products. It was about paperwork, the acquisition thereof, in a foreign land. But primarily, it was about simulating real-world pressure as best as the Delta trainers could devise.

There were 231 passengers on the flight from London. The team at customs was told in advance that a general threat existed; NSA had picked up chatter about a cell of terrorists trying to get into the country with a bomb through Dulles.

Dewey and the team had met in London. One of Dewey's teammates, Gus Johns, was a munitions expert; they quickly acquired the components of an RDX-based device, meting out the white powder form of RDX into a variety of cosmetics jars, toothpaste tubes, and other innocuous places they hoped would attract little attention. The paraffin wax needed for the device was similarly hidden in this way. The fuse was disassembled into more than twenty pieces, and taped into the inside circuitry of everyone's laptop. A bomb's worth of powdered aluminum was tucked into the battery case in each of the team members' wristwatches.

For passports, the team decided to intentionally not collaborate, fearing that if they did they might unwittingly show a pattern in terms of the design of the passport, the background, even the country of origin.

Dewey had traveled by train to Edinburgh, where he got a motel room in the neighborhood of the University of Edinburgh. He cut his hair short, shaved, and pretended for a few days to be a student, blending in. On his third night in Edinburgh, he went to a local student pub and got into a conversation with a student, a tall Scotsman named Langham, finding out Langham's background, the fact that he was studying to be a poet, that he played golf four times a week, that his father and mother were both dead, eventually finding out where he lived.

Within an hour, Dewey had broken into Langham's apartment, stolen his passport, and was on a London-bound train.

And three days later, as Dewey stepped off the British Airways 747, Dewey was Terence Langham, future poet, golfer, and orphan. He believed it, believed the story that he was about to tell the customs agents.

Of the fifteen Deltas to step off the British Airways flight that day, ten Deltas were taken out of line for further questioning, including Dewey. And of the ten who were interrogated, only Dewey failed.

He would never forget the question that had stopped him in his tracks that day.

"Recite us a poem, Mr. Langham," the grinning customs agent had said. "Any poem. Let's hear it."

It was a lesson Dewey would never forget.

Dewey had gotten into Delta anyway. His record during training was too good. His physical abilities were among the best his trainers at Fort Bragg had ever seen.

But he knew he wasn't a good liar. It was his Achilles' heel.

His truck rumbled to the point in the line where the trucks split into five lanes beneath a corrugated green steel roof. He moved his truck into the first lane.

"Be cool," he said to himself.

Inside the trailer, Dewey knew, was enough to get him in serious trouble. A duffel bag, sitting like a bag of groceries, was filled with compact submachine guns, carbines, handguns, a sniper rifle, and antipersonnel rounds. Of course, the trouble those got him in would pale in comparison to what lay above the duffel, courtesy of Borchardt. Yes, thought Dewey, that would raise a few eyebrows.

Strapped to his ankle, Dewey felt his SOG double-serrated fixed-blade combat knife: Seal Pup.

Duct taped beneath the steering column, to the right, out of sight: Colt M1911 .45 caliber handgun.

He looked at his watch: 10:20 A.M.

An Iranian customs agent, dressed in a black uniform, nodded at Dewey as he pulled in. He asked him something, in Persian, and Dewey looked back quizzically.

"English?" the customs agent asked, his accent thick.

"Yes," mumbled Dewey quietly.

He handed the agent his passport.

"Where are you going?" asked the Iranian.

Dewey watched as two soldiers, clad in long black boots and khaki uniforms, began to circle the truck.

"Tabriz," said Dewey. "The refinery."

"Gasoline?"

Dewey nodded as the customs agent stared at him.

"And then what?"

"Then back."

"Back where?'

"Erzurum," grunted Dewey. "Gas stations."

In front of the truck, Dewey became aware of a plain-clothed Iranian with mirrored glasses. He had on white pants, a blue shirt that was untucked. He had a holster on, the handgun on his right hip. He was smoking a cigarette and walking in front of the parked line of trucks. In his hand, as he smoked, he held a piece of paper. Dewey couldn't quite make out what was on the paper, but the way the man looked at each truck driver then back at the paper, before moving onto the next truck, indicated it was a photo.

"Do you live in Erzurum?"

"No," said Dewey. "In the country. Narman."

The Iranian agent nodded. He turned to the other agent, turning his back away from Dewey, and said something to the other agent.

At the same time, the plainclothed man roamed to Dewey's truck. He stared at Dewey from the passenger side of the truck, then glanced back at the paper in his hand. He kept looking at Dewey and moved to the driver's side, staring up at Dewey.

Dewey didn't move, except his hand, which he felt

along the steering column, until he felt the familiar butt of his Colt.

Let me through, he thought.

From his pocket, the second agent took out a small object; a stamp. He handed it to the first agent, who took it and stamped Dewey's passport.

"Have a good trip," said the agent.

As he went to hand the passport back to Dewey, the plainclothed Iranian grabbed it out of his hand. He flipped through it.

"First trip over Bazargan?" asked the man.

Dewey nodded.

"Yes."

"Why?'

Dewey looked and for the first time could see the piece of paper. It was a black-and-white photo, an image of a man; short hair, American. Him.

Dewey willed himself to not do a double take. Reflexively, he reached for his handgun.

"Esendere," said Dewey, his voice low and hoarse, accented. "Now Bazargan. I go where I'm told."

The man nodded. Dewey gripped the handle of his .45 caliber. Then the man handed his passport back to the agent.

"Go ahead," the plainclothed man said, waving Dewey through, staring with suspicion as Dewey stepped on the gas and drove into Iran.

46

Taris entered a drab concrete office building that housed *Al Jazeera,* took the elevator to the third floor, and went inside the suite that housed the Tehran offices of the news agency.

As usual, immediately upon entering the *Al Jazeera* offices, Taris removed her headdress. Her short black hair was combed neatly back, parted in the middle. A small cowlick made it stick up just a bit.

Taris had grown up in Tehran, the daughter of a writer named Katchmin Darwil, a failed novelist who worked as a janitor at a hotel and who used all of the little amount of money he earned to self-publish his books, which he would then leave in the hotel rooms in the hope that somehow, someday, he would be discovered. His wife—Taris's mother—was a beautiful woman who became embarrassed and then embittered by Katchmin's failures and ran away with an American journalist when Taris was just two. Katchmin had raised her as best he could, and taught her the one thing he knew, which was to love the act of writing. Taris had studied hard and gotten into Tehran University on a full scholarship. Her senior year, she was the deputy editor in chief of the student newspaper. While women were not allowed to be the editor in chief, everyone knew it was really Taris who ran the paper that year. She'd been hired by *Al Jazeera* the summer after she graduated.

Taris inherited her mother's large nose and innate shyness and her father's love of writing. At twenty-nine, she was one of *Al Jazeera*'s top reporters. While most Westerners despised *Al Jazeera* because of its pro-Islamic, anti-Western point of view, on one issue, the question of women's rights, *Al Jazeera*'s management was, surprisingly, even ironically, remarkably enlightened. Taris was one of the company's top reporters, serving as Tehran bureau chief and was, some thought, in line for even bigger things.

Taris walked quickly down the worn red carpet to her desk. The small message light on the phone was lit up.

Taris picked up the phone.

"Taris, this is Mohammed," came the voice on the first message from her boss. She skipped the message. The second message came on.

"Mahdishahr," came the faint, pain-filled voice of Qassou. "Golestan Street, a yellow warehouse . . ." Then, the unmistakable sound of gunfire.

That was all. The message ended. Taris replayed it twice, then deleted the message.

The message had come in at 9:16. She looked at her watch; it was 10:34.

Her mind raced. She fought to control her emotions. Who had killed him? Police? VEVAK?

If they killed him, they would have the phone. The phone would lead them directly to *Al Jazeera* and to her.

Yet, there was a rational explanation. If they asked her why Qassou called, she would say that he calls every day. At least once a day. That is what reporters do. He's a source. An important source.

Yes, she could bluff them easily enough.

But what if they took her in, and interrogated her? What if they tortured her? What if they did what VEVAK does to so many citizens from whom it wants information: what if they took her father in and threatened him? Taris knew she wouldn't last long if they tortured her.

She needed to run. She went to her desk and was about to shut down her computer when she heard a noise that made her heart stop. It came from outside. A car door slamming, then shouting.

She walked across the office to the window. What she saw made her gasp, then put her hand to her mouth.

In the busy street out in front of the office building, four black sedans were stopped in the middle of the road. Traffic was already beginning to back up. Horns were blaring, and several drivers, caught behind the vehicles, were shouting. The dark sedans' occupants didn't care about the fact that they were stopping traffic on one of downtown Tehran's busiest streets. A loose line of officers in black uniforms was sprinting from the vehicles toward the front entrance of the building.

Taris closed her eyes.

Be calm now, dear girl. She heard the voice of her father.

"What's happening?" asked another reporter, looking up from his computer as Taris walked calmly across the office.

Taris ignored him. She signed into her computer. She moved to "private browsing." If they really looked, she knew full well, they would be able to find out which sites she'd gone to, but perhaps it would buy her some time.

She signed into a Yahoo account she had set up for this singular purpose. She would use this account once.

"Mahdishahr." She typed in quickly. Down the hallway, she heard the sound of people entering the offices. "Golestan Street, yellow warehouse."

The first VEVAK agent stormed into the room as Taris completed the e-mail.

"Taris Darwil!" the lead man shouted to one of her reporters, Katim, who looked as if he would faint. Katim pointed to her.

The agent raised his handgun and aimed it at her head as a swarm of other agents entered behind him.

"Stop whatever you are doing!" the agent yelled.

"What do you want?" Taris said, indignant. "I've done nothing wrong."

Her fingers moved across the keyboard. She hit SEND just as the agent arrived at her desk and pushed her off her chair. She went tumbling to the ground. He looked at her screen.

Taris said nothing. Instead, she crawled a few feet away, acting fearful.

"What have I done?" she asked quietly.

"Get Haqim over here," said the first agent, staring into the computer screen.

The agent stepped from the computer and aimed his weapon at Taris. He moved the muzzle of the weapon closer, then knelt down next to her. He brought the steel of the weapon's tip against her forehead.

"What did Qassou say?" he asked, anger seething in his voice. "Speak or you die. What did he tell you?"

"When?" Taris asked. "We speak all the time."

"At nine sixteen!" the agent barked. "*What did he say?*"

"I wasn't here. I haven't spoken with him today."

"She logged into a private directory two and a half minutes ago," said another agent, now scouring Taris's computer screen. "That's all I can determine without running some diagnostics."

"What does that mean?" asked the agent still pointing his gun against her forehead.

"It means she did something on a private setting. We might not be able to retrieve it."

He turned back to her.

"What was it?" he demanded.

Taris ignored him, looking up from the ground as tears came to her eyes and began to roll down her cheeks.

"Answer me!" screamed the agent.

She said nothing.

The agent stared at Taris.

"So you're going to be a problem, yes?" he asked. "That's too bad."

The big Iranian swung the handgun across her face

and smashed the butt into her nose, crumpling it. Taris screamed as blood began to pour from the nose.

"You used to be a very pretty girl," he said as he leaned over and grabbed her arm, pulling her up, as the other agent hastily packed up her laptop.

Taris glanced around the newsroom at her colleagues, who stared at the scene in silence.

"Get back to work," she said.

47

Meir let his mind drift to Israel. Then, for whatever reason, he thought of his mother. He remembered how she would come to his school, every day, and walk home with him. Until he was in fourth grade, he would hold her hand on the small sidewalks between the school and home. Every day, when they arrived at home, there would be a snack waiting on the kitchen table. Home-made cookies or fruit. Those days were like a gift, a simple present; the love of a mother. He closed his eyes and tried to imagine his mother's smile. Meir felt her presence.

What if the time had indeed arrived for Israel to be wiped from the earth? There is no incontrovertible rule that guarantees Israel will always exist. There are countries that once existed, but are no longer. Perhaps the time had come, and perhaps he was but a player, a small player, in a battle that on this day, in this unique way, began the destruction of his country and his people?

Don't give up, Kohl, came a voice. *Don't give in.* It was the voice of his father. *You must fight until you are dead. That is the way of your family. It is the way of your country.*

Meir had endured a terrible night of half sleep, waking every few minutes, fearful of what was to come. Now that the day of his execution was here, he tried to will himself to sleep. But he couldn't, not on his last morning alive. He settled into a sort of twilight half-consciousness.

Sometime later, a noise startled him and made him sit up. Through his grogginess, he heard footsteps coming down the corridor. They were louder than those of the guards. His feet hit the ground in a steady, heavy, menacing rhythm.

Meir's ankles and wrists were shackled. He lifted himself, then sat up and stood. He moved toward the doorway. As the footsteps grew louder, he inched to the left of the door, his back pressed against the wall.

The ring of keys on the other side of the door jingled like a pocketful of quarters as whoever it was found the key to Meir's cell. The lock slid and the door pushed in.

As Meir had hoped, whoever it was had neglected to peek inside the door hole.

As he raised his shackled wrists above his head, Meir thought of Achabar, his lawyer. *Perhaps it is Achabar. That would be especially nice,* he thought.

The large steel door swept inward and harsh light

spilled into the cell from the corridor. A dark figure stepped into the room. Meir waited, pressed against the concrete wall. As the intruder's head crossed the door jamb, Meir leapt into the air and swung his shackled wrists down, wrapping his cuffs around the intruder's neck, like a noose. He yanked back with every ounce of strength he still had in his body.

The intruder choked and grunted in pain as Meir yanked back as hard as he could.

It wasn't Achabar. He couldn't smell any of his lawyer's foul cologne. But more to the point, as Meir struggled to strangle the intruder, pulling with lethal strength, he found the man suddenly fighting back, pushing Meir against the concrete wall. He knew it couldn't be Achabar. No, this one was powerful.

The man dropped a folder, then shot his hands to his neck, trying to get his fingers between his neck and the chain, which was rapidly cutting off oxygen. He slammed Meir backward against the concrete. Meir let out a pained grunt. The man stepped forward, then lurched again backward, this time with all of his force. He slammed Meir hard into the concrete wall, as his fingers were finally able to get between the chain and his own neck. Meir felt the wind get knocked out of his chest.

The man wheezed, catching his first breath of air in almost half a minute as his powerful hands created space between the chain and his trachea.

Meir held the chain tight, yanking back again. But the man was too strong.

Slowly, the figure moved toward the middle of the cell, lifting Meir from the ground as he eased the chain up, pushing against Meir who was pulling as hard as he could. Both fighters were grunting hard. Meir raised his knees and smashed them into the man's back, but the strike barely registered more than a pained grunt. Most men would have died under the assault by the Israeli, but this one was an animal.

Meir kicked from behind again, this time using his knees and lifting them up against the middle part of the intruder's back. He pulled back, yet as hard as he did, the strength of the stranger's hands was even more powerful.

It was at this precise moment that Meir knew who the man was.

Paria lifted the chain to his chin. His right hand reached back and grabbed Meir at the wrist, squeezing, then abruptly twisting, trying to snap Meir's wrist. With his left hand, he grabbed the other wrist. Then, clenching both of Meir's wrists tightly, Paria lifted Meir's two-hundred-pound frame, then, when the shackles were above his head, hurled Meir through the air. Meir crashed, back first, against the toilet, then screamed out in agony.

Looking up, he saw the large silhouette of Paria stepping toward him like a caged beast.

Paria was panting.

Meir lay on the ground, struggling to catch his breath, looking up at Paria, who stepped closer. He could see red at his neck, blood, skin that had scraped off in the initial assault with the chain. Paria let the wound bleed, not even registering the pain. He looked as angry as Meir had ever seen a man.

"I thought you said you could kick my ass," said Paria.

"Take these shackles off and find out for yourself," said Meir.

As Meir coughed blood onto the ground, both men knew his words were hollow.

"I'm here to save your life," said Paria.

Meir tasted blood. He shifted his torso to try and understand how much damage the toilet had just caused. He could move, but felt sharp pain in his lower back.

"Save me?" asked Meir. "Fuck you."

Paria came closer. He knelt down. His eyes were wide, furious pools of black. His bald head shimmered with sweat. He threw his right hand out and gripped Meir's neck. He squeezed until Meir began to struggle and air no longer could pass into his lungs.

"You like the way that feels?" asked Paria. "It feels good, doesn't it?"

Meir attempted to push Paria's hand away from his neck, grabbing the wrist with his two manacled hands. But Paria moved his black boot and stomped down on Meir's shackled hands.

For a full minute, Paria held tight, cutting off air. Then he let go of Meir's neck.

Meir gasped for breath, coughing up more blood as he writhed on the ground, desperately trying to refill his lungs with air.

Paria moved back toward the door. He picked up the folder that had fallen on the ground. He stepped to the bed and sat down. He waited until Meir stopped coughing and caught his breath.

"I'm prepared to offer you a deal," said Paria.

Meir stared up at Paria from the ground, his lips and ground-facing cheek covered in blood. The Israeli looked confused and disoriented. Pain stabbed at several places throughout his body.

He said nothing.

"All I want is information," said Paria. "You give me information, and your life will be spared. It's that simple."

"Information?" asked Meir.

"Yes. Just information."

"And then what?" asked Meir. "I spend the remainder of my life in this fucking prison? No thank you."

"No," said Paria. "You'll be delivered back to Israel. You're a free man. In addition, I will see that you're removed from the capture-or-kill list. I will also see to it that your sister's name is removed."

At the mention of his sister, Meir's eyes sharpened.

"You're a liar and we both know it," said Meir.

"I won't kill you if you give me the information. You have my word."

"The word of a thug and a murderer. The man who gives Hezbollah and Hamas the missiles they need to kill my countrymen."

"The word of a warrior, like you. That is all."

"The word of my enemy."

"Yes, you will have to take a leap of faith, Kohl," said Paria. "But then, what other options do you have? You're sentenced to die this afternoon. I am your last refuge."

Meir stared into Paria's eyes. A small grin crept across the Iranian's lips.

"I would rather die than give you something you need," said Meir. "Even if I thought you would live up to your end of the bargain, I wouldn't do it. And I don't think you'll live up to your end of the bargain."

Paria nodded.

"Just what I thought you'd say," said Paria. "The confidence of a man who still believes he's going to be freed. Is that what you think? Was this part of the plan all along? You're sent to prison and Qassou will somehow free you?"

Paria stared at Meir's eyes intently, looking for the spark of recognition. Meir gave it to him, if by accident, just a moment, a single movement of his head as Paria mentioned the name Qassou.

"Well, if he was your escape plan, I have some sobering news for you, Kohl."

Paria reached into his pocket. He removed a cell phone. He aimed it down at Meir. The image on the small screen made Meir flinch. The photo showed Qassou's prostrate, bullet-riddled corpse, his tan button-down shirt covered in blood, a black hole the size of a golf ball in his neck, his eyes wide-open, staring out into space.

"We have Taris Darwil in a cell down the hall," said Paria. "It's only a matter of time before she speaks."

Meir felt his heart sink like a thousand bricks tossed into an endless ocean.

"Was she your escape plan?" asked Paria. "Was Qassou? Your 'knight in shining armor'? Well, suffice it to say, Qassou or the reporter won't be in a position to participate in your little operation any longer. And as we speak, we are rapidly digging through Qassou's network and through the reporter's. I'll kill anyone and everyone who was involved in this thing."

"What thing?"

"This conspiracy."

"I've never seen this man, and the name Qassou means nothing to me," said Meir. "I don't know what you're talking about."

Paria tossed down a third picture to the ground. It was a photo of Dewey.

"I don't know who he is."

"You don't know him?" asked Paria. "You saved his life in Beirut. You saved Andreas's life less than two weeks before this photograph was snapped. Now stop the bullshit. Your escape hatch is gone, Kohl. *Start talking!*"

Paria stood up and moved closer. Meir looked up at him, but said nothing. Then Paria kicked his steel-toed boot into Meir's torso, striking his ribs. Meir screamed in pain.

Then the voice of his father spoke again. This time, his father was louder, commanding him.

You must keep fighting. That is the way of your family. It is the way of your country.

"I would rather die with honor than live in shame," said Meir, shutting his eyes and bracing himself for the kick he knew would soon come from Paria's boot.

48

South of the city of Abhar, Dewey got off the freeway in what would be his third attempt to retrieve any e-mails Taris might have sent.

Both previous attempts had failed. An hour past the large city of Tabriz, Dewey had gotten off the freeway and found an Internet café at the truck stop where he refueled the semi. But Taris still hadn't sent him a message. In Zanjan, at another truck stop, Dewey had pulled into a gas station and noticed a pair of Iranian policemen walking around the parking lot, each holding a piece of paper that they were asking truck drivers to look at. At the sight, Dewey had stopped filling his tank and left before going inside to check for messages.

He had little doubt the policemen were looking for him. A border crossing is one thing, but a gas station signaled an altogether higher level of urgency to the search. And if they were looking for him at a truck stop

in remote Zanjan, they were looking for him everywhere.

Dewey thought back to his Delta training and was
thankful for two things during that long truck drive
toward Tehran. The first was the week spent learning
how to drive a semi. It was extremely difficult work,
especially on congested roads. He was also thankful
for the simple, contrarian, and uniquely Delta perspective on operating across enemy lines. Delta taught the
importance of immersion within the most crowded, pop-
ulous centers of activity, blending into bustling environ-
ments, filled with people, and not venturing off into
remote areas, where you could stand out. It took more
balls, but it rewarded with a higher degree of anonymity.

He would soon be in Tehran. He was, at most, an
hour away. There was a strong possibility Qassou and
Taris had been captured before finding out the location
of the bomb. Dewey had already formulated a backup
plan. If he didn't hear anything by Tehran, he would
keep heading east, toward Afghanistan, and pray he
could figure out a way across the border.

Dewey checked in with Calibrisi twice. The CIA
director was coordinating with Dayan and the Israeli
special forces team already on the ground in Tehran. It
was a tight kill team, composed of Kurds who Mossad
had recruited out of northern Iraq years ago. They were
waiting for Dewey's go.

Calibrisi wanted Dewey's e-mail account, lest something happen to him, such as being apprehended, so that
the team could still move on any potential information
from Taris. But Dewey had refused. He remained

worried that if Taris e-mailed the location, Calibrisi or Dayan might move preemptively without him. They might simply opt for destroying the bomb altogether. Dewey knew that would spell death for Meir.

He exited the crowded freeway in downtown Abhar. At a large SPC gas station, he wheeled the semi to a set of pumps, then went inside. The truck stop had a small, brightly lit restaurant attached to the main building. A neon sign that said INTERNET was in the window. Dewey went in and sat down at one of three old desktop computers. When a waiter came by, he handed him a small wad of rials, then went on. He quickly signed in to his e-mail account. There was one message, from Taris.

Mahdishahr. Golestan Street, yellow warehouse.

Dewey studied a map of Iran, identifying the city of Mahdishahr and Golestan Street. He memorized the location, signed off, and walked back to the truck.

Back on the Qazvin-Zanjan Freeway, Dewey phoned Calibrisi.

"I got the address," Dewey said when Calibrisi answered.

"Where is it?"

"Before I tell you, I want your assurance that nobody moves until I give the word. No preemptive missile strikes. No sending in the Sayeret team. Nothing."

"Dewey, if you're worried about Kohl, we believe he's already been executed. So stealing the bomb and trading for him is probably not realistic at this point."

"Do you know he's been executed?"

"No," said Calibrisi.

"I want your word, Hector. I want Menachem Dayan's too."

"You got it. We won't move."

"It's in Mahdishahr, in a yellow warehouse on Golestan Street," said Dewey. "I'll call when I'm getting close."

"How far out are you?"

"An hour. Maybe less."

49

KHOMEINI SQUARE
TEHRAN

Meir looked up from the floor of the room, straining to open his eyes, which were both long since bruised shut.

His head was concussed, and the floor was littered with small piles of vomit. All of it, every drop, was his. Had he attempted to stand, it would have been no use. Paria had, at some point in the long, painful session discovered the bullet wound on his left thigh. In one horrific moment, Paria had taken one of the clips from the car battery and clipped it to the raw, pink scar atop the bullet hole. Then he'd turned on the machine, sending bolts of electricity into the wound. It was by far the worst pain of the night.

Meir sat against the concrete wall, trying to get a glimpse of the clock on the wall, above the two-way mirror, but could not. Is it morning? Is today the day? Meir didn't want to die. But he had resigned himself to the fact that he was going to. With that resignation, he counted the minutes with anticipation.

Paria had begun in the morning, using the promise of freedom to try to get Meir to confess. But that kinder, gentler phase of Abu Paria hadn't lasted long. Next came the beatings. Paria had struck Meir more times than he could count, punching him, slapping him, kicking him. He would lose consciousness, only to be woken up sometime later by water being poured on him. The beatings would begin again.

"Where is Andreas?" Paria would scream. "Why are you in Iran? *Answer me!*"

At first he had answered.

"You're the one who abducted me, Abu," said Meir. "I was minding my own business in Brooklyn."

But then, inevitably, he tired. He went in and out of consciousness. Yet still, he held on.

Paria stared at Meir through the two-way mirror. His own fists were raw and bloody, as was his shirt, covered in spots of blood that had splattered off the Israeli's damaged face.

The door behind him opened, but Paria did not turn around.

"General," said one of Paria's deputies, "would you like coffee?"

"Yes," said Paria, without turning.

The aide peered in through the dimly lit room, at the clump of flesh that was balled up in the fetal position in the far corner of the interrogation room.

"Nothing?" he asked.

Paria did not respond. Finally, he turned.

"No, nothing," Paria said. "He's stronger than I anticipated."

"It's almost three," said his aide. "They'll be coming for him. The firing squad is assembling now. They're in the locker room, putting on uniforms."

"What about the computer?"

"Nothing yet."

Paria glanced in the interrogation room. Was it worth one more attempt to break Meir?

His aide left as Paria tightened his belt and opened the door to go back inside. The door opened again, the same aide with a Styrofoam cup filled with coffee in his hand.

Next to the door, a green light on the phone started flashing. The aide picked it up.

"Yes, sir." He looked at Paria, extending his arm toward him.

Paria picked up the phone.

"What," he said.

"General," came a soft male voice. "Please hold for the Supreme Leader."

Paria nodded at his aide, indicating that he wanted him to shut the door to the interrogation room.

The phone clicked.

"Abu," came the voice he knew so well, the voice of his boss, Suleiman. "Good morning."

"Good morning to you, Imam."

"Where are you?" asked Suleiman.

"I'm . . . at Evin," said Paria. "Checking on the Israeli prisoner."

"Checking on him?" asked Suleiman. "What exactly needs checking, General?"

"I was just trying to see if I could elicit a bit more information out of our prisoner," said Paria. "Before he's no longer with us."

"Well, that is fine, but I would like you with me today," said Suleiman. "After my speech."

"Of course," said Paria. "It would be my honor."

"Well, Abu, you of all people deserve credit for this day," said Suleiman. "It will be a truly historic event. You have led the fight against Israel. I want you there with me when Meir is executed."

"It would be an honor, Imam."

"To think that in a matter of only hours the bomb will leave for Tel Aviv," said Suleiman. "This is the beginning of the end for Israel."

Paria felt a sudden, warm spike of heat in his head, then down his spine. His eyes shot to the interrogation room, to the motionless, blood-covered prisoner on the concrete floor. He reached into his pocket and removed the small, black Porsche key he had taken from Meir's belongings, the only possession the Israeli had on him when he was abducted. Why had he kept the key? He realized now it was because he knew something was wrong with it. He'd known it all along.

"Oh, God," he whispered.

He pressed his thumb into the bottom of the key. A small silver attachment suddenly flipped out; not a key, as he expected, but the end of a USB flash drive.

Paria dropped the handset. It crashed to the ground.

"What have I done?" he asked aloud to no one, as he reached desperately for the door.

50

ALONG THE A83 HIGHWAY
IRAN

By 4:00 P.M., Dewey was through Tehran. He steered the cab of the Mack truck east on the A83 highway toward Mahdishahr.

The A83 highway was an aging four-lane road, crowded with traffic. It wound like a ribbon around low brown desert hills with little vegetation. The vistas were, in their own way, mesmerizing; beautiful brown hills and behind them mountains that spread for as far as he could see, tinted with pink and orange. Dewey stayed in the right lane as small sedans, many coated in rust, sped by, some in the other lane, but if both lanes were occupied with vehicles, the occasional car would veer onto the dirt shoulder, sending up clouds of dirt and dust as they broke the law to get where they were going.

Dewey dialed the SAT phone.

"Control," said the voice.

"Calibrisi," said Dewey.

"Hold."

A few seconds later, Calibrisi came on.

"Dewey, I have General Dayan on. Where are you?"

"I'm on the A83 highway, approaching the area. Do you have the team in place?"

"We have two vehicles positioned a hundred yards on either side of the warehouse," said Dayan.

"*If* this even *is* the warehouse," said Calibrisi. "We've seen no activity. Nothing. I have to tell you, Mahdi-shahr is not on any of our radar screens. This location comes as a surprise."

"Dewey," said Dayan, "Commander Nehoshtan has six F-16s awaiting my command. If you ask me, we should just blow the fucking place up."

"No," said Dewey. "Not yet. If we fail, you can wipe the place out, but give me the opportunity to take the bomb."

"Fine. But if anything goes badly, Israeli Air Force is going in."

"Understood. When did the Sayeret Matkal team get there?"

"Fifteen minutes ago."

"How many men?"

"Five."

"What kind of weapons do they have?"

"They're armed to the teeth."

"Is there news on Kohl?" asked Dewey.

"According to *Al Jazeera,* there's a big rally in downtown Tehran," said Calibrisi. "Nava speaks at five, followed by Suleiman. Either they'll execute him before the speeches or after, we don't know and they're not saying."

"Do we have a UAV overhead?"

"We have a KH-13 satellite overhead. More than enough."

"What do you see?"

"Dewey, this is Bill," said Bill Polk, the head of the CIA's National Clandestine Service. "It looks empty. We haven't seen anyone move in or out. Are you sure your source got this correct?"

"No," said Dewey. "But it's all we have. I'll call you when I'm there."

The outline of the city of Semnān arose from the desert like a mirage. A panoply of gray dots suddenly littered the horizon, as Semnān's homes and low-slung buildings came into view from the highway, scattered mud and adobe, some of which were painted in bright hues of red, orange, and green.

As he came closer to Semnān, he saw a sign that said MAHDISHAHR. Taking the exit, he drove for several miles through choppy, thin streets, cutting through Semnān as he aimed north to the smaller city of Mahdishahr. On the right, the undeveloped brown hills suddenly turned into warehouses in the distance. Ahead, Dewey saw a street sign.

Golestan Street.

He went right, down the thin street, past more than a dozen warehouses. Then he saw a brown van, which appeared empty: Israel one. He kept driving. When he came to a yellow warehouse, he didn't even look twice; but from the corner of his eye, he counted a pair of security cameras, along with two men near a gate, watching him pass by.

He passed an old white Land Cruiser, parked to the side of the road.

A mile down the street, he pulled into a large parking lot and turned the truck around. He came to a stop, then redialed Langley.

"Calibrisi."

"Any movement?"

"Yes," said Calibrisi. "We see at least a dozen men behind the warehouse."

"Is that our guys, brown van, white Land Cruiser?"

"Yeah. Team leader is a Kurd named Baz."

"Can you patch me in?"

"Yes."

He heard some static, then a couple of clicks.

"It's Dewey. Is this Baz?"

"Yes."

"Are you guys ready?"

"Yes, we're good to go," said Baz.

"I need someone with me. Someone who can handle a truck. I'll pull up next to the Land Cruiser."

"Okay, I'll give you Cano. What's the OP?"

"A truck is going to come out of the building. We hit it on the service road. I'll handle the truck with Cano. You need to eliminate whatever they accompany it with."

"There's not a lot of time," said Baz.

"Make the best of it. They won't be expecting us."

"Got it."

Dewey checked his submachine gun, an HK MP7A1 with a suppressor. He checked the magazine on his Colt. He moved the truck slowly back down the road.

When he came to the white Land Cruiser, he stopped. From the back left door, a man in a baseball cap and sunglasses emerged, dark-skinned, a carbine held out in front of him. He sprinted to the passenger door of the cab and climbed in. It was Cano.

Dewey nodded, but said nothing.

Cano handed him a small, gumdrop-shaped object. Dewey stuck it in his ear.

"Is that working?" whispered the commando.

"Yeah," said Dewey.

"I've got you on COMM," said Baz, who was in the brown van.

"Move to COMM, Hector," said Dewey into the phone. "I'm hanging up."

"I've got movement," said Polk, now patched into the Israeli closed frequency.

"Where?" asked Dewey.

"Back of the warehouse," said Polk. "We've got one, two, three SUVs. Now we have a big truck. One more SUV. That's it. You got four SUVs and the truck."

Dewey floored the gas and moved past the ware house entrance. From the corner of his eye, he saw the first SUV at the side of the warehouse, in the distance, behind a fence.

"Can you handle four?" asked Dewey.

"Yeah, no problem," said Baz. "It might get a little bloody."

"Take them on the road. I don't care what you do with them, but don't touch the truck. And do it out of sight of the warehouse so they don't send more people."

"Understood."

"Hector, how about some support on this?" asked Dewey.

"What do you mean?" asked Calibrisi.

"You need to destroy that warehouse and everyone in it. Can you do anything from the sky?"

"You're going to get me fired, Dewey. Let me see what we can do."

Calibrisi and Polk were monitoring the operation from a windowless tactical operations room on the third floor of CIA headquarters. The room looked like NASA control center. The walls were lined with plasma screens. One screen displayed a live video feed of an overhead shot of Dewey's truck moving slowly down a street. Another screen showed the warehouse, also a live shot, the image clear enough to make out half a dozen soldiers milling about the entrance area to the warehouse. Another screen—the largest of them all—showed a regional map of Iran and the Persian Gulf; several flashing lights moved on the screen, showing in real time the various assets the United States of America possessed in the region, including vessels, UAVs, and troops, all displayed in real time. On yet another screen was a live network feed from Khomeini Square, where a massive crowd awaited the arrival of Mahmoud Nava.

Three CIA engineers sat in bucket seats, smaller plasmas in front of them.

"Chris," said Calibrisi, "what do we got in the area?"

"Yes, sir," said the CIA engineer in the middle seat.

He typed into his keyboard. The large screen showing Iran and the region suddenly went black except for bright yellow lines, indicating the borders of the countries, followed by brightly lit, flashing starlike clusters, some in green, others in orange, which indicated the UAVs in striking distance; sixteen in all.

"The closest assets in theater are over the Strait of Hormuz, Hector," said the engineer. "We have enough Tomahawks to level the town, sir."

"How long will they take to get there?"

"Hold on."

As, Chris typed, a red line shot across the screen, showing the flight path of a hypothetical missile from one of the UAVs, hovering off the coast of Iran and Semnān. Then a number jumped on the screen: 4:34.

"Four and a half minutes," said Calibrisi.

He hit the phone console.

"How much time do you need, Dewey?" asked Calibrisi.

"Send 'em right now."

Calibrisi looked at the engineer to the right.

"Send in three, on my go," said Calibrisi. "And don't miss."

"No, sir."

"One, two, fire."

Dewey watched in the side mirror, looking behind him, as the front of a Range Rover pushed slowly into the street, several hundred yards behind them.

"Thanks, Hector."

"No prob. I just hope they fixed that thing that was screwing up the targeting."

Dewey laughed.

"Did I make you laugh?" asked Calibrisi.

"Yeah," said Dewey. "You don't have any more coming out of the building, Bill?"

"None," said Polk.

"Hector, I need you to do me a favor," said Dewey.

"What is it?" asked Calibrisi.

"You need to call Katie," said Dewey.

"What do you want me to tell her?"

"Tell her to get Bhutta ready."

"Ready for what?" asked Calibrisi.

"She'll know."

"I know she'll know," said Calibrisi. "*I* want to fucking know."

Dewey exhaled and shook his head.

"To call Mahmoud Nava."

51

Paria ripped the door to the interrogation room open. In his right hand, he held a photo of a nuclear bomb, taken from the Israeli's USB drive.

Paria's aide, who was standing above the Israeli, turned, surprised by Paria's sudden entrance. Paria swatted him with the back of his powerful left forearm, sending his aide flying to the ground.

He stepped to Meir and threw the photo through the air, where it landed next to Meir's head.

Paria kicked his boot viciously toward Meir's head.

Yet somehow, through the thin slit still remaining in his left eye, Meir saw the boot. His adrenaline spiked. He lurched right, avoiding the kick from Paria, then grabbed the big Iranian's boot and, with every ounce of strength left in his body, ripped the foot sideways; he listened as Paria let out a blood-curdling scream. Paria fell to the ground, clutching his ankle, as his aide stood up and withdrew his handgun, aiming it at Meir's head.

He fired just an inch from Meir's ear, the bullet striking the concrete wall and raining dust all over Meir's shoulder.

Paria stood, limping. He began to say something, then turned toward the door.

"You're too late," said Meir as Paria hobbled from the interrogation room.

"Maybe," said Paria, grunting in agony, which he swallowed. "But you'll never know."

Paria picked up the phone next to the door of the observation room. He dialed a number, then waited for a response.

"IRGC command," said the voice.

"Get me Colonel Hek now!" he yelled into the phone.

A minute later, the phone clicked.

"General Paria," came the voice, a deep, scratchy voice.

"You must divert the movement of the bomb," said Paria. "It's a setup!"

"What are you talking about?"

"Listen to me. Stop the bomb. It's a trap, Ali!"

"It's too late, General," said Hek. "The device has left Mahdishahr."

Dewey waited at the side of the small industrial road, a hundred yards ahead of the brown van.

"Here they come," said Polk on COMM.

From the parking lot, a pair of black Range Rovers emerged first, moving down the street toward Dewey and the brown van. Then, the Iranian semi turned onto the street, behind the pair of lead Range Rovers guarding the bomb.

The semi was followed by two more Range Rovers, which fell in line behind the truck carrying the missile.

"Get out," Dewey said to Cano.

Dewey moved across the seat, toward the passenger door. He carried his silenced MP7A1, then inched along the side of the trailer, out of view.

Three Israeli commandos climbed out of the van. Two took up positions behind the van, kneeling. Each commando held shoulder-fired missiles, and they brought the weapons to their shoulders, out of view of the approaching convoy. They calibrated the targeting mechanism, then flipped the safeties off.

Cano crabbed along the side of the van, out of view. He clutched a silenced M4, whose safety he flipped off as he came to the rear bumper. He saw the side of the street darkening as the shadow from the semi moved slowly along the road toward him.

Behind the convoy, the other two Sayeret Matkal commandos climbed from the back of the Land Cruiser. They knelt, backs against the back bumper, out of sight, while they waited for the rear Range Rovers to get onto the main road. Each commando brought their shoulder-fired missile into position on top of their shoulders.

The Israeli team was communicating on a closed cell frequency, the COMM devices jammed in their ears.

Baz, who was team leader, and was running the OP for the Israeli team, put his hand to his ear.

"Everyone set?" he whispered.

Each commando, along with Dewey, said yes.

"On my go," said Baz. "Watch your backgrounds; shoot straight."

On his knees, through the back glass, Baz watched as the pair of lead Range Rovers came closer, now only twenty feet away. A high-pitched whistling could be heard above the Iranian semi's engine.

"Three, two," said Baz, pausing. "Go."

In front of the van, two Israelis stood, trained the black barrels of their shoulder-fired missiles on the Range Rovers, then fired.

Behind the Land Cruiser, at virtually the same moment, the other commandos stood, aimed, and fired their missiles.

Four distinct, loud booms echoed in the air, followed by the telltale smoky trail as the missiles stormed across the sky.

Three of the missiles were triggered at the same moment; and exactly two seconds later, three of the Range Rovers were hit dead square by the missiles. Each vehicle exploded, two behind the truck, one on front.

The fourth missile missed; it went sailing past the Range Rover, then skimmed within just inches of the Iranian semi, barely missing the front of the Iranian truck.

The Range Rover that had been spared lurched left, trying to get away. The semi driver also hit the gas and the Iranian truck bounced forward.

Dewey ran from the side of the trailer, his MP7 set

to auto-hail, and started firing at the fleeing SUV, ripping slugs first into the tires, then through the passenger-side glass, destroying the two soldiers inside; the Range Rover slammed into a telephone pole.

Dewey turned toward the Iranian semi, firing at the driver; the glass was bulletproof, the truck kept moving forward, as Dewey's bullets sunk into the thick protective glass.

"Fuck," Dewey said. He came to the side of the truck, staring inside from the ground at the soldier who was seated in the passenger seat; he stared back at Dewey as Dewey unloaded his submachine gun, but to no avail.

The air around the truck was clouded in smoke and fire.

Dewey suddenly heard high-pitched whistling noises: the telltale screams of incoming Tomahawks.

The missiles came into view at the horizon, then cut through the last quarter mile of air unwavering: two black objects trailing waves of dark smoke behind them.

The missiles sailed just overhead, a hundred feet above the convoy, then, a millisecond later, a pair of explosions shook the ground, as the Tomahawks ripped into the warehouse and exploded, leveling anything within a hundred yards of the target.

Cano sprinted back to Dewey's truck. He jumped into the driver's seat as the Iranian truck barreled down the road, trying to get away. The commando put his truck into gear, then slammed the gas, moving in front of the escaping Iranians. He cut them off.

Baz came alongside Dewey. They stood, staring at the Iranians, who were trapped inside the cab of their truck, but protected by bulletproof glass.

"That's thick," said Baz, firing a few rounds from his carbine into the glass. "What do you want me to do?"

"We need the truck," said Dewey. He inserted a new magazine in his MP7. "It's gotta break at some point."

They were joined by two other commandos. The four men stood abreast, weapons aimed at the passenger-door glass. They started firing, putting hundreds of slugs into the glass. The street, which was clotted in smoke and fire, reverberated with the sound of automatic weapon fire. At some point after several minutes of firing, a bullet penetrated the worn-down glass; the slug tore into the head of the frightened soldier. Another slug, a minute later, killed the driver.

Dewey climbed the passenger-side steps, then punched the glass out with the back of a hatchet, handed to him by one of the commandos. He reached in and unlocked the door. He pulled the bodies of the two dead Iranian soldiers out of the cab and left them on the road.

He ran to the first truck, looking at Cano.

"Let's get the hell out of here."

"Here," said Cano. He handed Dewey his SAT phone and the weapons duffel.

The van and the Land Cruiser sped along the back of the truck.

Dewey pressed his ear.

"Thanks," said Dewey.

"You need anything else?" asked Baz. "We need to scoot before the cops show up."

"No, we're all set."

Dewey ran back to the semi as the sound of sirens could be heared in the distance.

Cano straightened the semi and headed toward Mahdishar's main road, followed by Dewey. On the road south of the city, Dewey passed him. The two semis climbed onto the A83 highway, headed toward Tehran, as, behind them, a fleet of police cars and fire trucks descended on the grisly scene. In the air, a steady stream of black smoke formed a cloud visible from the highway.

Dewey picked up the SAT phone and pressed two preprogrammed buttons.

In a suite at Claridge's Hotel, Foxx handed Bhutta the phone.

"Yes," Bhutta said into the handset, looking at Foxx.

"Make the call," said Dewey. "Paria and Meir, that's it. Anyone else and the deal is off. Anything suspicious and the deal is off. If I see a jet overhead, choppers, anything, the deal is off."

"Paria and Meir," said Bhutta. "Got it."

"Just remember, Amit, you get your family back when Kohl Meir is safe. I'll call you in one hour with the location."

52

Meir sat at a steel table. On the plate in front of him was a chicken breast, with sliced tomatoes on the side, rice, and a sugar cookie. In front of the plate, a plastic cup held red wine.

"Eat," said a soldier to his left. "It's your last meal. That's real wine."

Meir turned slowly toward the soldier. Meir didn't know the soldier's name, but he had been the one who lifted Meir from the concrete floor of the interrogation room, brought him to his cell, cleaned him up, and brought him a fresh change of clothing.

Meir tried to make out his face. But his eyes were so swollen it was impossible to open them. For a brief moment, Meir allowed himself to fantasize, to hope, to imagine: *Is this the one who was sent by Qassou to save me*? Then he laughed, a low, sad laugh at the utter ridiculousness of his thought.

Qassou is dead. And so are you.

Next to the cup of wine was a leather-bound book. It was a Torah. Meir stared at it, then looked up at the guard, this time forcing his left eye open. Thank you, he thought, though he didn't say it.

But somehow, the Iranian guard understood.

"No man should die alone," said the guard, smiling kindly. "I'm sure, if the tables were turned, you would bring me the Koran and a glass of wine."

Meir nodded. *I wouldn't have,* he thought to himself. *I was a great man, but not a good one.*

He reached forward and picked up the cup of wine. He took a sip; it was very sweet and too warm. He gulped the rest of the cup down.

The guard laughed heartily.

"I'm glad you like it," he said.

The guard looked from Meir to the clock on the wall.

"It's time to go, I'm afraid."

Meir stood up from the steel chair.

"I would like to take your ankle cuffs off," said the guard. "So that you may walk in dignity. May I do that without you trying to hurt someone, Mr. Meir?"

"Yes," he said.

The guard leaned over, inserted a lock into Meir's ankle cuffs, unlocked them, and pulled off the heavy chains.

Outside the cell, two more guards joined the first. They went down three flights of stairs. Another corridor was brightly lit and clean. They passed what looked like a small auditorium with rows of chairs and a lectern at the front of the room, the Iranian flag on the wall behind it.

Two doors down, the guard opened a room. Sunlight came in through the door. Meir followed the guard to a courtyard. The ground was grass, brown and yellow in places. Three walls were concrete, and windowless. The fourth wall was two stories high; above it stood the white-capped summits of the Alborz Mountains. As Meir walked toward the wall, he noticed that it was spattered in black; the color of dried blood.

The guard led him across the courtyard.

"Good luck to you, Mr. Meir," he whispered. "Would you like a blindfold?"

Meir stared at the black strip of material in his hand.

"No," said Meir. "But will you say a blessing?"

"A blessing?" asked the guard. "I'm not Jewish."

"A blessing in your religion," said Meir.

The guard smiled and nodded. He closed his eyes and put a hand on Meir's forehead.

"And the dawn came to the trusted ones," he whispered, closing his eyes, "and He who had cast them out returned, and it was then that the light was shone . . ."

Bhutta stood in front of the leather sofa, flipping between the BBC and *Al Jazeera*. It was already twenty minutes after he'd called Nava and still the Iranian president had yet to call him back. Bhutta paced the room nervously. For he knew that the moment Meir died, his own reason for living would be gone.

The door to the suite opened and Danny stepped in.

"Try again," Danny ordered.

Bhutta went to the desk and sat down. He dialed a number. After several moments, it began ringing.

"Office of the president," came the voice.

"Qasim, this is Ambassador Bhutta again," said Bhutta. "I must speak with him. It is an emergency."

"Mr. Ambassador, he's away from the office," said Nava's executive assistant. "I tried. He can't be reached."

"You must reach him," said Bhutta. "It is a matter of national security."

"I can't," said Qasim. "Even if I wanted to—"

"*They've stolen the bomb!*" screamed Bhutta. *"Find him!"*

There was a short pause.

"Hold the line," said Qasim.

Nava's motorcade pulled through the front gates of Evin Prison, then moved swiftly to a side entrance, where the commandant of the prison was waiting, along with a photographer to record the historic moment.

"Good morning, Mr. President," said the commandant.

Nava followed him through the door and down a brightly lit corridor. At the end of the hallway, Nava stepped into a dimly lit room. A soldier went to the wall and moved a curtain aside, revealing a long, thin window. Through the window was a sun-splashed courtyard. Against the left wall of the courtyard stood a line of soldiers, rifles aimed at the ground; the firing squad.

Across from the firing squad, against the far wall, stood Kohl Meir.

Nava stepped to the window.

"Are you ready, Mr. President?" asked the commandant.

"Yes," said Nava, rubbing his hands together.

Footsteps were heard as someone approached, running from down the hallway. As the commandant turned to give the orders to proceed, the door to the room flew opened. A young soldier burst in, his face contorted in a sheen of perspiration. He held a cell phone.

"How dare you interrupt!" barked Nava.

"I'm sorry, sir," said the soldier frantically. He extended the cell. "It's your assistant. He says it's a matter of national emergency."

Nava grabbed the phone.

"What do you want?" Nava yelled. "I'm in the middle of something that is more important than—"

"They have the nuclear device," came a familiar voice, though not Qasim's. Nava quickly processed the sound of the voice and knew who it was.

"Amit?" asked Nava. "Where are you? We thought you were dead."

"The Americans," said Bhutta. "They've stolen the bomb."

"No, it's impossible," said Nava.

"*It's over, Mahmoud!*" yelled Bhutta. "They kidnapped me for the single purpose of making this phone call. They have the nuclear bomb. They've known about it, stolen it, and now they have it. If you don't believe me, go to the warehouse in Mahdishahr and look for it."

Nava's face turned ashen. His excitement was gone, replaced by a look of sadness, then anger.

"If you don't believe me, call Colonel Hek or Paria,"

continued Bhutta. "It's gone. And before you do anything to Kohl Meir, you had better listen to what they have to say."

"What do you mean 'the Americans'?" asked Nava. "The U.S. government has no idea—"

"One American. A rogue sent to free the Israeli. Andreas. He has the bomb. They were working with Qassou."

Footsteps echoed down the hallway. The door to the room opened; it was Paria, a pained look on his face.

Nava stared at Paria's sweat-covered face.

"Is it true, Abu?" asked Nava.

Paria looked at the soldiers in the room, then pointed at the door.

"Get out," Paria ordered.

When they left, he slammed the door.

"You speak of this in front of prison guards?" asked Paria. "You stupid idiot."

"Is the bomb gone or not?" countered Nava.

"Yes, it's gone."

Paria reached for the cell phone, pressed a button that put the call on speaker.

"This is Abu Paria. What's going on? Who is this?"

"It's Amit," said Bhutta. "As I was telling President Nava, an American—Dewey Andreas—has stolen the bomb. They'll make a deal for it, but they want the Israeli back."

"Shut down the borders," interrupted Nava. "Stop him!"

"Shut the hell up, Mahmoud," said Paria, who towered over Nava, looking as if he might punch the

Iranian president. He looked at the phone. "What do you mean a deal?"

"A trade. The bomb for the Israeli."

"Why would America, or Israel for that matter, trade a nuclear bomb for him?" asked Paria.

"It's not America or Israel," said Bhutta. "It's Andreas. He's not interested in anything other than getting Meir back. Meir saved his life after the Pakistani coup. He has conditions."

"What are they?" asked Paria.

"He wants you and you alone at the handoff, Abu."

Paria glared at the phone.

"Why me?"

"I'm just a messenger, General," said Bhutta.

Nava shook his head, staring at Paria, then held his index finger up, moving it back and forth.

"No," Nava said. "No, no, no, no, no. This was *my* day."

Nava pointed at the courtyard, at Meir in the distance. A pained look crept across his face as he realized Meir would not be executed.

Paria raised his right arm, then swung it through the air, striking Nava with the back of his hand and sending the short, frail Nava tumbling to the ground.

Paria opened the door. He looked at the commandant.

"Bring him in," said Paria.

He pressed a button on the cell phone, taking the speaker off, then put the cell phone to his ear.

"The bomb is our priority," said Paria to Bhutta. "What are the details?"

"We have the great-grandson of Golda Meir!" pleaded Nava from the ground. "The people demand his death. We must proceed with the execution! Let him keep the bomb, we'll make another!"

"Mahmoud," said Paria calmly. "I'm afraid that's not your decision to make."

Ten minutes later, Paria walked into the command center of the Revolutionary Guards headquarters. Colonel Hek, the head of IRGC, stood, a phone on each ear, staring at a large plasma screen, which displayed live on-the-ground video of Mahdishahr, taken by an IRGC videographer. Firefighters were spraying water at the Range Rovers. Another screen showed the warehouse, which was now a burned-out bomb site, with flames dancing along the scrub bushes surrounding the crater where the structure had once stood.

A third screen had a live *Al Jazeera* feed of Khomeini Square.

Hek looked up at Paria, moving the phones to his chest. His look said it all: *It's true*, their serious, furious edge seemed to say.

"It's gone," said Hek.

"What are we doing to get it back?" barked Paria.

"I have more than thirty reconnaissance planes in the air," said Hek.

"Where are you looking?" asked Paria.

"We're scouring every road between Mahdishahr and the border," said Hek. "I assume he'll go to Iraq and the waiting arms of the U.S. Army, but I'm also looking at Turkey."

"We can't let him escape," said Paria.

"Every border crossing will be a fortress," said Hek. "A chipmunk won't be able to get out of Iran without my say-so."

"What about Afghanistan?" asked Paria. "Azerbaijan? Turkey?"

"Every border is shut," said Hek. "Every border crossing, every road, every dirt lane leading from a small village. It's a nine-thousand-pound bomb. He won't get it out of Iran."

"How much time do we have to find it?"

"The logical border is Iraq. That's where the search is concentrated. But Turkey is only a seven- or eight-hour drive. That's where our focus is also. In a few hours, if we haven't found him somewhere between Mahdishahr and Iraq or Tabriz, then I'll put resources into the Afghan theater."

"Get more planes in the air," said Paria. "Helicopters. Get the State Police out on the roads."

"Yes, sir," said Hek. "It's already done. I must tell you, the plan to move the device to Tehran in an anonymous-looking truck is now our greatest challenge. There are many large silver trucks driving the roads. There was a battle and we're looking for bullet holes."

"Bullet holes?" asked Paria. He shook his head in frustration. "Now is the time. They left Mahdishahr only a few minutes ago. What about roadblocks?"

"Do you know how many roads spread out from Mahdishahr?" asked Hek. "Too many. Abu, be patient. We are searching everywhere. We will find the bomb. If not, we will catch him at the border. I have to repeat this. He's carrying a nine-thousand-pound bomb! There is simply no way to get it out of the country without a truck. A big truck."

Paria pointed at the *Al Jazeera* feed on the plasma screen. A sea of people filled the square and the streets. Signs with photos of Nava and Suleiman were everywhere. But by far the most signs showed photos of Kohl Meir, all of them with a red X across his face.

"What will we do about the crowd?" asked Hek, pointing at the *Al Jazeera* feed.

"Get rid of it," said Paria.

The 350-foot container ship *Milene* moved through the black waters of the Caspian Sea at twenty-two knots, a little more than twenty-five miles per hour. The ship was painted black, its name in bright yellow along its stern, along with the words BAKU, AZERBAIJAN painted beneath.

A skeleton crew of eight men were on board. The trip was a special charter, arranged by the ship's owner, an Athens-based shipping company called Caspian Trekker, LLP.

The ship's captain, a gruff, thin old Azerbaijani who spoke little English, was nevertheless smiling on this hot, windy day as his ship came into sight of land. After all, it wasn't often that he could make in one week what he was used to making in four or five years aboard the *Milene*. But it was true. The only condition was to keep quiet and not bother the pair of Americans responsible for the largesse.

When the captain caught sight of land, he nodded to his first mate.

"Go tell the Americans we're in sight of land," said the captain.

"Yes, Captain."

Two minutes later, Katie Foxx and Rob Tacoma emerged from a doorway on the main deck. Tacoma wore a blue sweater and jeans. Behind him, Foxx wore a red, white, and blue North Face raincoat, jeans. On Tacoma's face was a big grin; he looked like a kid out on his first boat ride.

They walked to the front of the *Milene*. At the front of the ship, they stood side by side, watching the approaching port city as it came slowly into view.

"That crap is going to kill you," said Foxx, shaking her head as she watched Tacoma put a pinch of Copenhagen in his mouth.

"And stealing nukes from nutjob Islamic fundamentalists won't?" asked Tacoma, taking one more pinch, then sending a stream of brown tobacco juice off the bow of the ship, where it meandered down into the black water.

The drive to Tehran had been white-knuckled. If they were going to catch him, it would've been in the first hour, Dewey knew. After that, the routes available to him increased exponentially. By the time he and Cano cruised by downtown Tehran on the freeway, despite the fact that he was in the belly of the beast, Dewey began to, if not relax, at least not grip the steering wheel so tight. He knew that Tehran would be the last place the Iranians would look; they would assume he was running for the Iraq border. Or, they would try and outthink themselves, guessing that Iraq was too obvious.

They would never expect Dewey to do what he was about to do.

When he was thirty minutes north of Tehran, Dewey called Bhutta again.

"Yes," Bhutta said.

"Nowshahr," said Dewey.

"The port?" asked Bhutta. "The Caspian Sea?"

"Paria and Meir, that's all. They fly in by chopper. I'll hand them the keys to the truck when they get there."

The road became perilously windy as they came closer to Nowshahr, stretching on carved-out shelves on the sides of the mountains north of the city. An hour after passing through Tehran, Dewey's truck crested a hilltop and the shelf of dark blue that was the distant Caspian came suddenly into view.

He picked up the SAT. Pressing a number, he waited.

"Calibrisi," said the voice.

"It's me," said Dewey.

"Where are you?"

"Nowshahr, the port."

"What do you need?"

"A couple more UAVs," said Dewey. "Just in case."

"Done," said Calibrisi.

"One more thing," said Dewey. "Send a C-130 to Baku."

They drove through the city of Nowshahr, a town almost a thousand years old, with pretty buildings clinging to the sides of vegetation-covered hillsides just above the cool waters of the Caspian.

Dewey drove along a residential street at the water's edge, by pedestrians out for strolls in the midafternoon sun. The beaches ended and an industrial-looking area began, where the port and its busy wharves teemed with activity.

After passing by several large wharves, with gantry cranes overhead, Dewey saw two people standing at the stern of a black container ship, parked alongside a set of container cranes.

Dewey stopped on the side of the road. He climbed out of the truck and walked back to Cano.

"Park it right here," said Dewey.

Cano pulled up to a chain-link fence along the port's service road. He turned off the engine, then climbed out. Dewey glanced around; seeing nobody, he aimed the suppressed .45 at the door of the truck and blew several holes through the thin steel.

Dewey returned to the first truck, glancing around as he walked, but seeing no one. Cano climbed into the passenger seat of the lead truck, handing Dewey the keys.

"Get down," said Dewey.

Dewey engaged the gears, driving the truck to the port's entrance gate. A lone security attendant, a man not more than twenty years old, looked up at Dewey.

"Papers," he said.

Dewey handed the man his passport.

"Which dock?"

Dewey pointed at the black container ship.

The attendant stared at the ship, then back at Dewey. Slowly, the attendant's eyes moved down to the steel of the door, which had several bullet holes in it.

He looked up at Dewey, his eyes shifting nervously. He abruptly reached for the door.

"The port police said to look for a truck with holes," he said as he looked up at Dewey, like a deer in the headlights.

Dewey pulled his Colt from the duffel, then trained it on the young Iranian. He fired a single round through his head, knocking him to the floor of the small wooden shack.

"Sorry about that," said Dewey.

He moved through the gates, turned right on the service road, then took his third left, down a long concrete dock. He parked the truck next to the ship, the word *Milene* painted on its stern.

Dewey climbed out of the cab of the truck. With Cano in tow, carrying their weapons, they ascended a set of stairs. At the top of the stairs, Dewey was greeted by Foxx, holding a handgun that was aimed at his head.

"Don't move," said Foxx.

Dewey dropped the duffel and raised his arms. He casually pulled his hijab from his head.

"Dewey?" asked Foxx, lowering her weapon. "Sorry about that."

The two started laughing as Cano climbed aboard.

A minute later, the large gantry crane on the deck of the *Milene* lifted the semi from the deck of the pier. As the truck swung gently in the air, moving slowly to the ship's deck, Dewey, Foxx, Tacoma, and Cano watched.

The crane then went back and hoisted the cab of the truck, setting it down in front of the trailer.

Dewey nodded to Tacoma.

"Let's go," said Dewey.

The *Milene* was quickly untied from the pier. Within five minutes, it was chugging north, out of the port of Nowshahr, toward the open waters of the Caspian. Five minutes after that, standing on the pier, it was hard to tell the *Milene* from any of the other ships.

"Do we know what kind of chopper he'll be flying?" asked Tacoma.

"No," said Dewey. "You'll do fine. I'm not worried about your flying."

"Well, you should be."

In the distance, Dewey became vaguely aware of a commotion coming from shore; looking, he saw police cars bunched at the port entrance.

He kept looking to the mountains for signs of Paria's chopper.

The port numbered more than a dozen individual piers, jutting into the water. Dewey and Tacoma watched as a swarm of officers walked onto the pier next to theirs, a few hundred yards away.

Then, in the air above one of the mountain peaks, a small black dot appeared. They heard the chopper's rotors cutting through the air. A few moments later, a light green Mil Mi-8 Soviet-made chopper crossed like a bird over the city, then grew louder as it descended toward them. Dewey spied the dark skull of Paria, headset covering his ears.

The chopper landed on the end of the pier. Dewey glanced up at the blue sky, looked at Tacoma, then began walking down the length of the empty pier.

Paria climbed out of the chopper, stepping down onto the concrete, eyeing Dewey. In his right hand, he held a small duffel bag. Paria was a massive man, dressed in a khaki uniform. He limped as he walked, though it did not diminish the speed with which he strode toward Dewey and Tacoma. He looked angry and dangerous.

"Check and see if he's alive," said Dewey as they drew close, without taking his eyes off Paria.

Tacoma nodded. As Paria and Dewey came toward each other, Tacoma kept walking, past Paria, toward the chopper.

Dewey and Paria stopped when they were face-to-face. Dewey said nothing, staring into Paria's eyes. They were similar in height, but Paria somehow loomed larger, like a gorilla dressed in human clothing.

"He's good!" yelled Tacoma from the side of the chopper, holding his thumb up.

"Where is it?" asked Paria.

"Follow me," said Dewey.

They walked to the end of the pier, then down the service road. They walked toward the entrance shed, now swarming with police. Several officers started to move toward Dewey and Paria; then, recognizing the notorious chief of Iran's Ministry of Intelligence, they recoiled and gave the two men berth.

Paria noted the bullet holes in the side of the cab as they walked by.

Dewey unhitched the handle at the back of the semi-trailer, then lifted it up. Paria climbed inside as Dewey waited on the street.

Paria removed a flashlight and a yellow handheld Geiger counter from the duffel. He limped into the truck, seeing the line of steel containers.

"Which one?" he asked.

"Third one from the front," said Dewey. "Combo is eight-eight-seven."

"And what does that signify, Mr. Andreas?"

"It's my IQ," said Dewey.

Paria nodded, chuckling mirthlessly.

"What are in the other boxes?"

"Machine parts for oil wells. Consider them a present from the U.S. government. There's at least a hundred dollars' worth."

Paria didn't respond, but his nostrils flared angrily as he glared at Dewey, who looked back without moving. Finally, Paria turned and walked to the steel container near the front of the truck.

Paria moved the dials of the padlock, then removed it. He lifted the top of the container, pushing the heavy steel top against the wall. He aimed the flashlight into the box, running it down the length of the bomb. He ran his other hand along the bomb. He spent more than a minute examining it. Then, he flipped the Geiger on. It beeped several times, then made a low clicking noise. He moved the small wand on the side of the device to the bomb; the clicking noise accelerated and became high-pitched.

After a minute of scanning the bomb with the Geiger, Paria shut it off.

He walked to the end of the truck, pulled the door down, then climbed down.

Dewey pulled the truck keys from his pocket. He handed them to Paria.

"How will you get home?"

"I need the key to the chopper."

Paria reached into his pocket. He pulled out a key.

"Look up for a moment," said Dewey, pointing.

Paria looked into the sky. He saw nothing.

"What is it?" he asked. "I don't see anything."

"Look again," Dewey said, pointing.

Paria then saw it, the first one, as small as a mosquito, but unmistakable; the shine gave it away, the temporary silver glimmer from the sun off its side: UAV.

"Count them, Abu," said Dewey.

Paria studied the sky.

"Reapers?" he asked.

"Anything happens to the chopper, someone in an office building somewhere back in America is going to press a little button and turn you into roadkill."

Paria smiled, then nodded.

"I understand. We're not going to shoot you down. That's not my style."

"Yeah, right," said Dewey. He walked away from the truck, back toward the waiting chopper.

Paria watched Dewey walk away. He went to the cab of the truck and climbed inside.

He called his deputy.

"Did you find a warehouse?" asked Paria.

"Number ten. They're waiting."

"Get Dr. Kashilla to Natanz. I'll meet him there."

Paria hung up without saying anything. He drove along the service road, across from the piers, then turned into a large brown warehouse. Inside were dozens of semitrailers and cabs.

At least ten men were standing inside the door waiting. A pair of them decoupled the trailer from the cab, then Paria drove forward, parked it out of the way, and climbed out. Another man backed a black semicab into the trailer. A crowd of men spray-painted the sides of the trailers in dark silver; another climbed onto the roof and spray-painted it black, covering over the silver that had been there.

Within ten minutes of arriving at the warehouse, Paria steered the semi back out onto the service road; he was the third in a row of seven trucks to leave the warehouse at the same time. He drove into Nowshahr, meandering along residential streets. He parked in front of a small white bungalow, then called his deputy.

"Is it done?" his deputy asked.

"Yes."

"Shall I send a chopper to pick you up?"

"I'll drive," said Paria.

"The Leader called for you."

"Put me through to him."

After a few moments, the soft voice of Ali Suleiman came on the phone.

"We'll need to review everything that has happened," said Suleiman. "This affair with Qassou, the Israeli. *Everything*. It's deeply upsetting. The reports from Mahdishahr are simply unacceptable, Abu."

"I'll resign if you like, sir," said Paria.

"No," said Suleiman. "That's not my point. You've retrieved what matters. But how do we now explain to our people what happened with the Israeli?"

"Might I suggest that our president shares some of the blame?"

"Of course he does. But perhaps there is something to be salvaged in all of this. I was always uncomfortable with the duplicitous nature of it all. On the one hand, possessing a nuclear weapon, on the other acting as if we would stop the nuclear program."

Paria steered the semi onto the freeway entrance.

"One thing that keeps running through my mind," said Suleiman. "Why would he give the bomb back?"

"The Israeli saved his life," said Paria, as he brought the truck up to speed on the crowded highway, headed toward Tehran.

"Sentimental Americans," said Suleiman. "Always placing value on individual human life. How ironic that it will someday be their downfall."

Paria stared ahead, stricken by a sudden inexplicable wave of anxiety.

Dewey arrived at the chopper and walked to the passenger door. Meir was seated, his eyes bruised shut. Dewey opened the door, causing Meir to flinch. He strained to open his eyes and look at Dewey. Dewey was shocked by Meir's appearance. Both eyes were deep purple, and there were cuts and raw skin along his cheeks, chin, and nose.

Dewey grinned.

"You look like a million shekels," said Dewey.

Meir smiled. He reached his right hand out.

"Thanks," said Meir.

Dewey glanced across the cabin at Tacoma.

"Let's get the fuck out of here."

"What are the odds this thing has a bomb on it?" asked Tacoma.

"Fifty-fifty," said Dewey. "At least we'll go quick."

They lifted off, bouncing awkwardly into the afternoon haze, then flew out over the port. Tacoma aimed the chopper to the north. Dewey counted eleven ships floating in the immediate port area, and several more either en route to the port or leaving. They flew for several miles until they saw the *Milene*. He swooped down and landed the chopper on the foredeck of the container ship.

After climbing out, Dewey walked to the crane operator, pointing to the Mil Mi-8.

"Dump it," said Dewey, thumbing toward the water. "Now."

53

NATANZ

South of Natanz, Paria took a left on a dusty road off the Isfahan freeway. The road seemed to lead nowhere. After a mile, he came to a chain-link fence. A lone soldier stood at the fence, opening it as Paria approached. The dirt road continued for several more miles, eventually dead-ending at an unusual, out-of-context sight—at the base of a small mountain was a nondescript garage door. After sitting in front of the door for a minute, it slowly started to rise. Paria drove forward, through a tunnel that was at least five hundred feet long, lit by halogen lights overhead. At the end of the tunnel was another door, this one thick silver steel, which slid sideways. Paria drove through this second doorway, into a massive open space, brightly lit, like a warehouse. This was the back entrance to Natanz.

The Natanz facility was Iran's most important nuclear facility. It was the first facility constructed by the Iranian government for the purpose of enriching uranium. It was at Natanz where the plans for the first bomb had been discussed and where the low enriched uranium had been processed into weapons-grade uranium. And despite reports in the Western press to the contrary, despite great acclaim by the media about the reported Stuxnet computer virus and the assassination of several key Iranian nuclear scientists, the fact was it was at Natanz where the processing of yellowcake into highly enriched, weaponized uranium continued unabated. It was also where the first bomb had been put together.

Natanz was constructed beneath a small mountain so that the facility could withstand any efforts to destroy the facility with aerial bombardment. In a feat of considerable technical accomplishment, Iranian engineers had turned the meandering old tunnels of a former copper mine into a fortified sarcophagus, an iron- and concrete-clad dome that went more than six stories beneath ground, while reaching upward seven stories into the mountain, aboveground. It had cost Iran nearly $6 billion to build Natanz. The Iranian reaction to the development by America of the GBU 57, the so-called bunker buster bomb was to move more core operations deeper underground, and to construct newer facilities in a handful of other towns across Iran, including Qum, Mahdishahr, and a dozen others.

Paria had been an early, vocal opponent of Natanz. He thought it too expensive and believed the decade of development would only serve to hamper his ability to fight Israel and America by siphoning off precious resources that he thought could be better spent building IEDs and funding Hezbollah, Al-Qaeda, and Hamas.

Once the decision was made by Ali Suleiman to construct Natanz and pursue a nuclear bomb, however, Paria had gotten on board. It was Paria's team of VE-VAK operatives who acquired key components of the centrifuges housed at Natanz that were used for uranium enrichment. It was a VEVAK operative who had purchased a uranium deuteride trigger from a former Russian general named Markov. Afterward, it was another VEVAK agent who had killed Markov, after the Russian had begun to brag of his $35 million payday from the Iranians.

As Paria pulled the truck slowly into the warehouse, he watched as a dozen men swarmed the truck. Dr. Kashilla walked on his cane to Paria's door.

"General," said Kashilla. "It's been too long."

"Yes, it has, Mohammed," said Paria, stepping down from the truck and gently shaking Kashilla's left hand. "How are you?"

"Well, I'm better now," said the scientist.

Kashilla nodded at the back of the truck.

"I'm told it was a close call," said Kashilla.

"Yes," said Paria. "But it's over now."

"Let's get this unloaded and make sure everything is intact, shall we?" said Kashilla.

The roof of the trailer was opened. A side boom moved into place. Over the next few minutes, the bomb was lifted inch by inch into the air as the expectant crowd, now numbering more than fifty workers, gathered below.

Paria stepped toward the bomb as it was hoisted into the air. The silver-black steel of the bomb had a patina of scratches and thin black welding seams that formed a line of slight bumps along the side like an inchworm meandering up the side of the bomb.

Kashilla suddenly gasped as the bomb climbed higher into the sky. He pointed at the bomb.

"What is it?" asked Paria.

Paria looked to the scientist. He appeared to be in a mild state of shock.

"What is it, Mohammed?" demanded Paria.

Kashilla stepped forward. He looked at one of the Iranian guards.

"A hammer," said Kashilla.

The guard ran to the side of the warehouse and quickly returned with a hammer. He handed it to Kashilla.

"What are you doing?" asked Paria.

Without answering Paria, Kashilla stepped forward, the sledgehammer in his left hand. Despite his weak legs, his advanced age, Kashilla seemed possessed. He smashed the hammer at the front of the bomb.

"*Stop!*" screamed Paria as the hammer struck the front of the bomb, but he was too late.

Kashilla's swing came down hard on one of the seams, which immediately cracked. Several rivets dropped to the concrete floor.

Paria grabbed the sledgehammer from Kashilla, pushing him aside.

"What have you done?" yelled Paria, running to the bomb. "Do you have any idea . . ."

Paria's voice trailed off as his eye was caught, for the

first time, by the Persian lettering running along the underside of the bomb. Where he'd expected to find the words *Goodbye, Tel Aviv,* a new message, also in Persian, was painted in the same ornate style: *Fuck you, Tehran.*

Paria stepped to the now torn seam along the side of the bomb. Through the seam, he spied the light gray of concrete. Paria jammed his fingertips into the seam and ripped it open. The thin steel peeled back easily. Beneath there was only concrete, with bricks of lead layered inside it.

Paria looked at the concrete for several seconds. He took the sledgehammer and smashed it into the side of the fake bomb. As a growing cluster of Natanz workers surrounded the big man, he swung down on the bomb and struck it once, then twice, then again, each time making a loud, deep guttural noise, primitive and animalistic. He didn't stop pounding at the bomb. The sweat began to pour down his face as he smashed into it, ripping apart the thin layer of steel, then striking into concrete and lead. Paria became manic, and the crowd, which at first had grown out of curiosity, started to disperse, as none of them wanted to be in the crosshairs of Paria's coming explosion.

After several minutes of smashing into the top of the bomb, the top section was torn completely away. Paria was soaked in sweat, his face beet-red. He dropped the sledgehammer. He ripped the section of badly dented steel from the bomb. He hammered away at the concrete. He pulled out brick after brick of heavy lead, throwing them like wafers across the warehouse, even striking the side of a centrifuge and sending a piece of it toppling to the ground. When, at long last, he had gutted the front half of the bomb, Paria stepped back. He looked around the warehouse; Kashilla was the sole individual remaining within a hundred feet of him. Both men stared blankly at the ground, littered in concrete and lead.

The *Milene* moved through the calm waters of the Caspian Sea with four mysterious guests and, hidden in the back of a semitrailer lashed to the deck, a stolen twenty-kiloton nuclear bomb.

Dewey called Calibrisi and Jessica on the SAT phone.

"I'll keep those Reapers overhead until you're in Baku in case Iran finds the fake bomb and scrambles some boats to look for you."

"You got a C-130?" asked Dewey.

"I scrambled one out of Bagram. We need to get that thing back here so we can look at it."

"Hector, it's Israel's bomb," said Dewey.

"Jesus Christ, you're a pain in the ass, Andreas."

The *Milene* enjoyed the security of three overhead UAVs—MQ-9s, or Reapers as they were appropriately named—armed to the teeth with Hellfire missiles. But there had been no cause for concern.

Meir was not in good shape; he spent the first few hours in a bunkroom, sleeping. He was dazed. In the past week he'd been electrocuted twice. He'd been severely beaten, and barely fed. Many people would have died from such abuse.

Nevertheless, by 6:00 P.M., as the sun was setting over the western strip of green that was the far-off coast of Azerbaijan, Meir had gotten up to join Dewey, Foxx, and Tacoma, who were in the small mess hall near the back of the ship.

Tacoma was able to find a bottle of vodka in a cabinet, and the four each had a few drinks as the night wore on and the *Milene* chugged at twenty-five knots to the north.

It was midnight by the time the ship steamed into Baku, capital of Azerbaijan, a large port city on the country's eastern coast.

They were met by the Baku CIA chief of station, a young, curly-haired American named Lew Vaphiades. Tacoma and Meir drove in Vaphiades's Mercedes, while Dewey and Foxx followed in the semi. They drove from the port across the eastern section of the capital to Baku Kala Air Base. Sitting on the tarmac at Baku Kala was a desert-camouflaged C-130 cargo plane, its rear hatch lowered. Next to the C-130 was a silver Gulfstream G150.

Dewey drove the truck up the ramp into the cargo hold of the C-130. Two U.S. soldiers attached steel cables to the semi in order to prevent the truck from shifting about in case there was turbulence. Dewey walked to the cabin, where two pilots were seated.

"Evening, guys," Dewey said. "What's the itinerary?"

"Tel Aviv," said the first officer. "Then back to Bagram."

"You got one guy with you," said Dewey. "He's in back. Make sure you check in on him."

"Yes, sir."

In the rear cabin, Meir was buckled into one of the canvas flight chairs on the side of the cabin. He strained to open his eyes, but he did, reaching out his hand to grasp Dewey's. Dewey shook his hand for several moments.

Meir reached to his neck and removed a necklace. He balled it up and handed it to Dewey; it was a Star of David.

"Thanks," said Dewey, smiling and taking it from Meir. "I'm not Israeli."

"Yeah, you are."

54

THE WHITE HOUSE

Jessica and Calibrisi entered the Oval Office at a quarter after one in the afternoon on Sunday.

Dellenbaugh was already seated in one of the two big tan leather chesterfield sofas in the center of the room. He was reading *The New York Times*. Dellenbaugh was dressed in a blue-and-red-checked flannel shirt that was untucked and a pair of jeans. He held a mug of coffee in his hand. He gestured to Jessica and Calibrisi to sit down also.

Dellenbaugh pointed at the silver coffee service on the table. "Would either of you like a cup?"

Calibrisi nodded and Dellenbaugh filled one of the small blue and white porcelain cups with coffee.

"Jess?"

"No, thank you, Mr. President," she said.

"So what's up?" asked Dellenbaugh.

"It's about Iran," said Calibrisi.

"Buenos Aires?" the president asked. "I assume everything is moving along?"

"Not the summit, sir," said Calibrisi. "Though it might influence whether or not you should go forward with it."

"There's been a fairly dramatic series of events in the past couple of days you need to be aware of, Mr. President."

"In Iran?"

"Yes, in Iran."

"Let me guess," said Dellenbaugh. "Dewey Andreas freed Kohl Meir. After stealing Iran's nuclear bomb."

Dellenbaugh took a sip from his cup, looking calmly at Calibrisi and Jessica. A smile slowly came to his face.

Jessica and Calibrisi exchanged glances, saying nothing.

"Prime Minister Shalit called me," continued Dellenbaugh. "To express his gratitude to the United States of America."

"Mr. President," said Calibrisi, "Jessica had nothing to do with Andreas. It was me."

"I'm not mad," said Dellenbaugh. "You did the right thing. His life *was* worth fighting for."

"What about Buenos Aires?" asked Jessica.

"The hope that was created by virtue of the fact that we were bringing Iran to the table of the civilized world was an illusion," said Dellenbaugh. "Obviously, Mahmoud Nava can't be trusted."

"No one can be trusted, sir," said Calibrisi. "You know that."

"I want to cancel the summit," said the president.

"Actually, we believe now is the time to push ahead, President Dellenbaugh," said Jessica. "If the public pressure and the lifting of sanctions are enough to get Iran to halt their nuclear weapons program—"

"Even if we know it's bullshit?"

"Even if we know it's a charade," said Jessica. "It will mean we have on-demand inspections, monitoring infrastructure, access to their scientists, and details about the centrifuge supply chain. It will be a lot harder for Iran to build another bomb. Frankly, we were caught by surprise on this one. So was Israel. Everyone was. If it wasn't for a man named Qassou who leaked word to Israel, we wouldn't have known until it was too late."

"You're missing the point," said Dellenbaugh. "If he was willing to negotiate while privately plotting to build a nuke, he can't be trusted."

"No one can be trusted," Calibrisi repeated. "Russia, China, North Korea, Pakistan. Certainly not the Iranians."

Dellenbaugh sat back and took a sip from his coffee cup. He smiled.

"I was naïve," said Dellenbaugh.

"It takes time to get used to the fact that, in our jobs, we're dealing with the most ruthless people known to man," said Calibrisi. "The president more so than anyone. You'll get used to it."

"I'm the one who trusted the Iranians," said Dellenbaugh. "What the hell was I thinking?"

"I should probably mention the fact that CIA drones

were employed in the operation," said Calibrisi. "We also fired Tomahawk missiles to destroy the warehouse in Mahdishahr."

Dellenbaugh stared for several moments at Calibrisi, then at Jessica, while remaining silent.

"Mr. President, I understand if you want me gone," said Calibrisi.

Dellenbaugh was silent for nearly a minute, sipping his coffee, then stood. He walked to the French doors that looked out on the Rose Garden.

"Do you want out of Langley?" asked Dellenbaugh.

"No, I don't," said Calibrisi.

Dellenbaugh stared out at the leaves on one of the trees along the edge of the garden.

"I don't want your resignation," Dellenbaugh said. "Your actions, and Andreas's, saved a lot of lives. I need you. I don't know what I'm doing."

"Then learn," said Calibrisi. "And don't be shocked or angry when your advisors talk straight to you. How do you think Rob Allaire got so good at this? He listened and wasn't afraid to have people disagree with him."

Dellenbaugh turned from the window. He looked at Calibrisi.

"I want you to honor everyone who risked their lives saving Meir and taking that nuke."

"A thank-you from you will mean a lot. I'll make sure to let Dewey know how grateful you are."

Dellenbaugh stepped back to the sofa and sat down.

"Let's talk about Buenos Aires," said Dellenbaugh. "I want to know if you two are serious."

"Serious about what?" asked Jessica.

"That I should go. That the United States should continue this thing. I mean, what's the fucking point?"

"Absolutely, you should go," said Jessica. "Iran knows we know about the bomb. They assume we were involved in stealing it. Nava and Suleiman have two choices. They can either back out of the agreement, in which case they will lose the significant economic package associated with signing the agreement, hundreds of billions of dollars, and incur the wrath of every civilized country in the world, and more important, their own people. Alternatively, Iran can proceed, sign the agreement, then attempt to subvert it. That's what we want. Because even if they're trying to build another nuclear device, the country will be crawling with inspectors. They won't be able to do it. We've boxed them in, sir."

Dellenbaugh nodded.

"Okay," he said. "Let's go to Buenos Aires."

55

It was a crisp, perfect spring day, a Saturday; a late April afternoon in Washington. The sky was deep blue, not a cloud anywhere. The temperature was in the mid-fifties. There was a faint aroma of smoke, coming from a few chimneys in Georgetown. The smell of burning firewood reminded Dewey of Maine.

He climbed out of the taxi on Wisconsin Avenue. To say he looked slightly out of place was an understatement. He still had on Turkish clothing, a pair of baggy pants and a tan shirt bought in Istanbul. He had, however, managed to sleep for a time on the CIA Gulfstream back from Baku.

As he walked down Twenty-fourth Street, Dewey suddenly realized that he had absolutely no idea what he was going to do next or where he was going to live. He knew, in a way, what he had was total freedom. He didn't owe anyone a thing. He had no obligations. He could live where he wanted, go where he wanted, and do what he wanted. His year on a ranch in Australia had made Dewey realize he could be happy in almost any job, in any environment, as long as certain conditions existed. He needed the feeling of physical labor. He liked being away from it all. On some level, being alone was what made Dewey happiest.

Yet Dewey knew that he couldn't be alone forever. Seeing Kohl Meir and the sacrifices the Israeli was willing to make in order to protect his own country had, on some level, revitalized him. He had once lived the same way. Those were the hardest days of his life, but also the most fulfilling, Dewey knew there was no greater feeling than fighting for something that mattered, for your country, for an idea, for America. There were few people in the world who could understand what it meant to use all of your skills, your physical abilities, your mind, your experience, and your training, to fight for the country you loved.

Still fewer could understand what Dewey was experiencing, having at one time felt the intense patriotism only to then lose it all. Perhaps it was the way Abu Paria had stared at Dewey, with pure hatred. There was a war going on, and Dewey was missing it. He wanted back in.

He walked past Standard Bakery, did a double take, then turned and went inside. He bought two raspberry muffins and two cups of coffee.

He walked along a thin, brick sidewalk, past the old, impeccably maintained brick, wood, and limestone town houses. He came to one particularly nice town house, a wide unit of red bricks, with a beautiful brass light fixture next to the door. Dewey paused for a moment. He knew Jessica was angry at him, for a number of reasons, but primarily for not telling her about the Iranian bomb. He bit his lower lip, then rang the doorbell. He waited nearly a minute, then the door swung open.

Standing in the doorway was Jessica. In her hand, she held a paintbrush with pink paint on the bristles. Her nose and right cheek each had paint on them, as did her yellow T-shirt. She had on a pair of cut-off denim shorts, also decorated in pink paint, and flip-flops. She stood inside the doorway, staring at Dewey for several moments. She didn't smile or show so much as a flicker of recognition whatsoever.

"Muffin?" he asked, holding the bag out toward her.

She stared at Dewey, then reached out and put her hand in the paper bag, pulled out a muffin, then transferred it to the same hand that held her paintbrush. She reached for one of the cups of coffee, pulled it from Dewey's hand, then softly kicked the door shut without saying anything.

Dewey stared at the door, then sat down on the front stoop. Eventually, he pulled the other muffin out of the bag and ate it, then drank the coffee. After finishing the coffee, he sat on the stoop for what seemed like an eternity but was in fact about an hour. On the stoop across from Jessica's was a stack of *Washington Post*s in plastic bags, the owners obviously away. Dewey crossed the street and took a newspaper, went back to Jessica's, and read. As he was finishing an article about innovative methods for baking outmeal cookies, the door again opened. Jessica had slightly more paint on her, including some in her hair. She stared at him without saying anything, standing in the doorway. Then she took a few steps back, so that only Dewey, sitting on the stoop, could see her. She reached down and pulled up her paint-splattered T-shirt over her head, then dropped it on the ground. She didn't have a bra on. She reached down and unbuttoned her cut-offs, then let them drop to the ground. She was wearing a pair of black lace panties.

Dewey folded the newspaper as his eyes moved up Jessica's legs, staring at her muscular, tan calves, then her knees and thighs. He looked at her panties, with their thin lace edges, then her stomach, toned but not muscular, with just the tiniest hint of voluptuous curve, above it her big breasts, the nape of her neck, and finally her eyes, which still held the same contemptuous stare.

Dewey stood up, walked inside, and kicked the door gently shut behind him, while gripping the two sides of the shirt, which after three days was very comfortable if quite rank in its aroma, and ripped it at the seams, sending buttons tumbling to the hardwood floor.

A small grin was on Dewey's lips, which he attempted to hide. He stepped closer to Jessica, and as he came within arm's length she reached her hands out and grabbed the buckle of his belt, yanking it harshly to unbuckle it, then grabbed and unbuttoned his pants, stepped closer, and then pushed her hands inside the back of his pants, making them fall to his ankles. He kicked off his shoes and then stepped out of his pants, naked.

She stared down at his body. He pushed against her. Behind her was the dining-room table. He pushed her back onto the table, and she sat on the edge of the table, wrapping her legs around Dewey's back. He reached down and pulled her panties gently aside, then watched as Jessica closed her eyes and leaned back on her elbows. They made love on the table then moved to the floor, where Jessica climbed on top of Dewey, saying nothing, her anger eventually dissipating as she moved slowly up and down on top of him, pacing herself, until finally she could feel Dewey begin to lose himself, and she allowed herself to lose control, letting the warmth come, and she closed her eyes, her breathing growing louder as he reached up and grabbed her tightly as she collapsed on top of him, into his arms.

"My God," she whispered afterward. "You really smell."

"I know," said Dewey. "It's even starting to bother me a little."

"When did you land?"

"I don't know. A couple hours ago maybe."

"Have they debriefed you?"

"No. I wanted to debrief you first."

"That was bad," she said, laughing. She leaned on her elbow. Dewey was on his back. She stared into his eyes. "What else are you hiding from me?"

Dewey grinned. She shook her head.

"Aren't you even going to apologize?" she asked.

"For what?"

"For deceiving me."

"Deceiving you? What are you talking about?"

"Your shit-eating grin doesn't work on me, Andreas," she said.

"Yes, it does," he said. "At least it's supposed to. Don't fight it."

"Asshole," she said. "I spent a week with you in Castine, fucking your brains out, and then you find out Iran has a nuclear bomb and you don't tell me."

"Oh, that," he said innocently.

"Yes, that. You owe me an apology."

"For stealing the bomb and preventing Iran from dropping it on Tel Aviv, or for rescuing Kohl Meir?"

She stood, leaving Dewey on the ground. "If you're not going to apologize, then get out."

"Do you have anything you haven't told me?" asked Dewey from the ground.

"Like what?"

"I don't know, some sort of secret thing with the president or some foreign country."

"Maybe," she said. "I mean, yes, of course, obviously. I'm the national security advisor."

"Okay, so you have stuff you haven't told me," he concluded. "Yet I should have told you? It seems kind of asymmetrical."

"You just should have told me, that's all."

Dewey stood up. He moved in front of Jessica.

"Let me ask you something," he said. "What if I promised you something then turned around and broke my promise? Would you like that?"

"No."

"I gave my word to someone," said Dewey.

Dewey reached out with his right arm and cupped Jessica's cheek.

"Do you want someone who'd break his word?" asked Dewey.

She stared at him, then shook her head.

"I don't know what I want, Dewey. I still feel like you deceived me."

"I did deceive you," he said.

"You didn't deceive Hector."

"I knew Hector would break the rules. If I'd told you about the bomb, would you have let the operation go the way it did? Or would you have gone to the president?"

She stared at him.

"I would've told him."

"And would he have allowed that sort of operation to move forward? Or would the Pentagon have been brought in?"

Jessica nodded.

"Probably."

"There's a war going on out there, Jess," Dewey continued. "Our enemies don't have rules. Had I told you about the bomb, it would've gotten back to Tehran. They would've moved it, hidden it, and then where would we be? Kohl would be dead. They might've leveled Tel Aviv by now. You want to stop these maniacs, you have to break the rules."

Jessica stepped forward and wrapped her arms around Dewey's back, then pulled him in close.

"Tough guy," she whispered, looking up at him and smiling.

He stared down, a slight scowl on his face.

"Of course you could make it up to me," she whispered, kissing his chest and then his shoulder.

"How?" he asked, kissing her back.

"Really?" she whispered in between kisses, their eyes closed.

"Yes," he mumbled. "Yes, anything."

Jessica kissed his lips for several more moments. Then, abruptly, she pushed back and stepped away from him. She looked at his waist, smiled mischievously, then moved her eyes up at his surprised face.

"Paint," she said. "I'll get you a brush. We only have two more rooms to go."

Turning, Jessica ran upstairs as Dewey followed.

"That was mean," he said, chasing after her. "You're worse than Mahmoud Nava."

56

MIDDLEBURG, VIRGINIA

A long, somewhat dilapidated pine harvest table sat in the middle of the manicured lawn behind the rambling farmhouse. The moon looked like a tennis ball overhead, bright yellow, and the sky was so clear and filled with stars that the Milky Way appeared as if someone had thrown a splash of confectionary sugar across it in a long, beautiful wisp.

Surrounding the eight-and-a-half-foot table, at each corner, on long sticks, stood lanterns burning a citrusy concoction that kept bugs away and provided soft, peachy light to the table.

The table itself was covered in empty wine bottles and several more that were half full, bottles that were still being passed around. A line of empty beer bottles looked like an assembly line at a brewery. The plates that had, at one point, held big grilled steaks, corn on the cob, and potato salad, sat largely empty, as did the bowls that had been filled with homemade strawberry ice cream.

It was past midnight, and were it not for the more than five hundred acres surrounding the big farm, the raucous laughter from the five people at the table would have guaranteed a visit from the Middleburg police department.

At this particular moment, all eyes were on Dewey, who stood next to the table, a grin on his face, leaning forward, a quarter in his right hand, staring down at a large mug full of beer. Suddenly, Dewey listed to his side. He began to fall over, but Jessica righted him.

"Jesus, you're in bad shape," she said. "You need to hit this."

"I'm fine," said Dewey, holding the table. "Rob tried to trip me, that's all."

"I'm on the other side of the table," said Tacoma, laughing. "How could I trip you?"

"Don't ask me," said Dewey, moving his hand up and down as he prepared to bounce the quarter on the table and try to land it in the beer. "You CIA guys are the tricky ones."

"Oh, my God," said Jessica, leaning forward and giggling.

"Come on, Dewey," said Tacoma. "You haven't made anyone drink all night."

Dewey suddenly stopped smiling. He looked at Tacoma. Without looking at the table, his eyes locked on Tacoma's, he tossed the coin at the table, where it bounced off the wood, lofted into the air, struck the lip of the mug, soared across the top of the mug, struck the opposite lip, bounced even higher into the air, and then came down with a splash into the beer.

Dewey kept his eyes on Tacoma as the crowd erupted in clapping, hoots, and laughter. A big shit-eating grin spread across his lips as he pointed at Tacoma.

"Drink up, killer," said Dewey.

Tacoma reached forward. The beer in front of him was more than twenty ounces, the big mug having been added on to several times as he and Dewey went through a series of "double or nothings" until Calibrisi finally intervened and declared that this would be the last quarter toss.

Calibrisi, Jessica, and Dewey had all come out that afternoon to the farm. Foxx and Tacoma were both stateside for a few weeks. It was Foxx's idea to celebrate July 4th at the farm. She and Calibrisi had planned it all. They had probably pictured something slightly more elegant and sophisticated, but somehow the combination of Dewey and the twenty-nine-year-old Tacoma had resulted in a rapidly escalating level of immaturity.

Still, not more than a minute had gone by all night without the sound of boisterous laughter.

Dewey sat back as Tacoma lifted the mug. He put it to his lips and began chugging the beer, slowly draining the entire mug, standing back, then letting out a ferocious belch.

"So I have a question," said Calibrisi, looking at Jessica, then Dewey. "Can I ask a serious question?"

Calibrisi took a sip of red wine. He was dressed in a madras shirt and jeans. He took his cigar and took a puff.

"Oh, no, Hector," said Jessica.

"It's for Dewey," said Hector.

"Are you going to ask me about my intentions, Hector?" asked Dewey.

"No," said Calibrisi, shaking his cigar through the air to reinforce the no. "No, that, my friend, is none of my business, even though you should know that Jessica here is like a daughter and also that you would be crazy to not at some point marry her because she is arguably the most beautiful woman in the world, or at least tied for the most beautiful."

Calibrisi turned and winked at Foxx, who with her long blond hair free, combed back across her shoulders, looked as if she'd just stepped off a Hollywood set.

"But that is none of my business, as I said," continued Calibrisi.

Dewey rolled his eyes, smiled, and glanced at Jessica.

"Okay," said Dewey. "Ask your question. Just remember I'm not the sharpest lightbulb in the drawer."

"Knife in the drawer," said Jessica, correcting Dewey.

"It was a joke," said Dewey. "Get it?"

"Oh," said Jessica, pausing, thinking about it for a second, then laughing. "That actually was funny."

"Thanks."

Calibrisi held his wineglass high.

"Okay, Dewey, here it is. What is the greatest threat facing the United States today?"

Dewey nodded and glanced about the table, thinking for a few moments.

"High-fructose corn syrup?" Dewey said.

The table erupted again in laughter. Tacoma hurled

the heel of a piece of garlic bread at him, hitting him in the forehead, which he barely noticed.

"Come on," said Calibrisi. "Can't you be serious?"

"Um," said Dewey. "Radical Islam. No question. Number two, the Chinese. Three, the knuckleheads in Congress. That's it. Those are the big three."

Calibrisi nodded. He smiled.

Then he shook his head back and forth.

"Wrong," he said. "Not even close."

"He went to BC, Hector," chimed in Tacoma.

"Hey, fuck you," said Dewey. "BC's a good school."

"Yeah, right," said Tacoma.

"You two could argue over anything," said Calibrisi. "And by the way, Rob, BC is a good school. My idiot brother went there."

"Hey, fuck you, too," said Dewey, glaring at Calibrisi, but with a smile on his face. "Where did you go? Like Mexico City University or something?"

"Hey, watch it."

"Well, don't make fun of BC. They have an excellent art history program."

"Okay, sorry," said Calibrisi. He paused. "Here's the answer. The gravest threat facing the United States comes from within, when our best people refuse to get involved. When the men and women we need to fight those threats you mentioned—radical Islam, China— stay on the sidelines. That's our gravest threat."

Calibrisi stared at Dewey. He leaned out and patted Dewey on the knee.

Dewey said nothing. He stared at Calibrisi, his arms crossed on his chest in front of him. His smile turned icy.

"I just almost single-handedly stole a nuclear weapon that would have wiped out Tel Aviv, a month after leading a coup d'état in Pakistan," said Dewey. "And you're going to tell me I'm staying on the sidelines?"

"So you're planning on coming back in?" asked Calibrisi.

Dewey was silent.

"So you're not?" asked Calibrisi. "You're going to run away to another ranch in Australia? Another oil rig? You're going to run away and leave the rest of us to fight it all. Is that right? Am I right?"

The table was silent. All eyes were on Dewey and Calibrisi.

"What do you want from me?" asked Dewey finally, his voice barely above a whisper.

"Your country needs you," said Calibrisi. "You know it. Everyone at this table knows it. We're losing these wars. We need you, and not just when you feel like it."

Dewey stood. The table was silent. He walked toward the field, away from the house. His back was turned for several minutes. Finally, in the dim light from the lanterns, he turned.

"I'll think about it," said Dewey.

"We're at war," said Calibrisi.

"I said I'd think about it," he said, candlelight flickering shadows on his face.

"You really think you'd be happy working for Chip Bronkelman?" asked Calibrisi.

"I wouldn't mind making a little money, Hector."

"Babysitting his kids," added Calibrisi. "Taking out the trash."

Dewey stepped back to the table. He glanced at Ta-coma, barely a nod, and yet Tacoma knew what he was asking for. He reached into his pocket, pulled out the quarter, and tossed it to Dewey. Dewey caught it. Then he looked at Calibrisi, halfway down the table. A mis-chievous smile appeared on Dewey's lips. He raised his hand slightly, then threw the quarter at the table. It struck the wood, then bounced high up into the air. All eyes followed the silver coin, which reflected the light from the lanterns as it spun in the air. It came down with a splash in Calibrisi's wineglass. Red wine splat-tered across the front of Calibrisi's shirt.

Dewey smiled as he looked at the director of the CIA.

"I guess that settles it," said Dewey.

EPILOGUE

Ehud Dillman walked through the lobby of the hotel, stopping outside the sliding glass doors. It was just after dawn, and the sun was above the eastern horizon, bright orange above the black of the Mediterranean Sea.

Dillman stared at the rising sun, then glanced suspiciously around. It was habit. It was the habit of all career Mossad agents. There was a reason everyone inside the agency called it the "madhouse." Dillman had been looking around suspiciously for so long it was second nature, almost like breathing. Still, ever since the rescue of Kohl Meir, and the audacious theft of Iran's nuclear weapon, Dillman had been particularly nervous. They'd planned a vital operation in the heart of Tehran, Israel's mortal enemy, right under his nose, and he hadn't known a damn thing about it. They'd segmented Mossad out of the OP, the way a surgeon cuts around a vital organ to get at the cancer. It could only mean one thing: they suspected someone high up in Mossad of working for Tehran.

Going to Haifa, and to his favorite hideaway, the Dan, was meant to buy him a few days to think about what to do next. Should he flee to Beijing? He didn't want to. He didn't like China. But they'd made him a wealthy man over the past decade and asylum was a promise Minister Bhang, the head of Chinese intelligence, had made to him many times over the years. He didn't want to leave his homeland, even though he'd betrayed her so many times, in so many ways, over so many years. Dillman knew that if he was caught, he would be executed without even a trial. He'd get a bullet in the forehead, and then only after one of his madhouse colleagues first looked him in the eye and made sure Dillman understood that he'd been caught, tried, and found guilty.

Dillman was dressed in blue tennis shorts with white stripes running along the edge. He had a white shirt on and black and white tennis shoes. In his hand, he held a yellow Babolat racquet.

Dillman began his jog in the hotel's driveway. He ran down the steep, winding road toward the ocean, not fast, but certainly faster than your typical fifty-one-year-old male.

He jogged through the neighborhood called Carmeliya. He ran down a quiet street, past small stucco and brick homes. He came to a school, then ran across the parking lot. Soon, he would be behind the school, where the public tennis court was. He would hit the ball against the backboard for an hour or so, then jog back to the Dan.

As he came around the corner of the schoolhouse, he was surprised to find somebody already at the court hitting tennis balls against the backboard. Dillman thought about turning around. It was the only tennis court he knew of in Haifa, but he didn't feel like waiting God knows how long for the man to be done.

Dillman walked over to the court. The player was young, dressed in red sweatpants and a long-sleeve gray T-shirt. He wore a yellow baseball cap with a Maccabi Haifa logo on it, and mirrored sunglasses. He was bearded and scraggly-looking.

"How long will you be, my friend?" asked Dillman in Hebrew.

The player turned, raising his hands.

"I only just arrived," he said, slightly annoyed.

"No worries," said Dillman. "I'll go for a jog instead."

The man tossed the ball up and swatted it toward the backboard as Dillman started to walk away. Dillman listened to the serial thwacking of string against ball; he could tell by the rhythm and pace that the player was decent. A tiny bit of jealousy ran through him. *Oh well, another time,* he thought.

As Dillman came to the corner of the schoolhouse, he heard a whistle. He looked back.

The tennis player waved him over.

"Would you like to hit some?" the man yelled from the court.

Dillman shrugged. *Why not,* he thought.

"Sure!" he yelled back.

They rallied for the better part of an hour. At first, they hit the ball back and forth, without keeping score, but that grew boring. It was Dillman who suggested they play a set. The stranger was good. His strokes were a little unnatural, as if he'd picked up the sport later in life, but he was fast and was able to get to everything, despite a slight limp. The man beat Dillman 6–3 in the first set. Dillman took the second 7–5. Then, in the third, the bearded stranger jumped to a 4–0 lead.

In the middle of the fifth game, they both heard the stranger's string break, after a particularly nice backhand he'd ripped up the line out of Dillman's reach.

Dillman welcomed the interruption. Not only was the younger man thoroughly beating the crap out of him, but he was sweating like a pig and hungry for breakfast.

"That's too bad," said Dillman, breathing heavily as he ran to the net. "I guess that means I win, yes?"

Dillman had been kidding, an attempt at a joke, but the stranger, who still wore his mirrored sunglasses and hat, either didn't hear the joke, or, if he had, didn't think it was funny.

"I have another racquet," the man said, walking to the bench at the side of the court. Other than saying the score, it was the first thing the young man had said the entire match.

He unzipped his racquet bag.

Dillman walked toward him as he reached into his bag.

"Are you from the area?" asked Dillman, puffing hard as he came up behind the stranger.

The man didn't turn, keeping his back to Dillman as he searched inside his bag.

"No," he answered. "Tel Aviv."

"Are you a student?" asked Dillman. "Do you play at the university? You're very good."

The stranger turned. His brown hair was thick and long and it cascaded out from under the hat. He reached up and removed his sunglasses. His eyes were dark brown, almost black. Something in the way he looked at him triggered a memory in Dillman. The nose was sharp and slightly askew, as if it had once been broken.

"No, I'm not a student," he said. "I'm in the military."

"Oh," said Dillman "What unit?"

"Shayetet Thirteen."

Dillman stared into the stranger's eyes. Then, slowly, Dillman's eyes drifted down to the man's right hand. A trick of the mind perhaps; he had thought the stranger had pulled a second tennis racquet from the bag. He hadn't really looked. But this was no tennis racquet. Instead of a graphite shaft there was a thick piece of wood; instead of a racquet head and strings, there was the dull steel of a large axe, the kind of axe you could chop down a tree with.

"Your second serve needs some work," said Meir. "Other than that, you're actually not bad."

Dillman turned to run, but Meir swung the axe, catching him in the side of the torso, ripping a deep gash into Dillman's side just below the ribs. Dillman fell to the ground, with the axe stuck in his side, gasping for air. The pain was so severe he couldn't scream, as his mouth went agape, his eyes bulged, and blood abruptly filled his mouth, then stained his stomach, chest, and side. His white shirt was quickly ruined in crimson.

"Was it Bhutta?" moaned Dillman. "Did he give me up?"

Meir ignored him, staring from above.

Dillman yanked at the axe handle, trying in vain to pull it out.

Calmly, Meir knelt next to him.

"You like my axe?" asked Meir, smiling at him. "It's for chopping the heads off traitors."

Meir stood and placed a foot on Dillman's chest then yanked up on the axe handle, pulling the axe head from Dillman's body. Dillman groaned in agony. He was rapidly bleeding out, drifting into shock.

Meir held the axe in both hands, then lifted it high over his head. Before he swung down, he looked into Dillman's panicked eyes.

"Look at me," said Meir, seething. Dillman complied, opening his eyes.

" 'I will walk among you and be your God, and you shall be my people,' " said Meir, staring down at Dillman. " 'But if you do not obey me, I will bring terror over you.' Leviticus."

BEIT RAHBARI
TEHRAN

Nava sat on a wooden bench, his arms crossed in front of him, silent. He stared at Paria, who stood across from him, staring back. The feeling of hatred between the two men was visceral.

Seated behind the desk at the far side of the small room was Iran's Supreme Leader, Ali Suleiman, whose wrinkled face was red with frustration and anger. He'd been listening for more than half an hour to the two men, each blaming the other for the fiasco that had caused the loss of both Iran's first nuclear bomb and Kohl Meir.

"It was he who let Qassou into his confidences!" yelled Paria, pointing at Nava. "For years, right under his nose! And he has the gall to blame me?"

"You had the pieces for days, Abu!" screamed Nava, slamming his fist down onto the bench. "You suspected Qassou and yet you didn't tell anyone! Would I have taken him to Mahdishahr? VEVAK is supposed to be good at this! My job is not to sniff out traitors! It's to lead!"

"Then lead!" bellowed Paria. "So we spend a decade creating a nuclear device, and all you want to do is use it to kill Israelis. If not for your blood thirst, Iran would possess a nuclear bomb. We would have a deterrent!"

Suleiman's eyes were closed as he listened. Finally, he looked up. He slapped his hand on the desk, silencing the two men.

"Silence," said Suleiman. "It was my decision, Abu, not Mahmoud's."

"Nava tricked you," said Paria, looking at Nava with contempt. "He's nothing more than a politician. They talk people into things. It's what they do. It's not your fault, Imam."

"Shut up, Abu," said Suleiman calmly.

"Yes, Abu, shut—" added Nava.

"*Both of you!*" screamed Suleiman, pointing to Nava. "Shut up! You're like little children."

Suleiman took a moment to catch his breath. He reached for a glass of water and took a large gulp. He remained silent for nearly an entire minute, breathing deeply. Finally, he cleared his throat.

"We're not here to talk about what happened," said Suleiman. "It was both of your faults, and mine, if truth be told. But it doesn't matter anymore. It's over. We are here to discuss the proposed agreement with the United States and whether we will sign it. That is all we're going to talk about. Do you understand?"

Nava glanced at Paria, then looked at Suleiman and nodded. Paria did nothing.

"Obviously, the Americans know we had a nuclear device," said Suleiman. "And yet, they're still willing to sign the agreement. The question is, why?"

"Obviously," said Paria, "because it allows them to get their spies inside Iran. They're making the cold calculation that some transparency is better than none at all, even at the price."

"Do you agree?" asked Suleiman, looking at Nava.

"Dellenbaugh loves the idea of Iran and the United States on the same stage," said Nava. "Yes, of course I agree with Abu, they want their cameras inside the country, their little inspectors, all of that. But it's also about Dellenbaugh's ego."

"Do you think we should do it?" asked Suleiman.

"Both of you know the IMF loans are badly needed,"

said Nava. "The sanctions are crippling us. But if signing the agreement means we'll be unable to continue to develop weapons, I'm against it."

Suleiman looked at Paria.

"Well, General," said Suleiman. "Can you figure out a way around the inspections?"

Paria looked at Suleiman. He shrugged his shoulders.

"I think so," said Paria. "Of course, it will be hard. The first few months are the hardest part, but then the inspectors grow lazy. We learn their patterns. We should be able to do it. There is sufficient highly enriched uranium now for a weapon or two. We'll need to be very careful."

Suleiman stood. He turned his back to Nava and Paria and stepped to the window behind his desk, which looked out on snowcapped mountain peaks.

"You'll go to Buenos Aires," said Suleiman. "Both of you. Mahmoud, to do what you do best, be a politician, shake hands with Dellenbaugh, say a few silly, obnoxious things. And Abu, you will go because you need a few days away. You're strung too tight. Go to Argentina. I've been there. It's a beautiful country, with beautiful women. Take a few days off. Drink some wine."

Suleiman turned. He pointed to Paria.

"That's an order."

MIDDLEBURG, VIRGINIA

Sometime long after midnight, Dewey was seated at the table, alone, his head to the side, boots crossed and up on the table. Everyone else had gone to bed. His eyes were closed; he'd long ago fallen asleep.

Something woke him; a noise from somewhere across the field. An animal? He stood up and blew out the candles on the table. Then he heard it again. It was fireworks, far off in the distance. He went inside the farmhouse. It was quiet and dark, except for a small lamp on a table in the living room. He walked through the farmhouse, then up the stairs.

At the top of the stairs, he turned right and walked toward the guest bedroom Foxx had pointed out to him earlier. Dewey went inside the room and shut the door. Dim yellow light shone from a lamp next to the bed.

Dewey sat on the edge of the bed and removed his boots and socks. He took off his jeans and shirt, then stripped off his underwear. He stepped to a mirror on the wall and inspected his left shoulder and the scar line from the bullet wound from two years before in Colombia. It was thick, and tougher every day, like leather.

He heard a soft knock on the door, and turned. The door opened. Jessica stepped inside the room, then quietly shut the door behind her.

Dewey looked at Jessica. A short, black, see-through silk robe came down to the top of her thighs. The robe was the only piece of clothing on her, and it was barely on her.

Dewey, for his part, made no attempt to hide his body from her.

"Mind if I come in?" she whispered.

He said nothing, letting his eyes move appreciatively up Jessica's flat stomach, barely veiled through the see-through material, to her face, familiar in the light, her eyes locking on to his.

Dewey stepped toward her as she reached up and slowly removed the robe, letting it fall silently to the ground.

"So you never answered my question," said Jessica, looking up into Dewey's eyes.

"I didn't?"

"You don't remember, do you?" she asked.

"No."

"I said, would you come with me to Buenos Aires?" Jessica asked.

She leaned forward and kissed his neck. She took his hand and led him toward the bed, as, in the distance, through the open window, the explosion of fireworks somewhere in the night rolled like a drumbeat across the plain.

ACKNOWLEDGMENTS

Two very close friends passed away from cancer during the writing of this book, and, with the firm belief that if there is a heaven, surely there are books there too (in fact they probably get released a day or two early up there), I want to thank them for their help on *The Last Refuge*.

Jim Windhorst was close to me in age, and was struck down far too soon, leaving legions of family and friends who will forever miss his big heart and wonderful sense of humor. Jim always read my books in their early stages, giving me constructive criticism which was immensely helpful. His greatest editorial contribution, however, came after he read a passage in an early draft in which I'd inadvertently named a large oil tanker after my wife. He called me up and said, "Ben, you might not want to name an oil tanker after your wife." "Oh my God," I said, "you're right." "Yeah, no s— I'm right, pinhead," he added. "What I want to know is who wrote this thing? Nobody stupid enough to name an oil tanker after his wife could have possibly written this." I'll miss you, Jimbo.

The other friend was more than a friend, he was my godfather, Frederick H. "Teddy" Marks, after whom our second son is named, and the basis for the eponymously named character, Teddy Marks, though the real Teddy Marks was more of a hero than the fictitious one. Ted was a goaltender on the 1965 U.S. Hockey team, a Navy SEAL, an award-winning foreign correspondent, a successful businessman, and an all-around great guy. He was brilliant, tough, opinionated, kindhearted, and wildly funny. I will miss everything about him, most of all his terrific, infectious laughter; at others, at himself, and most of all, at me. I sent Ted an early draft of *The Last Refuge,* and he called me up: "Ben, I'm a third of the way through the book and I just threw up all over the place." Needless to say, I was devastated. "What part made you sick?" I asked. "It wasn't the book, it was the chemo," he said, laughing. "The book's great."

I'm fortunate to be represented by the most talented agents in the world, Aaron Priest, Nicole James, Frances Jalet-Miller, Lisa Erbach Vance, Lucy Childs Baker, Arleen Priest, and John Richmond at the Aaron Priest Agency—thank you all for your hard work. In Hollywood, a special thanks to Chris George and Michael Ovitz.

I want to thank my extended family at St. Martin's Press, in particular Keith Kahla, Sally Richardson, Matthew Shear, John Murphy, George Witte, Matthew Baldacci, Nancy Trypuc, Stephen Lee, Judy Sisko,

Anne Marie Tallberg, Hannah Braaten, Stephanie Davis, Jeanne-Marie Hudson, the entire sales team, and everyone else. Thank you also to Trisha Jackson and everyone at Pan Macmillan in London, my wonderful publishers in the United Kingdom, Australia, New Zealand, and India. Finally, thank you to everyone at Brilliance Audio and Macmillan Audio.

The Last Refuge involves America, Israel, and Iran. During my research, I spoke with people in both Israel and Iran, and flew to Israel for a series of meetings with individuals involved with that country's political, military, and intelligence infrastructure. I would like to express my deep gratitude to Zvi Rafieh and Ophir Paz for their time, expertise, and insights. In addition, I would like to thank a certain former Israeli intelligence official, who asked that his name not be used, for his absolutely essential help. I also spoke with a number of people inside Tehran, all of whom asked that their names not be used. I would like, however, to thank them—they know who they are and I hope they get the opportunity to read *The Last Refuge* without being thrown in jail.

I would like to thank everyone at Harvard University's Kennedy School, in particular Professor Graham Allison, for his expertise on all things nuclear related; and Eric Anderson, at the Institute of Politics, for his invaluable help. Thanks also to Brad Thor, Vince Flynn, Mark Greaney, Brian Haig, Melinda Maguire Harnett, Will Donovan, Michael Murray, Mac Perry, Lee Van Alen Manigault, Amy and Jim Parker, José Gonzalez-Heres, and Joe Goldsmith.

Of course, none of this would have ever happened were it not for the inspiration, patience, profligate spending, and love of my family: Charlie, my future Boston Bruin, who can eat a gallon of ice cream, recite Tyler Seguin's scoring statistics, and kind of do his homework all at the same time; Teddy, the future dictator of a medium-sized country somewhere and the only macaroni and cheese–addicted concert pianist who sleeps in his goalie pads; Oscar, whose passion for back scratches is rivaled only by his love of stuffed animals, and whose inherent sweetness can only partially be explained by the vast quantities of bubble gum, chocolate chip cookies, and Twizzlers he puts down; Esmé, my beautiful, wonderful six-year-old daughter, who is living proof that you can survive and in fact be charming and magical on a steady diet of applesauce, bacon, and french fries, the one who has made me smile at least once a minute since the moment she was born; and Shannon, my partner, best friend, and love of my life: thank you.

PROLOGUE

UPPER PHILLIMORE GARDENS
KENSINGTON
LONDON
ONE WEEK AGO

I don't know."

The three words Amit Bhutta, Iran's ambassador to the United Nations, had repeated for the past day and a half; three words that Dewey listened to with a blank look on his face. It was, by his rough count, approximately the thousandth time Bhutta had said them.

He and Tacoma had been taking turns interrogating Bhutta. Two hours on, two off. They had distinctly different styles. Tacoma, the former SEAL, was less patient. Bhutta's bloody face showed the practical implications of that impatience. Dewey assumed it was

Tacoma's youth that made him slap the Iranian around. Not that he cared. But his style was different. With Bhutta, Dewey felt that screwing with his head had a better shot at getting them the information they needed. That and not feeding Bhutta or giving him anything to drink.

The interrogation room was soundproof and windowless. At the center of the room, a steel table was bolted to the wood floor. Behind it was a steel chair, also bolted down. The table had wet blood on it, not for the first time.

Bhutta was stooped over, leaning forward, his cheek pressed against the steel table. His left eye was shut, black and blue.

The heat inside the room was cranked up. Both men were sweating, but Bhutta, with his wrists shackled behind his back—and the muzzle of Dewey's Colt M1911 aimed at his head—was sweating a little more.

It had been a week since Dewey had infiltrated Iran and stolen the country's first nuclear device. Dewey's disguise, his overgrown beard and moustache, was gone now. His face was clean-shaven, his hair cut to a medium length.

Yet, as Bhutta had learned over thirty-six hours of interrogation, there lurked something beneath the attractive veneer of the kid from Castine, Maine.

Bhutta could see the toughness now, as he stared at the American. It was the same meanness and detachment that Bhutta knew had probably coursed in the blood of the men who so long ago had kicked the crap out of the British, a determination that, to the Iranian's mind at least, was as defeating as anything he'd ever experienced.

"What's his name?" asked Dewey.

"I told you, I don't know. He's China's asset."

Dewey was seated in a beat-up, torn, leather club chair. He had his right leg draped over the right arm.

"What's his name?"

"Fuck you."

"What's his name?"

"I don't know."

"Ambassador Bhutta, we can do this all night."

·"I don't know, asshole."

Dewey smiled.

"Language," said Dewey.

"Fuck you."

"If your mother could hear you swearing, she'd be really fucking pissed."

Bhutta's mouth flared slightly, nearly a smile.

"You laughed."

"Fuck you," Bhutta whispered. "You're not funny."

"Then why'd you laugh?"

"I wasn't laughing."

"Okay, I have one for you," said Dewey. "What do you do if an Iranian throws a pin at you?"

Bhutta paused, then finally relented.

"What?" he asked.

"Run like hell."

"Why?"

"Because he's got a grenade between his teeth."

Bhutta laughed.

"You're worse than the other guy," whispered Bhutta,

shaking his head. "That's stupid. Just beat the shit out of me, will you?"

Dewey laughed, then pumped the trigger on his .45. The bullet struck Bhutta's right kneecap. Bhutta screamed, lurching against the chair, pulling at the shackles.

"Jesus, I didn't think it would hurt that much," said Dewey.

Bhutta turned and looked at Dewey, a horrible grimace on his face. His knee was bleeding profusely.

"I don't know his name! How would I know China has a mole inside Mossad?"

Dewey ran his fingers back through his hair.

"Here's the deal," said Dewey, wiping the muzzle of the gun on his jeans. "You can either tell me the name of the mole, or you can tell Menachem Dayan and those nice fellas at the madhouse. I have a feeling their jokes aren't going to be as funny as mine. Also, they'll kill you."

Bhutta screamed again.

"You tell me the name and the only one who gets hurt is the mole," Dewey said. "You go free. We can arrange some sort of relocation program inside the United States. Some sunny state."

"What about my daughter?" asked Bhutta, tears streaming down his face.

"Her, too."

"I want something in writing. An affidavit from the CIA or the Justice Department."

"Not going to happen. If you want me to choose between shooting your kneecap off or calling some lawyer at Langley and explaining why I haven't already dumped you off to the Israelis like I was supposed to, all I can say is, that ain't gonna fuckin' happen."

"You're a bastard."

"Yeah, I am," said Dewey. "But if I say I'm going to do something, I'm going to do it. Tell me the name of China's spy inside Mossad."

"Fuck you."

Dewey stood up, then chambered another round. He aimed the gun at Bhutta's left knee.

"No!" Bhutta screamed. He looked at Dewey. "Dillman. His name is Dillman. That's all I know. Tell me you won't fuck me over."

Dewey stuck the Colt M1911 in his shoulder holster and walked to the door.

"I never break a promise."

Dewey walked down the hallway and pulled out his cell.

"Get me Menachem Dayan," he said into the phone as he walked upstairs.

A moment later, Dewey heard the raspy cough of Israel's top military commander, General Menachem Dayan.

"Hello, Dewey."

"I finished interrogating Bhutta," Dewey said. "I know the name of China's mole inside Mossad."

"Who is it?" asked Dayan.

"I want your word, General," said Dewey. "Kohl Meir gets to put the bullet in him. Then he's buried."

"You have my word."

"His name's Dillman."

1

Dayan stepped into Fritz Lavine's 12th-floor corner office, which overlooked the Mediterranean Sea, the U.S. Embassy, and downtown Tel Aviv. Lavine was the director general of Mossad, Israel's intelligence service. He was a tall, rotund man with receding brown hair, and big ruddy cheeks pockmarked with acne scars. Dressed in a white button-down shirt, sleeves rolled up, he stood behind his desk, inspecting a sheet of paper. Two men were seated in chairs in front of Lavine's desk: Cooperman, Mossad chief of staff, and Rolber, head of clandestine operations.

"What the *fuck* happened?" asked Dayan as he crossed the office, his voice deep, charred by decades' worth of cigarettes. "How many years did you three work with this sonofabitch traitor and you never suspected a goddam thing?"

"There'll be plenty of time for blame, Menachem," said Lavine, icily. "Right now, we need to find this motherfucker before he does any more damage and escapes."

"What *is* the damage?"

"It's extensive," said Cooperman. "So far, we can trace the exposure of at least sixteen MI6 and CIA operatives back to Dillman. As for Mossad, the number appears to be seven dead agents."

"Jesus Christ," Dayan whispered, looking in disbelief at Cooperman.

"He gave the Chinese everything. Every Far East operation we conducted over the past decade was known ahead of time by Fao Bhang and the ministry. Dillman passed on detailed aspects of anything Langley supplied to us. This includes nuclear infrastructure."

"Have we notified Calibrisi?" asked Dayan, referring to the CIA director, Hector Calibrisi.

Lavine nodded. "Chalmers, too," he added, referring to Derek Chalmers, head of MI6.

"And what was the reaction?" asked Dayan.

Lavine stared back at Dayan but remained silent. He didn't need to say anything. They knew Dillman had set all three agencies back years, decades even, and that both London and Langley would be extremely angry.

"Where is he?" asked Dayan, calmer now, his hand rubbing the bridge of his nose, eyes closed.

"We don't know," said Rolber. "We're looking, carefully. If he suspects anything, he'll run."

"If he goes to China, we'll never see him again," said Dayan.

The phone on Lavine's desk chimed, then a voice came on the speaker.

"Director, they're waiting for you."

"Patch us in."

The phone clicked.

"Hector?" asked Lavine.

"Hey, Fritz," said Calibrisi on speaker. "You have me and Bill Polk here at Langley along with Piper Redgrave and Jim Bruckheimer at NSA."

"MI6 is on also," said Derek Chalmers, in his British accent. "Where are we on this?"

"We have nothing," said Lavine. "We're looking everywhere. Last contact with the agency was two days ago. General Redgrave, has NSA developed anything?"

"No," came the soft female voice of the head of the National Security Agency.

"What's the plan if and when we do find him?" asked Calibrisi.

"We have three options," said Rolber. "One, we watch him, use him, plot an architecture of disinformation back up into Beijing. Two, we bring him in, interrogate, then let him rot. Three, termination."

"Why not two and three?" asked Calibrisi. "Grill him, then kill him."

"If we bring him in, China will find out, Hector," said Cooperman. "There has to be some form of check-in and tip-off. If he misses that check-in, Fao Bhang will immediately try to exfiltrate him, or, more likely, just kill him."

"Then Bhang will move on western assets before we have time to clean up inside the theater," said Chalmers.

"Every MI6, CIA, Mossad agent in China will die, not to mention anyone else Dillman has exposed. It will be a bloody mess."

"It already is a bloody mess," said Dayan.

"So what about option one?" asked Calibrisi. "What would the design look like?"

"We locate him, then hang back," answered Rolber, "carefully monitor his movements, and tightly control information flow to him. In the meantime, we put our assets in the Chinese theater on high alert. When Dillman is no longer useful to us, or he suspects something, we bring out our teams, then bring him in."

"Fuck that," yelled Dayan, hitting the desk with his hand. "We're not waiting. If I have to do it myself in downtown Shanghai with a dull butter knife, this motherfucker dies."

"Dillman is just a symptom, General," said Calibrisi. "It's Fao Bhang who's behind it all."

"Then let's kill that sonofabitch, too."

"Nothing would please me more, but we've never had a shot at him," said Chalmers. "He's as well guarded as the premier."

"Let's cut our losses and kill Dillman," said Dayan. "Let's focus on what we can do, namely kill what has to be the most important intelligence asset Bhang possesses in the west. That's at least something."

"I have an idea," said Chalmers.

"Even before this Dillman episode, Fao Bhang has done damage to all of us. Bhang and the ministry are a country unto themselves. He's the third highest ranking member of the Chinese state council but he's the most powerful by far. Premier Li fears him, as does the country's military. His tentacles extend into China's economic affairs. He's been an instrumental part of the currency manipulation that has plagued Britain and, on a much more dramatic scale, the United States, for years. For all I know, his hackers are listening in right now."

"What's your point?" asked Lavine.

"Bhang is rising," said Chalmers. "His malevolence grows. This is simply another chapter in a very dark book."

There was silence in the room, and over the intercom, as Chalmers paused.

"My question is, when are we going to do something about it?" he asked.

"So what's your idea?" asked Calibrisi.

"We have to find Dillman," said Chalmers. "Obviously. Then, my suggestion is, we use him. But not in the way you're thinking, General. No, instead of using him for disinformation, then killing him, we're going to switch the order around. Kill him, then use him. We're going to lure Fao Bhang out of his hole and Dillman is going to be our bait."

"I'm not sure what you mean," said Rolber.

"Bhang won't care about the loss of one human being, even his most treasured asset in the west, but he will care if the loss of Dillman exposes him as weak, as not in control," said Chalmers. "If we can undermine him in the terribly cutthroat drama that is Chinese leadership, it will endanger him. It will destabilize him. It will, potentially, signal to those who fear Bhang or who covet his power. It's time to destabilize Fao Bhang and let his enemies move against him. Otherwise, there will be no end to his reach and the damage he inflicts upon the west."

Cooperman suddenly reached for his chest pocket and pulled out a vibrating cell phone.

"What?" he whispered into the cell.

Cooperman listened, then signaled at the phone, indicating to Lavine to mute the conference call.

"We found him," whispered Cooperman, looking at Lavine, then Dayan and Rolber. "He's in Haifa."

Lavine pressed the mute button on the speakerphone.

"Haifa?" asked Lavine. "What do we have there?"

"I have a tight kill team in the city," said Rolber. "Boroshevsky, Malayim. They're good to go."

"No," said Dayan. "This is not Mossad's kill."

"You don't trust us now, General?" demanded Rolber.

"It has nothing to do with whether or not I trust you," said Dayan, his gravelly voice rising. "I gave my word to Andreas; it's Kohl Meir's kill. Get Meir up to Haifa, brief him en route, get him whatever weapons he wants. That's an order."

"Yes, sir."

"In the meantime, Fritz and I will coordinate with MI6 and Langley. I'm not sure I understand what the hell Derek Chalmers is talking about, but I like it. These British always have brilliant ideas, even if their food does suck."

X